The Twelve Points of Caleb Canto

By Sam Starbuck

The text of this book is set in Garamond and Courier New.
Cover image created by Vincent Le Moign, used under
Creative Commons Attribution 4.0. Original art at
http://creazilla.com/nodes/49782-guitar-emoji-clipart

This is the fourteenth volume published by
Extribulum Independent Press
extribulum.wordpress.com
Printer's Row, Chicago, IL

Nameless – 2009
Other People Can Smell You – 2009, Revised 2010
Charitable Getting – 2010
Dr. King's Lucky Book – 2011
Trace – 2011
By The Days – 2011
The Dead Isle – 2012
Six Harvests in Lea, Texas – 2020
The Found Fortune Deck – 2022
Fête for a King – 2022
Infinite Jes –2022
The Lady And The Tiger – 2022
The Shivadh Romances: Omnibus Volume I – 2022
The Twelve Points of Caleb Canto – 2023

ISBN 978-1-960785-99-2

This book contains material which may be triggering or upsetting, although generally brief. For a full list of content warnings, which may include spoilers, please turn to the end of the book.

For Cat, a good friend and invaluable source of Eurovision knowledge, without whom this book would not exist – or if it did, would be *wildly* inaccurate at best.

In 2022, the winners of the Eurovision Song Contest were Kalush Orchestra of Ukraine, and I must apologize for gently replacing them in this story; their win was very well deserved, and if you get a chance, do find and listen to *Stefania*. It is now an unofficial anthem for soldiers defending Ukraine against Vladimir Putin's ongoing persecution of their country.

In solidarity with Ukraine, for the duration of the war a portion of the proceeds from sales of this book will be donated to United24, President Zelenskyy's official government support initiative, split between the funds for medical aid and rebuilding. You can learn more and donate at https://u24.gov.ua.

I must also offer some small apology to Sam Ryder, the 2022 UK Eurovision representative, a lovely golden retriever of a man who took a well-deserved second place with *Space Man* and had to make way, in this book, for angry terrier Buck Haverd. One Sam to another, sorry about that.

PROLOGUE
Autumn, 2021

ASKAZER-SHIVADLAKIA, THE "little country by the sea," was delightful year-round – sun-kissed, with a tang of salt in the air and cool breezes off the water. As with many beach towns, the summer months in the capital city of Fons-Askaz were the busiest; in autumn, the bustle settled down to local affairs, with the dairy farmers driving the cattle south into the warmer winter pastures and the olive harvest taking the population out into the groves. After the harvest, usually following Yom Kippur, the air turned crisp – never too cold, rarely snowy except in the highlands, but chilly enough that people got their winter coats out.

And, Caleb thought, tired musicians huddled around fires on the lakefront to stay warm, as they enjoyed a break before heading home.

He had a decent jacket on, but he was still keeping close to the fire; Ava, his best friend and fellow musician, was sensitive to the cold and had swaddled herself in a massive quilted blanket over her coat, gray eyes and a tuft of short brown hair all that was visible.

They had spent the day in a recording booth of Reverb Studios, Askazer-Shivadlakia's first and only audio production company, recording an album. Reverb was in the bunker basement of the royal fishing lodge on the public grounds of the palace; the owners of the studio had converted the bunker into recording booths, mainly for podcasts, but lately local musicians had taken notice of their services. Word had gotten around that they did good work, and Ava had decided it was time to cut a studio album. Her folk duo, the Gay Twits, was aptly named, but Caleb liked Ava and the other Twit, Ben, and didn't mind sitting in as a third Twit to play Whatever Backup Instrument Required. Besides, he'd wanted a look at the old bunker, with its brutal concrete construction and mysterious tunnels. There was a rumor of a hidden wine cellar that had almost killed someone when it was discovered a few months ago.

Now, however, he was feeling uneasy about overstaying their welcome. They were sitting around a fire pit on the grounds outside the lodge, and Caleb could hear the noise of a dinner party from within – conversation, laughter, the occasional opening or closing of a door. The retired king, Michaelis, lived above the studios in the lodge, and was obviously entertaining guests.

"Should we be out here?" Caleb asked, scooting closer to the fire pit. It had been lit by Lachlan, an American immigrant and one of Reverb's owners, who had been engineering Ava and Ben's recording all day. "We're not bothering anyone, right?"

"No, we're fine," Lachlan said, basking in the glow of the fire, head tilted back to study the night sky. Firelight flickered over his tattoos and lit his wild salt-and-pepper hair, turning the lighter locks pale gold. "The conservation officers know people come and go from this part of the park all the time, and the lodge won't mind. I think His Grace likes that it stays busy these days."

"Is it a weird thought – " Ben started, and Lachlan, Ava, and Caleb all chorused *Yes* before he could finish, because they knew Ben well enough to know it absolutely would be.

"Okay," Ben persisted, "but *is it* a weird thought that this would be the easiest possible way to take out most of the ruling class of our country? The old king's definitely up there and I saw the new king and his man going in, and Lady Alanna Daskaz and the Duke of Shivadlakia, and other people too. Most of 'em work for the government. And they're all in one place right now, eating poisonable food, right by a convenient body dump."

He gestured to the lake. Lachlan, Ava, and Caleb considered this.

"It is a miracle you are not in prison for threatening the entire royal family," Caleb said at last.

"I'm not threatening them, I like them! I voted for King Gregory when he was elected. But is that weird to think?" Ben pressed.

"Maybe," Lachlan said, his voice doing an octave-skip that indicated *definitely*. Then he glanced up and grinned. "Look sharp, Benny, you wouldn't even have to go indoors to take out one of them right now."

Caleb twisted in his chair. A man was making his way down from the lodge to the lake's dock, passing them with a brisk nod for Lachlan. His features weren't easy to see in the dark, but they were still recognizable, being on half the currency in the kingdom – the sharp nose, clever dark eyes, and silver hair of the retired king, His Grace Michaelis, whose son currently ruled.

"What's he doing?" Ava asked in a hushed voice. "Going for a swim?"

The old king reached the end of the dock and cupped his hands around his mouth. The deep bass rumble of his voice boomed out, disturbing the serenity of the lake.

"TAVAT!" he bellowed, and far out in the lake something moved. "Come inside! Dinner's ready!"

"Coming!" a faint, higher-pitched voice echoed back. They watched, hushed and pretending not to be watching, as a small boat came skimming along the water, pulling up to the dock. A teenage boy – pale, slim, with short dark hair and heavy eyebrows – disembarked carefully, carrying an electric lantern.

"Have you set the fireworks on the bank?" they heard the old king ask as he and the boy passed them again, back towards the lodge.

"Yeah, it's gonna be awesome!" the boy replied, and Caleb thought he recognized the voice, or at least the American accent.

"I'm almost sure it'll work this time."

"Nice of them to put out fireworks for us," Ben joked.

"Was that Noah?" Caleb asked, watching the pair mount the steps to the lodge. "The one who was running around messing with the recording equipment? Ava's got him for classes, don't you?"

"Vocal lessons at the Academy, yeah," Ava said, nodding. "He just started at the school this year. I figured he had a part-time job at Reverb, but he's here awfully late."

"He's my godson," Lachlan said. "My co-founder's kid. They live up here at the lodge. By invitation of the king emeritus," he added, amused. "They were having trouble getting housing in town over the summer."

"That's convenient, living above the studio," Ava said. "Kind of intense, though."

"I mean, I live where I work too," Ben said.

"You live in a van, Ben," Caleb told him.

"By choice! And where do I do most of my work?" Ben asked.

"He's got you there," Lachlan said.

"Okay, but why did the old king call him Tabbat?" Caleb said, determined not to be distracted.

"Tavat," Lachlan corrected. "It's a term of endearment."

"What, like...kiddo or something?"

"Sort of," Lachlan said. "It's in the old Shivadh language, I think it's fairly obscure. Michaelis explained it to me once. It's a word for a person who's kind of daring, someone who gets away with things because they're audacious. It translates to little prince. Princeling," he corrected. "That's how he translated it."

"That's sweet," Ava said.

Caleb nodded agreement absently. He let the conversation drift on around him, turning this anecdote over in his mind. He'd watched as the boy and the old king walked up to the lodge, and seen Michaelis ruffle Noah's hair, an affectionate gesture, just before they went inside. *Tavat*. Interesting.

He got his phone out and opened the Shivadh National Resources App. It had been helpful when he'd finally moved permanently across the highlands from Galia and put down real roots; he knew Fons-Askaz pretty well, but there were places in the app to find housing, to figure out citizenship paperwork, and to learn more about the culture – not just what he'd gleaned from his summers in the city, when the place was full of tourists.

There was a Shivadh language dictionary that he'd found useful once in a while; most Shivadh didn't speak the old language fluently, but most still had more of it than he did. He spoke English well and with a Shivadh accent, but Italian, the national language of Galia, was his first, and the dictionary was a help.

It had an entry for Tavat, with a brief definition and a link to the digital national archive, which had a whole article on the term, with previous uses in literature. Most of them were from local folktales. Caleb skimmed through them, fascinated.

There was a song in all of this, somewhere. Something about legacy, about having to hold on and let go at the same time. It would be too much to explain what Tavat was in the song itself, but you could anchor a song around a Shivadh phrase that included the word and contextualized it. A song about watching a kid go off in the world, perhaps. Compelling, if he could come up with a good hook for it.

Every wave someday reaches a distant country's shore
But the tides follow on and the water here is pure –

"He's got the look," Ben said, and Caleb looked up.
"Sorry?"
"You got quiet, Caleb," Lachlan said, curious.
"He has his songwriting face on," Ava told Lachlan, which was permission for Caleb to open the recording app on his phone, get up, and walk away, carrying the ukulele he took pretty much

everywhere with him. Ava would explain it to Lachlan. Caleb needed a little more darkness and quiet to hear the song come together in his head.

He found a good spot down the trail that wound around the lake and dimmed his phone screen until he could just barely make it out. He settled down and began to compose, first mentally, then letting it flow out of his hands on the instrument while his phone recorded it, a good simple way to save it for later without having to start and stop to note down the tabulation. He didn't even notice the fireworks when they began going off across the lake, except to be irritated that it was occasionally hard to hear himself humming.

By the time he was done working out the bare bones of the song, his phone was on perilously low battery, and he could see the lights in the fishing lodge had dimmed. The others were just cleaning up and putting out the fire when he got back.

"Got everything out?" Ava asked.

"Yeah – can I have your charger?"

She tossed him a portable phone charger, wrapped in a cord. "Lachlan said to say goodnight and he'd see us back bright and early tomorrow morning to finish the last track."

"Sounds good," Caleb said, plugging his phone in and slinging the ukulele into its case, pulling the strap over his shoulder. "If you drop me on the high street in town I can walk the rest of the way."

He didn't hear much of what Ava said on the ride out of the grounds or into Fons-Askaz, but she wouldn't be offended. She knew he sometimes got contemplative, and if she really wanted to tell him something she knew to get his attention first. He only snapped back to reality when she said, "Sure you'll be all right?" as he climbed out of the car.

"Sure, it's Fons-Askaz, I'm perfectly safe."

"Well, don't get completely lost in daydream-land until you're home," she said.

"Promise," he agreed, and closed the door, watching her pull away. He got his phone out again, the cord disappearing into his pocket where the charger was, but in deference to her request that he not daydream on the walk, he didn't put headphones in.

Back when he'd lived in Levaldi, the capital of Galia, there were parts of the city where he wouldn't feel safe walking around with his phone out and his face stuck in it. He made an appealing target: a slightly-built young man with short, fine blond hair that made him look even younger than he was. He'd been hoping for a growth spurt for years, but at 24 he was beginning to suspect it wasn't coming.

One of the few Shivadh words he knew offhand was *ilef*, a word his mother had called him; it was a little sprite creature, and she'd tap the tip of his nose as she said it, smiling at his broad face with its sharp chin and high brow. In some ways an innocent face was an advantage, but he didn't come across as very imposing.

Still, Fons-Askaz was hardly Levaldi. It was a little smaller, but it was also simply too prosperous to be desperate, too friendly to tourists to be dangerous.

Caleb strolled down along narrow streets full of white-walled buildings, through alleys clogged by scaffolding, and past chained-off construction sites, all in perfect confidence. Recently, someone had lit a fire under the new king to make sure the infrastructure of the city was up to snuff; there had been a building collapse, and one or two near-misses. To his credit, King Gregory had immediately instituted new funding for inspection and repair, but there was only so much that could be done during tourist season. Now that most of the tourists had gone home, construction was springing up everywhere along the shoreline and slowly creeping through the town, a little further inland each day.

Pretty soon, Caleb thought, the scaffolding would reach his own building. He liked his boarding house, an elderly stucco job that had once been some rich person's home and now belonged to Ms. Costa, who rented out rooms and was generally kind, if a little absentminded. The bones were sound, as Ms. Costa said, but she also said (and Caleb agreed) that it could use some "sprucing up" and a new roof. She'd wrangled a grant from the infrastructure program for the roof, but she had yet to find a roofer with the time to do it. Caleb's ceiling had one small leak and it was over the bathtub anyway, so he didn't mind waiting.

It wasn't especially fancy, but he had friendly neighbors, a bedroom with a private bathroom, access to the kitchen whenever he wanted with a shelf in the fridge and the pantry just for his food, and a distant view of the harbor, with the sea beyond it. The first song he'd written when he moved in was about how he hadn't realized he'd been choking in landlocked Galia until he moved to the coast.

Water played a significant role in his music, and was perhaps a kind of common and obvious symbol, but he supposed it was nice to have a motif.

He spent the walk and even the climb to the third floor distracted, but when he let himself into his bedroom he became conscious he was footsore, cramped in various muscles, and exhausted. He put his ukulele in its stand by the door, shed his shirt and trousers, pulled off his binder with a long exhale, crawled into a t-shirt to sleep in, and just managed to put his phone down on the nightstand before he was unconscious.

The next morning, before they started their session, Caleb asked Ava, "Hey, can I have the first half-hour? I just need about three takes on something. Pay you back for it."

"Sure," Ava said. "We have it all morning and we probably won't need all of it. I can use the warmup time."

"What are you up to?" Lachlan asked Caleb, hands moving over the sound board, setting up for a single vocalist.

"The song I was working on last night, it's stuck in my head now," Caleb said. "I won't be of any use until I sing it a few times and know it's on record somewhere official. You don't need to make me sound fancy or anything."

"All part of the job. Just vocals – oh, vocals and a ukulele, okay," Lachlan said, laughing, as Caleb produced the little uke from his bag. He'd get the vocals and basic melody out in the first take, maybe do a keyboard follow-up, and see if he even wanted a third one. "Ready when you are, king."

> *Every wave someday reaches a distant country's shore*
> *But the tides follow on and the water here is pure*
> *Your sails spread wider now than mine*
> *But someday I'll still leave you behind*

They did two takes, and Caleb sighed with relief at the end of them; the song had flown out of his head, and he could feel the rest of the music – the stuff he was supposed to be playing today – flowing in to fill the gap.

Lachlan sent him a sound file for the recording, and Caleb stashed it with the digital sheet music in his "sell to whoever wants it" folder. He licensed the song a few weeks later to some kid who wanted to be a pop idol, something Caleb did all the time with his little ditties, and mostly forgot about it.

At least until the following spring, when it really came back to bite him in the ass.

CHAPTER ONE
Spring, 2022

BREAKFAST IN THE palace of Askazer-Shivadlakia was frequently chaotic, the product of a scattered family of busy people. It was served in the royal family's private dining room, but there was no formal seating time, and one could never be sure who would be there when. Jerry enjoyed the chaos, but he knew it for what it was.

Jerry's cousin, Gregory III, king and obnoxiously early riser, was usually the first in, and also the first out; sometimes Gregory and his fiancé Eddie missed each other at breakfast even though they shared apartments in the palace and ate within half an hour of each other. Jerry thought sometimes he saw Gregory at breakfast more often than Eddie did, if only because Jerry and Gregory had a standing twice-weekly morning run together. Eddie, in his own words and with a sensibility born of his California upbringing, only ran from the cops.

Michaelis, Gregory's father, might be at breakfast or might not, rarely with any warning. He might bring his partner Jes, or Jes's teenage son Noah, and the level of chaos Noah could cause was both a delight and a concern to much of the family. He never meant to, it just seemed to follow him around.

Alanna, Jerry's beloved and Gregory's head of Palace Operations, usually prepared Gregory's calendar, came in for breakfast, talked to Gregory without eating much, followed him out, and then came back in to eat and steal a few moments with Jerry. He wasn't sure why that particular administrative dance was so complicated, but it wasn't his place to question.

Jerry himself, the twelfth Duke of Shivadlakia and a grandson, nephew, and cousin of kings – without rigid employment and with a deep interest in human nature – often sat serenely through the entire breakfast shift. He worked on documents for the ducal estate, did Sudoku puzzles or scrolled his Photogram feed, and absorbed all the royal ambiance. Occasionally he even made himself useful as a human message board.

"Good morning, Gerald. Have I missed all of them already?" Michaelis asked as he arrived that morning, taking some eggs from the chafing dish and some toast from the rack.

"Gregory hasn't been in yet, and Alanna hasn't either; she said if he didn't come in by eight, she probably had to talk to him about something urgent, so I assume they'll show up sooner or later," Jerry said. "Eddie's on his way, I think. And you are here," he added with a flourish.

"More or less," Michaelis replied, settling in to eat. "I thought Gregory might be late. He's trying to get his minister of culture to sign off on a venue contract and it's a bit time-sensitive."

"The Eurovision thing?"

Michaelis nodded. "If I were the minister of culture I'd say Eurovision isn't my area, but that is why I am retired."

"Why, because Eurovision's not culture?" Jerry asked, laughing. "So sour! It's only a pop music contest, not a crime against nature. I bet that's why we've never entered Eurovision before now. You blocked it."

"Mm, not me," Michaelis shook his head. "Nobody wanted to pay the entry fee, but for my money it's always been pure old-fashioned Shivadh arrogance keeping us out."

"*Keeping* us out?" Jerry asked. Michaelis sat back, spreading his hands, preparing to expound.

"Obviously, so the reasoning goes, Shivadh musicians are simply better at what they do than other countries. The assumption is that we would win so handily it would be laughable," he said.

"I can feel my ancestors listening through me," Jerry said.

"I should hope so, that's generations of Shivadh ego lined up behind you," Michaelis replied. "The problem is, when you win Eurovision, you're supposed to host it the following year. You don't have to, but we'd never shirk, would we? And it sounds like an awful lot of work nobody really wants to do, not to mention the expense. So we never entered. Didn't want to put up with winning. Wasn't my decision, but I can't say I minded. One less thing to worry about."

"So why are we entering now? What changed?" Jerry asked.

"Gregory's been slowly and gently murdering people," Michaelis said, as Gregory himself came into the room.

"I have not, I could only wish for that kind of power," Gregory said, helping himself to breakfast. "What are we talking about?"

"You've been very gradually kicking out the oldest and most tediously conservative of the old guard," Michaelis said. "Filling Parliament with younger people with more progressive ideas."

"Is this about Eurovision?" Gregory sighed.

"I'm explaining to Gerald why we're entering this year."

"Eurovision is older than you are, Father," Gregory said. "It just so happens that people who are liberal in other ways think Eurovision would be fun. It'll bring in tourist revenue during the spring shoulder season before full tourist season, and it gives everyone something to talk about."

"And also," Jerry said, "because Eddie really, really wanted us to enter."

"You make it sound so frivolous," Michaelis drawled.

"Eddie suggested it because he thinks it'd be good for publicity," Gregory said. Michaelis fixed him with a look. "And yes, he loves Eurovision and asked me nicely."

"It's good to be the king," Michaelis told Jerry.

"Anyway, the contract is signed, so my part is over. Our National Final to select a song to send to Eurovision is now in the hands of event planners and the broadcaster, where it belongs," Gregory continued.

"You had better not have pushed Alanna into planning it," Jerry threatened.

"What do I look like, Jerry? I had to tell her specifically several times that she was to keep the name of Eurovision out of her mind, her mouth, and her to-do list," Gregory said. "I *made her* make someone else do it."

"Well, I appreciate that," Jerry allowed.

"Turns out the people she's making do it include Lachlan and Jes," Michaelis added. Jerry raised his eyebrows at Gregory and mouthed *ballsy*.

"Anyway, the musical acts have all been notified," Gregory said, ignoring him, "so they just have to do all the rehearsing and lighting and things. The fellow from the Royal Shivadh Broadcast Agency knows how to coordinate it all, or at least he's faking it well."

"I suppose we'll need to attend?" Michaelis asked.

"They're going to set up a box for the king and his guests, yes," Gregory said. "I hope you can attend. I'm supposed to select the winner, and I think the idea is that you and Eddie will be asked to advise me."

"How many seats?"

"Dad, I am *the king*. You of all people should know I can have as many seats as I want. I assume you'd like to have Noah and Jes there, even if they'll probably be backstage half the time."

"Jes doesn't care for the red carpet in any case," Michaelis said. "But yes, I would like two extra seats, for them and Noah."

"Jerry, you're on Alanna's arm?"

"Actually, if Jes isn't doing the red carpet, you might ask Al if she'd go with you," Jerry said to Michaelis, who nodded agreeably. "I have some very important drag queen friends to squire into the reception. They'll need audience seats."

"You say that as though I'm going to put a quota on drag queens," Gregory said. "At a Eurovision National Final, of all places. There's an invitation coming to your calendars, I'm sure it'll have all that information about who to talk to for tickets and such. Do not ask Alanna, you'll only encourage her," he said, pointing back and forth between them.

"Why don't you enter as a vocalist, Uncle Mike?" Jerry asked. "If you enter, Greg's got to pick you, eh? That'd be fun, sending a king to Eurovision."

"You are so good at sowing discord," Michaelis told him, and Jerry preened a little. "It really is a natural talent, I can't think where it came from."

"Just lucky, I guess," Jerry said modestly. "All right, I'm going to need an outfit and a little flag to wave, must get cracking. Think about it, though. You'd sound great over a hot dance beat."

He tango'd out, just to make Gregory and Michaelis laugh, and got a bonus chance to twirl and dip Alanna when he caught her just inside the dining room doorway. She laughed and kissed him and then shoved him off gently.

ASKAZER-SHIVADLAKIA NATIONAL FINAL
COMPETITION PERFORMERS

Bes and Naomi - *River Water*
David Lansky - *Fait Accompli*
Carne Mista - *Capital Chaos*
Kairao - *Young Prince*
Solo Olo - *We Drink Davzda*
Alia - *According To Plan*
Doozy Points - *Aim To Please*
The Maritime Academy Seniors' Quartet - *Chanty*

Caleb got the invitation to the Askazer-Shivadlakia Eurovision National Final concert on his lunch break, sitting on a picnic bench with Ava on the beach promenade, just outside the Maritime Academy.

It wasn't a particularly lucrative job, being a music teacher, but as Ava said it paid the bills and soothed the soul. Ava handled the older students at the Academy, generally; Caleb taught the under-twelves, which he'd felt was a little brave of the administration, but so far nobody had complained. When he'd ventured to ask about this, in his first performance review, he'd gotten a blank look from the headmaster.

"I wouldn't be allowed to teach little kids in Galia, probably, is all," he'd added with a squirm.

The headmaster had considered him, brows drawn together for a moment, and then nodded, addressing the issue frankly.

"Well, we do things differently in Askazer-Shivadlakia," he'd said. "You're entirely qualified and you passed the background check easily, which is what concerns the school's administration. You're young, but we have other teachers in their early twenties, and you seem to do excellently with the children, particularly ones we've had behavioral concerns about. Besides, odds are pretty good at least one of the kids you teach will be trans. Good to give them some role models, don't you think?"

It had taken Caleb a while to internalize the idea of himself as a role model. He wondered what the headmaster was going to call his involvement, however distant, with Eurovision.

The invitation to the National Final came by email, but it was an exceptionally fancy one. There were animations and everything. When all the bells and whistles were done and it was just the text remaining, he stared down at his phone, perplexed.

"You look like someone smacked your ass," Ava said around a mouthful of sandwich. "Bad news?"

"The Palace just sent me four tickets to the Eurovision National Final concert, with a backstage VIP pass," Caleb said.

"Or maybe a scammer posing as the Palace did."

"Really?" Ava asked, leaning in to study the email over his shoulder. "Why?"

"According to this, it's the standard complimentary package for all performers and songwriters who are participating," Caleb said, scrolling through it. "I think they think I wrote a – "

He stopped, eyes widening.

"Oh, no," he said.

"This is going to be good," Ava sighed.

"Remember when I sold a song to that irritating man who thinks he's going to be the next big thing in Europop?" he said.

"I remember telling you that he didn't deserve a song that good," Ava said, nodding.

"He's in the National Final. Singing that song."

"Oh whoa! That's great for you though, isn't it? If he does well, your song'll be everywhere."

"I guess," Caleb said. "I'm sure he did an ugly arrangement."

"Still. Bet you get some good opportunities out of it. Are you going?"

"Don't know. If I do, I'll stay backstage. Want my tickets?"

"Sure," Ava said. "I'll scalp the ones I don't use and split the take with you."

"See if Derek wants to come, he might have fun," Caleb said.

Ava nodded, folding up the wax wrap from her lunch and accepting the rest of the apple he no longer had any interest in eating. "Come on, let's go tell everyone! This is exciting – "

"Oh, do we have to?" Caleb asked, getting up to follow her back up to the school. "I can't imagine it'll win. Anyway, I'm just the songwriter. You know I don't like attention."

"A little more attention and you could be running the music scene in Askazer-Shivadlakia," Ava said.

"Who wants that kind of responsibility? I just – I don't like being looked at. You know what I mean," he added, because he and Ava had been in this debate before. On more than one occasion, Ava had pointed out that he liked teaching, where people did look at you all day long. It was different, he insisted. When he taught, he was in charge, and there were social scripts for teaching, a clear boundary between teacher and student.

"Think we might be too late," Ava said, bringing him back to the present. She pointed at the window of the music room in the big old industrial building the Maritime Academy had taken over and converted. A slew of children, ages six through eighteen, all in faintly nautical uniforms, were leaning out the windows and waving. One of them was blowing a trumpet (poorly).

"Mr. Canto's going to Eurovision!" someone yelled.

The headmaster met them on the front steps, beaming.

"The Royal Shivadh Broadcast Agency released the competitor list," he said, tilting his head at the cheering children. "Someone spotted your name in the songwriters' section."

"I'm not going to Eurovision," Caleb said, a little cross at all the noise. "It's just someone who bought a song from me. And he's probably not going to Eurovision either."

"Ah, they're still proud of you," the headmaster replied. "Go let them congratulate you."

"Well, I'll go teach class, in any case," Caleb said.

The children were rowdy, which made his ears buzz, but once he shooed the older ones out and got the nine-year-olds settled in their usual places, the buzzing faded. Caleb knew he was more of a creature of habit than most and that some of the children were impatient with the rote ritual at the start of every class, but it tended to settle both him and them, and especially today it was comforting. Nothing different from any other ordinary day.

They did their practice drumbeat and sang a little song to start class like they always did. He was just getting up off the floor, where he sat with the kids who didn't like chairs, when one of them blurted, "Are you going to be on television?"

Caleb weighed his options. If they were given an inch, the children would derail for a mile. On the other hand, until he addressed the Eurovision issue, he wouldn't have any peace. As a teacher he preferred to let children guide their own learning anyway, at least to an extent. He'd rarely had that kind of freedom himself as a child. He'd leaned into the title of The Weird Kid, but he'd rather nobody had to call themselves that in his classes. They could all be weird together, at least he hoped.

"All right," he said, taking his watch off and handing it to the nearest child. "You keep time. You get five minutes to ask yes or no questions. Then we have to do scales."

"Why yes or no?" a kid asked. Another immediately piped up, "That's not a yes-or-no-question!"

They blew a minute on this debate, which was less than Caleb expected, and then got back to peppering him with questions about whether he'd be on television, his career as a songwriter, if he'd get to meet the king at the National Final, and how he wrote music. The last one was interrupted by his timekeeper telling him time was up, but it was a good segue back into the lesson, at least.

He had two more classes that afternoon where he had to hold the same yes-or-no question sessions. Walking home, tired but pleased at how he'd handled things, he decided he would go to the concert. It would be interesting, and he sent all kinds of songs out into the world and never got to see what happened to them. None of the others had ever been hits, or anything more prestigious than a jingle on a local radio station.

Looking back, deciding to attend was either his biggest mistake or an extremely fortunate choice. Difficult to say which.

When the new king decided to enter Askazer-Shivadlakia in the Eurovision Song Contest, he did it with the appropriate flair for a country that loved pageantry. The concert was an evening extravaganza, hosted by a charismatic local news anchor, Isaiah Wynn, and shown live on the Royal Shivadh Broadcast Agency's

Channel One, as well as streamed on the RSBA website. They had non-competing acts performing between the official ones and apparently a couple of funny sketches planned. There was an extensive red carpet, intercut with footage of the pre-show reception once the attendees were inside.

Caleb arrived at the concert hall early to secure an out-of-the-way perch in the dark empty seating area off to one side; he sat in his little niche and watched people preparing for the show while at the same time streaming the red carpet on his phone, propped on the neck of his ukulele, settled in his lap. Lachlan, working with the stage crew nearby, waved at him and pointed him out to Noah Deimos and his parent Jes, who both gave him friendly nods.

Meanwhile, outside, the old king arrived with Lady Alanna on his arm – a slightly-built woman with pale brown hair, who was wearing the hell out of a burnished-gold dress with bright red highlights. The Duke of Shivadlakia, looking like a movie idol in a tailored navy suit, followed with a pair of gorgeous drag queens, raising him several notches in Caleb's estimation.

Like most of the country, Caleb was fond of the new king, and he liked what he'd seen of his American fiancé. Gregory III was a stickler for the royal uniform at public events – sober black trousers and a jacket with a banded collar, touched with gold. Caleb had read in an interview that Gregory III subscribed to the old Shivadh belief that a king should dress plainly in order to make his partner his brightest ornament.

The American fiancé, Eddie Rambler – newly titled as the Duke of the Orange – seemed to delight in being ornamentation. There had been a lot of speculation about what an American influencer with a loud aesthetic might wear to a Eurovision National Final, and Caleb watched with the rest of the country as their car arrived. He saw Rambler get out of the car wearing a black suit as well, with the same gold trim and braid as the king's uniform – and then he saw that the jacket was sequined.

He could literally hear people outside the venue go nuts

when, on the little screen, Rambler stopped for the cameras, did a turn, and then ran his hands up his own arms, turning the sequins backwards and transforming his black jacket into vivid gold. The king, clearly adoring, helped him with the back and shoulders.

Caleb stopped paying attention to the stream when it switched over to footage inside the reception, where various nobles, dignitaries, and celebrities were mingling and making small talk. They couldn't have paid Caleb to go to that, but before he switched it off, he recognized a few of the night's performers enjoying the open bar. He looked for Kairao, but didn't see him in the reception.

About thirty seconds later, he found out why Kairao wasn't in the bar – because he wasn't anywhere in the building. Lachlan skidded up to him, a panicked look on his face.

"Hey, do you actually, uh, do you *know* Kairao?" he asked, without preamble. Caleb blinked at him. "You wrote his song, right? Do you know him?"

"Only to speak to," Caleb said. "I mean, we have a contract for him to use the song but we're not friends."

"Do you know where he might be?"

"Is he not here?" Caleb asked.

"He is not, and the stage manager is going to start beheading people soon if he doesn't show, and I am crying mascara down my cheeks on the inside in panic. Is there any way you can think of to get in touch with him?"

"I can text him," Caleb said, scrolling his contacts. He found him under first name Kairao, last name Dickwhoboughttavat. Lachlan let out a nervous laugh.

Lachlan Hines wants to know where you are, you're supposed to be at the National Final, he texted, and then looked up at Lachlan. "I'll let you know if he replies."

"Don't bother, go straight to the stage manager," Lachlan said, and Caleb gave him a thumbs up. "Come backstage, they're about to open the house."

Things got significantly more frantic after that, not just because of Kairao but because they were fast approaching curtain. Caleb stayed tucked back against one backstage wall, away from the madness, and said hi whenever anyone stopped for a breather in the last-minute production preparation, or to update him on the mad search for their missing competitor.

Eventually he skulked his way to the wings just off the stage, peering out from the shadows. He was opposite the king's box, which sat to one side above the audience, and he had a clear view of its occupants as they settled in. There was Rambler in person, lion's mane of gold hair neatly combed back, gleaming like a comet next to King Gregory III, who was solemn as his uniform. The Duke of Shivadlakia, an attractive man in a stylish suit, was next to the equally stylish and attractive Lady Alanna, arm slung around her shoulders but eyes on his phone. The old king was behind them, speaking with a worried-looking stagehand.

"They still haven't found Kairao," a voice said, and Caleb looked over his shoulder to see Noah standing behind him, peering up at the king's box. "Jes is supposed to be up in the box, but they're still helping look."

"I can't imagine where he got to," Caleb said, turning back to the stage. "I don't know much about him."

"I heard he's kind of a jerk."

"That tracks." Caleb moved aside so Noah could have a better view. "Shouldn't you go get your seat?"

"I'm fine, I'm not expected up there for a bit. I like backstage, like you," Noah said. Caleb frowned. "I mean, you're back here instead of out there, aren't you?"

"Yeah, I guess so. What happens if we don't find him?"

"They're moving him to last in the lineup. At least it won't spoil the rest of the show. Worst case, I guess someone could get up and vamp for three minutes. Jerry's probably got a tight five," he added thoughtfully.

"A what?"

"You know, a five-minute set of jokes. He's pretty funny. And they'd like that, the viewers I mean. Duke of Shivadlakia doing a little entertainment routine. National Broadcaster'll find some sucker to fill the time, anyway," Noah finished. The old king Michaelis, up in the box, turned to face the stage; he tilted his head, clearly spotting Noah in the wings, and made a brief summoning gesture. "Agh. Guess I gotta go up. You gonna stay back here, Mr. Canto?"

"Yes – still waiting to hear from Kairao. Hope he hasn't died or something."

"He better have, honestly. If he hasn't, Lachlan'll kill him. Seeya later!" Noah added, and ran off. Caleb watched until he saw Noah slip into the king's box and settle in behind Rambler.

Eventually, determining that he wouldn't be in the way, Caleb dragged a wobbly stool over and perched himself with a decent view of the stage and the king's box, if not most of the audience.

Jes slipped into their seat between Noah and Michaelis just as the lights went down for the start of the concert. Michaelis had a moment of relief, until he saw the worried look on their face.

"Still no sign of your missing artist?" he asked in a low voice.

"No, but Lachlan told me to let it be his problem," they answered quietly. "Trying to relax about it."

"Good. I know how hard you worked on this. You should enjoy it," he said. Noah shushed them both. "Yes, all right."

Michaelis was willing to concede that it wasn't an unpleasant evening. If some of the music wasn't to his taste, at least it was brief, and it was good to see what kinds of art the culture was producing. He could tell from Gregory's posture that he was taking the same kind of mental notes, which was only sensible. Michaelis, having retired, could play politics for sport. Gregory took it seriously as his job.

In any case, he could tell Jes was happy he was there, even as they kept having to get up to help with backstage business. And it was good for Noah to be exposed to Shivadh culture, traditional or modern, after growing up in New York. He took his duty to educate the boy seriously, and also enjoyed the comedy of it.

"I think I liked that one best," Noah said to him, leaning across Jes's empty seat as Solo Olo, who'd been singing an admittedly catchy drinking song, left the stage.

"I think Theophile did as well," Michaelis agreed, nodding at Eddie, who had laughed his way through the song. "Haven't you got to support your Academy friends, though?"

"They know they won't win. They just think it'll be fun to be on TV," Noah replied, and then shushed Michaelis again with a gesture as the applause died away. Jes reappeared as he was leaning back into his own seat.

"No sign of him," they said in his ear. He squeezed their shoulder reassuringly. Kings had fallen and countries been laid waste, but not Askazer-Shivadlakia, at least not recently, and certainly not because of an absentee Eurovision performer. "Lachlan's working on a backup plan now."

"If it's the worst thing that goes wrong, everything will be fine," he murmured back.

It had been an excellent plan to situate himself where he was, Caleb decided. Not only was he out of the way, with a view of the performances and sights on the king's box, but he was central enough to have become a hub of the Search For Kairao. Which, once you got past the panic, was a little funny. People would run past his perch and toss out a word or two of update, and when Lachlan came by he'd pass on the lack of news, and Lachlan would flail some more and run off. He felt bad being amused, but only a little. It didn't matter all that much, in the grand scheme of things.

By the time they were headed for the second-to-last performers, the Maritime Academy kids, he'd decided on his vote, not that he really got a say in who would win. Each country had their own way of selecting acts to send; Askazer-Shivadlakia seemed content to let the king pick, as long as he considered the televote's favorites. For Caleb's money he was going to pick either the drinking song (which Rambler clearly liked) or the almost-as-catchy but much more somber song called "River Water," which represented the Shivadh love of drama poignantly. It was the kind of song to appeal to a man who had actively sought out a leadership role in a country that mostly called him king because it seemed more interesting than president or prime minister.

It was a shame Kairao clearly wasn't going to get to perform Caleb's song; he might have won. Almost fun to consider that, given that it wasn't going to happen and was therefore safe to laugh about.

Then, just as the Maritime Academy students were taking the stage, Lachlan arrived one last time, jerked his head in the direction of the dressing rooms, and said, "We have to talk, away from the stage."

Caleb followed him, curious, listening with half an ear to see if Ava had managed to school the quartet's tenor away from dominating.

"We've given up Kairao as a lost cause," Lachlan said. "Can't find him anywhere."

"Well, it's a shame, but it wasn't *that* great a song," Caleb said.

"I like it," Lachlan protested, "but that's not the point."

"What are you going to fill the time with? It's only three minutes, do you even need to?"

Lachlan blinked at him. "You can perform it, can't you?"

"I wrote it, of course I – " Caleb began, before he saw where the conversation was going. "Oh, no."

"He's got a backing track," Lachlan said. "You could go on. You know the lyrics – "

"I can't just go on for someone. I haven't even heard the backing track, though it's safe to assume it's dreadful," Caleb said. Lachlan's face did some complicated acrobatics Caleb wasn't even going to bother trying to interpret.

"It's not good," Lachlan said. "But you could make it work. Come on, you know you could."

"This is a nationally televised concert," Caleb hissed. "Streamed to all of Europe!"

"We need to fill three minutes and it's supposed to be with your song! Get with the program!" Lachlan insisted. "It's the song that's important, not really who sings it."

"What Eurovision have *you* been watching?" Caleb asked.

"They don't have Eurovision in Massachusetts! Look, there's going to be dead air or at the very least a weird gap in timing if someone doesn't play the song, and you wrote it. Don't you want to perform it?"

"No!" Caleb said emphatically. "I don't perform live! It's due to a health issue known as *social anxiety*."

"There's nothing social about a professional music career, even the socializing is business," Lachlan said, which was kind of a point, but Caleb just gave him a stubborn look. "You don't have to talk to anyone or anything. You just get your guitar, or someone's guitar, and play the song."

Caleb rubbed his eyes. "Ukulele."

"Gesundheit."

"I have my ukulele. I can play it on that, I don't have the guitar part in my head. Lachlan, are you going to make me play a song I wrote, on a ukulele, cold, in front of the king?"

"Would a hype-man backup dancer help? Kairao had three lined up," Lachlan offered desperately.

"Absolutely not. It's just – I hate being stared at," Caleb said, trying to breathe deep. "It's fine if I can't tell, but in front of a crowd I can see all their faces, I can see them reacting, or what I think is them reacting, it gets me in my head…"

"Look, I get it, but it's just for three minutes. The lights will be low, you'll barely – oh, hang on," Lachlan said, moving past Caleb to rummage in some junk on top of a nearby crate. "Do you need to see? Like do you need to have good vision, in order to play the song?"

"What?" Caleb asked.

"In order to sing. Do you have to be able to see?"

"Well, no. Just to get onstage, but otherwise…"

"Okay. Perfect. Here." Lachlan produced a pair of sunglasses, the rainbow-mirrored kind douchebags on the beach generally wore. "Put these on. Once the lights go down you won't be able to see a thing. Or just close your eyes, nobody'll be able to tell. No faces, no audience, you won't hear anything over whatever's coming in your earpieces."

Caleb took the sunglasses and stared down at them. "This won't look weird onstage?"

"It's Eurovision," Lachlan said.

"Point taken." He looked up at Lachlan. "Is this really that important?"

"It's…it's show business," Lachlan said. "It's simultaneously the most important thing in the world and the lowest stakes possible. Nobody dies if you don't go play the ukulele for the king."

Caleb looked back at the sunglasses and then at the stage, where the Maritime Academy quartet was beginning its performance.

"You owe me something I can't even describe right now," he said, gesturing at Lachlan with the sunglasses.

"If I didn't have boundaries I would kiss you," Lachlan told him. "Stay there, don't move," he added, and bolted away.

Thirty seconds later, a swarm of people *without* boundaries descended – a tech to mic him up, another to try and fix monitors in his ears, and one more to hook a pickup into his ukulele – incompetently, as it turned out, and Caleb ducked away from all the attention to do it himself. He took the monitors from the tech ("Please don't – don't touch my ears!") and fixed those himself as well, while he ran mentally through the chord progression.

The upside was, with no backing track or backup singers, nobody was going to be able to tell if he screwed it up and had to improvise.

Then Lachlan was hustling him towards the stage, and the host, Wynn, was doing a little verbal soft-shoe to introduce him. He was saying something that sounded confident, at least, about a minor incident and Kairao being unable to perform – but it was all about the song, after all, not the performer. (Again, Caleb thought, what Eurovision were these people watching?) And the songwriter had graciously agreed to perform the song himself, in a special arrangement just for the National Final.

Super special, Caleb thought, heart about to pound out of his chest. *Just the most special ever.*

He was glad he'd worn a suit; normally his only two outfits were the suits he wore to events and class, and the hoodie-and-cargos combo he wore everywhere else. It would have been nice to be wearing new Chucks, but the scuffs probably wouldn't show up on camera. And if he was going to go onstage, on national television even if it was a very small nation, in front of a live audience that included the entire royal family...at least he looked like a short, overly cool Tenth Doctor cosplayer.

Lachlan aimed him at the stage, where someone had thankfully put a single chair for him to sit in. And then, with applause, CALEB CANTO – YOUNG PRINCE was walking into Shivadh National Final history.

Things went black for a second, which he had sort of expected given the way his pulse was pounding and the darkness of the sunglasses. Then the music filled the world like it always did when he sat down to play –

And then something very unexpected happened.

CHAPTER TWO

THE SECOND SOMEONE came onstage for Kairao, the missing final artist, Noah could see Jes relax. He did too; Lachlan had come through, like he always did, and Noah resolved to talk to Gregory about what a good job Lachlan had done. He was still slightly intimidated by the king sometimes, but Gregory should know how hard Lachlan had worked on the National Final. Maybe there was a commendation Gregory could bestow, and who better than Noah to ask for it?

And Lachlan had found a *really good* replacement – that was Mr. Canto, the music teacher who'd written the song. He looked super cool coming out onstage in his high-tops and fitted suit and mirrored sunglasses that were just on the right side of tacky, the lights catching on his short blond hair like a halo.

Noah liked Mr. Canto and had wanted to get to know him better, but hadn't ever found the right excuse to talk to him much. Lots of people at school had been impressed that their under-twelves music teacher had written a song for the National Final. Noah hadn't heard it, but he knew through rumor that Mr. Canto didn't think much of what Kairao had done with it. Which just meant that this performance was probably how it was meant to be heard, and Noah was interested in that.

Mr. Canto seated himself and, after a brief pause, started to play the intro, a complicated combination of picking and strumming on the little amped ukulele. Noah glanced sidelong at Michaelis, sitting behind Gregory. He wondered what the royal family thought of songs about like…royalty and stuff. It must be

28

different when you'd grown up that way. Michaelis sometimes called Noah a princeling, but he meant it metaphorically.

He saw Michaelis shift, sitting forward with a controlled movement that meant he was carefully trying not to draw attention. Then the lyrics Mr. Canto had started to sing registered, and Noah's head whipped around to stare at the solitary musician, sitting in a single spot center-stage, instrument propped in his lap. From the corner of his eye he saw Gregory tilt his head curiously.

The song opened on a word that sounded an awful lot like *tavat*, the first vowel drawn out long like a sung prayer; there was a phrase Noah didn't understand, which sounded like it was in Shivadh, and then he launched into the English lyrics.

> *Every wave someday reaches a distant country's shore*
> *But the tides follow on and the water here is pure*
> *Your sails spread wider now than mine*
> *But someday I'll still leave you behind*
> *And until then, I'll be your guide*
>
> *Tavat —*
> *Enn tavat dach ois talah ta-nem*
> *And I've given you all I can…*

Noah, who'd been called Tavat often enough by Michaelis, and lately by Eddie and Lachlan (amused) and Jerry (when he was teasing Noah for being uppity), thought of the word as *his*. It was shocking to hear it from someone outside the royal family. From Michaelis's reaction, Noah wasn't the only one who was surprised.

"Did he just say that?" Noah asked Jes. His parent put their finger to their lips and gestured at the stage — not chiding him for talking over the performance, Noah realized, but because they wanted to hear what he was singing.

It was one of those pop songs where the tune was so catchy that you found your brain slipping away from the lyrics for the most part. Still, he got impressions – it was about a man talking to his child, who was getting to the age where he was starting to venture out in the world, and how worrying that was for his father. The kid himself was fearless enough to be…yes, he was singing *tavat*, and then that same Shivadh phrase, leading into the chorus.

"What's it mean?" he asked Jes, leaning in to hear their reply.

"The Shivadh? It's a proverb. In English, it means *a tavat buys his own birthright*," Jes replied.

"…what the heck does *that* mean?"

"Tell you later."

By the time he got to the high point of the song, where the singer was passing his crown to the prince, the audience had caught on to the bouncing cadence of the Shivadh proverb on the second line of the chorus, and was singing along. Noah could see Eddie's head nodding in time. Michaelis's face was a mask, but Noah had started to recognize that it was the expression he made when he was thinking deeply about something. Or amused and trying not to laugh, but this didn't seem like that kind of situation.

Mr. Canto let the last line of the song taper off, continuing to strum on the ukulele, then finished with a couple of finger plucks. He brought his hand down on the strings to dampen them to silence, and then sang a final drawn out *Tavat!* a capella.

Noah had worked mostly in audio media in his young life, but he'd attended more than enough live performance to know that sometimes the best thing in the theater to watch was the audience. He craned his neck and bent forward to see as many people as possible, and the lights from the stage were enough to pick out plenty of faces. Most were pleased, but more than a few looked like they were coming out of something like a trance, startled to be back in the audience of the National Final. Eddie, from his posture, might be one of them. Gregory was leaning back to speak to Michaelis, both of them carefully in shadow.

The applause was wild as Mr. Canto stood up, and the audience went bananas when he dropped into a low Shivadh bow.

"Well," Gregory said, turning to Eddie as they announced that the televote was open. "Apparently this isn't going to be an especially difficult choice."

"He's worried. What's he worried about?" Noah asked Jes, as Gregory got up to head backstage.

"He's king, worrying is his job," Jes replied.

"What does it mean, the thing about the birthright?"

"A tavat buys his own birthright," his parent repeated.

"That, yeah."

Jes sighed, looking at him – until a year ago they'd had to look down, but now he was taller than they were, and still growing.

"Birthright's a chance of fate," they said. "Someone's born first, or richer, or to a more well-connected parent. Birthrights aren't earned. But a tavat is very daring – he doesn't have to settle for whatever he used to be. He makes his own destiny."

"Huh," Noah said thoughtfully. He caught Jes and Michaelis exchanging a look, but wasn't sure what it meant. Michaelis leaned forward to speak to Eddie, and Jes got out their phone.

"You'd better vote," they said to him. Noah took his own phone out and considered – he'd been planning to vote for the Academy students, but…well, Mr. Canto was Academy too.

He voted, and then got distracted with text messages from his Academy friends about Mr. Canto's surprise showing, and before he knew it, Gregory was walking out onstage.

Caleb was glad he hadn't let Lachlan take the sunglasses away after the performance. He was reeling, confused by what had just happened, the strange chemistry he'd felt with the audience and with the music itself. It had been electrifying, easily one of the best performances he'd ever given, even counting the private recordings with no audience, the way he preferred.

He'd had a few minutes after performing, during the televote, to get a drink of water and compose himself, but not very long – almost immediately he had to go back onstage, because all the acts were supposed to line up behind the king in a little tableau while he announced the winner. Supposedly the king was consulting the televote from the National App, but Caleb sensed that Gregory III listened carefully to advice and then did whatever he wanted. You didn't get to be dating Eddie Rambler by listening to polls.

The king came onstage to immediate applause and a shrill whistle from his fiancé; he held up his hands for quiet, which took a moment, while Caleb felt more awkward by the second. The others were all in fancy performing clothes, costumes clearly selected specifically for this, and next to them he looked like the accountant for a flamboyant pop supergroup.

"Thank you so much for attending tonight and for that warm welcome onto the stage," the king said, clasping his hands together and beaming. "However, let's put this applause where it belongs, with our performers!"

He gestured behind him, and the hall erupted in more applause. Caleb glanced nervously at the others. They seemed okay with it.

"The televote is closed and being tabulated as we speak," the king continued. "Now, I'd like to remind you all that I am king and my word is law, but I'm told asserting a dictatorship this early in the reign is frowned upon, so I will be consulting the country's feelings on the matter. I personally think – "

"Gregory!" a voice called, and everyone's heads turned towards the wings, except for the king, who just pinched the bridge of his nose in annoyance.

"Yes, Jerry," he said.

Caleb had noticed the Duke of Shivadlakia leaving the box with the king and arriving backstage. He was prepared for this – unlike one of the other musicians, who muttered, "Oh great, they're doing a *skit*," under her breath.

The duke swanned onstage in a set of elaborate black robes

and a fake goatee. The audience roared.

"You look like a Shakespeare villain. What is this?" the king asked, waving at the duke's getup. His cousin struck a dramatic pose of offended shock.

"I am your vizier," he announced. "I am here to ad-vizier you. You can't make this decision without me!"

"And the goatee?"

"Evil vizier," the duke said, as if this should be obvious.

The audience was loving it. Even the performers were grinning. A stagehand darted out from the wings and thrust a sheet of paper into Duke Gerald's hands.

"Now, you can listen to the people, or your own good judgment, but then what are you paying me for?" he asked, holding the paper out of King Gregory's reach.

"I'm not paying you," the king said. Duke Gerald seemed to consider this.

"Well, in that case," he said, and handed over the paper. The king took it with a mock-annoyed look and cleared his throat. Duke Gerald leaned over his shoulder and pointed something out, then was elbowed away.

"Now, if the rest of my family has no input," His Majesty drawled, "It seems that my own personal choice is perfectly supported by the excellent taste of my subjects. So I would like to present to you the winning song of the Askazer-Shivadlakia National Final, the people's favorite and the king's choice: *Young Prince*, written and performed by Caleb Canto!"

It took the words a second to register. By the time they had, one of the other musicians had clapped Caleb on the shoulder. He stumbled forward, bewildered, and dodged out of the reach of two Academy students, who were trying to drag him downstage. The dodge took him that direction anyway, up to where the king and his vizier were waiting. The king gave him a low bow, which was a relief, and Caleb bowed back. The cheering was an endless, deafening roar.

"Encore!" The duke shouted into the storm, and the audience began to chant after him. Caleb looked at the king, who was smiling at him, gesturing for him to take center stage.

The chair had been cleared away and it was difficult to chord and strum while also trying to hold the ukulele with no strap. He pulled it out of the case on his back, looked around while it was amped up again by a stagehand (one who knew what they were doing this time). Then – seeing no other option – Caleb did what he would have done at school. He crossed his ankles, bent his knees, and dropped into a seat on the ground, tailor-fashion.

The cheering turned to laughter and for a mortified second Caleb froze. But then the king, standing next to him, raised a hand and gave the audience a warning look. Silence fell abruptly as the king shook his finger at them.

Then the king crouched, propped himself on his hands, and crossed his legs to sit as well, like a kid in one of Caleb's classes. Caleb watched, mistrustful, waiting for the punchline to this joke, but it didn't come.

"Go ahead," His Majesty said gently, and one of the students yelled *Play it, Mr. Canto!*

He gave the king one last look, still ready to stop the second someone laughed, but eight bars in, the king was still sitting there in his black and gold uniform, listening intently, hands folded in his lap. Ten bars in, the duke joined him on the floor.

> *And I know it good, and true*
> *How the crown has passed to you*
> *Tavat*

He got through the song for the second time in fifteen minutes without a problem, and nobody laughed again. When he was done, people clapped.

The king and his cousin stood up, and Caleb saw King Gregory reaching down to offer him a hand; he began to scramble up on his own, defensively, but the king never reached him. Instead the duke caught his cousin's wrist, arm darting out like lightning, and then gracefully twisted to pull the king away and into an impromptu dance step. His eyes caught Caleb's briefly – not that he could see Caleb's, behind the sunglasses – and he winked before he whisked the king into a twirl, distracting both the king and the audience so that Caleb could get offstage with the others.

By the time the show actually ended, the king's box was already half-empty – Gregory and Jerry had been onstage and now were backstage, probably going directly to the reception. Alanna had gone with Jerry to help him get into his silly costume, and Eddie was already at the door, waiting on Michaelis.

"I'm committed to at least half an hour of politics," Michaelis said, rising and kissing Jes, then leaning around to kiss Noah on the forehead. "You two take a town car home. I'll get a ride with Gregory back to the palace and walk from there. Be thirty minutes behind you."

"Not if you're trying to get a ride with Gregory, you won't," Jes said, looking amused at his optimism. "Don't worry about it – go do your work. We'll look after ourselves."

Noah followed Jes out into the hallway, avoiding the press of people below by slipping into the control booth and going down and out through the loading dock. The town cars – sleek, black, and adorned with the arms of the royal family – were nearly as fancy inside as limos, and they likewise came with drivers. Most of the time, Noah and Jes tooled around in a beat-up van, and he was still lobbying unsuccessfully to be allowed to try driving Michaelis's Jaguar, so the town cars were novel and fun.

"I wonder where Mr. Canto got the word tavat. Maybe it's more common than I thought," Noah said, as they got into the car. The driver turned around, giving them a friendly smile.

"Fishing lodge?" he asked.

"Please," Jes said, then turned to Noah as the car started up. "Mr. Canto teaches at your school, doesn't he?"

"Yeah, music for the younger kids. I don't really know him or anything."

"But you're new, so everyone knows you," Jes pointed out.

Noah nodded. "Guess so. Not that many new kids in Askazer-Shivadlakia. Did me a favor, for once."

"Didn't I say it would? And it's not a *secret* that Michaelis and I are seeing each other. He's called you Tavat in front of other people sometimes. Do you think he ever said it while he was dropping you off at school?"

Noah frowned until realization hit. "You think Mr. Canto got it from *me?*" he asked, shocked.

"I'm pretty sure, yeah. If it makes you – "

"That's *awesome!*" Noah crowed.

"…uncomfortable…" Jes trailed off, sighing. "Of course you think it's awesome."

"He wrote a song about me? And it's going to Eurovision? That's so cool!" Noah said, ignoring his parent's lack of enthusiasm. "Do you think I should, like, ask him about it?"

"I think someone will probably be speaking to him about it," Jes said. "Don't worry about it tonight, anyway," they added, throwing an arm over his shoulders. "You tired?"

"Yeah, but I gotta stay up and text Eddie about it, I bet he'll think it's cool, and look on Photogram to see if anyone else noticed…" Noah had his phone out and was just opening Photogram when Jes covered his eyes with one hand.

"You can text and surf until we get home," they said. "After that, no more screen tonight so you can sleep, okay? It's a Sunday night, you have school tomorrow and you hate being tired for school."

"Fine, deal," Noah said, and Jes took their hand away just in time for a text message from Eddie to pop up.

Screaming about this song, it read. *Metaphoric screaming. Greg thinks it's about you. Seemed Very Serious about it ten minutes ago, is now deep in discussion with mayor of nearby French village about road maintenance.*

Noah beamed. *I knew you'd think it was cool! Boss thinks it's about me too. Is Michaelis in on the road discussion?*

Michaelis is speaking Italian to someone. Study hard, being an American who only speaks English and culinary Spanish sucks, Eddie said.

Just checking. Going to bed when I get home so no more texting. Tag me in anything interesting, Noah finished.

Will do, kid. J & A say hi.

Noah sent a thumbs-up emoji, flipped over to Photogram, and poked around in the hashtags. Plenty of commentary on the show, on the king and his family, and even some remarks about Noah looking nice in his new suit for the performance, which was flattering. Nothing about the song being about him, though, at least not before they pulled up to the fishing lodge. He sighed, putting the phone in shutdown and showing it to Jes.

"Very mature decision," they said. "You're doing great at being a top of the line human right now."

"Maturity is boring, I want to play games on my phone until four in the morning," Noah said.

"When you're paying for your own internet, my son, you too can claim past-midnight gaming as your birthright," Jes told him.

As Caleb came offstage there was a flurry of activity. He found himself buffeted away from the rest of the performers by congratulatory stagehands, a few VIPs, and at least two reporters.

"Come on, come on, let the man get a breath," a voice said, and a pair of people were wading in to block him off, herding him into a side hallway. He saw Lachlan putting himself bodily in the entrance to the hall. A man Caleb didn't know was now standing with him in the otherwise-empty hallway, looking around cautiously.

"I'm Stephen," he said to Caleb. "Lachlan's husband. Let's get you out of here."

"I haven't got a ride home," Caleb blurted. He'd planned to walk.

"It's adorable you think you get to go home now," Lachlan called over his shoulder. Caleb scowled.

"As the winner, you have to go to the reception," Stephen said. "There's an interview set up and everything."

Caleb bit down on the retort that he didn't *have* to do anything, and instead gave him a measured look. "You're married to Lachlan?"

"Yes?" Stephen said, baffled.

"Got any kids?"

"Yes…"

"You owe me your firstborn," Caleb said. Stephen cracked a relieved smile.

"You can have her, babysitters are expensive," he said. "Come on. This way – "

There was a smattering of applause when Caleb walked into the backstage bar that the pre-performance reception had also been in, but the people here were too polite to crowd. He looked around for the cameras – there and there, the live feeds. He turned his face to the nearest one and gave a polite wave.

Stephen, who was being nice enough that Caleb was rethinking demanding his firstborn, delivered him to a brightly lit little stage at one end of the room, blocked off by camera equipment. There were two men there – one Caleb didn't recognize, in a conservative brown suit, and the other the host of the show, Wynn the news anchorman, still in his flashy velvet-and-glitter stage outfit. Caleb couldn't help but think of the ads for the local news hour – *Isaiah Wynn has news for you!*

"Mr. Canto," Wynn said, coming forward to greet him, his

conservatively-dressed companion hovering behind him. "Don't know about you but I am absolutely fucking beat."

Caleb smiled at his frankness, a welcome relief. "You probably did a marathon out there, the way you were running around."

"We can't all give encores sitting down with the king. Can you give me ten minutes of live interview? I mean, contractually you'd have to," Wynn said, gesturing at the other man. "RSBA Channel One has a contract with most of the performers. On the other hand, you weren't supposed to perform tonight, so I assume you didn't sign a contract."

"We'll have to fix that," the other man said.

"Leave him alone, Rob, he can sign your contract tomorrow," Wynn said, before turning back to Caleb. "Anyway, I'm tired and you look done, so I could be bid down. I'd settle for five minutes now and a half-hour later this week sometime."

"That," Caleb said, and Wynn nodded agreeably. "Uh, can I...keep my ukulele with me? I know that sounds weird but it's comforting."

Back in Galia, he'd taken to tapping the strings of whatever instrument was nearby, as a stim; in Fons-Askaz he just always had his ukulele with him. It was very calming and pretty subtle, but would probably look weird on camera. Wynn's eyes darted from the instrument to Caleb's face, assessing.

"I don't see why not," he said, watching Caleb's fingers tap the strings where he held it at the neck. "We can keep it off-camera if you'd like."

"Please," Caleb said, and Wynn waved him into the interview chair. While the cameramen got the feed going, Caleb peered around the camera, taking in the room. Some of the other musicians were at the bar; the king and his family were trickling in, and the mayor of Fons-Askaz was shaking hands. Various other rich or powerful (or both) people were scattered around, but the room wasn't too full, at least.

The interview turned out to be a lot like his question times with the kids, only he had to answer slightly more complicated questions.

"Now, this is a little embarrassing because we don't have a bio on you," Wynn said, after making their on-air introductions. "You were a last-minute replacement for Kairao, is that right?"

"Yes, I wasn't meant to perform," Caleb said.

"Can you tell us anything about why you had to step in?"

"Well," Caleb said measuredly, "I'm the only other person who knows how to sing the song."

He hadn't been trying for a laugh, but he got one; when Wynn stopped chuckling, he said, "I suppose that's what I get for trying to get gossip about a hot young rising star. So, Caleb, tell us about yourself. Are you a full-time musician?"

"No, I'm a teacher," Caleb replied. "I teach music at the Shivadh Maritime Academy."

"Ah! So you must have enjoyed their performance."

Caleb suppressed the urge to say *They were a little flat in places* and went with, "We're very proud of our students," which was neutral, pleasant, and true.

"Did you attend the Maritime Academy yourself?"

"Oh – no, I was raised in Galia," Caleb said.

"Galia!"

"I spent summers here – my mother was Shivadh, and I visited her during holidays. But I went to school in Galia. I didn't move here until recently – actually, it's been a few years now. I left when I was 18, and I'm 24. So six years."

"You seem to have settled in! What made you decide to move to Askazer-Shivadlakia?"

"Oh – well, I liked that the king is elected here. And everyone could see King Gregory was probably going to be the next king."

"Ah! You voted for His Majesty? I suppose now he's paid you back, picking your song as the winner."

"Yes – I always liked him," Caleb said, trying to show a

measured amount of earnestness. "I think a lot of queer people come to Askazer-Shivadlakia – gay, lesbian, trans like me, what have you – because we know the king's...on our side isn't quite right, but it's like that, isn't it?"

"I suppose so," Wynn said.

"Besides, he sat down with me."

"During your encore, you mean."

"I thought that was very polite," Caleb said. "And he didn't let anyone laugh at me. Plus," he added, considering, "He's not that much taller than I am, which is comforting."

"A couple of short kings have to stick together," Wynn said, and then turned to the camera. "Later this week we'll have Mr. Canto in studio to talk with us about his song and his plans for Eurovision. Thank you, Caleb, for your time."

"My pleasure," Caleb said, and only when the camera light blinked out did he realize he'd been in the sunglasses for all of it. He fumbled the glasses off his face, standing.

"You know, don't take this the wrong way," Wynn told him, "but I've never met such a naturally entertaining person in an interview who was also as insanely awkward as you."

"I had my sunglasses on!" Caleb told him, horrified.

"Exactly! You looked deeply cool, and I could tell you'd just forgotten they were there," he replied. "You gave me nothing with one hand and poured gold in my lap with the other. Truly amazing. Can't wait to see you in studio. Let me give you my number and we'll get it set up."

He took Caleb's phone and tapped his number in; Caleb took the phone back and sidled slightly behind the camera so he could study the room some more without being seen, but he was too slow. Lachlan noticed he was free and bounded over.

"Caleb, I am so sorry, I am so sorry," he said. "Stephen said we owe you Bonnie, do you want her in the car seat or the stroller?"

"Babysitter for tonight expensive?" Caleb asked.

"We didn't really need to save for her college tuition," Lachlan sighed. "Seriously, what can I get you? A drink? Something to eat? Xanax? That's not a joke, I know people."

"I'm a musician, I can get my own drugs," Caleb said wearily. "Ride home? Do I have to circulate? Also, why is the Duke of Shivadlakia staring at me?"

Lachlan casually glanced over his shoulder. The duke was leaning on the bar; he'd shed the robes and was back in the nice suit he'd been wearing earlier, but he'd kept the fake goatee. He was standing with Lady Alanna, apparently holding a conversation – but he was watching Caleb.

"Maybe he was enthralled by your raw magnetism," Lachlan said, turning back. Caleb shot him an appalled look. "Or he's like a bird, he saw himself in your sunglasses and now he's imprinted. Do you want to say hello?"

"Don't think I have a choice," Caleb said, because the duke had definitely seen Lachlan look at him, and was now moving across the room to where they stood, removing his fake goatee as he came.

"You'll be fine, I've met him, he's a goofball," Lachlan said.

"I see my reputation precedes me," the duke remarked, grinning at Lachlan as he arrived. "I am, indeed, the foremost goofball of this great country of ours."

"Caleb Canto, this is Gerald, twelfth Duke of Shivadlakia," Lachlan said, gesturing between them. "This is Caleb, our new Eurovision man."

"Jerry's fine," the duke said, and gave Caleb an elegant bow. Caleb wondered if he was doing it on purpose or if all the nobility just bowed instead of shaking hands for preference. Caleb bowed back. "It's a pleasure. I enjoyed your song tremendously."

"Thank you. Glad I could pull you away from your phone," Caleb said. Jerry beamed, and Caleb filled with the pleasure of a smartass remark properly made.

"It takes some doing, let me tell you," Jerry replied.

"Lachlan!" someone called, and Caleb tried to convey *please don't leave me alone with the king's favorite advisor* but Lachlan just said, "I have to go – shepherd him," to Jerry, and darted away.

"Don't worry, I don't bite unless provoked," Jerry said. "And I'll keep the rest of the sharks at bay. This must be a lot."

"I just gave an entire interview wearing these," Caleb said, holding up the sunglasses.

"You look great in them, if it's any consolation. Next week half the city will be in mirrored shades, trying to pull it off and failing."

"They helped, onstage," Caleb muttered.

"I imagine so," Jerry said, and Caleb was startled enough by the sympathy in his voice to make eye contact. There was a shocking level of understanding in the other man's face – enough that he realized it definitely hadn't been happenstance when Jerry pulled the king away from him onstage.

"You did it on purpose, didn't you?" he asked, without thinking about whether he ought to bring it up. "When the king went to help me up and you grabbed him."

"Ah – yes, I hope that was all right. I saw where you didn't want your students to touch you," Jerry said. "I…know some people with sensory issues. Greg's a good guy, he wouldn't have done it if he'd known, but that's what he's got me for," he added with a smile. "You should put it in your performance rider – you know, two bottles of spring water, three options of hot meals, warm damp towels, no unnecessary physical contact. They've definitely seen weirder."

"I don't usually gig," Caleb said. "Songwriting and studio work only. Not the kind of thing that needs a rider, for sure."

"Well, you'll have to have one for semi-finals."

"Oh, I'm not…" Caleb trailed off. "I'm not going to *go* to the semi-finals. The song is going."

Jerry frowned. "May I call you Caleb?" he asked. At Caleb's nod, he continued. "Caleb, you do understand you've won, yes?

You're going to Eurovision to represent us."

"No, they'll still send Kairao, right? He's the one who was supposed to perform it," Caleb pointed out. "I just wrote it."

"Does he own the rights?" Jerry asked. "I mean, do you still have any legal right to perform the song? Or sell it?"

"I...actually, I do," Caleb said, realization dawning. "I use the same contract every time. It says anything I license out, I still own, and I have the right to perform or record it."

"Clever of you, and my point exactly. Why would we send someone else? You did a great job and you've got a really fun schtick," Jerry said.

"It's not a schtick, it's just my life."

"I mean with the look, and the single spotlight with the ukulele. Though you might swap to guitar. Little more oomph," Jerry said.

"That's what I mean, though. Kairao has all the oomph," Caleb said.

"Well, there's such a thing as too much oomph. He can't, anyway, not after tonight. Haven't you heard? We just got the news, maybe not."

Panic filled Caleb suddenly, that all of the jokes about *He'd better be dead!* weren't actually going to be funny. "Oh, no. Is he – is he dead? We couldn't find him before the show, but..."

"Not dead, no," Jerry said, and Caleb's chest eased. Then he added, incredibly casually, "He was arrested about a half an hour before the show, in Monaco."

"*Monaco?*" Caleb asked, suddenly furious. "He knew the concert was tonight! Why was he in Monaco?"

"Apparently because that is where the cocaine is," Jerry said.

"Ugh, I should never have..." Caleb rubbed his forehead. "I have to stop selling music to anyone who wants to buy it. Background checks from now on."

The duke looked amused. "Good plan. But it does mean you're the one going to Eurovision, unless – " he turned briefly, because someone was approaching, some well-wisher Caleb didn't know. "Ah," he said to the woman, shaking his head. "Get on the waitlist, his dance card's full tonight."

She rolled her eyes. "Jerry – "

"Nuh-uh. It's been a long enough evening without having to make small talk. Shoo, go," Jerry said, and she pouted but turned and walked away. "Sorry," he added, turning back to Caleb, "but I didn't think you wanted ten thousand repeats of the same *Congratulations, you're so great, can I have a selfie* conversation, starting with Askazer-Shivadlakia's least interesting Photogram model."

"Can I hire you? Like as a bodyguard?" Caleb asked. Jerry smiled.

"I make a spectacular chaperone but my fiancée would probably veto," he said. "What was I saying?" he asked, and clearly actually did need an answer.

"I'm going to Eurovision unless," Caleb prompted.

"Ah. Yes! Unless you truly have to refuse. In which case we can just send the runner-up, but that's a bit anticlimactic for us as a drama-loving people. At a guess, the network would want you to act as a judge in some kind of one-night, pick-a-replacement reality show. Which could be fun, but also harrowing."

Caleb gave him an indecisive look. "So I could just refuse?"

"Of course. I'd back you if you did, nobody should be made to perform if they truly don't want to, but..." Jerry paused. "Look, this might be presuming, but I've had moments of clarity in my life so I know what they look like, and when you were onstage you looked like you were either having a moment of clarity or seeing the divine. And if the latter, I'd love to know what that looks like. I have a bet on with the Rabbi of the Grand Synagogue."

Caleb considered how to answer it, because he wasn't wrong, but he was also a stranger. This felt soul-deep.

"You don't have to say," Jerry told him, which actually decided it.

"I've never liked being in front of an audience. Teaching is fine, that's different, but I don't like being…seen. I don't like the way I think people think of me when that happens," Caleb said slowly. Jerry nodded. "But it wasn't like that this time. I couldn't see them, couldn't even hear them over the earpieces. I knew they were there but I couldn't tell what they thought which meant I was…I could make them think what I wanted. With the music. Which is all I ever really want, to make people feel something with it. It's just hard to know how it makes people feel."

"Huh. So you did get pretty close to seeing the divine, eh?" Jerry said.

"Not really big on religion but put like that, yeah, I guess. I don't think it would work in the gig work my friends do, like bars and weddings and stuff, but on a stage like that – there's a weird anonymity to it. Even being the only person onstage."

"No, I understand that," the duke said, and he probably did. He lived a lot of his life in public, like the king.

"It was euphoric. I'd like to see if that happens again," Caleb said. "There's just so much other stuff. Hair and makeup and the interviews, strangers thinking they're owed your time…"

"Hm." Jerry considered him. "If you could get around all that, though?"

"Yes. I'd be okay going to the semi-finals. Can't imagine a single guy in a chair with a ukulele – or a guitar – would make it to the Grand Final, so that wouldn't be a concern," Caleb said.

"With your permission, I'm going to see about pulling a few strings," Jerry replied. "Can I see your phone?"

Caleb, confused, unlocked his phone and passed it over. Jerry poked around in it for a second, then handed it back.

"Just put my info in there under Jerry Shivadlakia," he said. "When the Palace – or Eurovision – reaches out to you about plans for the semi-finals, call me and I'll hook you up. Or just call me if you're bored sometime, I love entertaining people."

"That's kind of you," Caleb said, opening the contact and texting a music-note emoji to him. "Now you've got my info too."

"Charming. So, would you like me to take you back to Lachlan, or to someone else, or walk you around and introduce you to people, or do you want to make your escape?"

Caleb could see, over his shoulder, Ava in the doorway of the reception, arguing with the guy on the door checking badges.

"If you could get me to the door, I think that's my ticket home," he said, indicating Ava.

"This way," Jerry said, and gestured for him to follow. He left Caleb at the door, gave Ava a bow and a kiss on the hand, and deftly blocked anyone from following.

In the hallway, Ava demanded, "Was that the Duke of Shivadlakia who just kissed my hand?"

"He said to call him Jerry," Caleb said faintly. "Can you drive me home?"

"Do you promise to tell me everything?" Ava asked.

"I just told the Duke of Shivadlakia about it, I guess I can tell you," Caleb said.

CHAPTER THREE

YOUNG PRINCE: King Emeritus Michaelis ben Jason, journalist Jes Deimos, and teen influencer Noah Deimos listen from the Royal Box as Caleb Canto performs his song *Young Prince*, which will go to Eurovision semi-finals in six weeks. The Deimos family is close to the royals, and sources say Mr. Deimos, a student at the Shivadh Maritime Academy, may be a candidate for heir to King Gregory III. (Photo Courtesy RSBA)

"GREGORY'S GOING TO adopt me," Noah announced the next morning, when Michaelis walked into the kitchen.

It was early, and – as Jes had predicted – Michaelis had been home from the reception rather later than he wanted. He went straight to the coffeemaker, which Noah had just turned on, and poured the meager, highly-caffeinated first-drippings that were in the carafe into his mug. Jes called him a menace for drinking the first cup out before the carafe was full, but the caffeine habit of a lifetime was difficult to break.

"No talk of succession before breakfast," he mumbled, seating himself at the table. Noah waved his phone in his face, so he plucked it out of Noah's grip and studied the news as he drank.

"I'm going to become the royal heir and be super fancy," Noah continued. "I'll go to some really good Ivy League school after all and give up all this podcasting nonsense."

"You can do better than American higher education,"

Michaelis said, playing into the joke. "Gregory went to the Sorbonne for university. And from there to the London School of Economics."

"A whole school of economics? I've had nightmares like that," Noah said.

"It is a real place full of extremely serious people," Michaelis said, handing his phone back. "Where do they come up with rumors like this?"

"Don't know. It's super dumb," Noah said. "I've seen what Gregory has to do. Being king is hard and boring."

"It requires a specific focus," Michaelis allowed. "Don't listen to the press, Noah. They're just stirring up trouble because it's a slow news week."

"I'm not bothered," Noah said with a shrug, and seemed to mean it. The resilience of the young, perhaps.

"I'm glad to hear it. How are you feeling about the song last night? I wanted to ask, but you and Jes were both asleep when I came in. Consensus in the family is that it's almost certainly about you, but the media doesn't seem to have caught on."

"I think it's cool. You know, like how nobody really knows who Carly Simon wrote *You're So Vain* about," Noah said.

"It was me," Michaelis said, sipping his coffee. Noah paused.

"Was not," he said uncertainly.

"Sure. You know anyone else who can gavotte?"

"AHA," Noah said, having consulted his phone while Michaelis was bullshitting him. "She wrote it in 1972. You were eleven years old!"

"Early bloomer," Michaelis said, laughing. Noah grinned at him. "All right. But you know if it made you uncomfortable, you only have to say."

"Boss said that too. I don't know why everyone thinks it would. It's less creepy than people taking pictures of us and writing weird fanfic that gets printed in the newspaper."

"Well, perhaps. But you should know it's an option; you're a minor and you haven't got much power over such things. Jes and I do," Michaelis said, getting up to fix himself some breakfast. "If something in the media upsets you, we want you to say so, and we'll do something about it. We can have the song withdrawn, and send someone else."

"No, I like it. It's catchy, anyway," Noah said.

"That is true. In that case, I'll see about tickets to the semi-finals in Turin," Michaelis said, returning to the table with a bowl of yogurt and granola in one hand, jar of jam in the other. "Gregory probably can't take the time, and we'll have to send someone to represent. Make a nice holiday of it, you and Jes and myself, if you like."

"Sounds fun. What did you feel about it?" Noah asked.

"Hm?" Michaelis asked around a mouthful of breakfast, raising his eyebrows.

"The song," Noah said. Michaelis swallowed.

"I was mostly concerned for you at the time. As you said, it's a decent song." Michaelis saw Noah's look and rolled his eyes a little. "What I think of it isn't really material."

"You still probably have, like, feelings about it," Noah said.

"I'm sure you've heard Gerald make the joke that members of the royal family are only allowed two emotions per year," Michaelis said. "When you and Jes moved in, I gave you each one of mine, so I haven't any left over for things like this."

"That is the sweetest and also the weirdest way of saying *I love you* that I've ever heard," Jes announced, walking into the kitchen. "What are you having no feelings about, my dear?" they asked, resting their hands on his shoulders, leaning against him gently from behind.

"The song from last night. Noah wants to know what I thought of it."

"What he felt about it," Noah corrected.

"Raising him to be emotionally intelligent was a mistake," Michaelis said, tilting his head back to look up at Jes.

"Did my best. You weren't there to micromanage my parenting," they replied, patting him and going to the fridge. "Noah, if he doesn't want to talk about it, he doesn't have to. Maybe he isn't sure what he feels about it."

"I just don't have any particular personal reaction," Michaelis said, beginning to be both annoyed and confused by the expectation that he would.

"Michaelis, you do realize you're probably the singer, right?" Jes asked into the refrigerator, rummaging for something.

"What?"

"It's written from your point of view," they said, emerging with a carton of milk. "You're the one singing. Well, it's meant to be some idealized, anonymized wise philosopher-king. But actually, obviously, you."

Michaelis paused, considering this. It took a while; it was a lot to suddenly process.

"He's having both of his emotions at once," Jes whispered to Noah.

"Surely not," Michaelis said, taking out his phone.

"Don't call Lachlan this early," Jes warned.

"Why would I be calling Lachlan?"

"Finding out where Mr. Canto lives, so you can order the hit?" Noah suggested.

"I just want to see the lyrics again," Michaelis said, digging in his email. Someone had sent the VIPs a songbook of all the lyrics; he hadn't bothered reading it, but now – there it was. He became aware of an air of expectation from Jes and Noah as he skimmed the lyrics of *Young Prince*.

He'd assumed the singer was meant to be Gregory, but on reading it was clear that the song was from an old king's point of view. The...the attitude was correct, too. Somehow Canto had grasped several layers of meaning in the word tavat, even personal ones he must have guessed at from circumstance.

It wasn't that he minded if anyone knew he cared for Noah.

He didn't hide the fact he liked the boy — would have liked him even if he wasn't involved with Jes. He wasn't concerned about people knowing that. But he did feel exposed for a few seconds, intensely seen, in a way he hadn't since early in his kingship, when all eyes were on him constantly.

"Michaelis?" Jes prompted, sounding less amused and more concerned now.

"Do *you* want to have it withdrawn?" Noah asked.

"Nonsense," Michaelis managed. "As you say, it's a fine song," he concluded, putting away his phone and also, metaphorically, his feelings. "Besides, none of it's incorrect. If it must be in part about me, at least it's properly so."

"I told him I was going to get adopted by Gregory and be a fancy future king," Noah said to Jes.

"Well, Wild Child, as long as you're happy," Jes said, pouring out a bowl of cereal. "Got everything you need for school today?"

"Yep, just gotta get my uniform on."

"Mind if I give you a ride to school?" Michaelis asked. Both parent and child Deimos looked at him. "What?"

"Are you going to yell at Mr. Canto?" Noah asked.

"Of course not. Nothing to yell about. Go and dress, Boss and I need a word," Michaelis said. Noah looked sulky about missing that discussion, but he flounced off the chair and out of the kitchen.

"Not that I want you to make a bigger fuss than this already is, but I'm glad you're going down there. Someone should talk to the man," Jes said.

"I agree. I know Noah's used to being a little in the public eye, but I'd rather not draw more attention to him like this than necessary."

Jes nodded. "I can do it instead, if you want. Noah's my kid."

"No, let me handle this, if you've no objection. I have some questions in any case."

"Thanks," Jes said, stealing a sip of his coffee.

"Part of the job." Michaelis glanced at them. "At least, I hope."

"At this point, I think it's unavoidable. Congratulations, you're a dad again," Jes said with a grin.

"You're just the type who'd shove a child on me right when they're at their most difficult," Michaelis mock-complained. "This won't get you out of parenting a teenager, just because I've already done it once."

"If you think this is his most difficult, I would like to put you in a time machine and show you what he was like at thirteen. This is the easy part," Jes replied.

"Hm. I'd better go dress for the occasion," Michaelis said. "Wish me luck."

"Good luck, have fun, don't be too scary," Jes told him as he left the kitchen.

"I promise nothing!" he called back, and heard them laughing.

When Caleb arrived at the Maritime Academy on Monday morning, it was apparent the children had been industrious, and at least one of them had access to a color printer. Arriving after a brisk and pleasant walk from home, enjoying the crisp early-spring air, he found the whiteboard at one end of his long classroom adorned with printouts of pictures of him.

Studying them, some of which were watermarked or had headers in the margins, Caleb realized it wasn't just the children.

Someone had snapped a photograph of him performing, or perhaps grabbed a frame from the digital stream of the encore. Caleb was sitting on the right side of the image, perfectly lit, hair pale and features sharpened by shadows. He was wearing those dumb but undeniably helpful sunglasses, and his hands were slightly blurred as he played. The king was sitting next to him on the left of the image, watching him, and the duke – Jerry – was looming over the king's shoulder, out of the spotlight but still visible, like he was about to attack the king.

In every image, all of them had different captions. The largest one, from someone on Reddit, had captioned Gregory III "New Friend." Caleb was captioned "My Autistic Ass" and Jerry, lurking in the darkness, was captioned "The Hyperfixation I'm About To Explain."

That was funny, admittedly, though he'd have to take it down before the kids could see it. The one next to it was even funnier: Gregory was "Me, A Cat Owner", Caleb was "My Cat" and Jerry was "The Impending Hairball."

He set his ukulele down on his desk and began, with only a little bit of regret, pulling them down so they wouldn't distract the children. He became so engrossed in reading them as he did so that he didn't notice anyone in the doorway until they cleared their throat. He turned, startled.

Which was how he found himself with a handful of memes and face to face with His Grace Michaelis, the king emeritus.

"Oh, shit," Caleb said, before he could stop himself. The nobility really should stop springing themselves on people, he thought. The old king gave him a smile as he stepped inside and closed the door.

"Not the worst reception I've had," he said. "Charmingly honest, actually."

"Sorry – sir – Your Grace," Caleb said, bowing. His Grace bowed back, eyes drifting over to the whiteboard.

"I see the internet has found us again," he sighed.

"I think the students probably made most of them." Caleb offered him the printouts in his hands. The old king looked at a few, smiled, and then handed them back.

"I apologize, I know this wasn't expected and you have a full day of work on top of performing last night," he said. "But we didn't get a chance to speak at the reception, and I thought we should. It was pointed out to me — as it was to young Noah, last night — that your song had certain personal implications for us."

It hadn't occurred to him that Michaelis would hear the song and recognize himself in it — that a song he'd written as an exercise, about the royal family but outside of it, still had an impact on them. Caleb realized that he had probably committed at the least a mistake, and possibly a terrible intrusion.

It wasn't easy to tell what the king emeritus was thinking. Still, this was the man who'd raised Gregory III, who was kind and understanding, at least in the few minutes they'd met. Caleb's mother had liked Michaelis when he was king, and spoken of him approvingly. So Caleb fell back on honesty.

"I'm sorry — I didn't consider what you'd think when I wrote it, and I should have," he said. "I don't know if that angers you?"

"No. It concerns me," Michaelis said. "Not because you wrote it but because you knew to write it. It's shocking to think of being so openly perceived that way. I've lived my life in the public eye; I don't mind. But Noah's a child — a very mature child, but still a child. As I'm sure you understand."

"Yes, of course. I don't teach him, but..." Caleb gestured around the classroom. "I didn't — I wasn't trying to hurt anyone."

"Lord knows what you could have accomplished if you were trying, but you don't strike me as malicious," the old king said. "How did you know, in any case? I'm curious if I've been indiscreet, using the nickname, or if you're simply observant."

"Both?" Caleb ventured. His Grace looked surprised. "It was last autumn, you were having some kind of party — I was out by the dock when you came out and called him in from setting fireworks. We heard you use the name, and Lachlan..."

He realized too late he was throwing Lachlan under the bus, but Michaelis just nodded thoughtfully.

"Ah, he explained it to you. That clarifies it. It's not a secret," he added reassuringly. "Lachlan didn't do anything wrong. It's simply private within the family."

"There's nothing in the song to say it's you. Or him," Caleb pointed out. "I made it anonymous on purpose. It was about the concept. I didn't get a lot of Shivadh culture growing up, because I was at school in Galia. Learned English, had my citizenship, but Galia and Askazer-Shivadlakia…" he made a weighing motion. "I like it here, but. I'm not Shivadh, not really."

The old king tilted his head. "But you're a citizen. You've lived here for years."

"I wasn't raised here. Just summer holidays with my mother, and sometimes Passover and stuff."

"Hardly matters. Neither was the king consort. You pay taxes here, don't you?"

Caleb nodded, perplexed.

"You live in Fons-Askaz, you eat the food, teach our children. Your mother is Shivadh?"

"Was. She passed a few years ago."

"I'm sorry to hear it. But as far as any right-thinking Shivadh is concerned, you are Shivadh. The rest is just a question of knowledge. And clearly, understanding the idea of tavat as you do, you have no lack of that, either."

"I liked the folk stories about them," Caleb offered. "I liked the idea, that's why I wrote the song."

"Good," Michaelis said. "In any case, you're off to the semi-finals eventually. I'd like to suggest that you stick to the line that you simply discovered a slightly archaic old term for a prince, and liked it. I'd ask you leave us out of the narrative – for Noah's sake – but I can't force you."

"It wouldn't even have occurred to me to share it," Caleb said. "Although it didn't occur to me I shouldn't sell a song like that to an asshole like Kairao, either – "

He clapped his hand over his mouth, realizing he'd just called someone an asshole in front of a king. Michaelis looked amused.

"I've called people much more important than him much worse names. Though I agree that it's a good song, too good for a fellow like Kairao. You'll do fine at Eurovision."

"No pressure," Caleb said.

"Pressure is a useful tool," Michaelis said. "The trick is to know how to apply it. Very few do. And I hear children," he added, gesturing over his shoulder. "I'll leave you to it. Do get in touch if you need anything. Lachlan knows how to reach me."

He left as quietly as he'd come, and apparently managed to dodge the children, since they poured into the classroom shouting about Eurovision, and not about the king in the hallway.

Ava met him for lunch that day, which was about the only normal thing that happened. The students were uncontrollable, and Caleb eventually decided to teach what he could, rather than what he'd planned, and spent the whole day talking to his various classes about what it was like to perform as a musician. If it wasn't music itself, it was at least related.

He vented to Ava about it over lunch, trying not to dominate the conversation but probably, ultimately, failing. Still, she couldn't have been too annoyed, because at the end of the day she arrived at his classroom and announced, "I'm making dinner and you're coming along."

Ava wasn't an inspired cook, but she was very good at plain, unchallenging comfort foods. Caleb never suspected her of ulterior motives, either, so he said yes. He didn't realize he'd been had until it was too late: he was sitting at her kitchen counter, chatting idly and watching her make buttered pasta, when there was a knock on the door and people began to arrive.

"Ava," he said, as their mutual friend Leah deposited a bottle of wine in the kitchen, "What are you up to?"

"Didn't she tell you?" Leah asked. Before moving to Askazer-Shivadlakia, Caleb had never met anyone like Leah — super tall, ultra-femme, impeccable makeup, flawless hair, never without a trans flag somewhere on her person. She was the loudest woman he knew and he loved her for it but she was also *so loud*.

"Does anyone ever tell me anything," Caleb sighed.

"It's because we want to protect you," Bill, Leah's partner, told him. "You're too pure for this world, Caleb."

"I feel attacked," Caleb told Ava.

"Four more people are coming," Leah put in. There was a clatter on the stairs. "Four more people in ugly boots," she corrected, as Ava's troop of friendly lesbians arrived in the company of Derek, who had given Caleb his first binder and still affectionately gave him endless shit for eating only three kinds of food. It had taken Caleb some time to realize the teasing was friendly; it gave him a warm feeling, now, every time Derek told him to eat a plant once in a while.

"Eurovision party!" Derek declared, adding a huge bag of crisps to the pile of food in the kitchen and tossing Caleb an apple.

"Ava," Caleb rubbed his eyes.

"Aw, come on, get your pasta and come sit with us," she told him, leading a parade into the living room, where she tapped open the video player on her laptop and shared it with the television mounted on the wall. "Askazer-Shivadlakia was one of the last countries to select their performer for Eurovision this year, so lots of the other acts already have previews online."

"Oh, guys, no," Caleb groaned. "I don't want to think about it tonight!"

"You've been thinking about it all day, might as well do it now and not spread it out over the week," Ava said pragmatically.

"Why do I have to think about it more at all?"

"You have to see your competition!" Leah interrupted.

"Gotta know their weaknesses, you know," Bill added.

"No, again, why? What do I care if they can't stay in tune, or in tempo, or whatever," Caleb complained.

"Because you gotta psych 'em out! Get in their heads! This is a contest," Ava told him, shadow-boxing in his direction.

"I don't like competing," Caleb said. "Collaboration is better. You should only compete against yourself."

"Told you he was too pure for this world," Bill said to Derek, who nodded sagely. Ava's lesbian squad was already passing around Leah's bottle of wine.

Ava raised an eyebrow at Caleb. "Do you want to see video of yourself?"

"You are a mean person," Caleb told her. "Everyone, Ava's mean."

"Look, there's only forty-two countries competing and thirty-six of them have their song picked. Songs have to be less than three minutes long, that's only – "

"An hour and forty-five minutes," Caleb said. "There's so much other stuff I could do for an hour and forty-five minutes!"

"And will you?" Derek asked. Caleb sighed.

"No," he admitted.

"So eat and let me DJ you a long set list," Ava said. "You're going to hate so many of them, it'll be great."

"Loathing does give me strength," Caleb said. "Fine, play it. If I fall asleep don't wake me up."

There was a crash from outside the doorway, and Ben's voice calling "I'm here! I'm not late! I'm here!"

"Quick, hit play to make him feel bad," Leah said, grinning.

"Poor boy. Come in, Ben, we're just starting!" Ava called, and Ben burst through the doorway with a large paper bag in one arm.

"I have beer and kedgeree," he announced.

"Why do you have kedgeree?" Ava asked.

"Next to the beer place?" Ben ventured.

"Not what I – oh, never mind," Ava said, hitting play. "Bring them over here and we'll figure something out."

Caleb tried to stay sullen about having to watch his competitors perform, but he did end up enjoying himself. Granted, Eurovision had a specific aesthetic and a reputation for kookiness, but that didn't mean the musicians were hacks. There was a level of skill required just to get to a place where you'd be considered; after all, Kairao might have been a screwup but he'd had a strong singing voice and he'd bought a song by – though Caleb said it himself – a skilled songwriter. You had to bring your best, and it made for interesting listening. He did hate a number of the songs, but he wasn't going to say they were badly done.

And it was fun to listen to everyone heckle the outfits.

About half an hour in, he had his phone out and was making notes. Not on how to crush the competition, as Ava and Leah clearly would have liked, but on the ways he'd have done some things differently, on what he liked about the other songs.

When the band from the UK, Strangelust, struck up a Devil's Interval as their opening chord, he was surprised but not especially impressed – metalheads had been using diminished fifths to unsettle their listeners for fifty years, and the blues had been incorporating them fifty years before that, if not longer. It was a sign of craftsmanship, perhaps, but not exactly of ingenuity.

But it kept repeating, over a heavy beat and a strange, almost unsynced bass riff, like someone had asked a bluesman to play Black Sabbath. Caleb looked up from his phone, curious, then fascinated. The song itself was about a specific kind of yearning, as far as he could tell, but in a shouty way that some people had, where Caleb could never discern whether the singer was angry or simply so full of emotion they had to yell about it.

> *You can't find me (can't find me)*
> *And you never will (ever will)*
> *I'll throw a punch as I walk away*
> *And nobody will know that it was me*
> *'cause I'm invisible*

The flatted fifth and the intense singing would have been enough to intrigue him, but the lead singer was also on guitar, a complicated proposition with a song like that, and he was *arresting*.

He looked young, not much older than Caleb, with vivid green eyes that the cameras were clearly trying to make the most of – he was constantly moving, hard to get in close-up. His short, wild hair was dyed a deep teal-blue that matched his guitar. Despite the shapeless black jacket he wore, slung over the guitar strap and some battered gray jeans, there was an obvious muscled solidity to him. He looked anchored, rooted, even as he moved around the stage, pulling the audience's attention with him.

"Do you suppose he wears makeup?" Ben asked, tilting his head. "I mean for his chest. Does he have nipple bronzer?"

"Imagine if he contours them," Leah added, laughing.

"Contoured anatomy aside, the song's a favorite to win this year," Ava said. "Well. One of them. People are always skeptical, the UK hasn't won or even gotten close in decades. They got zero points last year. But they have some flair, so it's up there now."

"I see why," Caleb said, watching intently. "Who did the arrangement? It's very technically interesting."

"Him," Ava said, nodding at the lead singer. "Buck Haverd. He wrote it. I read that he put Strangelust together specifically for the contest. Definitely his entry more than anyone else's."

"He's getting pretty famous in the UK, done some decent hits," Bill added. "People were surprised he wanted Eurovision."

"Why? Seems to me like it'd be a blast," Derek said.

"Dunno really. I guess it's a big risk to take."

There was a moment of quiet from the screen – the lead singer, Haverd, had played a single chord and then muted it, head bowed into the second of absolute silence. It reminded Caleb of the day he'd discovered Alanis Morissette. *Why are you so petrified of silence? Here, can you handle this?*

Onscreen, the beat ended with light flares that illuminated a single swift movement – Haverd raised his arms and spread them, like he was proclaiming something or inviting an attack, and unseen wires jerked his jacket off, leaving him topless except for the strap holding his guitar in place. Caleb sucked in a breath, half at the audacity of the stage trick and half at the previously-hinted muscles now on display. Ben wolf-whistled.

Haverd had round knotwork tattoos capping each smooth shoulder, one wrapping down around the bicep of his right arm. There was another tattoo, unreadable but clearly lettering of some kind, on his left pectoral under the strap of the guitar. He also had either a single symmetrical tattoo or two matched ones on his torso; they flanked his abdomen, disappearing under the waistband of his trousers, unidentifiable from the camera work.

"I think Disappearing Clothing is this year's Too Many Pyrotechnics," Ava said, oblivious to Caleb having a moment.

"Are you going to do any fancy staging?" Leah asked.

"I have no idea," Caleb admitted.

"Explosions," Ben suggested.

"It's…it's not really an explosion kind of song," Caleb said.

"It could be, if there were explosions. Explosions make any song an explosions kind of song."

"Ben, do not have ideas for our next gig," Ava said.

"Explosions notwithstanding, you should have some idea of what you want to do," Derek said to Caleb.

"I suppose it's up to the king," Caleb replied.

"Why?" Leah asked.

"I'm representing the country. Country ought to have some input."

"They already have," Ava pointed out. "They voted for you. The king said he liked you, too. I mean, I like a spectacle, and the country loves pageantry, but they liked you just fine when you were sitting on a chair in a spotlight. Play to your strengths."

"My strengths being sitting down?" Caleb asked, amused. Onscreen, Buck Haverd blew a kiss and then threw a rude gesture to the audience as the song ended. Voiceover on the video said *Twenty-six-year-old Buck Haverd, giving a taste* – before Ava muted it.

"Charisma, Caleb. You're attractive, you're mysterious, you have talent," Derek said. Caleb squirmed, uncomfortable with the compliments.

Ava sighed. "Keep watching. It'll make you feel better about yourself," she said.

It did, eventually. Caleb went back to alternating between drumming his fingers gently on the ukulele in his lap and making notes on his phone. If the king did want him to do some kind of special staging, the notes might even be helpful. Daunting to consider, though. Caleb didn't care for a lot of distracting stage tricks and could only imagine how boring they'd be to plan and rehearse, but at least if they wanted that, he'd have a list.

"What do you suppose you do after getting your top ripped off in the middle of the performance?" Caleb asked speculatively, because Switzerland's entry this year was understimulating at best, and he was still stuck back on Buck Haverd's vanishing jacket. "Do you suppose they have the jacket waiting for him when he comes offstage? Or a robe of some kind? Maybe one of those silver shock blankets, like foil-wrapped street food."

"Wanna snack on him, huh?" Derek teased.

"No," Caleb said with a scowl. "I'm just a curious student of human behavior."

"If he comes to the semis or you go to the Grand Final, you can ask him yourself," Ava said. "As a pick-up line it's not bad, has a certain unique flair to it."

"Make sure you mention the street food," Ben suggested.

"If I was suave enough to land someone like Buck Haverd, I'm pretty sure I could have wriggled out of going to Eurovision by now," Caleb sighed.

That week was strange and difficult, but in an oddly symmetrical way. Caleb found himself constantly at the center of attention, and at the same time a little distanced from his own life. He had to record a new backing track of *Young Prince* for the performances, as well as a studio version for the soundtrack; Lachlan, at least, smoothed the way at Reverb, getting him the studio time he needed. He also had to do another TV interview, but it was pre-recorded and he was allowed to wear his sunglasses again (requested, really, at this point) and keep his ukulele with him. Jerry turned up at the studio, interfering a few times when he didn't approve of the questions. At one point Caleb had to push back a little – "Jerry, I want to talk about it, autism isn't some secret I keep" – but at least he discovered that the duke was a pushover if you spoke firmly. They cut the interview down to ten minutes for air, and Caleb thought it went pretty well.

Even before the interview and definitely after, people would stop to congratulate him on the street, though at least that began to wear off by the weekend. Meanwhile, he had to tell the headmaster of the Academy that he'd need time off for Eurovision, of all nonsense, and also for meetings at the palace.

There was no way for a normal person to say "I have a meeting at the palace" without sounding like a pretentious fool. At least the headmaster was fine with it; the prestige of a Eurovision performer teaching there, he supposed.

As the attention slowly fell away, and he went back to being just plain Caleb, he began to realize how intense his participation in the rest of Eurovision would be. It started with the first meeting he had to have with Lachlan, Jerry, his very efficient fiancée Lady Alanna, and Rob Davidson, the conservatively dressed lawyer type Caleb had met after the concert. It turned out Davidson was some kind of executive at RSBA, the Royal Shivadh Broadcast Agency, and the Palace's link to the terrifying machinery of Eurovision pre-planning. Davidson was Head of Delegation, and it was his job to keep communication open between the country and Eurovision, get all the paperwork properly sorted, and make sure everyone else did the same.

For now, at least, Davidson was thus doing the bulk of the work, Jerry explained, and then looked a little sheepish as he added that he'd volunteered to serve as Assistant Head. He'd be managing more of the social end of things – PR, travel, events – but the first meeting was just to go over the calendar for the competition.

That alone was stressful enough that Caleb was secretly glad Jerry was there. He wasn't sure if anyone else knew that Jerry was a covert ally of some kind, so he didn't bring it up, but he appreciated Jerry's very evident awareness of certain limits, and deft negotiation around them.

"We're going to have to come up with your staging in the next few days," Davidson said, studying a digital manual for the submissions process on his laptop.

"Although the nice thing about being almost the last to have a National Final is that you won't have to stew in being a semi-finalist for long," Jerry said.

"There's only about six weeks until rehearsals start in Turin," Lady Alanna agreed. "Then semis, and Grand Final if you get through semis."

"And the regional pre-parties, of course," Davidson added.

"But nobody expects you to attend those unless you really want to," Lady Alanna said, giving Davidson a look. He smiled back faintly.

"I'd do the parties in Turin, London, and Amsterdam, myself," Jerry said. "The Palace will pay your travel costs, and you can get a look at the venue if you go to Turin."

"So why London and Amsterdam?" Caleb asked.

"Oh, London's good for publicity, and Amsterdam's got top-notch drugs," the duke said.

"Jerry," Lady Alanna said disapprovingly.

"I am of course a reformed dissolute, I don't do recreational drugs," Jerry said to Caleb, as if confiding a secret. "Left all that behind me. Still, for a young man in search of a good time…" he shrugged and grinned.

"I'm rarely in search of a good time," Caleb replied.

"Small mercies," Davidson put in.

"If I say yes to Turin, can I pass on the others?" Caleb asked.

"You don't have to do any of them," Jerry said.

"But you probably should show your face at Askazer-Shivadlakia's," Lachlan added, before Davidson could interject. "Hard to have a Eurovision pre-party concert without our Eurovision performer."

"I should do Turin, too," Caleb said reluctantly. It would be for the best if he did, even if it seemed like a nightmare from here. "It'll be good to meet some other performers and see the venue. Help to ease into it. I don't like...upheaval."

Lady Alanna looked up from her tablet.

"In that case, I sincerely apologize for everyone you meet in this building," she said, with what seemed like a mixture of amusement and earnest kindness.

"I'm getting used to it," Caleb replied. Jerry snorted.

"I'll put you down for our party and the Turin party," Lady Alanna decided. "London on option if you want it. Our office can arrange all the travel," she added to Davidson, who nodded.

"Going to have to write up that rider, now," Lachlan said to Caleb. "Make sure you ask for a hotel where they leave a mint on your pillow."

"In all seriousness, the clearer you can make your needs and requests, the easier it'll go for everyone," Lady Alanna said. "The king's is three pages long. Although that's mostly because he likes to be extremely specific," she admitted.

"Do you have one?" Caleb asked Jerry, who shook his head.

"I don't really Make Appearances, I just sort of show up places," he said. Davidson looked faintly horrified. "Wasn't there some band or other who wanted a bowl of M&Ms with all the blue ones picked out?"

"Van Halen, and it was brown," Caleb said absently. "They did it to make sure that whoever was working on their stage setup while they were on tour had read the contract. It was a safety trigger. If they found brown M&Ms in the bowl it meant they had to do a full check of the lights and sound equipment because someone wasn't paying attention."

There was a beat of silence, and then Lachlan said, "Huh," in a considering voice.

"David Lee Roth is a smart guy," Caleb finished, wondering if that had been an awkward overshare.

Apparently not; Jerry looked at Lady Alanna and asked, "If you were going to pull an M&Ms, what would you do?" and everyone around the table, even Davidson, looked thoughtful. Before Lady Alanna could respond, there was a knock at the door and a head poked in.

"Al, they said you were – oh, hello," the king said, sweeping everyone with a look, sidling through the open door. "Sorry to interrupt."

"Hi, Greg. Need something?" Lady Alanna asked.

Caleb had heard it said that certain politicians were just naturally magnetic, effortlessly charismatic; the king appeared to be one of these and unaware of it. His smile was wide and friendly, and Caleb liked him more every time they met.

On the other hand, the number of times they'd met unintentionally was beginning to get unsettling.

"I'm supposed to meet with the engraver about the portrait for the Galian bond thing, but I'm not sure where to go," the king said. "There's no meeting location in the invite."

"Ah, he's coming to your office – I'll fix it," she said, tapping away on her tablet.

"The country would fail without her," the king said to Caleb. "By the way, love the meme about us, where I'm watching you play while unaware that Jerry is about to murder me. Very fun. I hope you're okay with it."

"My students really like it," Caleb said. "Jerry doesn't seem to mind."

"Jerry loves attention," Gregory said, with an affectionate

glance at the duke. His phone beeped and he checked it. "Thanks, Al. Hey, bring everyone to lunch if they've got time," he added, and left as quickly as he'd come.

"I will not make you have lunch with the king with no warning," Alanna said immediately.

"Thank you," Caleb said, still considering what he'd just seen. "You know, I think I have an idea for staging the performance."

Lachlan raised his eyebrows. Jerry grinned, clearly having figured out Caleb's sudden inspiration.

"Do tell," Davidson said, looking up from his laptop.

"He's going to need two hype men and a couple of spotlights," Jerry said to Davidson, who didn't bat an eye, just began making notes. Alanna and Lachlan both looked at Caleb.

"We can try it out at the pre-parties," Caleb agreed, beginning to warm to the idea that in the palace he could simply ask for something and it would be procured.

CHAPTER FOUR

CALEB WAS LESS sanguine about being the Palace's pet Eurovision performer two weeks later, sitting in the Lingotto Fiere courtyard in Turin, waiting for his turn at sound check. The pre-party was outdoors on the plaza of the convention center, and the venue was a lot bigger than he'd anticipated.

He at least had the advantage of being a native Italian speaker. It helped him feel more at home, and certainly helped with the nerves, since Lachlan and Ava often needed translation, which was a good distraction. Lachlan had taken French in his American high school, and Ava's Italian was evidence of the fact that she'd spent her time in school mostly in the music room. In any case, he was glad they'd accepted his offer to come as part of the act. Ava had readily agreed as long as she didn't have to dance; Caleb had debated asking Jerry to be the other onstage presence before realizing that it would probably be weird, and asked Lachlan instead.

There were posters all over Turin for the event, with the major headline acts (Italy's performers listed first, of course) in huge font at the top, and progressively smaller fonts beneath for the others. Caleb himself was the third name of three on the last, smallest line. He knew a lot of musicians hated the format, hated seeing where they fell in the hierarchy of fame, but Caleb liked that at least the hierarchy was acknowledged, and it showed him his specific place in it. Earlier that day he'd stealthily pulled one of the posters off the inside of a shop window and absconded with it as a souvenir.

He should have been first for sound check, since he'd be performing first at the event; essentially lobby music, not that he minded. People would still be arriving, and the celebrities and some of his fellow performers would still be doing the "turquoise carpet" – the Eurovision equivalent of the red carpet – by the time he took his bows. But Davidson had informed him that, given the backing music was now pre-recorded, his lighting cues were literally three downlights, and really it was only his single voice that they had to contend with, the techs had relegated him to a late slot for run-through and sound check.

So Caleb had settled in to wait his turn near the front of the audience, to the left of the "green rooms" – little clutches of sofas that made up seating for the performers, down at the front. It was perhaps a little uncharitable to think it, but he was pretty sure the seating was arranged so that people could watch both the performers onstage and the reactions of the other competitors simultaneously. He didn't love the public nature of it, but he wasn't the one running things. In any case, he chose not to sit there for now, instead hanging out with Lachlan and Ava in regular audience seating as he spent the afternoon watching the other sound checks.

He couldn't blame the techs for wanting to budget more time for the labor-intensive performances – or sometimes just for divas who thought they were. All of it was interesting to watch; he mostly noodled along on his ukulele, learning the chord progressions of the other performers' songs in order to keep his nerves steady. Nearby, Ava had her headphones in and her well-loved copy of *Please Kill Me* for pleasure reading, while Lachlan reviewed podcast scripts on his tablet.

The last sound check before Caleb's was Strangelust, the band out of the UK. Caleb pretended to be tuning his uke, watching sidelong as Strangelust trooped onstage and began running through the staging. It seemed needlessly complicated to Caleb, but it also seemed very intentional.

Every cue was diligently checked by Haverd, who was in full performance costume – from this close, Caleb could even see the little mounting hooks in his jacket for the wires that would pull it off. It was evident now why it was so baggy and shapeless, not only because Haverd probably thought it looked cool, but because it had to be about two sizes too big for him in order to pull away effectively. But they ran through the performance several times without the jacket stunt, and Caleb was beginning to disappointedly wonder if they'd cut it from the act.

Still, he was enjoying watching; at this distance he could also see the dramatic dark roots that highlighted Haverd's vivid teal hair, and every now and then there was a tantalizing glimpse of his tattoos under the jacket. Caleb thought the ones flanking his belly button might be wings, but too much was covered by the jacket and trousers to tell for sure.

He understood why they hadn't yet practiced the wirework when Haverd finally said, "All right, let's try the jacket thing," with a resigned sigh. There followed half an hour of Haverd getting increasingly irritated as the infrastructure for a trick involving wires pulling a coat offstage in an open-air pavilion proved…inadequate.

It took ages for them to rig it properly, and the stagehands pointed out that the only functional rigging also made it a tripping hazard, which meant they had to attach visibility ribbons to it, which did ruin the effect. By the time everything was sorted, to a certain functionality but no real satisfaction on anyone's part, Haverd was visibly frustrated and Strangelust was fifteen minutes into Caleb's time slot.

Caleb was annoyed, because he preferred to start on time when possible, but he also felt sympathy for Haverd. It was difficult when you wanted something to be a very specific way that wasn't easy to achieve, and nobody seemed much inclined to help. Even Haverd's band hadn't offered any particular assistance in brainstorming.

So, when he saw Haverd coming offstage in his direction, Caleb thought he'd cheer him up and show him there were no hard feelings about running over time. As Haverd passed, Caleb leaned back in his chair and strummed out the bridge of Haverd's song on his ukulele, loud as the little instrument would go.

It backfired *immediately*. Haverd turned sharply, glared at him, and pointed.

"The fuck was that?" he demanded. Caleb blinked.

"Your bridge," he replied. "Scored for single ukulele."

This seemed to enrage the man more; he scowled and asked, "You think that's funny? Are you making fun of my song?"

"What? No," Caleb said. This was not how he'd anticipated meeting any of the performers, let alone a hot one with a penchant for the Devil's Interval. "It's a very nice bridge. I'm sorry, I only meant to amuse."

"I don't think that or your fake accent are fucking funny," Haverd retorted. Stagehands were nonchalantly watching the exchange; hopefully, Caleb thought, one of them would intervene if Haverd threw a chair, which he looked like he was considering.

"This is just how I talk," Caleb said, bewildered. They did sound a little alike, he supposed. Shivadh English had a Welsh lilt to the accent, and Caleb knew from covert research he felt only slightly guilty about that Haverd had been born and raised in Wales.

"Oh yeah? Where are you from? The hell are you doing here anyway?" Haverd demanded.

"I'm performing. I'm here from Askazer-Shivadlakia," Caleb said.

That, weirdly, seemed to mollify him. "Ah, you're that ukulele guy," he said, but there was still an edge to his voice – which came out like a blade before Caleb could reply. "Didn't recognize you without the dumb sunglasses."

Objectively, Caleb knew that the sunglasses were pretty dumb-looking, at least when they weren't on his face, but it didn't seem polite to say so. It seemed intentionally offensive, though it could simply be obliviousness. He'd found that in most cases, going with the kindest interpretation was usually best; if someone didn't have bad intentions, it helped the conversation along, and if they did, it often disarmed them.

So he took the sunglasses out of his pocket, popped them onto his face, and grinned. Haverd's face did a complicated transition from angry to confused. It occurred to Caleb that the other man didn't have a witty comeback as a response to pure silliness.

"We were occupied by Welsh soldiers that the English threw at us hundreds of years ago when they invaded on their way to a war with France," he said, because the history of English in Askazer-Shivadlakia was, after all, pretty interesting. "A lot of them realized it was like Wales, only less cold and rainy, so they stayed, and that's why we sound like this. Prevailing theory is, we kept up speaking English after we punted English rule off our backs because it was a funny way to annoy the French, who were also not in our good books just then."

Then, because he'd spent a lot of time with Lachlan lately and picked up some of his sass, he added, "Don't try to troll a Shivadh, honey. We invented it."

The other man blinked his bright green eyes, opened his mouth, then closed it again.

There was a cackling laugh from off to the left, and Caleb turned to see Lachlan standing in the aisle, doubled over, losing his shit. Ava was next to him, giggling.

"That'll teach you to try to be cool," Lachlan called, shaking a finger at the other man. "You shouldn't step to a king if you aren't prepared to get ruled, baby rocker."

Haverd looked back and forth from Lachlan, laughing, to Caleb, grinning in his dumb sunglasses, and stomped off through a row of chairs, heading for backstage. A voice over the PA system summoned "Askaz...Aszak...Skaz...Caleb Canto to the stage please."

"I'm going to have little cards printed up that explain how to pronounce Askazer-Shivadlakia," Lachlan said, as they headed for the stage.

"I think they put those in the press kit," Caleb said. "Maybe we can get some copies for us to hand out."

"I had no idea Buck Haverd was such an awful man," Ava said. "I know he's hot, Caleb, but what a jerk."

"I try to cut kids his age a lot of slack," Lachlan said.

"He's two years older than me," Caleb pointed out.

"Trust me, when you're forty, everyone under thirty looks like a child," Lachlan said.

"I thought you were twenty-nine," Ava teased.

"For the last eleven years," Lachlan replied, laughing. "Anyway, genuine question, does what just happened make him less hot or more hot? I vote less, not because he was a jerk, but because you owned him so effortlessly."

"That doesn't make him more hot, being so easily owned?" Caleb asked.

"Kinky," Lachlan said.

"But are you okay? He got pretty far in your face," Ava pointed out.

"He was just frustrated," Caleb said. He had begun the process of relabeling Buck Haverd from *very pretty, wouldn't mind meeting him* to *very pretty, stay out of his way*. You could, after all, enjoy looking regardless of personality. "That wasn't about me, and I won't take it personally. Even if it were, it's not the first time I've accidentally annoyed someone, and it won't be the last."

Too late, he glanced into the wing of the stage nearby; Buck Haverd was standing there, guitar in one hand, apparently in the process of packing it away. He was close enough to have heard the whole conversation. Caleb could see his face, and while he couldn't easily read the emotion on it, it was evident that he *had* heard it all.

Caleb could also see his abdomen now, without the guitar covering it, which confirmed that the symmetrical tattoos were indeed wings of some kind.

He had no idea what to say, but it hardly mattered; Haverd backed away, bumped into one of the stagehands, raised his free hand in apology to the person he'd collided with, and hurried off.

"Awkward," Caleb murmured, but then it was time for sound check, and with the limited window he had left he didn't have time to be distracted.

That evening, about to leave the dressing room to perform, Caleb got a text from Jerry. It simply said, *We're in our seats,* and was accompanied by a photograph taken just outside. It showed Jerry smiling photogenically in a bright Shivadh-blue suit, a Shivadh flag pin on his lapel. He had his arm around Lady Alanna, who was also in a suit, equally vivid, in Askazer orange. They looked like movie stars.

Uncle Mike said to tell you 'no pressure', came a second text. Caleb smiled and sent back a guitar emoji. Then he put his phone on do-not-disturb and added it to the lockbox in the dressing room.

They would go onstage from here, but come offstage and go straight to the "green rooms," the public artist seating down below the audience seats. The lockbox and whatever was in it would be taken from dressing room to green room directly. It mostly had their phones, wallets, and a couple of bundles from Ava in it; he'd seen other performers putting stuff like flower arrangements and costume changes into theirs.

Lachlan closed the lid and rolled the box to the door, into the hands of stage crew; one of the assistant stage managers led them to their space in the wings in time to hear the host, over the chatter of the audience, introduce them. Caleb put his sunglasses on.

"Showtime," Lachlan said, unnecessarily dusting off the cuffs of his jacket. Ava adjusted the delicate circle of gold in her hair.

Ava and Lachlan walked out together, finding their marks from little dots of glow-tape on the floor. It wasn't quite as impressive as it would be, Caleb hoped, on a more advanced, indoor stage, but when the spotlights came up they were standing center stage, apparently having a conversation. Both were in black suits reminiscent of the Shivadh king's uniform, with white trim instead of gold at the wrists and shoulders, around the collars of their jackets, and down the sides of their trousers. The crown of Askazer-Shivadlakia was bulky and a little inelegant, and the king almost never wore it anyway, so instead they had fine wire circlets that Lachlan had commissioned from someone, and which Caleb privately thought looked like something out of Tolkien.

When he joined them, wearing his sunglasses and carrying a ukulele – likewise black, trimmed like the uniforms, which he and Ava had done with black spray paint and a glitter stick in Ava's hot glue gun – they each took a step backwards. Caleb counted a beat, based on instructions Lachlan had given him for the most effective level of drama, and then did what he'd done at the National Final: dropped slowly and calmly into a sitting position on the floor, legs crossed, instrument in his lap.

Nobody in the audience laughed. Lachlan and Ava sat on either side of him, composing themselves to listen. Then the backing track fired up, and Caleb launched into the song.

> *Tavat!*

> *Every wave someday reaches a distant country's shore*
> *But the tides follow on and the water here is pure*
> *Your sails spread wider now than mine*
> *But someday I'll still leave you behind*
> *And until then I'll be your guide*
> *Tavat —*

From the sound of it, the hush rolling back through the audience, it was as effective as he'd hoped. Clearly the image of the king and the duke listening to him play had been a powerful one, if more comedic than dramatic. It was easy to riff on that, to transform it into a king and a prince as his audience. It was equally easy to pretend Lachlan and Ava, his friends, were the only ones listening. So he let the song do most of the work, and trusted in the image of the musician, seated between kings, singing about succession, to do the rest.

He could feel that dizzying rush again as he sang; there was a sense of a thousand eyes all fixed on him, but without the terror that usually accompanied the idea. Unable to see their faces, barely able to hear any reaction they might have over the monitors in his ears, he could still sense their attention, and for a few brief moments he understood exactly how to guide it, how to make them feel what he'd felt that night on the lakeshore, watching the old king shepherd the princeling inside for dinner. If other people felt like this, the power without the terror, no wonder so many people chased fame so desperately, he thought.

> *I could never live forever*
> *Never really wanted to*
> *And I know it good, and true*
> *How the crown has passed to you*

He struck the final chords on the ukulele, even though only Lachlan and Ava could hear it, and the backing track faded away; Caleb lifted his chin a little higher and sang the final word into the silence.

Tavat!

He waited for the applause, then stood and bowed, Lachlan and Ava bowing as well before following him offstage. It was a calm, dignified stroll; once they were behind the curtain they immediately lost all of their onstage dignity and most of their calm.

"That went *great*!" Ava said, bouncing up and down, hugging Lachlan and then Caleb. Caleb submitted to having his monitor and mic pack removed with the others before replying.

"It went well," he agreed, pleased and still floating a little. "It felt…right. Not just the song, the kind of…everything."

Ava hugged him again and kissed him on the cheek, mindful of his ears, which were still recovering from the monitor earbuds. Lachlan held up a hand and Caleb nodded, giving permission for Lachlan to clap him on the shoulder.

"And now the pressure's off," Lachlan said, as they came out into the open space in front of the audience seating, following a stagehand to their green room – three sofas in a rough U shape facing the stage, surrounding their lockbox from the dressing room and a little hutch with food and drinks in it. "We get to sit and drink margaritas all night and be admired."

"Are you all right in those uniforms?" Caleb asked, as Ava took off her crown.

"Well, I might loosen the collar," Lachlan said, flopping onto one of the couches. Ava opened the lockbox and fished out a blue object that turned out to be a rolled-up Shivadh flag, which she shook open and draped over one of the couches.

"Caleb!" Jerry's voice called, and then he was there too with Lady Alanna, both beaming. "Fantastic performance. Thank you for making the staging of your song about my uncle all about me."

Caleb grinned. "Only mostly about you."

"He'll take what he can get," Lady Alanna said. "How did you enjoy performing?"

"It's good – it was a good choice to come," he replied.

"Glad to hear it. We'll keep you company for a few minutes and then let you rest," she said, settling gracefully on the sofa, next to the flag.

Lady Alanna's suit, the same orange as the star on the flag, created a striking image against the blue. It reminded Caleb that he'd read somewhere – probably in the National Resources app – that Alanna Daskaz, granddaughter of the Duchess of Askaz, was descended directly from Gilles Roman y Askaz, who had founded Askazer-Shivadlakia and whose descendants had often ruled it. Watching Jerry settle in next to her, Caleb considered the fact that she was in love with the current Duke of Shivadlakia, son of eleven generations of landed nobility, who had served as companions and advisors to her family for centuries.

There was a song there, too, perhaps a someday-companion piece to *Young Prince*. Something about how the echoes of history could be a comfort, not just a warning. He set it aside for later, but Lachlan had clearly seen it, and nudged him.

"I can cover if you need a few minutes," he said.

"Just making a mental note," Caleb replied.

Jerry kept up an engaging stream of chatter, as the set changed over and the hosts entertained the audience. He and Lady Alanna sat through the next two performers after Caleb and then made their excuses, heading back to their seats. As they left, Jerry bowed goodbye over Ava's hand, and then over Lachlan's as well.

"Do you suppose the Duke of Shivadlakia just likes being chivalrous or is it unconscious, when he does the hand thing?" Ava asked. "I mean, do they teach you that kind of thing when you're born into nobility?"

"I bet it's both," Lachlan speculated. "Loves the drama, our duke, but he's pretty self-aware. It's funny to subvert those systems when you were raised in them. I bet he likes to do it and then likes to make fun of himself for it."

After that, it was mostly a matter of enjoying the evening, at least for a while. They sat and watched the other performers while Lachlan mixed margaritas for himself and Ava; Caleb took a few sips from Ava's before settling in with a bottle of water, cautious of his voice.

He tried not to spend too much time judging the other

performers as they took the stage. He didn't want to think about what they were doing wrong, but rather why they did what they did. If he was going to get to know any of them, or be on good terms, he'd like to not make the misstep he had with Buck Haverd.

Haverd's performance was stressful, because Caleb knew how long they'd spent trying to get the vanishing-jacket maneuver right. He watched half-anxious about the jacket and half, still, trying to see more of the tattoos on his hipbones. Once the jacket went off without a hitch he could relax a little, at least.

Strangelust's performance was nearly last, and Caleb could feel himself getting tired – the roar of the crowd, the loud music, the high-energy hosting meant to keep it all going were starting to press on his nerves. None of it was helped by the knowledge that he was constantly *visible* here, even if he was deliberately turned away from the audience.

The panic attack hit, sudden and sharp, during one of the breaks between acts. There was only one more song to go, but it was Italy's, and they were in Italy, so the hosts took their time hyping up the crowd, and the roar increased. The air, which had been pleasantly warm and only a little humid, felt like it turned thick. A ringing started up in his ears, and his breath started to come short. He recognized the signs, at least, and braced for it as best he could.

Just in case, he popped the under-arm strap on his binder first, but loosening it didn't help; he splayed one hand on the couch cushion next to him for balance and hoped Lachlan and Ava wouldn't notice. Panic attacks were never pleasant – understatement of the year when it felt like he was dying, and worse, dying very publicly – but he knew how to ride one out by now. And, well, if he was dying, a small frantic scratch of a voice told him, Ava was there, she'd call an ambulance if she had to.

The room tilted and spun as his heart thudded slower than he thought possible, given how his head pounded. He saw, through tunnel vision, Ava startle when she looked over at him, and then heard Lachlan's voice in increasingly panicked tones – someone was yelling and someone else was running, motion at the edge of his senses.

Then it felt like everything was suddenly blocked out – all the noise, all the worry, all the…public of it. Something was in front of him, so close it obscured his view of anything, even around the edges of his sunglasses. Caleb choked on a sudden inrush of air. The pressure in his chest eased for a second.

A face dropped to level with his, not entirely unfamiliar, and a murmur made it through the noise – "Can I touch you? Is that all right?"

He nodded and hands gripped his head behind his ears, pulling his face forward into dusty-smelling fabric with a thick, solid shoulder underneath it. The hands shifted forward to cup lightly over his ears, muffling all sound, and the voice was back. "Everyone leave him alone. He's fine. Hey, Shades, you're fine," the voice said, closer to his ears and clearly to him, which was when Caleb realized it was Buck Haverd's voice.

Caleb jerked in surprise and Haverd's hands immediately let him go. A lot of information rushed in at once but the pure shock of Haverd here – Lachlan leaning over his shoulder, Ava playing interference on what looked like EMTs at the edge of the couches, Jerry and Davidson both skidding to a stop in front of them – settled him back in his body.

Buck Haverd was balanced on his toes as he squatted, hands with palms splayed harmlessly at shoulder height, shapeless black coat hanging open over his bare chest, right in front of him. A little corner of Caleb's brain picked out the text of the tattoo on his left pectoral, which read **99 ½ WON'T DO** in block letters.

"All right?" Haverd asked warily.

"Did you call me *Shades?*" Caleb asked. It was all he could think of to say.

"Did I just give you the coolest nickname you'll ever have? Yes," Haverd said. "Sorry, I know I'm the git who got owned by you about eight hours ago and richly deserved it, but you looked like you needed help."

"And you thought you'd help me?" Caleb asked faintly.

"Can't argue with results," Haverd pointed out. Caleb considered this, then leaned in exhaustedly and rested his forehead on Haverd's shoulder.

"Can you get rid of the cops?" he managed, although cops wasn't the right word.

"The medics? Probably not, but I can keep this from getting to be a scene. Sit still and try not to cringe," Haverd said in his ear, and then stood up. Caleb watched as he put on a huge, theatrically visible grin and threw the rock horns – both arms went up, palms facing the audience. He spread his forefingers and pinkies wide, tucking his middle and ring fingers under his thumbs, and jerked his hands forward.

In Galia it was an appallingly offensive gesture, meant to indicate the recipient had an adulterous spouse, and Caleb wasn't sure if Haverd knew some Italians might take it amiss as well...and then he realized of course he knew. That was why he was doing it: being ambiguous on purpose, offering what everyone knew really meant that things were fine, simultaneously gesturing obscenely like a clueless tourist. One of the hosts said, in Italian, *"It appears Haverd is up to his usual tricks..."*

Haverd turned to the stage and gave him the horns specifically, which made the crowd laugh. The host grinned and went back to his pre-established patter as one of the medics moved past Ava to sit next to Caleb.

"I think you speak Italian, Mr. Canto?" he asked in Italian. Caleb nodded. "Are you feeling all right?"

"Panic attack. It's not unusual, I get them sometimes," Caleb replied. "I'm in no danger. It's over now."

"I'd like to measure your oxygen and blood pressure – it's pretty standard, just to be sure."

"Do you have to?"

"You can refuse treatment but I'd really like to, sir," the man said. "I'd say we should do it privately but it'll be a bigger deal if we have to take you out of here."

"What's he saying?" Haverd asked.

"Blood pressure," the medic said, in English.

"I don't want everyone seeing a big fuss," Caleb added, also in English. Haverd nodded and scooted over until he was between the green room camera-bank and Caleb.

"I can block the cameras, so you won't show up on the jumbos," he said, pointing to the big video screens. "I don't think they want to show you anyway. It's not very Eurovision, eh?"

The medic looked at Caleb, who nodded and shed his jacket, rolling up the sleeve on his left arm.

"Where did you come from?" Caleb asked Haverd, trying to distract himself as the medic clipped an oxygen meter on the index finger of his right hand.

"Our green room is right over there. When King #2 started panicking, I noticed," Haverd replied, jerking a thumb at Lachlan.

"Excuse you, off the stage I am Queen #1," Lachlan replied.

"Beg your pardon, milady," Haverd retorted.

"Oooh, Mr. Big Stuff is touchy," Lachlan told Caleb.

"Leave him alone, he helped," Caleb said, and then "Thank you," ending on a grunt as the blood pressure cuff tightened.

"No thanks needed. You'd do the same. And unlike you, I wouldn't deserve the help," Haverd replied.

"Everyone deserves help," Caleb said.

"Well, I wouldn't *expect* the help. I was going to come apologize eventually," Haverd added. "It's no excuse, but – "

"I saw the coat thing," Caleb interrupted. Haverd raised his eyebrows. "I mean, obviously you were having a garbage afternoon. Easy to get touchy when you're frustrated because the world won't bend to your will."

"You don't pull many punches, do you?" Haverd asked, but he seemed amused.

"Neurologically incapable of it," Caleb answered, a little emboldened. "Constitutionally, too."

"Aren't you lucky. I just have rage issues," Haverd said.

"Blood pressure's in a reasonable range," the medic interrupted in Italian. "Oxygen's good. And cognitively you seem fine. Are you breathing easily?"

"Yes, thank you."

"Then unless you're worried it'll happen again, I can do my disappearing act."

"I'd appreciate it," Caleb said. "And look, someone might offer you money to talk about this, and I can't match whatever they'll give you – "

"It's not worth losing my job to sell your medical information, and this is a non-event," the man replied. "Besides, I get the feeling your friend would be willing to deliver a beating."

"He just said something about me," Haverd said immediately. "I don't speak Italian but he definitely said something about me."

"He said you did a good job," Caleb said in English. The medic winked and stood, gathering up his things calmly.

"Caleb?" Jerry called, as Davidson stopped the medic, probably having much the same *please don't talk about this to the press* conversation they'd just had.

"I'm all right," Caleb said. "Momentary hiccup."

Jerry nodded and tilted his head at the audience; Caleb realized he was asking if he should go, and nodded back.

"Is there anything else you need?" Haverd asked, as the medic strolled away casually. The others began to move away too – Davidson leading, speaking quietly with Lady Alanna, and Jerry following with backwards, worried glances.

He felt a little disoriented but otherwise fine, and half of the confusion was probably from a guy he didn't think particularly liked him, standing there offering to help. He shifted his weight, testing his steadiness even sitting down, and felt the binder under his shirt ride up.

"Stay there in front of me?" he said, fumbling with the first two buttons of the shirt. He reached under his armpit and, with practiced skill, tightened the strap of the binder. It shifted back into place and he adjusted the fit, fiddling with it until it was comfortable, the pressure evenly distributed and not too tight. Haverd, once he saw what was happening, looked away.

Caleb finished buttoning up again just as the lights went down for the final performance – Italy, and the crowd falling silent, waiting for the opening chords.

"Thanks," he muttered, hoping Haverd could hear him. "You can move now if you want."

"No problem. Make a great photo op. Hey, as long as I'm here, what'd the medic really say?" Haverd asked, crouching again.

"Not now," Caleb said, pointing at the stage.

"But   "

"Shush! I want to hear Italy," Caleb said.

"Are you seriously going to make me wait until Italy finishes?" Haverd asked, turning to settle on the ground, back against the sofa next to Caleb's legs.

"I owe you for that crack about the sunglasses," Caleb replied, and then held up a finger when Haverd opened his mouth. "Italy first."

He did watch Italy perform, but he also watched Haverd watch Italy, curious now. Panic attacks could be subtle, and could also look like a lot of other things. Being able to identify one wasn't a skill everyone had, and knowing how to react was even rarer. Not everyone needed to have their senses cut off that way; some people found it as terrifying as Caleb did comforting.

There was a perceptive edge to Haverd's attention on the performance that was interesting. The same perception he'd used on Caleb, perhaps. Didn't one of his songs have a line, something like *I only look this stupid cause that's what you want to see...*

"They're strong competition," Haverd said, as Italy took their bows and the crowd settled down. He leaned up a little as Caleb leaned down to hear him better. "They're great vocalists and they've got a strong points base but Italy won last year, and most countries don't win two years running."

"Who do you think you'll have to beat?" Caleb asked.

"I'm not worried about what I saw tonight. Italy'll be a challenge and you're a contender but some of the others…just not very dynamic, and that counts with Eurovision, you know."

Caleb wasn't sure he agreed, but perhaps it was something Haverd needed to tell himself. Still –

"Everyone onstage during my number is sitting down," Caleb said. Haverd turned, blinked at him, and laughed.

"Intentionality, Shades! You're meant to be sitting down. They're *spiritually* sitting down. Not the same at all!"

"So what am I spiritually doing when my ass is on the stage?" Caleb asked.

"Fucking great question. You're an enigma wrapped in a ukulele. I'll let you know when I work it out," Haverd told him. "Hey, if I go back to my green room now, everyone'll know you're really fine. But I won't if you aren't really fine."

Caleb took stock, giving the question real weight. Haverd waited without apparent impatience.

"Yeah, I'm okay," he said. "Thank you. You helped a lot."

"At least I did something right today," Haverd said. "Nice meeting you again, Shades. Mind how you go," and he was gone.

Lachlan slid over next to Caleb and said, in a voice of great concern, "So. How close did you get to touching his abs?"

Caleb looked up at Lachlan and burst out laughing.

Buck Haverd had never been to Turin before and didn't speak much Italian, but after the day he'd had he wasn't about to let that stop him. He left the concert hall, barely stopping to put on a shirt, wipe off the stage makeup, and apply some real-life makeup instead, and in half an hour was climbing into the party bus one of the VIP attendees had hinted he'd be welcome on.

They'd all had media briefing packets, him and the band and likely the other competitors as well, about representing Eurovision and behaving themselves appropriately. Buck, however, was more or less the designated black hat and could get away with making trouble that others couldn't, at least to an extent. The UK was one of the Big Five, the countries bankrolling the bulk of Eurovision, so while they could be fined if Buck misbehaved too badly, it wasn't like Eurovision could kick the country out, and the UK knew what they were getting when they picked Buck. He wasn't going to make trouble for the sake of it, but he'd never pretended he was going to win for best-behaved.

So he and the band went out, first on the party bus and then into the club it stopped in front of. Buck wasn't as famous as he'd like, but he was well famous enough to walk up to the front of the line, cock an eyebrow at the bouncer, and get ushered inside to a good table. He ordered beers for the table and settled in while the band ran off to make friends.

Good place to start the night; the vibe and the music were both energetic. He let the rhythm bounce around in his head for a while, still coming down from the excitement of the evening. Of the whole day, really.

Even if Canto had said it was fine, he was still furious with himself at picking the fight during rehearsal. Not just because he didn't actually like being That Guy, but because he'd been so transparent about it. Canto had seen that none of it was about him, had put Buck neatly in his place, and then had proceeded to *forgive him*, because he'd seen how frustrated Buck was. It was humiliating to lash out in anger, but it was worse when the other person saw it and treated you like a child, even if you deserved it.

He took a long swallow of beer. At least they'd mended fences. The adrenaline from performing had barely leveled off when he'd seen Canto's panic attack and it kicked back up, but he was glad he'd been there. It was good to be able to help someone like that —

"Hey."

Buck looked up from his beer and his thoughts. Someone was leaning on the edge of the booth, voice raised to be heard over the music. A man about his age, pale with long dark hair and a white-toothed smile — attractive, in the goth kind of way Buck sometimes fancied.

"I was hoping you were coming over. Your whole band's over there," the man said, tipping his head at the bar. He had a faint Italian accent. "But you've stayed looking very cool over here, and I couldn't wait forever to say hello."

"Ah, they go to the bar. The bar comes to me," Buck said grandly, spreading his arms and giving the man a smile.

"I've played into your trap, then. I'm Giulio. I'm a big fan."

Buck's grin widened. "Nice to meet you, Giulio. If you're stuck with me now, might as well come have a beer."

Just as well to have a distraction. He had a lot to consider, between the fight with Canto and the concert, but his mam always said he did his best thinking when he wasn't thinking. He wasn't fond of putting it that way — it carried a sting of condescension, as though she thought it was sweet but pointless, his trying to make anything of himself. He tried to view it differently, telling himself that he thought so deep he had to be doing something else while he was thinking, to keep from getting in his own way.

Giulio was fun to talk to, anyway, cool enough that he didn't gush, interested enough in music that they had something to talk about. And he knew of a more interesting venue with better drinks, so after about an hour of trying to gather everyone up and keep them in one place long enough to get rides to the new place, they ended up in a really cool underground music club. It had the promised better drinks (also cheaper), and it had some friends of Giulio's, which meant the party with Buck at the center was getting bigger and louder and thus much more fun.

He could figure out the rest tomorrow – what to do about Canto, if anything, and maybe even what he felt about it. Or he could do that never, if he wanted. He could get on with life, avoid Canto at future performances, and forget it ever happened.

Around three in the morning, coming off the dance floor, some of that deep-thinking paid off. An idea sparked across his brain, clearly the result of unconscious cogitation.

They'd be headed back to the UK day after tomorrow, or something like that. He had some space on his calendar, which his agent wanted him to keep open for publicity leading up to Eurovision but which he was secretly hoping he'd find the balls to use to just fuck off somewhere for weeks on end. Show up at Eurovision with a tan and an apologetic grin. Write his album on a beach, maybe.

Now he had an actual idea of a destination. The insanely hard-to-spell country, the one Canto came from. That could be…good for him, perhaps.

"What're you doing?" Giulio asked, leaning over his shoulder to study what Buck was up to on his phone. He rubbed his nose against Buck's ear, which was endearing but also distracting.

"Buying a plane ticket," Buck said. "Had an idea for a holiday."

"Right now?"

"Nah. See? I'm in Turin, with you," he said, and Giulio blushed a little. "Flight's in a week or two. Now, in an hour or two, we could both be in my hotel suite in Turin, if you're patient."

"Buy whatever you need to," Giulio said grandly. Buck tilted his head at his phone. He was definitely drunk, but he was pretty sure he'd spelled Askazer right at least. "You can't fly into Askazer-Shivadlakia," Giulio added, still spying.

"I can't even pronounce it," Buck replied. Giulio laughed.

"Closest airport is Nice. There's a train," Giulio said.

"These complicated fuckers," Buck muttered, as Giulio reached around his shoulder to tap on his phone's screen. Make fun of him *and* make it difficult to get there? The lack of fucks they must have.

Giulio took the phone out of his hands eventually and took over; Buck picked dates when asked, put in his payment information when required, and shortly found himself with a plane ticket from London to Nice and a first-class reservation on the train from Nice to Fons-Askaz.

"I owe you," he said, putting his phone away and turning to give Giulio his full attention.

"I'll collect," Giulio told him easily.

It was a shame they weren't in Turin for longer, really. Giulio seemed cool and knew his way around the scene. He could be fun to run around with. But Buck knew even if they stayed longer, or even when they came back to Turin for the Grand Final, it wouldn't matter. Giulio hadn't gone out looking for a romance, he'd been looking for a fun night.

Well, having fun had worked out for Buck so far.

"Let's go back to mine and negotiate," Buck suggested, and Giulio nodded, grinning. "I'll let the band know I'm going. Some of 'em might want to ride back with us."

Giulio pressed up against him in the crowd, hands wandering pleasantly. "They can't come to your room party."

"They can have their own," Buck said, starting to look around for the band and hangers-on, because he might be bailing on them but he wasn't going to abandon them without making sure they had a way to get back. "If we start trying to find everyone now, we might actually get back by breakfast."

Caleb and the others had a late dinner after they managed to escape the concert plaza, with Jerry and Lady Alanna treating. The privilege of being a duke, even in another country, was evident – Jerry effortlessly got them a quiet, private room in the back of a restaurant and a several-course meal with minimal interruption. They left full of good food and generally satisfied, even Caleb, who sometimes found himself unsettled for days after a panic attack.

He didn't expect to sleep much, and he was right. He caught a few hours, but between the strange bed and strange room, he was up with the sunrise, more or less. After a futile half-hour of trying to grasp at more sleep, he threw on a hoodie and some cargo shorts and went downstairs to take a walk, and maybe to find a cafe that would feed him this early.

Because some vengeful force of fate liked to laugh, he came face-to-face with Buck Haverd again in the lobby.

He was clearly coming in from spending the entire night out, walking a little unsteadily, with the rest of his band and some strangers in tow. Caleb almost slipped past, but Haverd called, "Canto!" and stumbled up to him, beaming.

"Hey, you're up as late as me. Been out at the clubs?" Haverd asked.

Caleb squinted at him and decided he was joking.

"Well, you know me, the party animal," he said. Haverd laughed. "You look like you've had a good time."

"Yeah, when in Rome. Or Turin," Haverd said. "Hey, by the way."

"Yes?"

"I was gonna use this as an excuse later but I still wanna know what the medic really said about me."

"An excuse for what?" Caleb asked, caught on the first half of the sentence.

"What?" Haverd said.

Caleb decided to let it go. "He said he wasn't going to tell the tabloids what happened to me," he said. "Because you looked like you'd beat him if he did."

"Huh. Sure would have. I'm gonna have to work on being harder to read," Haverd said.

"Please don't. Obvious people are a real relief," Caleb told him. Haverd mimed being hit in the face. "Told you I wasn't capable of pulling punches."

Haverd held up a hand questioningly, asking permission. Caleb wondered where he'd learned good manners in this, but he suspected he wouldn't get a real answer just now, so he simply nodded. Haverd carefully cupped the side of Caleb's neck, just below his jaw, and pressed their foreheads together. He smelled like dust and cheap liquor.

"You're solid, you are," he said.

"Buck!" someone called, and Haverd pulled away; over his shoulder, Caleb could see one of the people he'd come in with, hands on hips, looking amused but impatient.

"That's my cue," Haverd said, turning to go. "See you around, Shades!" he called over his shoulder as they left.

"See you at semis!" Caleb called back.

But it was much sooner than that, as it turned out.

CHAPTER FIVE

ALL THINGS CONSIDERED, the panic attack got remarkably little play, which was probably a relief to Davidson and the RSBA. Eurovision wasn't interested in mental health struggles being part of its branding, he supposed. He didn't see commentary on it from anyone who'd been there – not Jerry and Alanna, not the medic, not even Buck Haverd.

His performance got equally little play, at least outside of Askazer-Shivadlakia, which was just as well. Besides, there was only so much attention you could possibly get in a country that small – his landlady had to run off the paparazzi the morning after he got back, but since that consisted of sweeping the front step threateningly in the direction of the reporter from the one local radio station and the reporter from the one local television station, she didn't particularly mind doing it.

His students continued to attempt to become ungovernable, but Caleb had their number now, and usually managed to get them back on track.

A few days after they returned, he got an invitation to Saturday brunch at the palace. An informal meal with the royal family, Jerry's email said, just to discuss a few things. He sent a full list of attendees, which Caleb appreciated, although he was less appreciative that Gregory III, his father Michaelis, and Eddie Rambler would be there in addition to Jerry and Lady Alanna, Jes and Noah, Lachlan and Ava and Davidson.

"More on our side than theirs, though," Ava said, when he brought this up.

"Are there sides?" Caleb asked, alarmed.

"No! You've met the king, he's fine. I'm just saying there are more people there you like than people you're nervous about," she said.

Which was true, and very helpful, because it turned out when you wound up the royal family and let them loose on a topic, they did not hold back. It was a lot to deal with while trying to eat a croissant.

The topic was, amusingly enough, Caleb's public image, which had only been improved by his performance in Turin, but it also meant more attention was on him now. The royal family spoke over and around each other, managing to simultaneously argue about Palace publicity, social media in general, Photogram in specific, Caleb's representation of the country, and the Shivadh attitude towards Eurovision. Lachlan, clearly accustomed to the chaos, joined in, and after a few minutes Ava did as well. Caleb sat quietly, absorbing it with interest. Davidson, who was equally quiet, looked like he was reconsidering his career choices.

"The issue is that he hasn't got any social media at all," said Lady Alanna – who had asked him to call her Al, something he was finding oddly more difficult than calling the Duke of Shivadlakia "Jerry".

"I don't think that's an issue necessarily," Jes Deimos replied. "He doesn't have to if he doesn't want to. I personally think it adds to his mystique," they said, grinning sidelong at Caleb, who smiled tentatively back. He liked Jes, felt the instinctive siblinghood of transness in them, and so far had been validated in trusting their opinion.

"Of course not, it's only that without a platform, he doesn't control the narrative," Eddie Rambler replied. It turned out that nothing Rambler did in his videos was an act, and he really was that friendly and loud.

"There doesn't actually have to be a narrative," Ava said tentatively.

"Not from us, but there will be one regardless," Lady Alanna said. "This is Eurovision. Someone's telling the story. Whether you care about that narrative is the question," she said to Caleb.

"I kinda do," Caleb said. "There's…a lot of nasty things you can say about me."

"Mm, no. There are a lot of things people *think* they can say," Michaelis replied. "They can be corrected if they try."

"You don't mean there are scandals, do you," Rambler said, his voice kind. "You mean there are slurs."

Caleb nodded. "I'm trans, I'm autistic, technically I'm an immigrant, whatever you have to say about it," he added to Michaelis, who was opening his mouth to object. "But I've been myself my whole life, it's not new. I know how to hit back if I need to. Anyway, if you're not on the internet you don't hear or see all that garbage."

"We're the ones putting you through this, so you have the protection of the Palace when needed," Gregory III said. "If you choose to engage on that level, we have resources we can offer."

"As does the RSBA," Davidson put in, looking relieved to have the chance to speak. "We're grateful the Palace is choosing to help, but the agency wouldn't leave you to hang."

"Father," Gregory III added, and Michaelis looked over at him. "You've got that face."

"Your bored-at-the-UN face you get when you're thinking," Jes added.

"I hardly ever even go to the UN. This is just my face," the king emeritus replied. "I was thinking that Theophile works for our communications office, and Gerald's involved with our Delegation for the event. Surely one of you two would be willing to take point on whatever PR is required."

"No need," Noah said. He'd been quiet for a while, but only Caleb had noticed; now every adult in the room looked at him. He held up his phone. "I just set up the user name CalebCanto on every social site worth having a presence on, all fed by Photogram.

I've got a ticket in to the VIP helpdesk at Photogram to get you verified. I'm verified and Photogram friends with Eddie, so they'll take my word for it."

"When did you do that?" Eddie asked.

"While you were talking," Noah said. "It's not like it takes long. I just did the same stuff I did for myself when I started getting in the news."

"When you were in the news?" Michaelis echoed, perturbed.

"Not, like, a specific article or anything," Noah told him. "Just generally. I'm newsworthy now, so I wanted to make sure nobody else made a fake account for me somewhere."

"Should we be doing this?" Michaelis asked Gregory.

"We are," Eddie replied absently. Gregory and Michaelis both looked at him curiously. "Communications office monitors your media presence. Social and other stuff. I didn't tell them to do it – they've been doing it since before I got here. I didn't think about adding Noah to the list. I think the team assumed Reverb was handling his business."

"…yeah, we probably should be," Jes said thoughtfully.

"That's what I'm doing," Noah said. "I mean, I work for Reverb and I'm…doing it…for me. I can handle it," he added, a little defensively.

"I'm sure you can, but that's the kind of thing that should come up in a producer meeting, so that you don't have to invent a media strategy all on your own," Jes told him. "And if you're going to do it for someone else, they should have input."

"I wouldn't post for him unless he asked me to," Noah protested. "I just wanted to make sure we got his username on all the stuff."

"You still need to ask," Jes said.

"Sorry," Noah muttered, then turned back to Caleb, looking more authentically contrite. "Sorry. I should have asked. But it's all set up so at least there's that, right? And uh." He glanced at his parent, who sighed and gestured for him to continue. "There's a new PR email account for you. All the passwords are going there but I've got 'em too so I can help run stuff. I'm your publicist now!" he added brightly.

"Aren't you sixteen?" Davidson asked.

"Probably keep him out of a good deal of trouble," Michaelis said. Jes nudged him, frowning. "Well, the deed is done, and I hate to tell any child to sit still and play on a smartphone but Noah is a self-driven wrecking ball. He could use the distraction."

"And also five percent on any endorsements," Noah said. "Negotiable. I'll send you a contract, Mr. Canto."

"That solves that, I guess," Eddie said. "One less thing for me to do."

"Hit the max number of Photogram accounts allowed on the app?" Jerry guessed.

"I'm one away and I'm saving it for emergencies," Eddie agreed.

"*Anyway*, you can run the accounts if you want, or I'll do it for you," Noah told Caleb. "Like if you only want to make sure you 'control the narrative' or whatever, I can just post for you when needed, but if you want to post video clips of your music or selfies and stuff, you can. Want me to follow all the other performers for you?"

"Can you do that?" Caleb asked.

"Sure, there's lists and stuff. And you've got a hashtag, but it's pretty quiet right now," Noah said. "Here, lean in with Jerry and smile!"

Jerry leaned forward and turned up the wattage on his smile; Caleb did his best to grin convincingly, while Noah snapped a photo.

"Throwing this on Photogram to prove it's you," he added.

"The tag for you is very complimentary, actually," Michaelis said, studying his phone. "Lots of photographs of you on stage. Well-lit. I imagine your fans have downvoted the negativity. They generally do for the royal family."

"I thought you didn't know how hashtags worked," Jerry said. "Or about downvoting."

"I live with these two, I'm learning whether I want to or not," Michaelis replied, gesturing at Jes and Noah.

"You are the longest-term troll I've ever met," Jerry said.

"Don't you have a Photogram of your own to maintain?" Michaelis asked mildly. Jerry was opening his mouth to retort when Noah interrupted.

"Look, Buck Haverd tagged you! He mentioned you in a post, the day after Turin," he said.

"He did?" Caleb asked, intrigued. "Oh, no, is it a picture of me freaking out at the concert?"

"No, it's nice," Noah said, passing his phone over. It showed a photograph of Caleb sitting on the couch, Buck on the floor next to his legs. They were watching the stage, oblivious to the picture even being taken. Buck had tagged it *Making friends with #calebcanto so I get some of the Ask's points in #eurovision Grand Final.*

"Want to reply?" Noah asked. "It's logged in as you."

Caleb took the phone and typed *Sunglasses don't look so nerdy now, do they?* in Italian, then hit send. Noah laughed.

"That's cool. You're a natural," he told Caleb, but Caleb was watching Photogram load Buck Haverd's profile page. The most recent image was...unsettlingly familiar.

"Um," he said, and showed it to Noah. "Is that our boat? The Academy's, I mean."

"What?" Ava asked, leaning over his shoulder. "Why..."

The image was a selfie, Buck's grinning face with its light green eyes and deep teal hair; he was wearing a faded Poly Styrene t-shirt and standing on a dock, a tall ship in the background. Caleb had rarely been out on the ship that the Maritime Academy used in training its older students, but he saw it every day, and knew what it looked like.

"Yeah, that's the *Dychev*," Noah said, taking the phone back from him. "When was this – huh."

"Would you like to share?" Jes prompted.

"Buck Haverd's in Askazar-Shivadlakia," Noah said. "Posted ten minutes ago. Says *Doing a little touristing. Didn't think I'd do this pre-party but I like their style. Catch #strangelust at the...* well, he spelled Shivadh wrong, but he's got the spirit," Noah interrupted, "*shivahd pre-party next month.*"

"Why is he here a month early for a pre-party he didn't even want to go to?" Caleb asked, confused.

"Couldn't say," Noah replied, tapping away on the phone.

"Don't think he's told us, either," Jes said to Lachlan.

"He definitely hasn't informed us," Davidson said.

"What's a month's warning among friends," Lachlan sighed.

"Hope you've got a setup for that jacket stunt," Ava added.

"Why shouldn't he come to Askazer-Shivadlakia? We're delightful," Eddie put in. "Besides, there's been some buzz about you, Caleb. Couple of in-the-know vloggers think you're a contender. Might get a few unexpected guests at the party."

"How do you, son of California, know more about Eurovision than I do?" Gregory III asked. "I've *been to* Eurovision. And I still don't fully understand how the points work."

"Nobody understands that," Eddie said dismissively. "I'm just a very enthusiastic man."

"Do tell," Gregory replied drily.

"Noah," Jes said, the warning in their tone evident as they read something on his phone over his shoulder.

"I was going to tell him!" Noah protested. He turned to Caleb. "I followed Buck Haverd for you and he followed you back and I was just gonna ask him in private messages if he wants to have lunch at Reverb, down at the fishing lodge."

"Why would he..." Caleb began, and then frowned. "Why would either of us want to have lunch at Reverb?"

"I want him to come to the fishing lodge because he's becoming a big deal recording artist and I want him to see the studios," Noah explained. "You want to go to the fishing lodge and have lunch with him to find out why he's here."

There was a beat of silence, and then the deep rumble of Michaelis, who had begun to laugh.

"This is what you get for befriending a tavat," he said, shaking his head. Caleb glanced at Noah. "A tavat buys his own birthright indeed. And one for everyone around him. He's networking on your behalf, Caleb. You don't have to let him unless you agree."

Caleb looked down at the phone Noah was holding out. The private message just said, "Lunch? 1pm," with a pin-drop for the underground entrance to Reverb Studios.

"Might be the first time you ever speak to him while he's wearing a shirt," Jerry pointed out.

"He really loves to give those pecs an airing," Ava added.

"I think I speak for nearly everyone when I say I love it too," Lachlan put in.

"It's okay," Caleb said, surprising himself. "I do want to know why he's here. And – and I like the fishing lodge," he added, glancing at Michaelis. "The lake and the footpaths and everything. It's a pretty park. More people who come here should see it."

"Well," the old king said, still looking amused. "I agree."

"Okay, I'll send it then," Noah said, hitting the little button to fire off the message. "Let you know what he says. See, I'm already doing a great job managing your socials!"

"This is a whole lot to happen at breakfast," Caleb observed.

"You should see us at a party," Gregory said.

"What are you planning on for lunch?" Eddie asked.

Buck Haverd knew he wasn't the brightest man in the world, but he wasn't a fool; when the CalebCanto Photogram user friended him, he studied it carefully. Even with the photo of Caleb with that duke guy, it could be a weird catfish of some kind. Still, it was pending verification, and Eddie Rambler's official account was following it. He took a chance and followed back.

When the private message came through, he'd been sitting out on a cafe patio, knit hat pulled down over his very visible hair, trying to blend in and apparently succeeding. Everyone in Askazer-Shivadlakia was sporting Caleb's style of sunglasses these days, so it wasn't weird that he was too. With his hair and most of his ink covered up, he really was just a nondescript white guy.

He'd felt his eyebrows shoot up at the lunch invite, because he didn't think Canto really wanted to see him again, and he...

Well, he hadn't come here to see Caleb, but he couldn't deny he'd wondered if he would. Fons-Askaz was relatively small, he knew Caleb lived here, and how many music venues could there even be? And now he was asking Buck to lunch.

Buck barely hesitated before sending a thumbs-up emoji back. The odds of the account being a catfish still weren't zero, but Reverb Studios was a real place and looked, actually, like the kind of place he could make use of.

So here he was: the UK's latest not-really-that-bad bad boy, hundreds of miles from home, rocking up to an old-fashioned looking building in the middle of a park in his rented car, following the GPS directions into a weird underground garage.

There was plenty of parking, at least, and when he got out of the car there was a sign on a nearby door reading REVERB STUDIOS. It looked like the kind of place you'd get murdered in a horror flick, but so did most of the bars he'd played before turning twenty. And Buck hadn't got anywhere in life by using good sense, so he pushed the door open and stepped inside.

There was a long hall with a row of doors to the right; the hallway eventually opened at the far end into what looked like a bigger room. He'd gotten about halfway down the hall when a teenage kid bounced up to him, looking like the one you'd cast as the Nice One in a boy band.

"Mr. Haverd, welcome to Reverb Studios," he said, very professionally. Buck eyed him. "I'm Noah, I'm Mr. Canto's social media manager and a junior producer at Reverb. This way."

"Make 'em younger and younger these days," Buck said.

"Yeah, I'm getting extra credit in my intro to business class at school," the boy said, apparently unironically. He led Buck the rest of the way down the hall, into a big open room with an ancient kitchenette off to the side and, perplexingly, a giant elderly map of Europe on one wall.

"I know it looks super weird. It's an old bunker from World War Two," Noah said. "Great soundproofing for the studios."

"How many do you have?" Buck asked, on firmer ground here.

"One for voice only because the acoustics are strange, three for general use. Only one has a separate booth for the producers, which can be a pain, but it means people who want to self-produce can," Noah said. "Just finished putting in a rehearsal space but the hours are a little restricted because there's some sound bleed upwards and it pipes right into Michaelis's bathroom."

"Like the king, Michaelis?" Buck asked, taking a single-saor cash bill out of his pocket and holding it up. The man on the front managed to look stern while smiling.

"Yeah, he lives upstairs. Tough to get a shower with an epic drum solo going on under your feet," Noah said with a grin. "Anyway there's also office space for meetings and the big room here."

"The king lives above a recording studio?"

"King emeritus. He'll correct you if you say that. He's cool though, don't let him fool you."

"Oh, sure," Buck said. "Wouldn't want to get hoodwinked by the ex-king of Askazer-Shivadlakia."

"Hey, good job pronouncing the name! Mr. Canto should be here soon, he ran up to the palace to get some food."

"I merit royal catering?"

Noah gave him a grin. "It's not tea with the queen around here."

"That's not what the guy playing the king for Caleb said to me," Buck said, and Noah gave him a startled look, then cracked up laughing.

"Lachlan makes an impression," he agreed, as the door in the far end of the room opened. Caleb appeared, a large square tote in one hand; behind him, Lachlan was carrying a small cooler.

"Hey, Mr. Haverd is here!" Noah called. "Lachlan, guess what he just said about you."

"Am I gonna have to make you hold my earrings?" Lachlan asked Noah.

"No! He was getting real freaked out about Michaelis living upstairs – "

"That is not true," Buck protested. It struck him that he was definitely ruining his cool-guy vibe around this kid, who was like ten years younger and yet somehow cooler than him.

" – so I said it's not like he's having tea with the queen and he said that's not what you said to him," Noah blurted.

Lachlan cackled. "Bless the child," he said to Buck. "I don't take sass like that from just anyone, but you're coasting on goodwill after helping Caleb out."

"You called yourself Queen #1!" Buck said.

"I did do that," Lachlan told Noah. "Mind you, that's only because Caleb's a king through and through."

"Short king, as everyone keeps reminding me," Caleb said, a little dourly, but he gave Buck a smile as he set down the food bags and took an instrument case off his back, propping it on an empty chair. "Hey, thanks for coming. Noah wanted to show off the studio and I'm dying to know why you're here."

"Mr. Canto," Noah said.

"Subtlety, buddy," Lachlan told him.

"Oh, no thank you, I'm allergic," Caleb replied. Lachlan and Noah looked at each other.

"There's a whole section in the Wikipedia article on Askazer-Shivadlakia about your sense of humor," Buck remarked into the silence. "I can't believe I read the whole thing and still didn't get it until just now."

"I know we're not supposed to be so blatant about this kind of thing," Caleb continued, unpacking the insulated tote onto the table. Amazing smells began to drift around the room – onions, something vaguely herbal, the faint acrid tang of salt. "But why bother? I told you I liked obvious people, it'd be hypocritical of me not to be one."

"I say this, aware that we haven't known each other very long," Buck managed, "but you aren't actually obvious in the least, Shades. Anyway, feed me and I'm an open book."

"Noah, how about we let Caleb handle Mr. Haverd," Lachlan said, plucking up one of the cartons Caleb was unpacking. "Come on, kiddo, we can go upstairs and do our wigs there."

Buck saw Noah looking a little irritated at the adults having stolen his march; he dropped the kid a wink and said, "Give me a tour after, yeah? I'm in the market for someplace like this."

"Don't let him forget," Noah said to Caleb, a little imploringly, and then it was just Caleb, opening up cartons, and Buck, standing by like a knob.

"I had no idea what we were going to do about lunch," he said, drawing closer to the table, looking over the food. "You didn't actually have to cater, I was ready to buy you a sandwich down the high street."

"Good, I think you make more than I do," Caleb said. "Not a problem, though, I had help. In deference to your heritage, quoting Eddie there, he made fish and chips. But there's seaweed salad, Askazer twist-bread, some cheesy pasta. Didn't know if you were vegetarian."

"Nah, grew up too broke to be picky. I will have some of the seaweed salad with the fish and chips, though," Buck said, seating himself. "Eddie, that's Rambler, the chef, yeah? Saw he was following your Photogram."

"He's very enthusiastic about lunches," Caleb said, as if he didn't quite understand why. "Although he's enthusiastic about everything, really. There's beer and soda in the cooler."

"Generous," Buck said, popping the lid open and fishing out a bottle of beer. "Serve you something?"

"I have water, I'm good," Caleb replied.

"Sure. More for me," Buck said with a grin. "So the kid wanted to showcase the studio. And you're just curious why I popped up on your turf?"

"Hardly my turf. Lots of people live in Askazer-Shivadlakia," Caleb said. There was a certain charm to the way he handled small talk — or perhaps didn't handle it. He treated everything one said as if it was important. Which, Buck had to admit, was particularly novel for him, who had generally been relegated to unimportance unless he had a guitar strapped on.

"Most of them aren't repping at Eurovision, though," Buck pointed out. "And I don't know any of them."

"Hardly know me," Caleb said.

"I'll get your number yet," Buck said with a grin, then had to stop because he'd put a piece of fried fish in his mouth and was having a *moment*. "Wow," he added.

"Eddie's cooking is pretty good," Caleb replied, having apparently opted for the cheesy pasta.

"This is outstanding," Buck agreed. "Fuck, now I'm staying for the fish."

Caleb burst out laughing. "You're representing the UK and you want Shivadh fish cooked by an American? Better not tell the folks back home."

"Ah, fuck nationalism," Buck said. "Yes, I am now officially here for fried fish."

"Not really, though. Not originally," Caleb prompted. "Got a shock seeing you at the harbor this morning."

"I keep hearing how quaint this is," Buck said, waving a chip around him, indicating the whole country. "And you have a pre-party coming up. Thought I'd be a big fish in a smallish pond."

"But you said you're looking for studio space? Is your band here?"

"Nah. Truth is, whatever happens with Eurovision, I have to get an album out sooner or later. I need to be ready to take advantage of the exposure from the competition. And if I don't do well, I'll have to have a comeback waiting."

"Seems very stressful," Caleb said dubiously.

"You don't think about things like that?" Buck asked.

"I don't make a living that way. I'm a teacher. Never have to worry about your career when you're up against nine year olds."

"Couldn't pay me to do it," Buck said, chest tightening a little at the idea of going back to school, even as a teacher. "Anyway, I've been trying to get some songs down but the bigger the buzz gets, the harder it is to get any peace, you know? Back home they want me to do signings and performances and interviews and all, and normally that's fine, but between all that and Eurovision and like, social media...dunno, I just wanted some quiet. In the meantime," he added, diverting attention from the train wreck of noise and marketing and unpleasant emotion that had been his life lately, "I can spend the month doing songwriting, getting some riffs down, getting some inspiration. Like, you know. Going into the desert to figure life out or whatever."

Caleb was quiet, studying him, features grave. His eyes never quite met Buck's, but that didn't signify much, and it was much more interesting that they often darted down to his hands.

"You make it sound very peaceful," he said finally.

"Isn't it?"

"I live here and I have a day job, so it's just normal for me."

"Ah yeah, that's a point," Buck said. "Can I ask you something?"

Caleb gestured with his fork, mouth full.

"You sell most of the songs you write. I hunted some up online."

Caleb swallowed and opened a small carton, full of what

looked like apple slices. "I don't make much from them, if that's what you're asking."

"No, it wasn't. The lyrics, they're all really different. The arrangements sometimes too."

"Most of that's not me, it's them redoing my work. Some better than others."

"Still. You're not like...repeating on a theme. Where do you get it all?" Buck asked. "You live here, right? Do you travel much? Is the scene here really good? Where's the music come from for you?"

He hadn't meant to ask all that quite so intensely, but if Caleb thought it was weird, he didn't say so.

"It sort of strikes me," Caleb said. "Conversations, or books. I don't travel a lot, and I don't actually go see much live music. I just look around and see stuff and write about it. I wrote *Young Prince* because I heard someone say the word tavat and looked it up in the dictionary. You know the Duke of Shivadlakia?"

"Tall, with the annoyingly good hair?"

Caleb laughed. "Yeah. Jerry. He's dating Lady Alanna – she works for the king too. He's the Duke of Shivadlakia, she's going to be Duchess of Askaz."

"What, like Askazer-Shivadlakia..." Buck considered this. "Oh, that's...cool, unless...I mean they're not related, right?"

"I don't think so. Anyway, that's a fun theme to try and write a song about. The countries were united centuries ago. And now they're dating. The hook lyric I'm playing around with is *we are nations.*"

"Huh. I like that. She was the one in orange at Turin? They're both scorching, can't blame either one of them," Buck said. "Though if it were me writing it, I'd write about – "

"The weird part where they might be related? Yes, I looked up your music too," Caleb said.

"My music could very well be defined entirely as 'the weird part'," Buck said.

"There's plenty of weirdness here. The Shivadh sense of humor is just the start."

"Noah said if you play a drum solo in the rehearsal room here, the king emeritus hears it in his shower upstairs," Buck said.

"If you can make a pop hit out of that, you should have my job."

"Musicians love to talk about being musicians," Buck mused.

"Yeah, like *Piano Man*," Caleb said. Buck choked on a chip.

"I was thinking more like *Killing Me Softly*, but sure, why not. *Piano Man*, hell," Buck said.

"*Bobby McGee*," Caleb added thoughtfully. "That's a song about music, sort of."

"Bobby Mc – first *Piano Man* and then *Bobby McGee*? How old are you?"

"Twenty-four."

"I meant metaphorically."

"Oh. Probably about five hundred," Caleb said. There was a brief, fleeting expression that crossed his face – a little pained, struggling with something deep – but it was gone quickly.

"At least pick something from this century," Buck challenged.

"Like what?"

"I don't know – *Uptown Funk*."

Caleb lifted his chin, clearly taking the challenge –

"*American Pie*," he said.

...or perhaps just taking the challenge as un-seriously as possible.

"You are a monster," Buck said. "Fine. *Shake It Off*."

"Barely," Caleb said.

"She's got that music in her mind," Buck informed him. "It says it's going to be all right."

Caleb sat back, smiling, and shook his head. "Don't make me do it."

"What?"

"*Jailhouse Rock.*"

"Elvis Presley was a thief," Buck cried. "He stole everything he did from the blues and ruined it! He should have been on his *knees* thanking Big Mama Thornton and Sister Rosetta Tharpe."

Caleb's smile widened. "*Sing And Shout.*"

"All right," Buck acknowledged. "I can't speak against Sister Rosetta," he added, touching his chest, the left pectoral where a line she'd written was inked on his skin. He sat back, stretching out. "Point is, I'm here for a month to take a holiday and write some music. Find a little peace before Eurovision really strikes. Did you record your stuff here?"

"At Reverb? Sure. The album cut of *Young Prince*, and the backing instrumentals for semis and the pre-party – did the guitar first and then layered the ukulele over it, so it's all me playing. Reverb's the only game in town, but they do good work."

"Would they let a studio long-term? Could I just put down cash and get a booth to myself for the month?"

"I don't know, but I don't see why they wouldn't. Noah's going to be very impressed with my salesmanship if you do," Caleb said. "Why not just get a rehearsal space?"

"I could, but I have the money, finally, to get a studio whenever I want one. And I like to do a lot of remixing and relistening, so access to the tech is nice."

"You do a lot of the music yourself too," Caleb observed. "Ava told me you basically put together Strangelust just so you could take a band to Eurovision."

"Got to be a bit independent. You're a musician, you know how it is, most of them can't be depended on, so I just hired some reliable people. Sometimes you can only trust yourself," Buck said. Caleb frowned, then shrugged.

"No harm in asking if you can rent a studio," he said, which sounded to Buck like he was trying to be diplomatic.

"You should come round sometime if I do," Buck said, steering away from whatever that was. "Give your opinion and such. Refreshing to find someone willing to hit me where it hurts. *Jailhouse Rock*, fuck's sake."

"Bet you fifteen saorh you can't write a song about the rehearsal room sound bleed," Caleb said.

"What's that in real money?" Buck asked.

"The Shivadh saor is real money! It's got the kings on it and everything. It isn't even pegged to the Euro like Galia's currency, it's that strong."

"Shivadh Sour. Sounds like a boiled sweet your granddad gives you," Buck said. "What's the exchange rate?"

"Dunno, I never have to buy anything in pounds sterling," Caleb retorted, taunting. "Too cheap to take the bet, Haverd?"

"I'll take that bet and when my single *Shower Drum Solo* goes platinum I will accept whatever you use instead of small change around here," Buck said. He hummed a few notes, considering what the song might sound like. It felt nice to be challenged. Usually he was just making things up as he went along. Which was working fine, for now, but you couldn't live your life that way.

Well, you could, and he did, but it wasn't ideal.

"And if it doesn't go well, I can take comfort in the idea that I single-handedly destroyed your career," Caleb said.

"If my career is destroyed I will definitely have had a hand in it," Buck told him. "Nobody like a musician for self-sabotage."

"I suppose we'll see." Caleb began picking up half-empty cartons, combining them. "Want me to get Noah back down here to discuss the studio with you?"

"He's upstairs, yeah? I'll run up," Buck said. There was a door in one wall marked *Lodge Stairwell* and he popped it open without waiting for reply, bounding up the stairs.

Perhaps he shouldn't have been surprised that the door at the top of the stairs didn't open into another big concrete room; after all, he'd seen the building on his way in and knew that above-ground it was a large, pretty building. Still, it was startling to step out of the stairwell and into a nicely-furnished living room.

Across the room was a kitchen, divided from the living room by a bar; a man was standing at a sink on the other side of the bar, washing dishes.

"Ah, I'm looking for Noah – " Buck began, and the man looked up. "...and you're the king. Emeritus," he added, recalling Noah's admonition. "Sorry, I'm in your living room, aren't I?"

"You're old to be one of Noah's schoolmates," the king emeritus said, looking faintly amused.

"No, I'm pretty much a total stranger," Buck said.

"It's Haverd, isn't it? From Eurovision, Caleb's friend."

"Sort...of?"

"Michaelis," came another voice, as someone passed down the hall towards the kitchen. "Did you steal the book I was reading? I had notes in – oh, hi," they finished, coming to a stop nearby, blinking at Buck.

Jes Deimos, in person, wearing ragged cutoffs and a fraying black tank top. Buck gaped.

"Jes, this is Buck Haverd, Caleb's friend," Michaelis said. Deimos turned to the king emeritus and gave him a look like he was being deliberately obtuse.

"Yeah, he's a little more famous than that," they said, and then turned back to Buck.

"Noah is Noah *Deimos*," Buck said, before they could speak. He couldn't believe he hadn't worked it out sooner. "This is *that* Reverb. The one *The Echo* records in."

"I believe Noah's out on the dock," Michaelis put in.

"I think you're the person I actually need to talk to," Buck said to Deimos. "About renting some recording space."

"Huh. Well. Life is chaos," Deimos said. "Noah was the one who wanted to show you the studios, though, and he'll be annoyed if I steal his glory. He won't have gone far," they added, leading him out of the front door and down the steps of a wide porch.

Beyond the lodge, on this side of the building, was a little clearing of dirt and grass, with a footpath leading down to a dock on a scenic lake. Noah, who was standing in a boat moored to the dock, clambered back onto land and came to meet them.

"I see you met Boss," he said to Buck.

"More or less," Deimos said, because Buck was still working out how to handle them. "Did you abandon him with Caleb?"

"Lachlan made me," Noah replied. "I was gonna come back down and check in a minute."

"It's fine, I'm just not a patient person," Buck said. "Wanted to ask you about studio rental."

"Oh sure! You want the full pitch?" Noah asked eagerly.

"I don't know," Buck said cautiously. "I'd really just like to…have one for a month. Personal use. Don't need a technician or anything, I know my way around the equipment, mostly."

"You want a studio for a whole entire month?" Noah asked, voice cracking.

"He gets a commission," Deimos said fondly. "Although you'll get it cheap regardless – this is public property, so we only charge for equipment use, plus a convenience and cleaning fee."

Noah squared his shoulders. Buck hadn't realized Noah Deimos, of *The Echo Junior*, was quite so young. He sounded older on the podcasts.

"Why don't you come to the office and we'll discuss particulars," Noah said. Buck glanced at Deimos, who looked both amused and proud.

"That sounds fine," he agreed, remembering being sixteen and trying to get into clubs to gig, trying to get *anyone to just listen for three minutes, for fuck's sake.*

"Then come this way, Mr. Haverd," Noah said, and began the walk back to the lodge.

Buck turned to Deimos. "I'm going with your kid but I have to tell you I am a huge fan and at some point I'm going to ask for your autograph," he said, and then scurried away, catching up with Noah, before Deimos could reply.

CHAPTER SIX

WHEN BUCK RETURNED, it was because Noah was leading him through the bunker to the little business office in the far corner. Noah looked determined enough, and Buck confused enough, that Caleb decided it was probably best to leave them to it. He put the leftovers in the ancient refrigerator of the bunker's kitchenette, messaged Buck through Photogram that he could take the food if he wanted, and then, after consideration, added his phone number. That way they could text instead of using Photogram, which was awkwardly parasocial in addition to being uncomfortably hackable. Satisfied with a job well done, he went home with a light heart and spent most of the afternoon working on *We Are Nations*.

Late that evening, his phone pinged; he rolled over in bed and picked it up, expecting Ava or some musician looking for a last-minute gig fill-in, but it was a number without a name.

Thanks for lunch. I'd owe you, but I'm going to make you bring me more fish because Eddie Rambler likes you. I'll just owe you until I leave here, it read.

Caleb smiled in the darkness, labeling the contact with Buck's name before replying.

He was just being nice, he said. *Did you get your studio?*

Buck answered with a microphone emoji first, then a line of text. *Did. Meant that invitation, drop by sometime. I don't believe about Rambler. Bring fish for admission.*

A month living on fried fish might kill you, Caleb warned.

I'll risk it for that fish, Buck replied. Caleb didn't really have a funny or interesting response for that, so he was about to put the phone away when Buck added, *Come out tonight if you want, found a karaoke place with cheap drinks.*

There was no way Caleb was getting out of bed, let alone getting out of bed to go somewhere with karaoke. *Not my scene. Send embarrassing photos if you take any.*

Ten minutes later his phone dinged again, but Caleb was already asleep.

When he woke in the morning, it was to a photo of Buck, dimly lit, in one of Fons-Askaz's two karaoke bars, wearing a pair of mirrored sunglasses like Caleb's. He replied with a sunglasses emoji as he was getting up to fix himself some breakfast.

Morning, sunshine, Buck texted back.

You're up early, Caleb replied.

Not yet been to bed. Shut down the bar. Epic hangover coming, probly not till lunchtime though.

Caleb grinned. *When you're done suffering, look up Shivadh Fried Breakfast and find somewhere close to the beach that serves it. Thank me later.*

He didn't get a response for the rest of his Sunday, but he didn't really expect one; he hoped Buck was peacefully sleeping it off.

It didn't occur to him until Monday morning that he could have checked Photogram to see what Buck was up to. By then he was already in classes with the children, who were young and impressionable and absolutely should not see him checking his phone, so it stayed locked in his desk drawer until lunch like usual. Ava had grading to do, so he went out to the quay and sat alone with his apple and his phone, savoring the quiet, scrolling through Photogram.

The most recent image of Buck, from that morning, was of the studio he'd rented at Reverb. He'd hung a little sign reading Motherfucker At Work over the sound board. Back past that (and a lot of posts by other Eurovision people Caleb hadn't met but probably should care about) was an early morning selfie in a mirror captioned "Woke up like this" showing Buck in a pair of pajama shorts and a smile, teal hair standing straight out from his head. From the look of the room, he was staying in one of the more upscale small bed-and-breakfasts for tourists, and from the mess it would seem he'd made himself at home.

A few photos past that, Caleb stopped scrolling and grinned.

The post from early Sunday afternoon showed a metal table somewhere, the latticed kind favored by beach food shacks. A square wooden tray was sitting on it, lined with a sheet of paper. Resting on the paper was a heap of gleaming golden food – a slice of fried bread topped with a runny fried egg, two pan-seared kreplach dumplings on a bed of sauteed mushrooms, a perfectly round scoop of hashed potatoes, a doughnut with a visible dot of jelly indicating it was probably strawberry, and a pair of chicken wings with a little cup of hot sauce. He must have gone to one of the trendier places; traditional grubby beach shacks never included chicken wings, but all the newer, nicer ones did.

The second image in the photo set was a picture of Buck's face, eyes wide in awe. The whole thing was captioned *I'm going to die but I'm not going to die hungry.*

Caleb considered matters and then commented, *You usually only get the doughnut if you order the meal "king's touch". Rumor says because michaelisbenjason liked sufganiyot with fried breakfast when he was king.*

Noah must have been on Photogram at lunch too; as he was heading back to the classroom, Caleb's phone informed him that Photogram user *noahtheterror* had commented to confirm that the king emeritus always ate the doughnut first and usually let someone else have his potatoes. Buck had responded to Noah with a potato emoji and to Caleb with a crown. Various other comments from his fans ranged from equal levels of awe to deep disgust. An entire thread seemed to be dedicated to the great and ongoing Chicken Wing Debate, which would probably make for extremely fun reading later.

Caleb scrolled back down, stopping for a moment to re-examine the "woke up like this" picture because he was, after all, only human. With more lighting, he wasn't sure the tattooed wings on Buck's abdomen were bird's wings; perhaps they were bats. Caleb spent a little while contemplating this, then moved on, wondering if he should post something. He couldn't come up with anything especially funny after a few minutes' thought, so he blanked his phone and got up, intending to go inside and get ready for afternoon classes.

Noah met him in the doorway, beaming.

"You see Mr. Haverd's post about fried breakfast?" he asked excitedly. "He replied to my comment! I mean sort of. With a potato. Good enough for me."

"Me too," Caleb said. "What do people put on Photogram, anyway? I scrolled around for ideas but I haven't got well-defined abs or interesting hair or a horse to show off."

Noah laughed. "You should still post a selfie. Here, hang on," he said, and held out his hand for Caleb's phone. "Smile really big."

Caleb obeyed, curious, and Noah got almost uncomfortably close with the camera; when he turned it around to show Caleb the photo it was only a narrow slice of his face – one up-curved edge of his mouth, a dimple just above it, the smooth skin of his wide cheek, and a single dark blue eye under a pale gold eyebrow.

"Here you go, we'll say *You woke up like that? I was born this way*," Noah said, typing out the message. He glanced up. "I mean, if that's okay, Mr. Canto."

"Yes, I like it," Caleb decided. Noah pushed the post button and the phone made a little whooshing noise.

"Okay, I have class. You should come out sailing with us some Friday. We'll do a Photogram shoot on the *Dychev*," Noah called over his shoulder as he ran off. Caleb didn't roll his eyes, but it was a near thing. The last thing he needed was to add the complications of Photogram shoots to his life.

Just before he put his phone back in his desk, a notification popped up on the screen. Buck had commented – *Shades with the strong selfie game.*

If Buck was goofing off in the recording studio, Caleb might as well go up to the fishing lodge after school and see what he was up to. He'd been invited, after all.

Caleb's last class let out at two, but he usually lingered to walk into town with Ava; he swung by her classroom to let her know he was heading to the fishing lodge, then shouldered his ukulele case and strolled up to the high street, stopping in one of the little closet-sized convenience stores that sold overpriced sunscreen and silly keychains to tourists. It had begun to be very strange, being in one; a lot of the tourist merchandise had pictures of the royal family on it, which landed differently when you'd hung out with them. He wondered what Jerry thought of pint glasses with the Shivadlakia ducal coat of arms on them. Knowing Jerry, he might own a set. In any case, he wasn't there to buy pint glasses today.

Supplies secured, he headed for the footpath to the fishing lodge, enjoying the warm afternoon and the gentle hike past the lake. People were out on the grounds now that tourist season was beginning, and he stopped to give one very lost American couple directions back to the palace. Jes Deimos was on the porch of the lodge, speaking with a couple of people he didn't know. He sidled around without being spotted and let himself in through the underground garage, the bunker dim and cool after the warm walk outside.

Each of the studios at Reverb had a little indicator light installed above the door, two of which were on. The one nearest to the big open space had a little sign on it reading *Bastards Only.* Buck was really leaning into a theme.

Caleb leaned up against the wall opposite and loitered, playing around on his phone. It didn't take more than about five minutes for the light to flick off. He leaned over and rapped on the door.

It was flung open a few seconds later, and Buck poked his head out; he blinked when he saw Caleb, startled.

"Do you always wear suits and waistcoats?" he asked without preamble, taking in Caleb's school outfit.

"Weekdays I do," Caleb said. "Impresses the children. Am I interrupting?"

"No! Hi. Sorry. Nice suit. I'd ask you in but I don't think you qualify," Buck replied with a grin, pointing to the *Bastards Only* sign.

"I brought fish," Caleb said.

"You did?" Buck asked.

Caleb reached into his pocket and produced the tin of anchovies he'd bought from the convenience store. Buck's jaw dropped, eyes narrowing. Caleb tossed the tin at him and slipped past him into the studio as Buck fumbled to catch it.

"You said I should come by. I did stop specially just for the fish," he announced, hoisting himself onto a stool and eyeing the guitar on the stand next to it. Buck had made himself at home quickly, rearranging the equipment so that he could reach it all from a central location, propping up music stands here and there. He'd also installed a keyboard, an electric drum kit, and an entire collection of guitars, also mostly electric, with one acoustic nearby. There was also a banjo, tucked into a corner, that Caleb was not going to ask about.

"You didn't have to come *today*," Buck said, placing the tin of anchovies delicately on top of a computer monitor.

"I wasn't doing anything more interesting," Caleb said, still peering around as he set his ukulele case down. "And I was curious. I suppose I could have waited a few days for appearance's sake, but why? Besides, I'd never get the timing right."

"How do you mean?"

"Oh, I'd wait too long, and then it'd be awkward, or wait longer than I want and still not wait long enough, which would be worse. I'm always doing one of those," Caleb said, studying the waveforms on the monitor. "You're blowing out the mic."

"I'm calibrating," Buck told him with exaggerated dignity.

"You just like being loud, I think."

"That too," the other man said, grinning. "But I'll calm down once I get a feel for things. For now, I just want to make sure everything works. Good way to get settled in. I won't do any real work for a few days yet," Buck said. "Just replaying old stuff for now."

"I suppose you know how it's meant to sound, that must help you to know the tech's set up right," Caleb said.

"That's it exactly," Buck said. "And if something sounds weird, it's fun to mess around with that, too. Boring process overall, but," he shrugged eloquently. "Been switching off between setup, decoration, and thinking about what I want to work on. I have a month, anyhow."

"What does your band think of this?" Caleb asked, gesturing around. "You coming here, I mean, when you could be doing promotion back home."

"They're being paid extremely well to tolerate my behavior," Buck said. His tone was light, but there was something in the phrasing, in the way he said *tolerate*, that made Caleb wonder if Buck felt tolerance was the most he could expect. "Most of them have studio gigs in the meantime, so at least it's making their lives easier, not more complicated. And they have an interest in me finishing the album, they'll be on it."

"I suppose that makes sense. What've you got planned?"

"To work on?" Buck asked. "Couple of hooks. Two strong melodies. One anthem, that one's nearly complete. Bunch of lyrics to nothing."

"You write the lyrics first?" Caleb asked, interested. Buck

picked up a notebook and tossed it to him, skimming it like a flying disc. Caleb let it hit his chest and then caught it on the rebound. The notebook was slim and cheap, spiral-bound, smaller than a school composition book but too big to fit into a pocket. Endearingly, there was a sticker on the front cover of a skeleton playing a tuba.

When Caleb opened the notebook to the first page there was no pretension about it; each sheet was covered, front and back, with scrawled lyrics, tabs for guitar chords, and what looked like some kind of personal notation system. There were reminders, here and there, phone numbers and email addresses and notes to self, but the vast majority of the filled pages were dedicated intensively to the composition of music. Messy, repeating sometimes, but undoubtedly single-minded.

"Do you mind if I read it?" he asked, looking up from the book.

"Wouldn't have pitched it at you if you couldn't," Buck said, ducking under the table that held the sound board, apparently following a cord to somewhere. "There's most of an album in it eventually," his voice echoed up. "Needs a lot of work."

He seemed to be intent on something, so Caleb kept quiet and went back to studying – ukulele propped on his lap, left hand tapping the strings, right hand paging through the book. The most interesting part was the cryptic notation: a series of dots, hashes, and five or six different repeating squiggles. It looked like a code, perhaps to indicate rhythm or time signature. Maybe emphasis for the words. Possibly all three.

One of the first pages had a song from Buck's last album that Caleb had heard a few times, which helped to decode it; he paged slowly through the rest of the work, testing his theories about the notation in his head, studying the chords, noticing where he'd do something differently, perhaps change the words around or move a bridge or chorus. There were only two or three finished songs, and then it got less cohesive; first the notation vanished, then the tabs became messy and incomplete, and finally there were just pages of lyrics without any other indicators, essentially a book of poetry.

"I see what you mean about the lyrics to nothing," he said, flipping back slowly to the front of the book. "They come across very personal, when you see them without any music."

"Fortunately, I'm an exhibitionist," Buck said from under the table. "Hey, is there a red light blinking on the monitor?"

"Not yet," Caleb said, glancing at it.

"Right, I'll try something else then."

"Can I use one of your guitars?" Caleb asked. "Promise I'll be kind to it."

"Which one? The Fender's really fussy."

"Just the acoustic."

"Sure, have fun."

Caleb set his ukulele aside and picked up the guitar, testing the tuning. He flipped to the page in the notebook headed ANTHEM in scrawling, blocky letters, and propped it on the nearest music stand.

He picked out a few notes here and there, getting used to the feel of the song, and then tried the intro, using the notation code as guidance. It worked, or at least seemed to, and it was a nice tune; he kept going, adding in the sung lyrics, working his way steadily through. He didn't quite manage it at tempo, between reading the unfamiliar notation and switching around words when the meter didn't fit, or when a different word would convey meaning better, but he got close.

He struck the last chord and added a little flourish to finish it off, then muted the strings and grinned to himself, pleased. The song was solid, good bones, just needed some adornment. He began to turn to where he'd thought Buck still was, under the equipment table, then startled when he realized Buck was right there next to him, arms crossed over his chest, body rigid.

"I should not have played that," Caleb ventured, because it

was clear something was wrong and he didn't know what else it could be.

"Don't care you played it," Buck said, voice low. "But I know you never heard that song before. I've never played it all the way through out loud. Haven't even played it at all since I got here."

"…okay?" Caleb managed.

"How'd you know it? How'd you know how to play it?"

"You wrote it down," Caleb said.

"I don't mean the chords. How'd you know the rest? How'd you know *how to* play it?"

Caleb glanced at the notebook. "Oh, your notations. I read the little squiggles – did I get it wrong…?"

He trailed off, because Buck's rigid tension had faded into something different – curiosity, or perhaps confusion, his arms falling to his sides.

"How'd you work out my notation?" he asked.

"It wasn't difficult. Kind of a nice change. Not very nuanced but for your purposes you don't need nuance really," Caleb said.

"So you can just…read it? Could you play it a second time?"

"S'pose," Caleb said warily. Buck tore a sheet from the back of the notebook and sat down next to him, turning one of the music stands flat so he could write on it.

"Play that one again? Please," Buck said, remembering his manners. "You changed some lyrics, I want to write them down."

Caleb nodded, a little confused but game to see where this went, and ran through the song again, almost at speed this time. Buck nodded along, scribbling down the changes.

"That's actually gorgeous," he said, when Caleb had finished the second run-through. "Your playing, I mean. Song's getting there but it still needs work. Still, you're giving me something to chew on."

"Glad to help," Caleb said. "Sorry about playing without asking."

"No, I made it weird, that's on me," Buck said. "I had an ex who used to steal my hooks – I'd walk into the room and he'd just be playing some half-finished song I was working on, and somehow they ended up becoming *his* songs. He's been on my mind lately. Other reasons," he added, waving a hand as if he could brush it off.

Caleb studied him. "If that's the case, it was brave of you to show me your notebook."

"Not really. He only ever stole them when he heard me play them. Couldn't read my notations. Most people can't."

"They're not very difficult to learn."

"Well," Buck said, tone slightly brittle, "then let's say he never bothered to try."

"Sounds like a dick," Caleb said.

"He was, but he was hot and I was stupid, so I let him do it for like a year," Buck sighed, studying the notes he'd made while Caleb was playing. "I just wasn't expecting to hear someone playing my stuff. Still kinda sets me off."

"I can ask, next time."

"Don't worry about it, it's my problem, not yours. Anyway, nice to have someone who can read the notation. Usually I have to just play it and get someone to listen and write down the proper sheet music for people."

"Do you not read music?"

Buck shrugged, ignoring the question. "What do you think of the song? I know what you'd change, I guess."

"I like it. You don't use major keys like this much. Is it meant to be in earnest, or making fun of something?"

"If you can't tell, I'm probably in trouble," Buck said.

"A lot of knowing something like that is in the inflection," Caleb said. "You do sarcastic songs sometimes, I know. But you don't seem to have notations for sarcasm. Imagine if we systematically notated in prose for that," he added. "Some people on the internet do it, apparently, but it hasn't really caught on yet. It'd make my life easier, for sure."

"It's mostly earnest," Buck said, studying his notes. "It's meant to be a bit outside my usual. People like it when they think you're not nice to know and then you do something wholesome. I think people think it means they could fix you."

"You don't seem like you need fixing to me," Caleb said, peering at him.

"Then I'm not trying hard enough," Buck replied, amused.

"Why would you try to seem broken?"

"Oh, the drama of it." Buck stretched. He cracked his neck and turned back to Caleb. "Most of what I do onstage is an act. Well, most of what everyone does all the time is an act, but especially onstage. And you want some real honesty about that?"

"Sure," Caleb said, not sure at all.

"If people think you're broken in some obvious way, they don't see where you're actually broken," Buck said. "And then they can't get their fingers into it."

Caleb considered this; he could tell Buck expected him to be horrified, or at least weirded out by it, but...well, it wasn't untrue.

"Never been very good at that kind of misdirect," Caleb told him. "But I see your point. This way you control what people think is wrong with you *and* how they react to it."

He couldn't tell quite what Buck's reaction was, but it didn't matter – it didn't last long. Then Buck picked up the notebook, tucking the new notes into it.

"Something like that," he said, turning to set it on the table. "Anyway. By the time I leave for Eurovision, I want to have at least half the album written. More if I can swing it."

"That's awfully fast," Caleb pointed out.

"Good. I like the pressure," Buck said with a sharp grin. "Hey, want to help me test the equipment out?"

"If you want. What can I do?"

"You stay there and sing and do a little guitar, and I'll sit back here and make sure everything's working how I want it to."

"Easy enough," Caleb said. "Any particular song? Or key?

Your voice is deeper than mine."

"Whatever you want," Buck said. "You working on anything right now?"

Caleb thought about trotting out *We Are Nations*, but it wasn't quite done yet.

"Here, I'll give you some culture to listen to while you work," he said, and started playing an old Shivadh folk song he'd learned when he first started teaching at the Academy. He could tell Buck must not hate it, because after a few bars he nodded along with it as he tested equipment and set levels. Caleb worked his way steadily through a couple of Ava's songs and most of the folk music the Academy taught, while Buck fiddled with technology.

"Got a nice beat to it," Buck muttered, mostly distracted by the work, as Caleb brought the last song to an end.

"It's a sailing song. Most of the coastal songs are. Inland a little, you get more melodic stuff. You ever see that video of the Swedish woman singing to call in the cows?"

"The *what*," Buck asked, looking up from the sound board.

"It's called kulning. It's Swedish mostly, I think, but there's Shivadh kulning videos too…" Caleb dug out his phone, setting the guitar aside, and opened the national app, paging through the resources until he found the playlist he was looking for. He opened the video titled *Eerie Shivadh Kulning* and turned the volume up. Curious, Buck got up and came to stand next to Caleb's stool, leaning over his shoulder, head cocked.

"Holy shit, look at the cows," he said, baffled. In the video, a woman was standing on one side of the fence, singing in Shivadh, her voice a high soprano. Cows were emerging from the fog in the distance, most of them with blue leather bell collars on, ringing merrily as they came towards the woman. "How do they know to come?"

"I assume she did it while feeding them at first, but maybe they just like the music," Caleb said.

"That'd make a funny Eurovision number. Open with

someone – kerning?"

"Kulning."

"That, and then have the band come onstage dressed as cows," Buck said, grinning. "Isn't like we haven't seen weirder."

"Not your usual aesthetic," Caleb pointed out.

"No, wouldn't do for me. And I think that's all we can do today," Buck said, stepping back and beginning to shut down the tech. "Thanks for helping."

"My pleasure. So this is yours for the next month – do you mind if I come by again?"

"No, that'd be fine, long as you don't mind me swearing up and down about the music. Part of the creative process, swearing."

"I don't mind."

"What are you up to now?" Buck asked, checking his watch. "Getting to be past mealtime. I was going to grab some food and go bar hopping, maybe find a good club. Want to come?"

"Oh, I...can't," Caleb said, caught off-guard and aware he didn't sound particularly convincing.

"Sure you can," Buck said breezily. "We can swing by your place if you need to change clothes or something..."

"No, I...it's...my clothes are fine," Caleb said uncertainly.

"I think so," Buck agreed.

"I don't, uh, like nightclubs, which wouldn't matter, I think probably you'd make it fun but. I need. Warning," Caleb said.

"Warning about a nightclub?" Buck asked.

"Warning about dinner and a night out, including a nightclub, yes. Preferably two weeks written notice," Caleb said. Buck looked incredulous. "That was a joke, Buck. Mostly," he added.

"Oh..." Buck looked like something was smacking him in the head. "Ah, fuck, Shades, I didn't think. Clubs are probably a *nightmare* for you."

"They're not great," Caleb said. "But that's fine, I know how to deal, it's just. Anywhere, really. I was planning to go home and...it's – "

"Difficult not to stick to the plan," Buck said. "It itches your brain."

"Yes," Caleb answered, relieved. He'd never heard it put quite that way, but that was a good phrase for it. The incorrectness of it, of having one plan and suddenly being thrust into another, clung to the mind. "You understand."

"Yeah, crazy enough, I do," Buck said thoughtfully. "All right. Well. I'm still gonna go, but don't worry about it. I'll send daft photos if you want and I definitely won't if you don't want. And if I want you to come with me next time I'll make sure to have an invitation engraved."

It sounded like a gentle joke, but it might be a passive-aggressive jab. Caleb was considering asking which (asking that kind of question generally put an end to people being passive-aggressive at him, since nobody liked having it pointed out, and also it usually got him a straight answer) when Buck added, "That was also a joke, mostly."

Caleb felt his shoulders drop in relief. "I would like daft photographs," he said. "And permission to roast you about them."

"Doubly-done. Off you run, Shades," Buck said with a grin, and made a shooing motion. Caleb got down from the stool and gathered up his things.

"I like *Anthem*," he offered, at the door. "Work on that one first. You could build an album around it."

"Ta. And thanks for the lyric doctoring."

Caleb let himself out into the silent, evening-dark bunker, and took the footpath back into Fons-Askaz cheerfully.

CHAPTER SEVEN

IN THE NEXT two weeks, it became a new routine – some days he met up with Derek or Bill and Leah to hang out after work, and sometimes he still walked home with Ava, but if they were busy or even if he didn't want too much company, instead of going straight home Caleb made the uncomfortable but ultimately gratifying decision to walk up to the fishing lodge and spend his evening at Reverb. Buck, turning and polishing and disassembling and reassembling *Anthem* and other songs, seemed happy to see him, but equally happy to ignore him. He could play backup, or offer his thoughts on the songs, or just sit to one side, tuning out Buck's experimentation in favor of his own work.

He kept a list in his phone of things he was supposed to remember to do in order to keep his life running smoothly – the dishes, his grading, at least one meal out a week to make sure he didn't turn into a hermit. To the list he added one post a day to Photogram, although he still never felt particularly inspired. He'd ask the kids what they thought he should post, or see what Buck was posting and try to riff on that, like Noah had. Ava always had good ideas for posts as well.

In any case, his follower count climbed steadily, so he must have been doing something right. Sometimes the comments were stupid, or cruel, or irrelevant, but they were only words, and not even words flung at him in real time – like notes on a chalkboard left by someone ten years before. Most of them got voted into oblivion by his other followers before he even saw them, and the rest were the reason the delete button had been invented.

"I just zap them like bugs," Caleb said to Buck, late on a Saturday morning. Buck had seen him scrolling Photogram and asked how he liked it; they'd gotten into the kind of discussion he thought few people would, about how to manage the volume of comments and tags and requests they got, and how to deal with the inevitable hate messaging.

"That's obscenely healthy," Buck replied. "Doesn't it mean you have to read them all, though?"

"Only whatever's left – Noah sometimes gets on there and deletes a bunch, I can tell when he's been through," Caleb said. "Don't you read your comments?"

"Sure, but not like...regularly or anything. I just see things and sometimes I answer. Mostly I talk to people I follow. Sometimes a fan says something funny that gets upvoted enough it hits my eyeballs," Buck said.

"You do have a lot more followers than me," Caleb replied.

"Yeah, but I bet you get more shit than I do."

"Why would you say that?"

"Well, I'm obnoxious," Buck began, "but – "

"I don't think you're obnoxious," Caleb objected. "There's a temper on you, but you're not malicious."

"Thanks, I think. What I was going to say is that I'm also...shielded a bit. White cisguy," Buck said with a self-deprecating shrug. "I get flak for being bi, but comparatively, probably not much."

"Maybe. I suppose it doesn't really matter who gets more." Caleb deleted one final comment and set his phone aside, leaning back and stretching. "End result's still the same. Fuck 'em."

"That's your full philosophy? Fuck 'em?"

"I can try to make someone like me all day long but some people aren't going to like me no matter what and most of them seem to live on the internet. Like...all I did was write a song about how generations pass things on to other generations, but because I happened to be writing about kings and princes, and our king is elected so he's a true head of state, people keep saying my song is *political* and shouldn't be allowed because politics aren't allowed at Eurovision. You and I both know I'm not trying to make some kind of statement, and it should be pretty obvious to everyone else, too. Are they pedants or are they transphobes or are they just assholes or what? The Broadcasting Union's already said it's fine, and I haven't got time to figure that out, so…yeah, fuck 'em. Life's hard enough without all that nonsense."

Buck studied him, brushing teal hair out of his eyes. "And you really believe that?"

"I don't say things I don't believe."

"Don't I know it," Buck replied. "Have you ever given a single shit what other people think of you?"

"Yes – all the time," Caleb said, puzzled. "It's why I wore the sunglasses in the first place. Social anxiety, rejection sensitivity…they kind of come with the brain. But the internet never feels real like that. And it only gets worse if you try to fake like you're okay with it. So I'm just me and I deal with the fact that I embarrass myself a lot by not wasting energy pretending I won't."

"Wait, go back to the sunglasses," Buck said, frowning.

"What about them?"

"You wear them because you're anxious?"

"Yeah – I can't perform onstage. Well, couldn't," Caleb said. "I still hate playing small stages. But the sunglasses are dark enough that on a real main stage, with the right lighting, I can't see the audience. Which means I stop caring what they think. I thought you knew that."

"Why would I know that?"

"In Turin, the first thing you did was cover my eyes," Caleb said. "You pulled my face into your coat."

Buck seemed to be digesting this, so Caleb picked up the acoustic guitar he'd started to think of as his, even just on loan, and busied himself tuning it.

"But you seem fine, one-on-one," Buck said at last. "And there's the whole fuck-the-dickheads thing."

"Mostly I can handle a person on their own, it's big groups that are hard. That random guy on the internet isn't here, in person – I can't see him and he can't physically hurt me, so I can handle him, too. You're here in person, but like, being human. You're trustworthy, and I know you, so I can handle you," Caleb said. Buck was silent for an almost awkwardly long time, so he added, "Although, you should see me with someone like the king. I do not do as well."

"He's a king," Buck said. "I probably wouldn't either."

"He *is* nice," Caleb allowed. "It's just he's got a lot of power. And he's super charismatic."

Buck grinned. "And I'm not?"

"Doesn't matter whether you are or not. I've got you figured out," Caleb answered absently.

Another silence, and he looked up from the guitar, suddenly worried. Buck was still, green eyes on him, mouth pulled into a frown.

"I didn't mean it as an insult," Caleb added carefully. "Are you upset by what I said?"

"I don't know," Buck admitted. "You can be a little uncanny. Nobody just says things like that."

"Well, I do."

"I know. And weirdly, I believe you. You probably do have my number," Buck said.

"The truth can be upsetting, so I'm told, but I prefer it. You always know where you stand that way."

"Sometimes people don't actually want to know where they stand," Buck pointed out. "Mostly when they're standing somewhere uncomfortable."

"Does that include you?"

Buck threw his head back and laughed. Caleb startled.

"Good fucking point, Shades! It does not, or anyway, I don't want it to. Cut you a deal. I won't be upset when you tell the truth, but you'll have to remind me every so often that I asked for it. Keep me humble. Your job now."

"Keeping you humble could probably be a full-time job with paid salary," Caleb said.

"Many have tried," Buck agreed. "So that iconic sunglasses look, that's just nerves?"

"Lachlan found them backstage and put them on me so I'd go onstage at all. I actually have no idea whose they are. I owe whoever it is a new pair," Caleb said thoughtfully.

"You set a global fashion trend by weaponizing your social anxiety," Buck pointed out.

"Probably not global. I doubt it's gone much past Fons-Askaz."

"I dunno, it's at least made it over the highlands," Buck said.

"Just the one highland," Caleb replied.

"What?"

"Never mind. Old joke. Over the highlands? Like into Italy?"

"I heard someone saying Galia copies everything the Shivadh do," Buck said. "Mirrored shades are making it big over there."

"Huh. I could wish Galia was like that with anything more important than accessories. Askazer-Shivadlakia could give Galia some short sharp lessons," Caleb told him. "You couldn't pay me to go back. Anyway, we aren't spending much on Eurovision – not as much as Kairao would have – so if I need to replace someone's sunglasses, it won't be a big deal."

"You're going to stick with the arse-on-stage thing?" Buck asked.

"It's apparently pretty compelling. Besides, I like sitting on the floor. Lots of my kids prefer it. Makes life easy for the stagehands, and it's very cheap."

"How much did that ukulele for the Turin pre-party run you? Can't have been much spent there, either."

"The glitter glue we used on it was almost as much as the

ukulele," Caleb admitted, and Buck laughed. "Jerry wants me to have a guitar for the semi, though. More romantic, he says."

"It's not like you have to play it for real, the music's pre-recorded. You could walk out there with a tuba if you wanted."

Caleb's laughter startled him so much he almost fell out of his chair.

"Can you imagine?" he asked, righting himself. "Lachlan and Ava walk out all dramatic in their king and prince uniforms, I step into the spotlight and it's just me, wearing a giant tuba – "

"Sousaphone," Buck suggested, and Caleb howled. "Bigger than you are. They could just wheel it out and you could climb out of it with a ukulele in hand. Actually, there's something to that," he said, more speculatively, as Caleb continued to laugh. "Maybe next tour I do, I could have this big fuckoff drum onstage or something, and for the opening number I'm flung out of it."

"You like the big staging, huh," Caleb said.

"Sure. What's the fun of doing a show if you don't make it a *show?*" Buck said.

"I don't know, I'm not really there to have fun," Caleb said. Buck frowned. "I mean. I enjoy it, it's not that, but...it's hard to connect with people. When I write music it's because there's something I want to communicate. Not very good at doing it any other way."

"You seem to me like you do fine."

"Well, you're you," Caleb said. Buck's frown deepened. "Some people are better at...translating than others, I guess."

"How do you mean?"

"Look, I notice, okay – you ask permission before you touch me. You knew what to do when I was flipping out in Turin. It's not stuff neurotypical people generally think of unless they know someone who needs it. Maybe you're just really...aware, I don't know, but – "

"Friend of mine," Buck said, nodding. "Music class at school. She was being bullied by some of the kids because she was, you know," he made air quotes, rolling his eyes, "weird. I was being bullied by the teachers because school's shit, and I was mad about that and looking for somewhere to put it. It's one thing when a teacher goes after you, you can't do anything about that, but I could do something about the other kids. Wasn't even about her at first, but turned out she's really cool."

"Huh," Caleb said.

"Not proud of just doing it because I was a pissed off twelve-year-old," Buck admitted.

"But you stepped in even when you didn't know her," Caleb pointed out. "It's easy to defend family. Harder to stand up for a stranger."

"Shades, when you're me, you're standing up to everyone all the time anyway," Buck said. "If I could give the whole fucking world a black eye, I would."

"Even now?" Caleb asked, surprised.

"Maybe not anymore. Or anyway I'd only give the bullies a black eye now. I'm so mad I missed the peak of punk, I'd have been such a good punk!" Buck said with a self-deprecating laugh, flopping back in his chair to contemplate the ceiling.

"Haven't lost your chance. Maybe punk isn't dead, it was just waiting for you to show up," Caleb said. Buck snorted. "Being soft when the world is hard is really punk, anyway."

"I'm not soft."

"All that swagger's covering something," Caleb said, and Buck scowled at him. "Soft punk. New genre. Easy listening punk."

"Easy listening – !" Buck gave him an outraged look, but he picked up his guitar and broke into a jazzy riff. He messed around with it for a few seconds, trying out some flamenco flair before pulling back into something more folky. Caleb listened, head cocked.

"Is that *Hitsville UK?*" he asked, and Buck tilted his head back and broke into full-throated song to the muzak he was playing.

Caleb plucked up the ukulele and began improvising around it, adding a tropical riff and following Buck's baritone in his high tenor.

The band went in and knocked 'em dead
In two minutes fifty-nine
I know the boy was all alone
Till the Hitsville hit UK…

"The Clash is easy to adapt," Buck said, when the last lick of sound had faded off. "Great songwriters, but they could have gone harder."

"You think everyone could go harder, Buck," Caleb said.

"I think you go – oh, shit," Buck said, interrupting himself, rising to his feet and setting the guitar aside. "Did you know we were recording?"

"Are we?" Caleb asked. The monitor in the room was lit up, and when he got up to look over Buck's shoulder he could see waveforms; Buck exhaled, stopping the program.

"For like twenty minutes, yeah. I'm surprised the computer didn't explode," he said. "We weren't broadcasting to the exterior monitors, though. Nobody outside heard us pissing about."

"We weren't saying anything awful. Wait, don't delete it," Caleb added, as Buck went to erase the file. "That was a cool cover, you should save it."

"I was just fucking around, and I kept dropping that one chord – "

"But it was still cool. Here, listen," Caleb said, and clicked back to just before the song started.

Maybe punk isn't dead, it was just waiting for you to show up. Being soft when the world is hard is really punk, anyway, they heard. Caleb smiled, hearing the warmth in his words.

I'm not soft, Buck protested in the recording. Buck shot Caleb a self-deprecating look.

All that swagger's covering something. Soft punk. New genre. Easy listening punk, Caleb replied, and there was Buck's squawk of outrage.

Easy listening — ! he cried, and then there was the clang of him picking up his guitar. Buck narrowed his eyes, listening to himself riff. They could barely hear Caleb demand *Is that Hitsville UK?* and then Buck was off; after a few bars Caleb was there with him.

"It's not bad," Buck said, over the music.

"Shh, I want to hear if I was flat there," Caleb said.

"Stop shushing me, you're always shushing me."

"You're always talking!"

They listened through until the song ended, Buck flagging a few places where he had indeed dropped a chord.

The Clash is easy to adapt. Great songwriters, but they could have gone harder.

You think everyone could go harder, Buck.

Buck stopped the playback and crossed his arms, staring at the waveforms.

"Yeah, it's all right," he said at last. "I mean yes, it's a decent cover. But especially with that setup – sampling our conversation, and ending with that crack about going harder. That's a really fun B-side."

"You want to throw it on Photogram?" Caleb asked. Buck blinked at him.

"You can't just throw a song on Photogram," he said.

"Why not? People do stuff like that all the time. They film themselves doing a monologue from Shakespeare or they make funny little skits and they put it out there so other people can enjoy them. Just because we do this for a living doesn't mean we can't make stuff that's not perfect and just…let other people enjoy it," Caleb said.

"But the – "

"Ah, fuck the dropped chords, nobody cares but other musicians," Caleb told him. "That's a good song, you're right, and it was fun. Trim it up, export it, send it to my phone. I'll post it if you don't want to."

"I'll get shit for saying The Clash could go harder."

"Probably what'll happen is everyone else will just fight about whether it's true," Caleb pointed out. He nudged Buck out of the way gently and dove into the sound file, snipping it out into a new editing window, starting with himself saying that punk wasn't dead. He trimmed out a few seconds of Buck experimenting before the song actually started, then let the song play through. The sound quality wasn't perfect, but that just meant it took even less time than usual to export it and drop it to his phone. Buck had his thumb pressed to his lips in thought.

"We have to put a photo on it," he said finally. "Photogram won't take a straight audio file with no visual element."

"I have about five selfies and a picture of dinner from my last birthday on my phone, what've you got on yours?" Caleb said.

"Dick pics," Buck said with a grin. Caleb rolled his eyes. "Okay, not as many as you think."

"Well, we're in a bunker next to a lake, there's no lack of dramatic artistic stuff we could do," Caleb said. "Come on."

Out in the main room, Noah was sitting at the conference table, working on a tablet. Michaelis was with him; Caleb wasn't sure he was ever going to get used to seeing the man who'd been king for most of his life, slouched in a chair, feet up on the table, glasses perched on his nose and a book in his lap.

"Noah, we need your help," Caleb announced. Noah looked up. "We have a song to post but it needs an image. We want to take a pretentious dramatic album cover type photo."

"Wine hole," Noah said.

"Beg pardon?" Buck asked. Caleb frowned, confused.

"Come on," Noah said, rising. "I'll show you the wine hole, I can take the photo for you."

"If you die, don't come running to me," the king emeritus said mildly, without looking up from his book.

"Nobody's going to die, it's been reinforced," Noah assured them, as Caleb and Buck followed him curiously down a hallway. "The bunker used to be like an actual bunker, with food supplies and stuff. There's a wine cellar, we call it the wine hole because the first time we found it I kinda fell in," he added.

"Oh wow, that was you?" Caleb asked. "I heard rumors about some wine cellar nearly killing someone."

"Yep. Last summer, before I started at the Academy. It's not my fault, stuff just falls apart around me," Noah complained.

"Very heartening, given we're following you into a hole in the ground," Buck pointed out.

"I know, right? It's super atmospheric."

There was a shored-up gap in the hallway wall about halfway down, and inside was a small room full of scaffolding, with a dimly lit hole in the floor. A weird little platform that looked like it might be some kind of cargo elevator went down on one side of the hole, and next to it was a flight of steep but sturdy-looking steps. Caleb and Buck followed Noah down the stairs, then blinked when Noah flipped a breaker and the room was illuminated.

"Whoa," Buck said, when he reached the bottom.

The wine cellar was actually a natural cavern, a huge oval with an arching ceiling; empty wine racks had been grouped into a mass to one side, and bright bare bulbs hung from support scaffolding, thick electrical cords winding up and down temporary metal columns. Noah led them through it, picking up a lantern on the way, and slipped through a large gap in an elderly brick wall at the back of the cavern.

"They're excavating bits of the cave, but only during summer; rest of the year it just kind of sits here, and we give tours of it sometimes. Here ya go," he said, holding up the lantern.

Someone had carved something into the rock, at what would be eye level for a man slightly taller than Caleb. Two lines of text, and a rough oblong shape below them. Buck leaned in close.

"What's it say?" he asked. "It's not in English."

"It's Latin," Noah said. "Michaelis says it says *We have conquered both above and below.*"

"Latin? Like Roman? Or newer?" Buck asked.

"Someone could've put it there any time before the forties, I guess," Noah said. "That's when the wall went in, and the wall was still whole when the cellar was sealed. But the archaeologists are pretty sure it's from at least 1800 years ago. Maybe older. That's when the Romans were here. And there's the dick."

"The what," Caleb said. Noah pointed to the oblong shape, which on closer inspection had a specific bend to it, and two ovals beneath it. Buck sniggered. "Someone had a high opinion of himself," Caleb remarked.

"Michaelis says I have to ace my Italian exam this year before he explains the Latin to me, but I'm pretty sure the literal translation says something a lot more obscene than 'conquered'," Noah said.

"There," Caleb said, pointing to one of the words. "Futuimus. Fottere in Italian means – ah, it's a rude word."

"We've fucked 'em both above and below," Buck inferred.

"Taking your picture with a Latin engraving automatically looks cool," Noah said with a grin. "And if anyone does read it…"

"I'm pretty sure we can't put the dick on Photogram," Caleb ventured.

"No, but you can block it out. Here," Buck said, gesturing him forward. He held up his hands, and Caleb nodded; Buck guided him into place with a light grip on his shoulders, turning him so that he was in profile, his head blocking the carving. "Stay put," Buck said, and moved around behind him, passing his phone to Noah.

"Oh, I see," Noah said, snapping photos. He moved the lantern around a few times, taking more.

"Come on, get the good shot," Buck said.

"Can't hurry art," Noah replied.

"I do that all the time," Buck replied.

"Just hold still for the love of – Caleb, hang on, don't move your body but turn your head," Noah said, then paused. "Uh, I mean, Mr. Canto."

Caleb twisted a little, looking at Noah. "Caleb's okay when we're not in school. As long as you think you can remember at school."

"Awesome," Noah replied. "Okay. Uh. Right into the lens – there. Pretentious, perfect."

Caleb hadn't realized how cool and dry the wine cellar was until they climbed the stairs back up into the warmer, humid air of the bunker, which had an almost plantlike smell to it compared to the cavern. At the conference table, Noah sat down and Buck and Caleb both leaned over him, studying the photos.

In each image, the two of them stood back-to-back, at one end of the inscription; Buck's head was next to *Futuimus*, and Caleb's neatly blocked out the obscene image below the rest of the inscription. Most of the shots looked dramatic and interesting, but Caleb couldn't deny the best one was the last, where Buck was still looking off to one side, but Caleb's face was turned to the camera, his eyes big and dark in the black-and-white filter as he looked into the lens.

"That's the one," Buck said. Caleb nodded. A hand came into view; Michaelis, still not looking at them, reaching out for the phone. Noah rolled his eyes and put it in his palm. The old king held the phone and studied the image, lips twitching upwards.

"Caleb told me what Futuimus means," Noah said, tone reproachful.

"It's always good to have two sources for your research," Michaelis told him. "I know Photogram has an obscenity filter, but I don't think it speaks Latin. Approved," he concluded, and passed the phone back to Buck, nodding at them.

"You can't adopt them, they're too old," Noah said, as Buck sent the image to Caleb, who opened Photogram and stitched it onto the audio file before posting it.

"I can adopt anyone I please, I'm *incredibly* old," Michaelis replied calmly. "My biological son is older than all three of you."

"Don't ask me, I could use a dad who isn't a knob," Buck said. "Must be a ton of perks to getting adopted by a literal king."

"Not as many as you'd think," Michaelis said. "But lunch is on offer, if anyone's hungry. Noah, run and get Jes if you would, see if they'd like to come with us."

It was strange, alien in the nicest possible way, to be taken to lunch by the former king. It was a short walk from the lodge down a footpath into Fons-Askaz, with Caleb playing the *Hitsville UK* cover over a portable bluetooth speaker Buck had, so that Noah could listen and offer commentary.

They'd barely finished playing it when the footpath let out onto the high road above the harbor and Caleb muted the sound out of politeness. Michaelis herded them into a nearby bakery-cafe that was clearly accustomed to the royal family dropping in, and they sat on a terrace at the back, overlooking the water. They ate fresh fruit and focaccia served with little bowls of tapenade, soft cheese, cold pesto, and warm bagna cauda. Buck was uncharacteristically quiet while Noah spoke with Caleb in Italian for practice, and Michaelis and Jes expounded on the history of Rome and Askazer-Shivadlakia.

"He's the history buff," Jes said at one point, indicating Michaelis, "but I can't say I'd mind doing more research into the Roman occupation. It lasted a while, and it's not particularly unique – the Romans invaded everyone they could anytime they could. But there isn't much left in the way of settlement here, which is unusual."

"Not like finding a Roman bath under a pub or something," Buck said, around a mouthful of bread.

"Exactly. Pretty much all we've found in the last what, fifty years? Is what's in the wine cellar." Jes glanced at Michaelis, who nodded.

"Before that, they only started finding artifacts to begin with because of the war. We weren't bombed heavily, but we did get a few — one of them left a crater in a field at the northern edge of the Daskaz estate, and they found some pottery shards and a coin or two in the bottom," Michaelis said.

"I keep waiting for all of Gregory's infrastructure projects in town to turn something up, but no joy so far," Jes concluded. They were leaning back, face turned up to the mild afternoon sun; the old king had his arm over their chair, smiling sidelong at them, and they both looked…comfortable. At ease in themselves. Caleb glanced at Buck and wondered if he ever wanted something like that. It wouldn't be so hard to put an arm over his shoulders, not the way Buck was slouched.

Instead, though, he just leaned sideways a little and bumped his shoulder against Buck's, pressing their biceps together as he took his phone out.

"Song's getting some plays," he said, studying the post. He'd tossed it up with a quick *music appreciation all morning with buckhaverd so we can knock 'em dead in two minutes fifty-nine.* People were, in fact, arguing in the notes about whether The Clash could have gone harder.

There was a little green flag next to one of the threads, where someone had simply written "Being soft when the world is hard is #reallypunk : a WHOLE ASS MOOD." Caleb expanded the thread, curious; the green flag was next to every use of #reallypunk.

"Noah, what's it mean when there's a little green doodad next to a hashtag?" he asked.

"You are actually older than Michaelis," Noah said.

"Mind yourself, young man," Michaelis said, amused.

"It means it's trending," Noah continued. "Why?"

Buck leaned over and tapped the green flag. Thousands of

comments unspooled on Caleb's screen.

"Oh," Caleb said faintly.

```
Being soft when the world is hard is #reallypunk.
It's #reallypunk to punch a Nazi.
Fellas is it #reallypunk to cut a cover of a Clash song
with your Eurovision bestie?
Feeling #reallypunk this morning, might delete later.
```

"Well, look at that, you're trending," Jes said, giving Caleb a smile.

"Calebcanto knows being autistic is inherently hashtag reallypunk," Buck read aloud from his own phone.

"I think that one might be making fun," Caleb said uncertainly. Buck shook his head.

"That's from my mate Maggie's account," he said. "She's my friend from school."

Caleb blinked at him. "Oh. So she really means it."

"Maggie's forgotten more about music history than I'll ever learn, so yeah," Buck said. "This time tomorrow she'll probably have a response video up explaining in detail the history of punk philosophy. Possibly with costume changes."

"I like her already," Jes said.

"When did punk...happen?" Michaelis asked, looking contemplative. "I think I was busy at the time."

"Seventy-five or so, until about eighty-five, that was the best part," Buck said.

"Ah. I was at boarding school. And then king," Michaelis said, nodding.

"What, did you go from graduation to coronation?" Buck asked.

"More or less. I left school around 1978, was elected in 1981..." Michaelis shrugged. "If it's coming back now, I suppose I'll catch it this time round."

"Fuck me, you were king when you were twenty? I'm twenty-six and not even mayor. I've been wasting my time," Buck said.

Michaelis smiled at him. "I very much doubt that. Although we have, I think, lingered long enough over lunch."

"He wants to go look up punk music in Askazer-Shivadlakia," Jes said to Caleb. "You can see he's got his research face on."

"Come on, Caleb, got an album to finish," Buck said. "Can't keep struggling along on track three without my muse."

"Still not getting paid to keep you humble," Caleb reminded him, but secretly felt a little pleased at the idea of being anyone's muse.

CHAPTER EIGHT

NOAH'S ALMOST-FORGOTTEN suggestion, that Caleb come out sailing with them on the Academy's tall ship some Friday, turned into a gently insistent demand that week. Some of Noah's classmates thought it would be fun to have music like they might have had in the age of sail, and also lobbied for it. Caleb didn't see the point of doing something just "for the Photogram," but he didn't really see the harm either, so he agreed, and asked if Noah thought Ava might like to come too.

"You guys could play sea shanties while we work," Noah said excitedly. "I'll do a video for your Photogram. Jamie knows how to dance an actual hornpipe, he's wanted me to film him on the ship doing one. Could you play one for him to dance to?"

"I'll brush up," Caleb promised. "Any other requests?"

"I'll ask the crew. It's supposed to be historical learning so it should be period if you play stuff for them."

"That shouldn't be difficult, there are lots of sea ballads and they're mostly easy to learn."

"Bet nobody would stop you if you played *Young Prince*," Noah said slyly.

"Eurovision at sea. What an idea," Caleb said with a laugh. "Hey, would anyone find it strange if I asked Buck if he wanted to come along too?"

"Maybe, but you should totally do it anyway, I like him," Noah said. "Besides, there's a lot of skepticism around my claims that I've met him."

"I can't make any promises, he might be the seasick type,"

Caleb said. "But I'll see, he might enjoy it."

Buck seemed perplexed by the invitation, but said yes anyway. Ava loved the idea, especially since she worked with a lot of the kids who served on the ship, and she made sure none of the school administration objected.

And that was how they found themselves early on a Friday morning, a three-piece band consisting of Buck with his guitar, Caleb with a recorder and a mandolin replacing his usual ukulele, and Ava with a concertina, trooping up the gangplank after a bunch of awkward teenagers dressed like 19th-century sailors.

"Can you actually play that thing?" Buck asked Ava, nodding at the concertina. It was a trim and pretty octagon only a little bigger than her hands, clearly of the accordion family.

"More or less. You know how it is, you can pick anything up if you've got a decent ear and you mess around long enough," she said. "Anyway it's cute, isn't it?"

"You know, I wouldn't have said cute as a first thought, but you're not wrong," Buck agreed.

Caleb had known, in theory, that the point of spending one day a week on the *Dychev* was to teach the children maturity, independence of mind, and teamwork. There were instructors aboard, of course, in case anything went genuinely wrong, but it was the job of the oldest students to serve as officers and command and train the younger ones, and the job of the younger ones to learn everything there was to know about the operation of a tall ship that ran purely on the winds and currents.

In practice, he realized, this meant their lives were in the hands of a bunch of teenagers. The ship was fitted with lifeboats and Noah had given them a little demonstration of the life jackets it carried, but it seemed both a lot bigger and a lot less stable once you were on it.

Admittedly the children seemed to have a pretty good idea of what they were doing, to judge by how they ran around, rigging ropes and calling out to one another. Hurrying out of someone's way for the third or fourth time, Caleb retreated to a sheltered area up against a wall where nobody seemed to need to be. Ava and Buck hastily followed, settling with him on some crates covered in burlap, Buck pulling his feet up to sit cross-legged, cradling the guitar in his lap.

In another five minutes, with timbers creaking and water churning, the brigantine *Dychev* cast off for Friday's sail.

As the ship left the quay and slowly made its way towards the harbor mouth, Buck grinned ferally at Caleb, flipped his pick in the air like a coin, caught it, and strummed the guitar thoughtfully. Once he launched into the melody, it didn't take long for Caleb to catch on.

"Is that *The Wreck of the Edmund Fitzgerald?*" he demanded.

"It's this or *My Heart Will Go On*," Buck announced. "It's probably considered good luck!"

"Not in any way!" Noah called as he ran past.

"Well, that's me told," Buck said, muting his strings.

"It's not a bad idea, though," Ava said. "What's a good setting-to-sea song?"

Caleb strummed the mandolin thoughtfully, then modulated into the opening bars of *Long Hot Summer Day*. Buck and Ava laughed.

"Deep cut, Canto!" Buck hooted, while Ava sang along.

> *For every day of workin' on the Illinois river*
> *Get a half a day off with pay!*
> *Tow boat pickin' up barges*
> *On this long hot summer day...*

They played the ship out of the harbor with John Hartford, and into the open sea with Hall & Oates ("Yacht rock, get it?" Buck said). The day was beautiful, the air warm and the sunlight not too intense. Out on the sea, with the French Riviera to starboard, Noah began setting up the tripod for filming, while his friend Jamie practiced the hornpipe to Caleb and Ava's playing.

"What does 'dychev' mean, anyway?" Buck asked. "I assume it's Shivadh."

"Are you ready to be angry?" Ava asked.

"Do you think I am ever *not* ready to be angry?" Buck replied.

"Dy means 'boat'," Caleb said, bent over his mandolin to make sure the tuning was true. "Chev as a suffix means 'extremely', it's an intensifier."

Buck looked at Ava wildly, delighted.

"Yeah, we named it The Boatiest," Ava said, grinning. "Well, not us personally, the students decided, but when the Maritime Academy bought it, they voted and the Headmaster let them keep the name they picked."

"*EXTREME BOAT*," Buck yelled.

"The Shivadh sense of humor at its finest," Caleb replied. "They only called it that because there's probably no elegant way to say Boaty McBoatFace in Shivadh."

"I wouldn't think a Shivadh would care about elegance," Buck said.

"Oh, of course," Caleb said. "If we can't be dramatic about something we won't do it at all. If we can't *elegantly* call this ship Boaty McBoatFace we're better off sticking to The Boatiest."

"Okay, camera's set up!" Noah called. "Caleb and Ava, you're up. Buck, do you want to be in the video?"

"I think I'm ruining the historical accuracy," Buck announced, running a hand through his teal hair. He patted Caleb's shoulder absently, leaning on it a little as he got up, then turned, startled.

"Sorry – forgot," he said, looking stricken.

"It's fine," Caleb said. Ava looked from Caleb to Buck, frowning. "Seriously, Buck, it's okay. Hey, they eat in the dining room off the galley and we'll probably do a sing at lunch, go see what the acoustics are like."

"Ah – yeah," Buck agreed, still looking a little annoyed with himself, but he strode off with his guitar, already adjusting to the gentle roll of the deck.

Dancing a hornpipe on a tall ship at sea was something of a proposition, but Noah's friend Jamie made it through a handful of takes without stumbling too badly or taking a fall. Caleb and Ava provided music for the filming, working through the hornpipes they'd learned, changing to a new one whenever Jamie asked.

At last, Noah said, "Okay, I've got enough for your video, Jamie," and the boy ran off back to his duties, passing Buck on his way as the rocker returned to them.

"Do you have classes this morning, Noah, or are you on watch?" Ava asked, clicking buttons idly on the concertina.

"Technically I have class, but I got a pass to film you guys and do the photoshoot," Noah said.

"Wish I could have done school like this," Buck said, looking up at the rigging.

"You'd have liked Maritime," Caleb said. "We like unconventional thinkers."

"Most of the time," Noah added. "Gotta learn to obey orders on the ship. Did you want to do makeup for the shoot, Mr. Canto?"

"Do I need to?" Caleb asked. "I don't like stuff on my skin if I can avoid it. I didn't bring anything."

"I got eyeliner in my jacket if you want it," Buck said. Noah and Ava both looked at him, Noah with raised eyebrows. "I don't look like this *naturally*," Buck added, gesturing to his face.

"Definitely not," Caleb said to Noah.

"In that case, you two stay here and keep playing so you earn your lunch," Noah said to Ava and Buck. "Mr. Canto and I are gonna do a shoot."

Noah's idea of doing a shoot was to drag Caleb all over the ship, up to the stern and out to the bow, into the galley, almost everywhere but belowdecks into the classroom where the hold had once been, because after all the whole point was to be shot scenically. Caleb's backdrops were the ship's rigging and railing, but also the distant French coastline, the open water, and the sky.

"Maybe I should do a class on nautical music," Caleb said, studying the water as Noah tried various angles with a selfie-stick held out over the railing; Ava and Buck were working steadily through old whaling songs in the background, currently on *Farewell to Tarwathie*. "Shanties and sea ballads and forebitters. This is nice."

"A lot of people would take that class," Noah agreed. "But if you wanted an excuse to get out on the ship while you teach it, you'd have to do it for the older students."

"I guess there's nothing saying I couldn't," Caleb said. "I just never have. People your age have much stronger opinions and…judgements, than the under-twelves. Harder to impress you."

"You may not believe me," Noah said absently, looking into the camera's viewfinder, "But impressing a bunch of sixteen-year-olds is not going to be a problem for you."

"That's right," Buck said, swaggering up, song finished. "After all, you're running around with me, aren't you? I'm very impressive."

Noah looked up and laughed. "Get out of the frame!"

"Shan't. Include me," Buck insisted. He glanced at Caleb. "Arm okay?"

"Arm?" Caleb asked, and Buck lifted his arm over Caleb's shoulders, not touching. "Oh, sure."

Buck settled his arm and leaned in to give the camera a punk grimace, tongue waggling out, eyebrows arched. Caleb tried to imitate him, meaning to tease gently back; Buck was too busy clowning to notice, but Ava laughed in the background.

Caleb reached out to take his phone from Noah just as the ship's bell rang out – eight bells on the forenoon watch, meaning that for most of the students of the *Dychev*, it was lunch time.

Caleb jostled into line with everyone, taking the bowl that was handed to him, topped with two slices of thick dense rye bread.

"What is this, exactly?" Buck asked, studying the meat and gravy under the bread.

"Burgoo," Caleb replied. "It's a kind of stew."

"Burgoo," Buck repeated, unimpressed.

"Surprised you're not familiar – some people think we got it when the Royal Navy dropped the Welsh invasion off a couple hundred years ago," Caleb said, moving down the line. Buck snorted. "Try it, you'll like it. I love school burgoo. Everything has the same flavor and it's easy on the mouth."

"Damnation by faint praise," Buck said.

"Not so faint when you're me. Nothing worse than biting into a pepper by surprise," Caleb said.

"Burgoo's the only protein he gets," Ava said, grinning at Caleb.

"That's not true, I eat protein bars," Caleb said. "I just favor compact nutrition. And burgoo."

He didn't immediately get a chance to eat, however; when he passed out of the galley and into the dining room, the students started up a chant: *Tavat! Tavat!*

"Better play it," Buck said, taking the bowl out of his hand. "They'll shut up if you do."

The students laughed at this, but he had a point. Caleb had practiced *Young Prince* on the mandolin, figuring this might happen, but he hadn't thought about how close this was. Like playing a crowded bar, or a small venue. The kind of thing that made him cringe and flee.

"They're only students," Buck said in his ear.

Caleb knew he meant they weren't anything to be afraid of, but it was a better reminder that there was a structure here – that he'd taught some of the youngest crew when they were still in the under-twelves, and that this was class, not a social gathering.

"All right, hush, quiet," he said, settling them down. "No

talking if I'm going to give you a private concert, my nerves can't take it. Now, I'm going to play *Young Prince* through for you and because this is school – it's *school*," he reminded them, as they groaned, "once I'm done we're going to do a little lesson in songwriting. Mr. Haverd, Ms. Jones, you don't get to talk, you know too much," he added to Buck and Ava, and there was a murmur of giggles. The table nearest him had some space clear; he settled himself cross-legged on top of it, so as to be visible, and balanced the mandolin on his thighs.

He waited until he was sure they were quiet before he sang the intro, the long fluting *Tavat*, and then struck the opening chords. He could see some of the kids – and Buck – mouthing along with the words. It still made him uneasy, the attention, but this wasn't so bad, at least; the general structure of teacher-and-student was still somewhat in place.

After the last chorus, he lifted his hands away from the mandolin, gesturing palm up for everyone to join in with him. They repeated the four lines of the chorus, with some notable mumbling on the line in Shivadh, and finished with applause.

"Job very well done," Caleb said, mostly to get them to quiet down again. "So, now everyone's heard it – is everyone mostly clear on the lyrics? Yes? All right. Let's start with the instrumental structure. What kind of music does this remind you of?"

Perhaps Noah had a point about doing a class with the older kids; they were a little more irreverent, but also gave way to each other easier, and required less guidance from him. They were more capable of talking to each other, not just for his benefit, and he only jumped in occasionally to guide them off a tangent or offer some insight. He was just about to step in to talk them out of the mire of *why does it start that way* when Buck interrupted, raising his hand.

"Ah!" Buck said, waving it a little. Caleb blinked at him. "You said I couldn't give answers, but I just have comments!"

"The floor is open for comments," Caleb said graciously.

Buck grinned.

"I think you open it like you do so that it sounds like a prayer," Buck said. "It sounds like something you'd hear from a muezzin."

"Or in synagogue!" one of the kids added.

"Right. Why do you suppose that is?" Caleb asked Buck.

"Well, the whole thing's about ritual, history repeating itself intentionally," Buck said. "Makes sense."

Caleb nodded. "Okay – that's a great point. Now, you don't talk, because they have to talk about what you just said," he said. "What does Mr. Haverd mean when he says it's about ritual?"

Buck's face was difficult to read, but he seemed to be feeling something very strongly. He didn't look negative, at least not entirely. He looked...conflicted. Caleb spared some thought for it while leading the discussion, but the look faded as Buck watched the children dissect what he'd said, picking the lyrics apart for further religious meaning, if any.

"But it's not like. Specifically religious," one of the students said. "It's about the way religion..." she frowned, working out how to say it. "The way it *works*."

"Is it about that?" Caleb asked.

"No," Buck said, not putting his hand up this time. Caleb raised his eyebrows at him. "I mean – as a song writer," he said. "It's about the king talking to the prince. That's the story. The story's inside of the other thing, like. The ritual. That's – the foundation, it's the language he uses, the language and the music. So it's like he made a frame out of ritual and hung the story on the frame," he finished.

The room was silent, and Caleb could see Buck flush with embarrassment, redness in his ears spreading across his cheeks. Buck was opening his mouth to say something when one of the students said, "Whoa."

Then three or four launched themselves at the idea, clearly fascinated, and Caleb had to play traffic-director for a moment.

By the time he got them sorted, Buck had slipped out onto the deck, and Caleb turned to Ava.

"I need to eat and see where Buck went," he said. "Can you handle the students?"

"Sure, they're off on their own journey now," Ava said. Caleb climbed off the table, leaving the mandolin with her, and grabbed his bowl of lukewarm stew, going in search of Buck.

He wasn't especially hard to find; he'd just gone up to the foredeck and settled on a pin rail there, a low plank full of large wooden pins meant to hold rigging. Caleb sat next to him, bowl in his lap, content to keep him company and eat until he was ready to talk. Buck fiddled with the wooden pin between them idly.

"Did I say too much in front of the kids?" Buck asked, after a while. "Or...was it stupid?"

"Not at all," Caleb said, around a mouthful of stew and bread. "They're still taking apart what you said. Very insightful."

"Good, s'good," Buck muttered.

"Guessing you were not the kid who spoke much in class," Caleb said, looking out at the water, rippling as the bow pushed through it.

"Not after about ten or so," Buck agreed.

"Shame. You're onto something with that ritual-as-foundation thing," Caleb said. "Got it on good authority that was a deliberate choice on the part of the composer."

Buck snorted. "I've studied his work."

"Easy to tell," Caleb said. He set down his stew and let himself sway with the motion of the ship, bumping into Buck and leaning up against his shoulder. He could feel the other man tense, so he leaned away again. Buck turned his head.

"Should've asked first?" Caleb said.

"About what?"

Caleb leaned in slowly and bumped him again.

"Oh – no, I'm good, just wasn't sure you meant to," Buck replied.

"I did," Caleb said, still leaning on him. "You don't have to ask every time, you know," he added. "We're not strangers."

"Sometimes that doesn't make a difference," Buck said.

"Maybe, but it does for me. I like touch, just not when strangers touch me. Especially without warning. But it's the surprise, not the touch, you know. Ava doesn't have to ask."

"Maggie likes me to always ask. I just assumed," Buck said.

"People are different. You should still ask her, if she wants you to. But I'm giving you permission. As long as I can see it coming, you don't have to ask."

"As long as you can see it coming," Buck repeated.

"Yeah. Don't grab me from behind, you know."

Buck nodded, then lifted his arm, settling it behind Caleb, tucking Caleb's shoulder under his.

"Thanks. That's cool. Really punk of you, Mr. Canto," Buck added, and Caleb leaned in hard enough to push him off balance for a second, in revenge.

Friday turned out to be their last glimpse of freedom; the next week filled up with rehearsals and prep meetings for the Askazer-Shivadlakia pre-party, and their time wasn't much their own.

Caleb had it easier, since his performance was simple and he was headlining this time. Buck, who had ingratiated himself with Lachlan by way of Noah and Caleb, got a little extra time in the venue to work out the coat trick, although really that just meant he spread his grumpiness across several afternoons instead of one.

Focus was ramping up on the Eurovision competitors in any case. Askazer-Shivadlakia was the last pre-party before the semi-finals and the country was getting attention as a new competitor; between that and the growing obviousness of Buck's presence in-country, more and more performers wanted to come to Fons-Askaz for the party — to see and be seen, if not to perform.

Davidson, more harried every time Caleb saw him, nevertheless seemed to be enjoying the challenge of herding Eurovision cats, Shivadh-style. Jerry positively reveled in it.

The concert was set for early Saturday evening, in the same venue where they'd held the National Final, but the people Caleb talked to – admittedly, mainly Buck and members of the royal family, because that was just his life now – were more excited about the Friday evening before. They'd all received invitations from the king to attend his Friday night gala, a special event for the Eurovision pre-party performers. Caleb was aware of the king's garden parties distantly, the way most people in Fons-Askaz were, but he'd never been asked to one before, and Buck was curious about them too.

"Gregory has them on the palace grounds almost every Friday night in the summer, and any time the weather's fine the rest of the year," Noah said, sitting with Caleb and Buck in the audience at the concert hall, watching the stagehands rehearse set transitions for the various performances. "Usually they're not very interesting, just government people and any fancy rich visitors who are staying in town to do touristy stuff. The food's really good though – Simon goes all-out, and sometimes Eddie pitches in. When there's music we can hear it from the fishing lodge."

"You ever go?" Caleb asked, an unstrung guitar sitting on his lap. He'd acquiesced to the suggestion that he play a guitar for the performances, but he refused on principle to be normal about it, so he'd bought a cheap guitar and painted it black. The sound quality wouldn't matter; all the musical tracks had to be pre-recorded anyway, to make the stage transitions faster. They'd only hear his singing and his original backing track, not the cheap guitar in front of him. So he didn't feel too bad about carefully adorning it with white puff-paint, in a filigree pattern to match the royal uniforms Lachlan and Ava would wear.

"Sure, I go sometimes," Noah said. "Boss knows some of the MPs from doing interviews and anyway it's a good opportunity to sniff out news, so I tag along. And Michaelis knows everyone, which means everyone knows me."

"How's that work?" Buck asked, looking up from his notebook.

"He introduced me to everyone, and people pay attention when Michaelis says things," Noah said. "I'm pretty much the only one my age running around the parties anyway – most of the MPs either have little kids, or they're old enough their kids are grown. Sometimes if the MPs can't find babysitters, they'll bring the little ones along and I look after them."

"That why they think you're going to be the next king? Because you're close to the royals?" Buck asked.

"That's just a rumor someone made up. Kinda cool, though," Noah said, settling back. "I was an unpopular weirdo at my old school back in America. Got here and made a bunch of friends at my cool new school, and *then* word got out I was hanging out with the king? I'm still a weirdo but now I'm the popular weirdo. It's a real, what do you call it? Reversal of fortune." He gave them a sunny smile. "Come to Askazer-Shivadlakia, seek fame and power!"

"They ought to put you on a poster," Buck agreed. "Huh, there's a song. *Poster Boy.* Couldn't write it about you, though."

"Why not? I told you, I'm popular now," Noah said, laughing.

"Well, if I wrote a song called *Poster Boy* it'd be making fun of someone," Buck said. "Not the cool kid, either. Not like you and me."

"Were you cool when you were my age?" Noah asked.

"I was so cool I left school at fifteen. Don't be that cool," Buck advised. Noah nodded, eyes wide. "Anyway, what I mean is the ugly popular kid, you know the one. Gets his kicks punching down. Wait, no," Buck added, humming a melody. "*Got to the top by punching down, gets his kicks in when you're on the ground...*Doesn't scan, but it's a start."

"Reverse 'em," Caleb said. "*Gets his kicks when you're on the ground, he climbed to the top by punching down.*"

"*You've no reason to frown when the Poster Boy's around,*" Buck finished, scribbling the lyrics into his notebook. "Hm, I like that. So this party, is it gonna be cool or lame?"

"Probably cool," Noah said. "It's a special invitation-only for the Eurovision people, so no politicians, or anyway only the interesting ones. Jerry's got a bunch of friends he's bringing from his old party crowd and Eddie called in some local influencers."

"This is not making it sound cool," Caleb said.

"Ah, that's because you like to go to bed early and have healthy boundaries and a sense of proportion," Buck told him.

"List my many flaws," Caleb drawled.

"I'm just saying, party people, influencers, and Eurovision performers sounds like a wildly entertaining evening if you know how to do it right," Buck replied. "The Shivadh jury voters won't be there though, right? Could get in real trouble if I'm seen consorting with people capable of giving me points directly."

"No – they invited a bunch of the acts, so Gregory told the jury to stay home," Noah said. "I heard him and Jerry talking about it. Anyway, should be lots of fun for Gregory. A gay king hosting a Eurovision dinner party for club kids and musicians? Can't be missed. You'll come, Caleb, won't you? At least for a while?"

"Well, put that way it does sound entertaining."

"You can come with me," Buck said. "I'll keep you out of trouble. The rest of Strangelust'll be there too, they can be our bouncers. We'll rent a limo, show up in style."

"I was just going to walk," Caleb said. "It's like…twenty minutes from home."

"Hopelessly practical," Buck sighed.

"Why don't you guys come to the lodge first, instead?" Noah asked. "Jerry and Alanna are coming over, Jes is gonna do Alanna's makeup. Maybe Jerry's too, if he wants a smokey eye.

We're all getting dressed there and then taking the van up to the palace."

"Rolling up to a party with half the royal family in a van driven by a teenage sound engineer is very on-brand for me," Buck said thoughtfully. "You in, Shades?"

"I don't think I've honestly had much of a choice in most of what's happened to me for weeks, why start now?" Caleb sighed.

"Aw, cheer up. If you play your cards right, Jerry'll buy you a boutonniere," Noah said.

It was actually pretty fun, arriving at the lodge to the controlled chaos of the royal family preparing for a party. Caleb was already in his usual suit and Chucks with shades at the ready, unwilling to break character at this point; he had his ukulele and a granola bar in his bag, so he felt as prepared as possible, and had settled at the kitchen counter to spectate. Jes was doing makeup in the kitchen, which had the best lighting for it, first on Alanna while Noah and Jerry showed off various potential looks for the party, then on Noah and Jerry while Michaelis argued with Jes about whether or not he was permitted to wear the royal uniform.

("I always wore the uniform when I was hosting." "You're a guest now, and you look nice in the gray suit." "It's not formal enough!" "Michaelis, do you see what Buck is wearing right now?" "Don't bring me into this!")

They ran late, rather naturally, which made Caleb anxious, but he reasoned that the event was hardly likely to start, or end, before the Duke of Shivadlakia arrived. It did not occur to him that he would be arriving as part of the Duke of Shivadlakia's entourage until they were walking into the garden, strung with fairy lights and dotted with torches, just as the sun went down.

He had to admit, it was probably one of the better parties he'd ever attended, and probably *because* he was a guest of the duke. Jerry dragged Caleb and Buck around with him, introducing them but never lingering, then sat Caleb at his table while Buck ran off to make mischief with Strangelust. People came and went; Jerry swung past every few minutes to make a remark or introduce a new topic of conversation or bring a friend over to meet him before whisking said friend off again. He made the experience so generally effortless and pleasant – at least for Caleb – that Caleb lost track of time, something previously unknown in his experience of social events.

It wasn't until he was leaning back in his seat, with a plate of nearly-finished food and an almost-empty wineglass on the table in front of him, that Jerry dropped into the chair next to him with a sigh and announced, "Pretty good party. Thanks for staying."

"Oh – yeah, it was nice," Caleb agreed. "Is it over? I mean – not to ask if we're going soon, I just wondered. I don't know how parties usually end."

Jerry smiled at him. "Whereas I have a lot of experience in staying until the messy finish. Not quite over yet, but soon. Anyone who wants to keep the thing going – all the influencers, most of the people I brought – took off for an afterparty in Fons-Askaz. Karaoke," he added with a comic grimace.

"You don't like karaoke either?"

"I love a nightclub. Karaoke's not my thing. Especially if you aren't drunk," Jerry added, waggling the glass in his hand. Caleb had seen wine and water available, but Jerry was holding a pint glass, and it looked like it had juice in it. The duke nodded at it. "Cherry-pomegranate. Every party's a smoothie, that's my motto."

"You don't drink?" Caleb asked, curious. He was pretty sure the tabloids for the last ten years would contradict that.

"Not anymore," Jerry said. He glanced sidelong at Caleb. "I don't bring it up much," he said. "Adderall and liquor don't mix. Mind you, forty milligrams of amphetamines makes the world a lot more tolerable without alcohol anyway," he continued.

"I didn't mean to pry – "

"No, I wanted to mention it. Don't have much experience being smooth at that, but it felt like a good time. I've got ADHD, extreme edition."

Caleb had a sudden realization and pointed at him. "That's how you knew about the touch thing. When you stopped the king from grabbing me onstage."

"I do a lot of reading about neurodiversity these days. And I talk to people. It's a lot to learn – I only got a diagnosis last year."

"Yikes," Caleb managed.

"Yikes does about cover it," Jerry agreed. "I know the way my brain works and the way your brain works aren't quite the same, but...when you meet someone cool and that radar pings and you think, *ah, he's like me, same hat*, you want to reach out."

"I understand that, I think," Caleb said. "Huh. Wish I could say you pinged the radar back but I thought you were just...very people-aware."

"Well, I am that too. Mostly I talk a big game," Jerry said, still smiling. "But then you seem to pull big talkers into your orbit."

Caleb glanced at Buck, who was laughing with a knot of other musicians – most of Strangelust, it looked like, among others.

"Not just Buck Haverd and the Duke of Shivadlakia, either," Jerry said, catching his glance. "You've charmed the king emeritus, who in his own way is the biggest talker of all of us."

Behind Jerry, Michaelis was sitting at one of the other tables; he'd lost the debate over the royal uniform, but had chosen a brown suit instead of whatever gray one Jes preferred. It had to be said, even out of uniform, that the best phrase for what he was doing was *holding court*.

"I suppose the king emeritus backs up any big talk he might make," Caleb said. As he watched, Buck wandered over with some of the musicians, pulling chairs up from elsewhere to join in the crowd. The old king nodded at Buck, smiling.

"Even without taking into account the forty years of rule," Jerry agreed. "Seems like he knows a little bit about everything, or he's good at faking it. He might not have thought much of us joining Eurovision, but he likes music too much to keep away."

"I thought he was more of a spoken-word man," Caleb said. "I know he works in audio now but it struck me that was a hobby. Not much time for music when you're king."

"We all got music hammered into us at school, but he's got some talent, too. Have you heard him sing?"

Caleb shook his head.

"Shame, but not unexpected. He used to enjoy it. Hasn't sung much since Aunt Miranda died. Although he's been doing better since last summer," Jerry added, brightening. He twisted around, resting his arms on the back of his chair. "Uncle Mike!" he called.

"Yes, Gerald?" Michaelis asked, turning to look at him.

"You should show them how it's done," Jerry said. "Give us a diva turn."

"They know their business, I'm sure," Michaelis said.

"I told him he should enter Eurovision," Jerry said to the assembled musicians, who grinned at one another. "Come on, Uncle Mike. One song."

"That's what you used to say when you were six and sleeping over with Gregory," Michaelis grumbled.

"And you did it then!"

"I'd like to hear it," one of the musicians said.

"So would I," Buck added. Michaelis tilted his head specifically at Buck, keen dark eyes curious.

"I don't suppose anyone knows *Mingulay Boat Song*," he said finally. Caleb did, because it was one of Ava's favorites, but he didn't fancy performing. He looked around and saw Buck giving the king emeritus a defiant, uplifted chin.

"I know it," Buck said. "Had to learn it for school, didn't I?"

"Then I'll have at least one backup," the old king said with a smile. Buck looked less certain at that. "Drummers, please?"

A few people raised their hands. Michaelis tapped out a beat and Caleb tilted his head, listening as people began to match it, thumping tables or pounding feet. Jerry winked and joined in.

Michaelis lifted his hand from the drumming, now that everyone had the beat, and ticked down on his fingers, then pointed at Buck. They started together, along with a few others.

> *Heel you home boys, let her go boys,*
> *Bring her head round into the weather*
> *Heel you home boys, to the ropes boys*
> *Sailing homewards to Mingulay —*

You could always tell a true folk song, Caleb thought, because nobody ever agreed on the lyrics. Michaelis was singing *Heel you home*, while Buck sang *Hill yo ho*, and someone else was singing *Hail ye home*. Some of the singers began to vocalize wordlessly instead, following the tune. Buck kept on stubbornly, voice spiraling around the old king's deeper one.

> *What care we how white the wave is?*
> *What care we, boys, for wind or weather?*
> *Heel you home boys, to the ropes boys*
> *Sailing homewards to Mingulay*

> *What care we how white the Minch is?*
> *What care we, boys, for windy weather?*
> *Hill yo ho boys, let her go boys*
> *Sailing homewards to Mingulay*

Buck had natural talent, but Caleb could hear that Michaelis had been trained. He kept a strong rhythm with the words and let Buck and one or two others improvise over him, harmonizing in higher registers.

> *They are waiting on the bank for*
> *Our return to cliff and heather*
> *Pull her round boys, and we'll anchor,*
> *Ere the sun sets, at Mingulay*

Michaelis held up a finger and the others fell silent; on the beat he kept singing, no longer in English now. It must be Shivadh; Caleb caught the word *Askazer* and a few other simple ones, and the old king ended with a repeat of the last line in English: *Sailing homewards to Mingulay.*

The musicians applauded, Michaelis as well; someone asked, as it died down, "Was that Gaelic?"

"Hah, no," Michaelis replied. "That was Shivadh. Our language," he said, gesturing at Caleb and Jerry. "It's a little deceitful. The song was only written about a hundred years ago. We were speaking English by then. Shivadh sailors liked it, but Mingulay's not our home – it's in the Hebrides somewhere. The last verse is about how every sailor has his Mingulay, and ours is the port here in Fons-Askaz."

"So it's in Shivadh just to be difficult?" Buck asked.

A few people laughed, but Michaelis nodded. "Very likely. It's how we are." He gestured to Caleb. "That one knows. He put a line in Shivadh into his song."

"Had to look it up," Caleb said. "I don't speak it."

"That could be remedied. But few bother anymore, and there's no strong reason to," Michaelis replied. "We're philosophical about leaving it to hobbyists and academics."

"Everyone knows tavat, now, at least," Buck said.

"So they do," the old king agreed. "And I believe my own port is calling me home," he added, rising. Caleb followed his gaze to where Jes was crossing the grounds, looking amused, arm slung over Noah's shoulders. "Until tomorrow. I look forward to seeing you all perform."

Caleb glanced at Jerry, wondering if they should go too, but he made no move to get up, and Caleb was, remarkably, enjoying himself. He stayed put – at worst he could simply walk home whenever he liked.

"Do you speak Shivadh?" one of the drummers asked Jerry, as Michaelis left.

"Ah, to an extent. Required reading when you're gentry, you know," Jerry replied. "Lost all but the swearwords and the pick-up lines at this point, I imagine."

"Go on, pick me up then," another one said. She looked like she meant it, too.

Jerry said something, brief and amused; when they pressed for a translation, he said, "Roughly it means, *My heart is already sold.* When I leave tonight, I go home to my duchessa, none other."

There was general amusement at that. Jerry caught Buck's eye and said something else, clearly to him.

"What, does your duchessa make an exception for foreign frontmen?" Buck asked.

"I'll let you figure that out. Come along, Caleb; I'm supposed to make sure you get a good night's rest. Friends," he said, nodding to them as he rose. Caleb followed him away from the others, curious.

"You weren't hitting on Buck Haverd, were you?" he asked, as they walked through the palace grounds.

"Ah, no. I was telling him if he'd dust that chip off his shoulder, someone might teach him Shivadh," Jerry said.

"Do you suppose he wants to learn?"

"It's a double-entendre – not surprised you don't know it, it's very old-fashioned. To offer to teach someone Shivadh, it's like suggesting they come up and look at your etchings," Jerry said.

"Jerry!"

"He doesn't know what I said. I'm sure he has his fair share of partners and probably more than his share besides, but I bet that's all he has. What I meant was that if he wasn't so prickly he'd find someone who'd put up with him for longer," Jerry said. "He wants that, you know. All his music's about what he's missing. Even the music that's not."

"How can you tell?"

Jerry shrugged. "I'm good at people. In the way you're good at music."

"What do you suppose he's missing?"

"At a guess, I'd say he needs a hug," Jerry said with a grin.

"Seriously, though," Caleb pressed. Jerry's hazel eyes turned on him and grew thoughtful. If he was as good at people as he said, then he was probably seeing right through Caleb, but Jerry wasn't cruel.

"I think he's had absolutely nobody at his back, probably his whole life," he said at last. "And he's painfully aware of it. There's no net if he falls, and that high wire just keeps getting higher for him. Probably he'd like to be someone else's safety net too – but I can't imagine he believes most people would accept that."

"I did," Caleb said. "When he helped me – in the green room, during the show in Turin."

"So you did," Jerry agreed lightly. "Do you want a ride home? I think Uncle Mike and Jes took the van, but I could wrangle a town car from the palace garage."

"No, I'll walk," Caleb said. "I like the quiet. Gives me time to think."

"You think a good deal," Jerry said.

"Can't help it," Caleb replied. "But I guess you know how that feels."

"You have no idea," Jerry replied. "Will you be okay, going home?"

"Yes – Fons-Askaz is pretty quiet, and the streets between here and home are well-lit."

"Good." Jerry nodded. "Text me anyway, huh? When you get home, I mean."

"Why?" Caleb asked. Jerry's brows drew together.

"So I know you're safe," he said. There was an oddly gentle catch to his voice. "You're in the Palace orbit now, Canto, and under the special protection of the Duke of Shivadlakia. We look out for each other."

"Huh," Caleb said, considering this. He'd pushed his shades up onto his forehead; now he tipped his head, letting them fall to the bridge of his nose, and gave Jerry finger-guns. Jerry laughed.

"See you tomorrow. Don't forget to text," he said.

When he did reach home, as he was climbing the stairs to his room, he considered what to send; finally he settled on a sunglasses emoji and a spiky, six-pointed Shivadh star. Jerry replied with a photograph of his hand, ducal signet ring prominent; the same star was part of the signet design. Caleb sent back LOL, and went to bed.

CHAPTER NINE

THERE WAS A final rehearsal at the concert hall on Saturday, before the evening performance, and Caleb was glad he'd arrived on foot. Crowds were already starting to gather, blocking the dense traffic, and Caleb was able to dodge around them and get in through the back with a little help from Noah. Strangelust rolled up about ten minutes later and arrived in a flurry of shouts and cheering from the crowd, but Buck seemed too tired and harassed to appreciate it.

"You look like hell," Caleb told him, as Buck slouched into the seat next to him, both of them waiting for their turn at final sound check. This time, Caleb was checking late because he was the headliner; just his luck to always come in near the end.

"Yeah, it's how I feel. Went out with the band after the party broke up. They just got in, you know, thought I'd show them Fons-Askaz hospitality."

"Shouldn't have had that last drink?" Caleb asked.

"Should have gone to bed two hours earlier. I was flirting with the bartender but he turned me down for a bigger tipper. Hard to blame him, she had...fantastic tips. Anyway, hangover's not so bad, just..." Buck leaned back, grunting, and propped his legs on the seat in front of him, knees over the back. "I woke up half an hour ago, so we're all lucky I'm clean and conscious. Didn't have time to get coffee."

"Why'd you do it? You know you're performing tonight."

Buck turned his head to grin at him. "Why didn't you? We're only young once, Shades."

"Yeah, and I'd like to enjoy it instead of spending it miserable."

"Eh, the misery's part-time, the fun is full-time," Buck replied. "To each their own, I suppose."

"I do love to sleep," Caleb said thoughtfully. "And I like being fresh for the concert."

"I'll be fine by then. Anyway, learned my lesson, haven't I? I'll make sure to get tucked in and have a good night's rest before the big event. You can yell at me if I don't."

It reminded Caleb that he was going to Eurovision; Buck talked about it sometimes, but to him it was something *Buck* was attending, something that was happening to other people. Perhaps even partly he didn't think of it because Buck didn't seem to. Caleb was going to the semis, but the UK was one of the Big Five, the countries that paid the most towards the broadcast expenses and so went straight through to the Grand Final. Buck could afford to take it easy – or to party before the semis, if he liked.

The idea that Caleb would be there, to yell at Buck if he tried to go out clubbing before the Grand Final, was an odd one.

"What, you don't expect me to come out partying with you?" Caleb asked lightly.

"Nah, why would you? Be thrilled if you did but you'd be miserable, and I can't have that," Buck said. "You remember the morning after Turin, when you were leaving as I was coming in?"

"Tough to forget," Caleb agreed. "I wasn't sure what you'd do, to be honest."

"Me either. Happy to see you, though. Felt like a weird constant, almost," Buck said. He turned away to stare at the ceiling of the concert hall, wistful. "It'd be nice to have someone to come home to, once in a while, instead of having to find someone to take home."

"No reason you couldn't have someone to come home to," Caleb pointed out.

"Eh. Most people don't love that."

"How do you mean?"

"Dunno," Buck said. "Few times I've dated someone, like a real relationship, if they don't go out with me every time I go out, things don't work. They get jealous even if I haven't done anything. Or they're mad I go out at all, when they don't want to."

"Huh." Caleb considered this. "I suppose it takes a lot of trust to do that. Just let your partner go off and have fun without you. But so long as you trust them…it'd be a relief to be with someone who didn't want me to do everything they did. To have a partner but to have my own life, too. I like my independence too much to try and force someone else to curb theirs."

"That's the size of it," Buck agreed. Caleb caught sight of Noah, down on stage watching someone wire something. Noah saw him too, and waved; Caleb waved back, then held up his phone. He texted Noah's number, *Is there coffee backstage? Buck's dying.*

Noah gave Caleb a thumbs-up, but instead of answering, he scuttled off. Caleb beamed at him, delighted, when he returned a minute later with a large paper cup.

"Hey, your luck's turning," he said, elbowing Buck, who opened his eyes and glanced at him. Then Buck saw Noah, gaped, and made grabby-hands.

"Are you paid for this?" Buck asked, clutching the coffee to him and slurping it. "Oh. *Oh.* Still hot, and you added sugar. You're about twelve years old but you should be paid for this."

"I'm sixteen, and I get union rate," Noah said, grinning. "The coffee is free, because Caleb likes you and I like Caleb."

"Mmh. I'm so glad you like me. Apologizing to you was the brightest thing I've done in a year," Buck told Caleb. "I should do it more often."

"Stick to not having to and you'll be fine," Caleb assured him. "Hey, did you see, by the way…" he reached over to one of the empty seats and picked up a little bag that was hanging on the back, presenting it to Buck. "The king consort had a great idea."

"What's…" Buck studied the black bag, which said *Shivadh Eurovision Party 2022* in gold on the outside. He pulled the drawstring at one end and shook the contents into his palm: a cheap pair of mirrored sunglasses.

"Everyone in the audience gets one, and when I come out on stage everyone puts theirs on," Caleb said, as Buck theatrically fell out of his chair laughing.

"Here, hang on, grab your guitar, put your shades on," Buck said, unzipping his jacket, under which he was already shirtless in preparation for performing. Caleb leaned over and picked up the guitar, settling it on his lap, and put his own slightly nicer shades on while Buck got the cheap souvenir ones situated. He threw an arm over Caleb's shoulders and they leaned in together, smiling for the selfie Buck took.

"Throw that on your Photogram," Buck said, sending it to him. "Now, let me finish this coffee and we can go and make some noise…"

With caffeine in him, Buck felt he survived the sound check and final dress competently. Once he was through that, the energy of the evening amped him up enough to give a hell of a performance during the actual concert. It was fun – lower stress than Turin, with a kind of community-theater spirit to it, even as professional as it was. Most of the other performers were from smaller countries and didn't put on airs, and the interval performances were all done by older kids from the Maritime Academy, most of whom Buck at least knew to wave at by this point. Lachlan and Ava were just buttoning up their costumes as Buck came offstage, and when Lachlan wolf-whistled him, Buck grabbed him by the waist and dipped him dramatically, which amused Caleb and made Lachlan scream in joy.

And he got to watch Caleb do *Young Prince* again, which got better every time, somehow. Not the performance, exactly, though Caleb was a good technical performer, anyone could tell that. But there was something about the song that sank down into your bones after a while. Bits and pieces of songs for Buck's new album – often the ones Caleb had helped with – were beginning to feel that way too, and he really liked it.

He really liked Caleb.

Now, sitting at the bar in the hottest nightclub Fons-Askaz boasted – which was not all that hot, but still a good time, and tonight full of famous people and musicians he knew – Buck nursed his beer and scrolled Photogram. Plenty of pictures from the concert, and more than one video; the one that kept popping to the top was captioned *King Consort Saxophone Cameo?* because the guy on sax in that particular number looked uncannily like Eddie Rambler. Buck knew it wasn't – he'd seen Rambler during that performance, air-guitaring to amuse the king – but he had to admit the resemblance was striking.

Another video that was sticking around was some phone footage from the night before, and he had to admit part of the reason it seemed to crop up is that every time it did, he watched it, and probably the app knew that or something.

Someone – difficult to see who, but nobody in Strangelust, for sure – had filmed him and the handful of others singing with Michaelis at the end of the party. It was dark and poorly lit, grainy, and the sound was awful, but there was an odd supernatural quality to it that seemed to pull you in. It felt like a mystery – like the half-lit faces and the haunting tune could conjure something, if they wanted to. But he kept coming back to the last few seconds before the camera moved and everything went blurry.

The film cut off completely just after the last chorus in English, before Michaelis sang in Shivadh, which was sort of a shame. But it meant that it ended on Michaelis and Buck, separated by about an octave, singing *sailing homeward to Mingulay…*

And just beyond the pair of them, off to the right, Caleb's

face, visible in a shaft of moonlight, eyes intent on Buck. His expression was difficult to read, but there was an intensity there that Buck, half-drunk in a bar after a concert, wanted to unlock. Everything about Caleb was so straightforward that this one central question, this locked door of what went on in that mind of his, didn't even irritate Buck, the way not knowing something normally did. It just pulled him in like a lure.

"You still surfing Photogram?" his bassist asked, nudging against him at the bar. "Come on, Buck, you've been in this backwater too long. You even remember how to have fun?"

"Ah, I'm having plenty of fun," Buck said easily. "Go, enjoy yourself. I'm having another beer."

He did go; they were used to Buck's occasional moods, and he knew they didn't take it personally when he wanted to fly solo. Buck considered another beer, realized the one he had wasn't even finished, and put his phone away in his pocket.

He closed out his tab and disappeared while the rest of the band was still trying to get in some local Shivadh pants.

"BOOOOOOOSS!"

Jes — exhausted after the concert, more than excited about going to bed for sweet delicious sleep, and enjoying it dreamlessly once they had — woke to a shout from their child.

They rolled out of bed to their feet, heading for his room, but at a reasonably sedate pace, trying to wake up fully as they went. Ten years ago they would have been running, but Noah was almost grown now, and in the intervening decade Jes had learned to distinguish, even half-asleep, between true panic and mild distress. Still in bed, Michaelis — clearly a master of this as well — rolled over and slept on.

"What is it, Wild Child?" they asked, blinking and yawning in the doorway of Noah's bedroom, down the hall from theirs.

Noah, sitting on the edge of the bed, held out his tablet, wordlessly. Jes looked down, trying to work out what they were seeing.

"Why do you have thirteen hundred unread messages?" they asked at last.

"Good question!" Noah said, throwing his arms up. "I don't! Caleb does."

"Caleb *Canto*? Why are you in his email at two in the morning?"

"I'm his agent, this is his PR email," Noah said. "I couldn't sleep. Please don't yell at me about screen time."

Jes squinted. "Wait, I recognize that name. And that one. Are these…"

"Label reps!" Noah said. "It's like…maybe eighty percent label reps, and the rest are weirdos who want to know if Caleb and Buck are an item. Which I don't know! And it's maybe pretty weird to ask!"

Jes minimized the email window and opened Photogram, a suspicion growing. There was the email address in Caleb's profile. And there was Caleb's latest post, made just before the concert. It showed him in the empty audience, leaning affectionately into Buck Haverd, both wearing mirrored sunglasses.

I'm not a performer, the caption on the photo said. *I'm an under-twelves music teacher and part-time songwriter. But tonight I'm headlining the Shivadh Eurovision Party with a song I wrote. In ten days I go to Eurovision semis representing Askazer-Shivadlakia and I couldn't be prouder. Ejechev Eurovision! See you in Shades!*

"What's Ejechev mean?" Noah asked.

"Sound it out," Jes told him, 'parent brain' just awake enough. Noah frowned.

"If Chev is intensifying Eje – conjugated…" Noah looked distracted. "It means *Let's go*?"

"It's like *viva*, or *daje*," Jes nodded. "It's a nice message. It means he's happy to go to Eurovision. Now," they added, sitting on the foot of Noah's bed next to him, "Which part do you think led to the emails?"

Noah took the tablet back, calling up the email app. "Well, I mean, they've been spending a lot of time together, I guess people are gonna wonder about the relationship stuff. That's just awkward gossip."

"And the rest?"

Noah frowned. "Buck regrammed it and Eurovision's official account regrammed from him, and they posted up Caleb's performance, too. Oh no," he said, realization dawning. "It's the songwriter part, isn't it?"

Jes nodded. "Caleb has a nice voice and a cool style but he's not Mick Jagger – or even Buck Haverd. He doesn't have that natural stage presence. What he *does* have is an earworm with a brutally catchy hook. People who hear his songs want a piece of him as a songwriter. And a whole bunch of people just saw tonight's performance."

"And so, emails. Ugh. What do I do?" Noah asked. "I know I signed on to be his agent but this wasn't what any of us had in mind. I have school on Monday, I can't read this many emails."

"No, that's true," Jes said thoughtfully. "Well, you have some options. First, take this to Caleb. If he's not interested in writing for others, full stop, you can just auto-reply to everything with a form letter. If he wants to consider the offers, he might want to read them all himself, which lets you off the hook."

"Maybe we don't show him the creepy ones."

"I think you should ask if he wants to see them, but yes, I imagine those can be deleted once he says so. And if he doesn't want to go through his email personally, you'll have to get some help. Caleb's representing the country, so you can probably ask the Palace. We can talk to Michaelis about it in the morning."

"Why wait?" a voice rumbled. Jes looked over to see Michaelis in the doorway, pajamas rumpled, smoothing his hair down.

"I thought you were asleep," they said apologetically.

"Inner alarm went off," he mumbled. "Child in distress. Took me a minute, that's all. What's going on?"

"Caleb posted about being a songwriter," Noah said. "A bunch of music reps want to hire him."

"Mmh. Palace could help triage the disaster?" Michaelis asked. Noah nodded. "Good idea," he said to Jes. "Alanna would enjoy a new challenge." He grunted thoughtfully. "Time s'it?"

"Just past two," Noah said. "Sorry. I couldn't sleep after the concert and I thought I'd check email."

Michaelis squinted at Jes, and they took the hint.

"There's nothing to be done about it tonight," they said. "So, Noah, what's a good plan?"

Noah considered this. Jes added, "When action grows unprofitable…"

"Gather information. When information grows unprofitable, sleep," Noah said. Michaelis made a confused noise.

"Ursula LeGuin. I'll loan you the book," Jes told him.

"Caleb's probably asleep," Noah said finally. "So I'll text him that I need to talk to him in the morning about some business opportunities. I can text Alanna too and warn her I need to talk to her about handling some of his PR but I won't know more until I talk to Caleb. Then I could go through the emails and get rid of any of the obvious junk and scams…"

"Or you could sleep," Jes said. Noah turned to Michaelis.

"Don't appeal to me, I'm here to back up Boss," Michaelis said, but he gave Jes a questioning look. They gestured for him to continue with whatever he was hesitating over. "If you want some help sleeping…"

Noah nodded. Michaelis came into the room, crouching down – then winced and sat on the floor instead, facing Noah, sitting on the bed.

"Close your eyes," he said. "Picture an underground cave – like the wine cellar. Somewhere dark and quiet."

"Guided meditation?" Noah asked skeptically, eyes closing regardless.

"Do you want help or do you want to sass me?" Michaelis asked.

"Help," Noah sighed.

"Good. Now, everything you're worried about, every separate concern, even just things like feeling too full of energy right now – sort them all out in your head. You don't have to do this now, in a minute we're going to go back to bed and you can do it when you lie down. For every worry, picture a little pebble. Something you can hold in your hand. They don't have to look different. In fact, it's better if they all look similar. Every worry is a separate pebble. When you've done that, picture your hands actually holding them, putting yourself in the cave."

Noah nodded, eyes still closed, fingers twitching. Jes watched, intrigued.

"Once you have that picture very firm in your mind, put down the pebbles in the cave, on the ground. And then you're going to walk backwards out of the cave, until you can't see them anymore, and turn around and leave everything there," Michaelis continued. "You can go back later if you need to, but for now it's all left behind. And then you can try to sleep."

Noah opened his eyes. "That's all?"

"Well, it's worked for me. If it doesn't for you, you know where we keep the wine, get yourself a glass," Michaelis said. Jes tsked. "Don't tell your parent I said that," he added, with an amused glance at Jes. He rose and kissed Noah on the forehead, heading back down the hall. Jes hugged Noah sidelong, gave him a last searching look to make sure he was okay, and then nodded.

"Send two texts, then go to bed," they said. "Don't set an alarm. If you oversleep tomorrow the world won't end."

Back in the bedroom, Michaelis was stretching, rolling his shoulders. He tumbled into the bed, on top of the covers, face buried in the pillow. Jes pulled the blankets back on their side.

"Who taught you that meditation?" they asked, sliding under the sheet. He turned his head to look at them out of one eye.

"Nobody."

"Nobody?"

"I invented it," he said. "After Miranda died. I had to find a way to put personal things aside when I needed to work, or to be there for Gregory. Or to sleep," he added, turning his face back into the pillow.

"Did it work?"

"It worked enough. Got me through," he mumbled.

"Through?" Jes asked.

"To you and Noah," he replied, clearly about to drift off himself. "Shh. Go 'sleep."

That led to about a million more questions Jes wanted to ask, but he was right, now wasn't the time. They considered, then gently threw a corner of the blanket over him, sliding across to curl up against his shoulder, an arm slung across his back. He heaved a sigh as his body went slack.

It didn't actually take that long for Jes to drop back down into sleep, either, though they dreamed about caverns full of emails for the rest of the night.

The next morning, Caleb awoke groggily to a text message from Noah. It read, *Don't read your email until you talk to me. Eurovision regrammed you and a lot of people emailed you. I'm gonna get the Palace on it. Text when you get this please? AGENT VOICE NOT STUDENT VOICE!*

He smiled at the end of the message – Buck had been teasing Noah the other day that when he was acting in Caleb's interest, he put on a special Agent Voice to do it.

I'm up, he texted, noticing that the message had come through past two in the morning. *I'll come to the lodge. Message if you want breakfast, I'm stopping at the bakery on the way.*

There was a text from Buck, too – a photo of him under the sign of one of Fons-Askaz's nightclubs, the neon turning his hair from teal to violet. The text said *Wish you were here, glad you aren't.*

It's the thought that counts, Caleb replied to Buck. *Going up to the lodge. Might work on the album a little. I'll leave notes if I do.*

He washed and dressed, slung his ukulele on his back, and had just left the boarding house when Noah hit him back.

Will pay u back for 3 pains au chocolat, 2 sufganiyot, 1 lamb sausage roll. We have coffee.

He sent back a croissant emoji and stopped at the bakery closest to the fishing lodge, picking up Noah's requests plus an apple danish for himself. He walked up to the lodge with the bakery box dangling from his fingers, enjoying the trail through the trees around the lake.

When the lodge came into view, Jerry and Gregory were sitting on the front porch, coffee mugs in hand. Jerry was in shorts and a race shirt that read A5K - RUN FOR THE ASK on it; the king was in joggers and a lurid floral Truly Tasty t-shirt.

"Good morning!" Jerry called. "You have pastry for us!"

"Do I?" Caleb asked, coming up the steps. "I thought maybe Noah was really hungry."

"There's some kind of summit," Jerry said, tilting his head at the lodge's front door. "Alanna got a text from Noah this morning about you, she told me she was coming out to the lodge. We were on a run, so…here we ran." He gestured with his coffee at Gregory. "We're backup in case of disaster."

"Apparently you're capable of making a stir whether you want to or not," Gregory said with a smile. "I think you have a pain au chocolat for me, and a doughnut for Jerry."

Caleb untied the bakery box and offered it to them, lid propped open; as they were making their selections, Alanna leaned out through the front door.

"I thought I heard trouble," she said with a smile. Caleb

offered her the box. "I retract my statement," she added, taking a pastry. "Come in. Noah's bouncing off the walls."

"Still mad at you for letting her get involved with Eurovision after all," Jerry said to Gregory, as Caleb followed Alanna inside.

"Can't be helped. Dad's the one who asked her. I can rule the country or keep him out of trouble, but not both," Gregory replied as the door swung shut.

Inside, Jes and Michaelis were at the breakfast table in the kitchen, sipping coffee and reading the news; Caleb leaned in the doorway and said, "Noah ordered catering," and got pleased looks from Jes (the last pain au chocolat) and Michaelis (lamb roll).

"We have a little meeting set up," Alanna said, indicating the more formal dining room behind the kitchen. Noah was inside, working at a laptop, with a tablet nearby.

"Impressive. Businesslike. What on earth happened?" Caleb asked.

"Did you look at your PR email?" Noah asked back.

"No, you said not to," Caleb said, setting the bakery box down next to him. "Guess the last doughnut is for you, unless you want to trade me for the danish I got."

"Thanks. We can expense the receipt to the Palace," Noah said absently, taking the doughnut, then the receipt that Caleb had stuffed into the box, and handing him a twenty saorh bill in exchange. An engraving of Gregory III gazed serenely up at him from the face of the bill. "Uh, so. Eurovision regrammed your performance last night. Turns out like. The whole world thinks they discovered you and everyone wants to hire you."

"...to teach?" Caleb asked, confused.

Alanna and Noah both looked at him.

"I mean, I posted about...being a teacher..." Caleb looked back and forth between them.

"And songwriting," Alanna said gently. "And then Buck regrammed you saying that you're a great lyricist, and Eurovision regrammed your song..."

"Oh." Caleb nodded. "Well, that makes — *what*," he added, as Noah turned the laptop around. The little header at the top listed a number of messages in four digits.

"You've got a few offers," Alanna said drily.

"Most of them are fanmail or trash," Noah said. "I've been looking through them. Some are asking for gossip about you and Buck."

"Like what?"

"Well, exactly," Noah said. Caleb squinted, but let it go. "Anyway, some are like, legit music label reps. Mostly smaller interests, but a few big names."

"What do I do?" Caleb asked, as his phone buzzed.

"That's what we're here to figure out," Alanna said. Caleb, looking down at his phone, saw that it was Buck: *At the lodge. R U here this morning or not till afternoon?*

"Hang on," he said, and messaged back, *Upstairs and things are wild. Please come help.* "Okay. Uh. This is not...normal, right?"

"I mean, not for me," Noah said. "Alanna has experience handling booking for the king and stuff but he's not like...in demand for album production."

"Though it would be hilarious if he were," she said. "No, I think we're all flying a little blind here — "

There was the slam of a door, a yelp of surprise, and then pounding feet; Caleb looked up as Buck, a little disheveled, skidded into the doorway.

"Hi," Caleb said. "You didn't have to run."

"You said shit was wild, I didn't know what that meant," Buck replied. "Ah. Hi Noah. Lady Alanna."

"Al's fine, I told you," she said. "My goodness, Caleb, you do collect defenders. Actually, Buck, you might be of use, come in, sit down. Sorry we just ran out of doughnuts."

"What's going on?" Buck asked, sliding into a seat next to Caleb. Caleb tore off half his danish and offered it to him, and he bit into it distractedly.

"Caleb got famous overnight," Noah said. "After you and Eurovision regrammed him talking about being a songwriter. Bunch of music reps want him to work on their albums."

"He can't," Buck said immediately, swallowing his mouthful of danish.

"I can't?" Caleb asked, exasperated.

"No. You're working on my album. I have you locked down," Buck told him.

"This is news to me," Caleb said slowly.

"Okay, uh – no, of course – fuck, now I sound like a dickhead," Buck said. "*Obviously* you didn't sign anything and you can do whatever you want. But I did ask my lawyer to make a contract because you've been doing all this work for free..." he gestured at the floor, and the bunker beneath it. "In the studio with me, I mean. I just hadn't given you the contract yet. But I want first refusal. Plus most music reps are man-eating sharks. You should sign with me instead and be my song doctor and get paid outrageous amounts of money by music industry standards. If you want."

Caleb stared at him. He wasn't even certain how to react; it was strangely sweet, the idea that Buck had been quietly considering his contributions and had decided he deserved some kind of legal protection. His initial wariness over Buck's assertion that Caleb was working exclusively for him began to fade.

"No pressure," Noah said into the silence, "but that would mean I could mass-delete a thousand emails."

"Although I feel compelled to add, Buck is probably not the only one who can offer you outrageous cash," Alanna said. "What we were going to suggest before he crashed in was that the Palace communications staff could sort through the email and present you with some of the best options."

Caleb's ears buzzed unpleasantly – not quite at panic-attack levels, he thought, but getting there. He knew why, too; this was a complication in his life he hadn't anticipated and didn't want.

Which at least made the choice easy.

"Delete them," he said to Noah, who made a little *yes* gesture. "Wait, no, can we – can we send everyone a letter, too? Like…sorry but I'm under contract?"

"Yeah, I can mass-email everyone," Noah said. "Still way, way easier, thank you."

"You're welcome. I really don't want to work for a music label. I like teaching. And I wasn't doing it for money," he added, turning to Buck. "I don't actually need a contract. It was just fun."

"Money for nothin' and your kicks for free," Buck said.

The buzzing stopped abruptly as Caleb gaped at him.

"*Dire Straits*? Really, Buck, Dire Straits right now?" he asked. Buck grinned. "It's not even the right lyrics!"

"What are you talking about?"

"It's *chicks* for free!"

"It is not!"

"It's chicks, everyone knows that."

"That's gross, it's not chicks!"

Alanna coughed politely. Both men looked at her.

"If you don't need me, I'm going to go enjoy this with my boyfriend on the porch," she said, holding up her pastry. "Noah?"

"He said delete, no take-backs," Noah announced. "Caleb, do you want to read the *thanks but no thanks* letter before I send it?"

"No, I know you're passing English Comp," Caleb replied. Buck was furiously googling Dire Straits lyrics on his phone. "Don't wear yourself out over it. Am I paying you hourly for this?"

"I'll get a commission from Buck's contract," Noah said.

"Hustling little bastard," Buck said affectionately, looking up. "Are you coming to the semis, Noah? I just need to know if I should warn the band to steer clear of you and your ways."

"Wouldn't miss it. Bet you Caleb wins them," Noah said.

"You can't win the semis, that's not how it works," Buck said.

"You don't get the semi-final score until after the whole thing's over."

"But I bet sometimes you just know. Like people's choice. Common acclaim."

"Fuck, I hope I don't," Caleb replied. "The whole point is I'm not supposed to go to the Grand Final as anything other than a spectator. Anyway, come on, leave him alone," he added to Buck, standing. "Let's go hang out in the studio, so everyone else can have their Sunday morning back. Noah, come get me if you need anything."

"I don't believe it's chicks for free," Buck said, as Caleb led him towards the door down to the bunker.

"Why not?"

"Because it means they think they're like. Getting a bargain. On women. Which is gross!"

"You know they use slurs in that song, right?" Caleb asked, propping the door open. Buck stopped in the doorway, eyes wide. "How long has it been since you actually listened to any Dire Straits?"

"Not long enough," a voice drifted out from the kitchen – Michaelis, who apparently had strong opinions. "If you're so desperate for inspiration you're listening to Dire Straits, Buckley, I have an entire music library I can send you that is leagues ahead of that."

"I realize I am having quite the morning but *what did you just call me?*" Buck asked, heading back to lean on the kitchen bar. Caleb rubbed his face.

"Joseph Buckley Haverd," Michaelis said from the breakfast table. "I looked you up. Speaking as someone named Michaelis, I'd have gone for Joseph, but I realize Buck is a much more dramatic stage name."

"If you call me Joseph, I don't care how long you were king, I'll shiv you," Buck told him, baring his teeth. Caleb shifted nervously, but there was a subtext he was missing, he thought;

Michaelis just laughed, and Buck's snarl turned into a grin. Caleb felt himself relax.

"I only use proper names when provoked," Michaelis said. "Ask Theophile or Gerald. Buck is a decent name, but I'd request the right to call you Buckley when you're being troublesome."

"I was just quoting a song!"

"Perhaps not, then?" Michaelis asked, eyebrows rising. Buck gave him a narrow look.

"You get three a year," he said at last. "You've used up one."

Michaelis looked amused at that. "Fair. Off with you now, go entertain Caleb. I have important work to do," and Caleb saw him flash the crossword as Buck retreated to the doorway again.

"Joseph Buckley," Buck muttered as they walked down the stairs. "Don't you get ideas either, Shades."

"Wouldn't dream of it," Caleb told him. "But you really should leave off Dire Straits."

"Yeah, well. Don't know if I've ever listened to that song all the way through, to be honest."

"Really?"

"I mostly know the cover."

"Which cover is that?"

Buck gave him a faintly guilty look. "Al Yankovic did a cover."

It took Caleb a second, and then he stopped dead in the middle of the bunker, while Buck more or less fled into his studio.

"*Al Yankovic is Weird Al!*" he yelled.

Buck's voice drifted out. "You catch on quickly!"

Caleb caught up to him, the *Bastards Only* sign on the door fluttering as he passed inside. "You are a secret nerd," he told Buck.

"I am an extremely cool rock musician," Buck replied. "Anyway, that's how you know you've made it, when Weird Al does a cover."

"Weird Al does parodies, not covers."

"Whatever. If I had what he has I'd be using my superpowers for revenge, but he's a better man than any of us deserve. And I have to make myself happy with writing my own music," Buck said, dropping into a chair and propping his legs up against the wall. He pulled the acoustic guitar into his lap. Caleb settled on one of the stools, shuffling through scribbled notes in his own handwriting and Buck's cryptic notation.

"Speaking of revenge, I finished my song," Buck added.

"One, what revenge, and two, which song?"

"Our bet-song. *Shower Drum Solo*," Buck said, shooting him a grin. "About the audio bleed from the rehearsal room."

"Buck, you didn't actually," Caleb replied.

"Of course I did, you bet me fifteen sours."

"Saorh," Caleb corrected.

"You want to hear it or not?"

"I suspect I'd get a bigger rise out of you if I said no," Caleb suggested. Buck rolled his eyes. "Okay, go ahead, play me this song and we'll see if I think it's worth fifteen saorh."

Buck plucked a few strings, then broke into a swingy, up-tempo melody, like something out of surf rock – very much like it actually, Caleb realized, with the same slightly dissonant chord progressions. When he started singing, it was very...very Buck, tight phrases and odd pauses that didn't seem like they'd fit until he pulled the whole thing together. It was pretty straightforward, about a guy who had a drummer for a downstairs neighbor and how the drum practice would shake the building when he was in the shower –

Halfway through, horrified, Caleb realized it was allegory. Buck saw his expression, broke off in the middle of a verse, and howled with laughter.

"Your *face*, Shades. Oh man, you should see it – where's my camera – " he flailed for his phone, patting his pockets.

"You can't sing that! You can't put it on an album!" Caleb said. "I said a song about audio bleed!"

That just made Buck laugh harder, dropping his phone and setting his guitar aside so he could lower his legs to the ground, bending to pick it up.

"Don't you like it? I think it'll be a huge hit," Buck said, taking his picture. Caleb scowled.

"It's supposed to be about the trials of being a musician, not – that's the king emeritus you're singing about!"

"You wrote a whole song about the king emeritus!"

"Yes, a dramatic ode to the passing of the crown from father to son and rites of passage, not a surf rock satire about *jerking off in the shower*," Caleb said. Buck went off into another gale of laughter.

"I'm sorry," he managed, wiping tears of mirth off his face. "Just. Your reaction. Don't even give me the fifteen sours. Your reaction has been worth diamonds." Buck shook his head. "Nobody'll ever know it's about Michaelis, including Michaelis. I wasn't even thinking about him when I wrote it. I was just thinking, if I was in the shower and heard a sudden drum solo, what would I do? But then I thought well, what am I generally doing in the shower? And I can't just leave and go yell at someone for drumming in the middle of personal time."

"You can't possibly...that often," Caleb said.

"Not every day, but most days. Cleans out the pipes, good for the digestion," Buck shrugged. "I think I did an extremely clever job. It's definitely going on the album. *Come on man let's go to town, good vibrations all around, can't get enough of that sweet sound –* "

"Noah's going to know and he's going to tell."

"Noah's going to laugh his arse off and if he does tell I'll bet you the king emeritus laughs too. It's only sex, Caleb, lots of people have it. I do. Michaelis almost definitely does, because Jes Deimos is a smoke show." Buck kicked the floor, sending his wheeled chair skidding over to Caleb.

"Bet you do," he said, leaning in to catch Caleb's gaze. Caleb, perched on the stool and a little above him for once, let him. "If you aren't, and you want to, you could be. Have your pick of half the willing in Fons-Askaz. Last time I was in a club I heard two guys talking about how good you look in those suits you wear."

Caleb shook his head. "I wouldn't mind it, but it sounds honestly exhausting. And anyway old habits die hard."

"Old habits?" Buck asked.

"I grew up in Galia, you know. It's not like it is here. It's conservative. If you make a pass at the wrong person there…" Caleb shrugged. "It's not that I haven't dated. I have, and I've had fun, but I'd rather have a boyfriend than a fling. Wouldn't you?"

"People are complicated," Buck said. "I have all the complication I need right now. Flings keep it simple."

"So does a drum solo in the shower but I don't see you being satisfied with that."

"There's a lot in life I'm not satisfied with," Buck said. "It'd be an ugly world if we all got everything we wanted all the time."

"Then…don't you want something more complicated than what you've got?" Caleb asked. "Come on, Buck. Are you going to sleep with groupies and hit on bartenders forever?"

"Are you not? You're poised to break big, Shades. Especially after last night. Why turn down what's on offer?"

"People offer me licorice, too, but that doesn't mean I always want licorice," Caleb said.

Buck lifted a hand and rested his palm on the back of Caleb's neck. He touched their foreheads together and Caleb watched his eyes close.

"What if I offered?" Buck asked. "Would you say no to that?"

A thrill went through him, a very basic sense of *I was chosen*, but Caleb had learned better than to trust in the visceral delight of being wanted. He knew a relationship with him would be complicated, and he knew that Buck was simply a complex person, not always easy to read. But this was, in one way, the easiest part of him – Buck didn't really do relationships. And Caleb didn't want anything so fleeting, even if it felt good to have it offered. Which meant that he had to handle this very carefully, something he wasn't generally adept at doing.

He knew he'd been quiet too long, spent too long thinking about it, when Buck's eyes opened again.

"I'm trying to figure out how to explain this," Caleb said.

"Explain what?"

"I don't want a fling with you. With anyone, but especially you. You're too important. If I have anything with you I want it to be – real isn't the word. Deep, maybe. I won't die if I can't have that, Buck, I'm not in love with you. I could be, someday. I like you a lot. I'd be willing to risk finding out. But I'm not going to take casual sex if that's all you're offering."

Buck snorted, bumping his head gently against Caleb's.

"You know what? That's fair, and I knew what kind of boy you were when I asked," he said. He didn't sound bitter, but it was tough to tell.

"What kind is that?" Caleb asked.

"Honest. Isn't the first time you've given me a hook to the jaw, won't be the last. I like boxing with you, anyway," Buck said, and leaned back. "Don't know if I want something more than a fling, Shades."

"Well, then I guess it's your call," Caleb said. "If you decide you do, you know where to find me."

"I wonder if I do," Buck told him. "Can I still give you that contract to sign?"

"You can give me a contract. Whether I sign it depends on what's in it. Are you sure you still want to?" Caleb asked. "I know this kind of thing can be awkward for some people."

"Not for you?" Buck tilted his head.

"No, Buck. Not for me," Caleb said. "You want to work on music?"

Buck gave him a faint smile. "Definitely. Just let me text someone about the contract."

CHAPTER TEN

THERE WASN'T MUCH time between the Shivadh Eurovision party and the semi-finals; performers began to pour into Turin that week, and Caleb and Buck both began preparing to leave Fons-Askaz.

Buck, true to his word, got a copy of the contract he'd wanted to offer Caleb. He thumped the huge stack of paper down in front of him during one of their album sessions, looking immensely pleased with himself. Buck spent most of the week packing up the rented room he'd been slowly filling with tourist treasure, takeout containers, the latest Shivadh fashions, and scribbled notes to himself. Caleb – only a little panicked – took the contract to Noah, who took it to Michaelis, who got an intense woman named Georgie to come to the lodge and have a look at it.

"It seems fine to me," she said, after reviewing the stack of paper. "Entertainment law isn't my specialty, but I did a little research and the terms are generous. He's offering you a decent upfront fee, residuals on album sales above normal scale, and you can dictate how you want to be credited, within reason. There's a lot of other stuff but none of it implies any kind of responsibility or liability on your part. Unless he gets sued because he slanders someone in a song. Having listened to some of Buck Haverd's music, I can see why he included that," she added thoughtfully.

"Has he been sued for…musical slander?" Caleb asked.

"What a term. No, and he probably won't be, but if I were you, I would request he not slander anyone," Georgie said. "You seem to have some influence over him, shouldn't be difficult."

"I'm not sure anyone tells Buck what to do," Caleb replied.

"If you didn't dictate anything in this, I'm twice impressed. Would you like to sign it now? I can notarize it for you."

In a way, it was stomach-clenchingly frightening – it was a very long, very binding legal document, and Caleb's previous experience had been of the *print out a form from a website for musicians* variety. But, well, he'd done the work. It seemed like this was just going to allow him to get paid, and give him claim over what he'd worked on. He was beginning to see the sense in that. He signed.

That evening, at Reverb, Buck paid Noah to bring them dinner from a pasta place in town that Caleb liked, as a celebration. After dinner he said he'd see Caleb at semis, didn't kiss him goodbye or seem mad about it, and the next day left Fons-Askaz, heading straight for Turin with Strangelust. It was fine.

Caleb left for Turin at the end of the week with an *entourage*, though Eurovision officially called it a Delegation. The trip was as exciting as it was nerve-wracking. He was more or less swept along in the tide of the royal family, and while it meant he didn't have to worry about much, it also meant he didn't have much control over what was happening.

Jerry, as Assistant Head of Delegation, had begun taking some of the heat off Davidson, mainly when it came to arranging their trip to Turin. It was a good thing on balance, but it did mean that a reformed party boy with ADHD and only a loose grasp on Italian was running things.

Still, Caleb had to admit Jerry had managed to get them all – Michaelis, Jes, Noah, Lachlan, Ava, Davidson, Caleb himself, Alanna, and half a dozen students from the Academy – to Turin without a hiccup. They were settled in a pensione close to the venue, and Alanna had even presented Caleb with an agenda of interviews, video spots, and meetups he was supposed to attend, interspersed with a remarkable amount of downtime.

"I appreciate the breaks," he said, studying the agenda document on his phone.

"Jerry said you would," she said with a smile.

"He seems to be enjoying the new responsibility."

"I think so. He likes organizing social stuff like this. But if it's still too much, you can text one of us and we'll come scoop you up. Or dip out on your own, you're a man with initiative."

"Not to worry," Caleb agreed absently, locking his phone and putting it in his pocket. "What will everyone else be doing?"

"Michaelis is minding Noah and his friends while they play tourist. Jes has interviews lined up for the podcast, and Jerry's running around doing Delegation things with Davidson. Lachlan and Ava have the same call times you do, I don't know what they're up to otherwise. And I," she added, "have errands to run on Gregory's behalf. Love it when I get to play the King's Avatar."

"Well, I'll let you get back to it," he told her, and she beamed at him and ran off to represent the king.

He wasn't due at the venue for rehearsal until the following day, so he hunted up Ava to see if she wanted to go rambling. He thought she might want to see Eurovision Village, but it was secretly a relief when she suggested they just wander instead.

"Feels like I haven't seen you much lately," he said, as they strolled down a narrow street lined with gelato places and trattorias, with promising-looking retail in the distance. "I hope you don't think Eurovision's corrupted me."

She laughed. "No, Caleb. I always miss you when I don't get to see you, but you've had new work to do, and that's good. Plus all that hanging out with Buck," she added slyly.

"We've been working on his album, that's all," he said.

"You wouldn't say *that's all* if you'd only been doing that," she told him. "I've seen the rumors on the fan blogs!"

"You can't listen to all of that."

"Oh, can't I?"

"Put it this way: anything serious has been going on only in our heads," Caleb replied.

"He's very cute. Seems like you like him."

"I do. He made a pass," Caleb added, and Ava whistled low. "It's...up in the air."

"It's not like you to be ambiguous about relationships," she said. "Are you okay with it?"

"Weirdly? I am. I told him if we had anything I wanted to try for something more than a fling. He isn't sure that's what he wants. I told him if he makes up his mind, he knows where to find me. To me, matter's closed," he said. "It's in Buck's court now."

"Hm. Well, from what I've seen, he's not the best decision-maker in the world, but he's far from stupid. I hope he pulls his head out of his ass, because you're a catch," she added, threading her arm around his elbow as the street grew more crowded.

"You have an odd definition of what a catch is," he replied.

"I don't know. You two have a lot in common, and finding someone who gets your art can be rare. He ought to appreciate that you're not in it just because he's famous, too. He knows you're serious. Anyway, there's a vintage store," she added, indicating a dusty shop window. "Come rummage in it with me."

"As the lady likes," Caleb said, affecting gallantry. "What are we looking for?"

"Leather jackets, musical instruments, and anything that looks like it might be haunted," she said. "I have to find either a cursed artifact or a lucky charm so that life stays interesting."

"Next year I'm making you write the national song for Eurovision. See how interesting life gets for you then," he said, but he followed her inside and enjoyed himself helping her shop. It took his mind off the impending performances, at any rate.

Rehearsals for the semi-finals were an intense affair. The machine of Eurovision was a very precise one, and Caleb became one of its moving parts, as did most of the musicians. Still, they made it as pleasant as they could for the artists – there was a lounge full of snacks (and unfortunately, often, video cameras), and if you knew you weren't going to be needed for a while, you could go take care of other responsibilities, like filming little ad spots or giving interviews.

Caleb did meet-and-greets and press conferences, rehearsed in costume and out, with sound and without, and prepared for the following week, when they'd have rehearsals in front of audiences. He filmed the little "postcard" segment they'd show before his performance, helping to promote Turin as a tourist destination; Jerry had been agitating for them to let Caleb take a turn around a test track in a racecar, but instead they got a professional stunt driver to teach him how to drive a Mini-Cooper, then filmed him re-creating a scene from *The Italian Job*.

Turned out you really could just drive a classic Mini-Cooper down a flight of stairs, provided the stairs were wide enough. It was tough to say who was more jealous, Noah or Buck. (Buck had to tour the Royal Library for his, which was a real decision on someone's part.)

He went to a few parties, squired by Jerry and Alanna, but he tried to spend most of his spare time resting, recovering from all the socializing he had to do. At one point he helped Michaelis shepherd Noah and his band of fellow teenagers into one of the Eurovision filming spaces to sing with him, since all of them except Noah were in one singing group or another at the Maritime Academy, and the organizers thought it would be cute. They sang a few folk songs and then did a very impromptu and rough but admittedly charming rendition of *Young Prince*, and the students looked like it made their year.

"We should send them next year," Caleb said to Michaelis and Jerry, who were watching the teens chatter excitedly together, studying Noah's phone footage of the song. "One of the Academy music groups, I mean. Maybe make a special group for it. They'd get more out of it than anyone else."

"I'll talk to Gregory. Technically it's his call, but the people have to be consulted," Jerry said. "They're really going to have to knock it out of the park."

"What if I helped?" Caleb asked. "Like a mentorship thing. My seal of approval for next year's candidate."

"Are you going to stay on at the Academy?" Jerry asked, surprised.

"Of course. It's my job."

"It doesn't have to be," Michaelis said. "You'll have other options. You already do."

"Sure, but that's one reason I said no to those. I like teaching. I like my life."

"May we all be so fortunate," Michaelis said. "I think I'd better round up the students before they wander off. Gerald?"

"Unless you need me, I have to do a thing with some stuff," Jerry said, consulting his phone, brow furrowed. "Ah, uh, I'm supposed to do five minutes with someone…that way," he pointed over his shoulder, "on this being our first year in the competition. Hey, look at me," he added, showing his phone to Caleb. "I even put the talking points in the meeting notification."

"What talking points are those?" Michaelis asked.

"Well, clearly we're thrilled to be participating for the first time, and we're looking forward to becoming part of a decades-long legacy of cultural exchange and musical excellence," Jerry said. "We're very happy that our entry contains such strong elements of Shivadh culture, and we hope it encourages people to learn more about Askazer-Shivadlakia…including how to pronounce it," he finished. He looked sidelong at Michaelis. "Also, we're extremely proud of how cool we look in sunglasses," he added, pulling a pair of mirrored shades out of his pocket and putting them on. "That's my finisher. I think it'll kill."

"Every day I am happier to be retired," Michaelis said to Caleb, then turned to the students. "Noah! Amani! Responsible ones, collect up the irresponsible ones, you all need some down-time and to email your parents. Yes, yes, I know you'd rather be out adventuring, but you promised to write them as a condition of being allowed to attend, and we must keep our word…"

The following day would be the opening ceremony and from then on Caleb's time truly wouldn't be his own, but he had one last commitment that afternoon – the organizers had them doing something called the Solo Sessions, where performers could take an instrument onstage, with a single microphone, and perform whatever they wanted, to be uploaded to the social media channel. Caleb wasn't sure who all would be there, but he was pleased – at least momentarily – to walk in and find Buck standing in the green room arena, waiting to give a performance, with his acoustic guitar and freshly styled, freshly-dyed hair.

"Hey, stranger," Buck said, as Caleb joined him in the aisle just outside the currently-empty Shivadh green room, with its little gathering of sofas for the delegation. At the mic, the act from Republic of Tolot – another micronation like Askazer-Shivadlakia, with about as much chance of winning but with a much longer history in the competition – was giving his performance. "Are you on the roster?"

"Yeah, pretty soon, I think. Hey, how's Eurovision treating you?" Caleb asked.

Buck seemed pleased, perhaps even a little self-satisfied, as he nodded. "Really well. Press conferences have all gone fine. Saw one you did, liked that one. You know how to keep your mouth shut when someone's baiting you."

"Really just don't often notice when someone's baiting me," Caleb replied. "You know that. Are you performing?"

"Yeah, but not after Tolot if I can help it."

"I think I might be next, so you're in luck there. Why don't you want to follow Tolot? Something I should know?"

Buck cut his eyes to the Republic of Tolot performer – Caleb was pretty sure he just went by *Patrice*, one name, like *Cher*, but he hadn't heard much one way or another about the man.

"Bit of a fraught situation," Buck said at last.

"Why?"

"I've been trying to avoid him. Knew he'd be here but I figured we wouldn't actually have to talk," Buck replied. "It's mostly just awkward, really. Remember my ex, the one I told you about, who used to steal my songs? That's Patrice."

Caleb cut his eyes to Patrice, newly curious. "He's not playing one he stole from you, is he?"

"No. He wouldn't dare, and I think they just brought him in as a ringer and gave him something to play." Buck's tone turned biting. "He's not even from Tolot, you know, he's from Brittany."

"You two didn't end well," Caleb observed.

"He's a bitter bitch," Buck said, looking mirthless about it. "Doesn't like that I've done well since we broke up. His career flattened out after he stopped being able to nick my shit."

"I can imagine," Caleb said. "If it were me, I'd be thinking about revenge."

"If you were Patrice?"

"No," Caleb said, frowning. "What's he got to want payback for? I mean if I were you."

Buck looked oddly pleased by this. "Ah, maybe. But what's it they say? A well-lived life is the best revenge?"

"Sure, but rank humiliation's a good second best."

Buck laughed at that, which was a mistake; Patrice had finished his song to polite applause, and it drew his attention as he came off the stage.

"Buck," Patrice said, adjusting the strap on his guitar, casually joining them. "Fancy meeting you here."

"Patrice," Buck said, and Caleb had never quite heard that tone in his voice before. Wary, and something else. A strange deference, perhaps.

"I'm Caleb," he said, because there was no point in being a basically awkward person if you couldn't make use of it. "Askazer-Shivadlakia. You're here for Tolot?"

"Ah, the rookie," Patrice said to him. "Buck take you under

his wing?"

"I think of it more as making a friend, but I know those are thin on the ground for you," Buck replied, before Caleb could say anything.

"You say that now, but the UK hasn't won Eurovision in decades. Friends are pretty thin on the ground for you, too."

"I wasn't talking about Eurovision," Buck said impatiently. "But I guess you still think everything's a competition."

"And you're still cheating them. What are you even doing here so early?" Patrice asked, and Caleb could hear the nasty edge in his voice getting broader, sharper. "You're Big Five, big boy. The UK pays to make sure you get to skate past the semis."

"I signed up for Eurovision, not Eurovision lite," Buck retorted. "I have a job as Big Five, you know. And it's fun, I want to be here for people and do things. I know half the people here, you included."

"Don't condescend on my account." Patrice sniffed.

"Oh, believe me, nothing I do is on your account, Patrice," Buck said.

"No, why would you? You always get ahead somehow, no matter how garbage you are at this," Patrice said.

"Buck," Caleb said in a low voice, because he could see Buck tense. "He wants you to take a swing. Then you're the bad guy."

"Ah, I'd heard you two were thick, but I guess you just found someone to be your conscience," Patrice said. "I don't care if you take a swing, Buck," he added, but Caleb knew immediately he'd pushed a little too far. His taunt only proved Caleb's point, and Buck knew it too – he visibly relaxed.

Then he smiled, clapping Patrice on the shoulders. The other man flinched.

"You have a great Eurovision, Pat," Buck said. "I'm sure I'll see you at the Grand Final. If you're in the audience instead of onstage for it, well, they do score partly on talent, after all."

That might actually have escalated things, Caleb never could be sure later, but just then fate intervened: the rest of Strangelust arrived to close ranks around Buck, and the PA system called *Caleb Canto to the stage, please*. He signaled to the booth and got a wave in reply.

"Hey," Caleb said, tugging on Buck's hand. Buck broke his stare with Patrice. "Loan me your guitar and take my ukulele. I'm going to cover one of your songs."

"I thought you were going to do that sea shanty – "

"Nah," Caleb said. "Guys, stick with Buck, huh?"

The band nodded, almost in unison, and Caleb traded the uke for the guitar, heading for the stage. When he turned he could see all the various acts waiting to perform or taking a break after performing, dotted around the audience, with Buck up near the front and Patrice...sitting on one of the Shivadh green room sofas nearby, just in Buck's blind spot. That one really was a bully; he knew exactly how to set Buck off.

Caleb cleared his throat, popping the monitor into his ear. "Let me know when you're recording," he said, putting his sunglasses on and checking the tuning on the guitar.

"Whenever you're ready," the voice in his ear said. "Introduce yourself, you get thirty seconds to say what you're performing and why, and then three minutes for the song."

"Thank you," Caleb said. He gave it a beat, then said, "I'm Caleb Canto, representing Askazer-Shivadlakia for our first ever entry into the Eurovision Song Contest. I met the UK Representative, Buck Haverd, at the Turin Eurovision party recently. I'm covering his new unreleased single, *Poster Boy*, which he was kind enough to share with me. I think it's a fitting follow-up to the song by the performer from Tolot."

Even through the sunglasses he could see Buck's head whip around when he named the song. He checked the tuning briefly, then strummed the opening riff to *Poster Boy*.

It had turned out typically *Buck*, brash and loud and unafraid of rhythmic pauses or key changes, but Caleb had those down.

The chorus was in third person, the way they'd started writing it back when it was just a joke to amuse Noah, but the verses were all in first-person from the point of view of a narcissist, a bully bragging about his own specialness. Some of the sarcasm was in the tone, which Caleb didn't know if he was hitting quite right, but the words were enough to poke sly fun at bad people who took themselves seriously, at their fawners and sycophants.

He'd helped with a lot of the lyrics, honing their mockery of bullies to a razor edge, and at one point Buck had said, "This must be cathartic for you."

"It isn't for you?" Caleb had asked.

"Fair point," Buck had said. "Guess we showed the bullies though, huh?"

Buck, obviously, understood what Caleb was doing, singing *that* song following someone who had just tried to take Buck himself down a peg. It was a shot right across Patrice's bow, a slap aimed at his face. It was also landing on its intended target: Patrice was furious, glaring around to see if anyone else understood what Caleb was doing before returning to stare at Caleb. Safe behind his sunglasses, Caleb couldn't have given less of a damn.

He picked his way delicately through the bridge, then launched into the third verse, the singer's inner monologue, which expressed how incredibly fragile it all was, how one blow could crack him into pieces and a moment's lapse in attention by his fans could drop him off a cliff. Glancing at Buck, his expression was hard to read, but he seemed some combination of confused and pleased. Glowing with schadenfreude at Patrice's discomfort, but also uncertain about something. Caleb couldn't think what, unless he was worried this would make Patrice worse.

Caleb was pretty sure it wouldn't. Nobody could fault him for this performance; it was a compliment to cover a fellow performer's work, and this was a fun way to introduce a new song off Buck's impending album.

And Patrice couldn't risk anything else in public, when the

whole point of Eurovision was peace, love, and friendship.

He finished to polite applause from the waiting performers, gave the booth a nod, and descended from the stage. Patrice was nowhere to be seen as he handed Buck back his guitar.

"Where'd poster boy go?" he asked. Buck was staring at him.

"He stormed off," Buck said. "I think if he'd stayed he was worried he'd be the one taking a swing."

"Good riddance," Caleb replied. "Are — are you okay? I can't tell what you're feeling and you're staring at me."

Buck Haverd to the stage, please.

"I'm fine. Are you going to — don't go anywhere, all right? Five — three minutes, I'll be back in three minutes," Buck said.

"Yeah, I know, you'll be right there," Caleb said, pointing to the stage. Buck was still staring at him, so Caleb gave him a gentle shove. He went, stumbling onto the stage, settling on the stool in front of the mic with his guitar, still bewildered. Then he seemed to notice where he was and compose himself.

"I'm Buck Haverd, representing the UK," Buck said. "I'm playing the first song I ever wrote. It's not on any of my albums but I used to play it in pubs, so there's some bootlegs flying around out there, but that's all. It feels like time I got it down somewhere, officially. So here, probably for the first time without the sound of beer being spilled in the background, is *Bound East*."

"Hey," one of the Strangelust guys said, as Buck performed. "You really fucked Patrice up. Buck wasn't kidding when he said Shivadh are brutal."

"We don't try to be," Caleb said, still watching Buck. "Can't help it, really. We just can't tolerate fools unless we're being one."

"I didn't say I minded. I don't know Buck that well, y'know, we're just the band, but he's a decent guy. And we all knew Patrice is an ass. Thanks for holding the fort until we got here."

"Of course," Caleb said. "But we've got days left and there's press conferences and all kinds of stuff." He glanced at the man. "We're going to have to keep Patrice away from him or there really will be trouble. You guys up to it?"

"Sure. Buck told us we're not allowed to party anyway. Which is kind of fucked up if you ask me, come all the way to Turin and not go clubbing, but I dunno, maybe he has a point. He says we can party all we want after Eurovision."

"Look at Buck Haverd, making strong life choices," Caleb said, mostly to himself.

When Buck was done, he came back to them and handed his guitar to his bandmates. "See you tomorrow," he said, which seemed to surprise everyone – definitely it surprised Caleb – and then turned to Caleb. "You have anywhere to be right now?"

"No…" Caleb frowned.

"Let's go grab a meal or something," Buck said, and Caleb gave the Strangelust guys a bewildered look, only to find they were giving him the same look back. Still, he could eat, and he hadn't seen Buck much, so he followed him down the aisle, around the stage, assuming they were cutting through the backstage to get out to the street. There was a pretty good gelateria near the stage door, and he was opening his mouth to suggest it when Buck turned down the hallway that led to the dressing rooms, pulled open one of the dressing room doors, and stalked inside.

Caleb followed, curious now, and the door had barely shut when Buck turned and stepped right up into his personal space. One hand took the ukulele case from him and set it aside; the other came up to cup his jaw. He had enough warning that he didn't startle as Buck crowded in and kissed him.

"That was the hottest thing I've seen in my life," he said, which seemed like a low bar for hotness, but Caleb wasn't going to complain with Buck's body pressed up against his, solid and warm, holding him against the closed door. "You playing my song to humiliate my ex right in front of me? Holy *shit*, Shades."

Anyway, Buck kissed him again and it was difficult to talk with Buck's tongue in his mouth, so he didn't bother.

In theory he *had* said he didn't want a fling, but his body did seem very interested in Buck's body at this particular moment, so Caleb rolled with it. There were a lot of steps between making out in some random dressing room and actually committing to the level of nakedness required to make this more serious, after all.

Then he realized he was doing a cost-benefit analysis on sex with Buck Haverd, and laughed. Buck pulled back, head tilted.

"I say something funny?" he asked, but he was smiling.

"No, just – sorry, it'd take too long to explain," Caleb said, raising his hands to rest them on Buck's chest. He was, for once, wearing a t-shirt – one of the free Eurovision ones they handed out like disposable napkins to the performers. It was thin enough he could feel the lines of Buck's pectorals. "Though I'm going to spoil a good time and ask what exactly you're doing."

Buck kissed him again, hands sliding under Caleb's suit jacket. Caleb tipped his head back, eyes closing.

"Offering more," Buck said. Caleb stiffened, eyes opening.

"What?" he asked.

"I'm an idiot. Maybe a coward, I'll sort that out later. I want more than a fling. I'm telling you I want more," Buck said, letting go of his waistcoat to try and work his jacket off.

"Do you actually?" Caleb asked, face pressed to his neck, moving his body anyway to help get the jacket off. It slid to the floor. "Or are you lying because you really want to get laid?"

"Listen to me closely," Buck said, leaning back, and cupped Caleb's jaw in his hands. "I am not lying. But if I am, do you care?"

Caleb considered. "No," he decided, wildly.

Buck's smile was knowing. "Make a rock star of you yet," he said, and he dropped his hands to Caleb's thighs. With a sharp lift, he hitched Caleb's legs up around his hips, holding him up against the door, and went back to kissing him. Caleb decided Turin was the kind of place where you went along with things, which suited him particularly well in this case. He'd almost got Buck's shirt off, or anyway pushed way up to his armpits, when Buck stopped kissing him, and the demanding press of his body eased a little.

"Fuck, we can't do this here," he said. "I know I'm not the responsible one but I'm not going to make you scream in some random – whose dressing room is this? I think it's Finland."

"You seem pretty confident about the screaming," Caleb said, as Buck set his feet back on the ground.

"Maybe you're the silent type, I don't know," Buck said, crouching to pick up Caleb's jacket. "Sorry I uh. Rumpled you."

"Still don't care," Caleb told him. Buck held up the jacket by the arms. Caleb blinked, then turned and let Buck help him into it. Buck smoothed the fabric, then bent and pressed his nose under Caleb's ear from behind, teeth grazing the skin.

"Come back to mine," he murmured.

"No, mine," Caleb said. Buck huffed against his scalp. "Has to be mine, Buck. You'll thank me, trust me."

"Right," Buck agreed. "Okay. Yours is probably cleaner anyhow. Please say we aren't going to have to take like, a tram or something to get there, though."

Caleb reached up and threaded his fingers through Buck's hair, holding him there for a moment.

"It's not far," he said, and felt Buck smile against his skin.

It turned out the wings on Buck's hips didn't belong to birds or bats – they were a pair of Welsh dragons, flanking Buck's abdomen, and Caleb laughed and kissed him and then laughed some more.

Later, although not too much later, Buck rolled onto his back, covered his face with his hands, and said, "Fuck. I can't believe you came to Turin this prepared to get laid. You brought supplies! You brought *implements*."

"There was room in my suitcase for a dick," Caleb said complacently. He was also lying in bed, on his side, drinking in a naked and post-coital Buck Haverd. He felt relaxed, pleased, unwilling to move even to get up and put clothes back on. Buck held up one hand; it took his sex-addled brain a second, and then he smacked Buck's palm with his own, laughing.

"That your usual charm move after sex, the high-five?" Caleb asked.

"Nope, saved that up for you," Buck replied. Caleb rolled into him, pressing his face into Buck's shoulder. "I haven't been done that thoroughly since...I think *ever*, actually."

"Happy to provide?" Caleb said, not sure this was normal pillow talk. Maybe it was; he wasn't exactly inexperienced, but he was pretty sure Buck had an order of magnitude on him to sample from. "Didn't hurt you, did I?"

"I might need a soak later, but no," Buck said. "This was such a good idea."

"Hm. I don't disagree," Caleb said, inhaling. Buck smelled good, like sweat and the last of his cologne. "Although at some point we should discuss your cowardice and my recklessness."

Buck made a low, amused noise. "Relationship talk. Yeah, all right, but I'm not being naked for that, and I'm not getting dressed right now."

"It can wait. I'm just warning you now it's happening eventually."

"I'll brace for impact." Buck rolled and tugged on Caleb's shoulders until they were lying face to face, Buck's arm wrapped around Caleb's waist and their legs tangled together. "You enjoyed that though, right? Not to be cliche – "

"Yes, it was good for me too, you insecure weirdo," Caleb said. Buck kissed his nose. "I'm writing a tell-all. Buck Haverd, the bad boy who isn't."

"Well, everyone who thinks I'm a poser will be pleased," Buck said. His tone was light, but Caleb could feel his body tense, a better indicator than his face of what he felt.

"You're not a poser, Buck," Caleb said. "Or anyway, if you are, it's intentional. You can't truly care whether people think you're really a social menace or not."

Buck opened his mouth to reply, but before he could there was the buzz of a mobile phone. Both of them pushed up onto their elbows, looking around for it; Buck found his phone under his trousers on the floor, leaning bare-ass in the air to get it. Caleb admired it for a few seconds; he had a tattoo, right at the base of his spine, of the fingering diagram for a G7 chord, which Caleb was planning to ask about later. Right now, after taking a moment for aesthetic appreciation, he dug around for his own phone, finally locating it under his boxers on the nightstand.

"Guess it's you," Buck said, settling back onto the bed properly, showing his blank phone.

"It's Alanna, dinner invitation," Caleb said. "Looks like her and Jerry, Lachlan, Ava, and me. I think Jes and Michaelis are chaperoning Noah and his friends. I guess Davidson's off doing whatever it is television executives do for stuff like this."

"Must be super weird to have that kind of family," Buck said. "Where there's like a million of you and you mostly like each other and do things together."

"Jerry said the other day that I'm in it now," Caleb said. "Kind of nice. A lot of chaos, though."

"Are you going?"

"Don't know, do you want to?"

Buck frowned. "I'm not the one they invited."

"No, but I want you there, and they like you. They'd be happy to see you. I'm not overly bothered to go if you want to get dinner somewhere just the two of us, or I'll go on my own if you've got stuff to do with the band."

"You think they like me?" Buck asked. It sounded half-joking, but the other half was, in its own way, tragically earnest.

"Of course they do. Why wouldn't they? Anyway, it might be

nice. Won't be as fun telling them how I owned Patrice if you aren't there to help."

"I'll dine on the duke's tab, fair enough." Buck rolled onto his stomach, propped up on his elbows. Caleb leaned up and kissed him. "Can I use your shower?"

Caleb gestured vaguely towards the bathroom, and watched Buck go, enjoying the slight wiggle of the G7 tattoo.

7pm is fine, bringing Buck, he texted the impromptu group chat. Lachlan responded with an eggplant emoji. *You are a child.*

Would have sent abs instead but there's a tragic lack of an abdomen emoji, Lachlan replied. *I'm in for dinner but I have to leave early, call with Stephen.*

We will carry on valiantly without you, Jerry sent. Caleb was checking his Photogram tag (mostly positive reactions to the video Noah had posted previewing the students singing) when a second text from Jerry came through to the group.

Purely theoretically, if I bought a sports car in Turin, what kind of tax/duty fees would I pay bringing it home?

Dinner was lively, another private-room affair with good food and no lack of conversation. Jerry had not actually bought the car, but Turin was a motor city and known for its sports cars, so there was a non-zero chance he would buy something before they left.

"It was an '88 Ferrari," he said wistfully, and most of the people at the table matched his look, to some degree or other. "My birth year. Beautiful rare bronze finish. Like-new condition, leather and chrome interiors."

"And how much was it?" Alanna prompted.

"About six hundred thousand euro," Jerry sighed.

"I realize I stereotypically can't do math but that sounds like a lot of money *without* doing any conversion," Lachlan said.

"I did the math – by which I mean I used an app, because same – and that's still over half a million saorh," Jerry said. Lachlan audibly gasped. "Now, I'm comfortable, and capable of keeping Al in style should she decide to be a lady of leisure instead of the breadwinner, but I'm not that comfortable."

"I'm going to be, one day," Buck said. "Music industry's a lot more brutal than it was twenty years ago but I'm going to play stadiums someday. Go platinum."

"Speak it into being," Lachlan said, deepening his voice like he was giving some kind of inspirational speech. "When you do, remember Reverb Studios gave you a discount on a month of studio space."

"My mam says a rising tide lifts every boat," Buck said. "Then again, mostly she says that when someone else's tide is rising and she wants a cut."

"You really won the parent lottery," Jerry said.

"Been reading the *Daily Mail*, have you?" Buck replied, grinning. "My parents aren't as bad as all that, that's just gossip-mongering. Can't say we're close but plenty have it worse."

Under the table, Buck's hand fumbled for Caleb's; Caleb caught it in his fingers and held on, squeezing gently. Buck's thumb tapped against his knuckles, a message he didn't understand, but he squeezed back, which seemed to be all Buck wanted before letting go.

"Anyway," Alanna said, "your mother's not wrong. Whatever happens at Eurovision, Caleb's really going to raise the Shivadh profile."

"Raise the Maritime Academy's profile, too," Ava said. "Bet we get a bunch of applications next year from music students."

"That's true, you could run a very prestigious music program if you build it right," Alanna said. "Be known for boats *and* pianos, et cetera."

"They offered sailing classes at our school," Jerry added, gesturing between himself and Alanna with his fork. "I did polo instead. Al, you did – "

"Fencing. But our sailboats were dumb," Alanna said. "Nothing as cool as the *Dychev*."

"What should we do about that, though?" Caleb asked Ava. He hadn't considered the long-term impact of Eurovision; he'd just got settled into his classes and his ways of doing things. He felt a momentary thump of panic in his chest at the idea, ridiculously outsized. He was in Turin, a place he'd only ever been once before, performing in Eurovision, where millions of people would watch him, and he hadn't felt at home in days, but this – some far-off maybe-not-even-happening difficulty with the school – was what made his lungs feel like they twisted in his chest.

"About more music students? Hire more staff, I imagine," Ava said. Buck rested a hand on his leg, fingers rolling through a rhythm in perfect 4/4 time. "You could dictate your terms, Caleb, I wouldn't worry. Nobody's going to risk our Eurovision guy walking."

"I suppose more staff would be fine," Caleb said, tension easing a little. He tried to put conscious thought into breathing normally, in time with Buck's rhythm.

"You could probably get someone to take one of your other classes and teach a songwriting class instead," Ava said. "Maybe I could take your twelve-year-olds."

"Thought I'd get Buck to teach the songwriting class," Caleb tried to joke. "He got on well with the older kids."

"I find," Buck said thoughtfully, "I do get on well with kids. Mainly because they think I'm cool."

"You have the hair," Lachlan said. "Luscious. Like a muppet who escaped containment."

Buck stared at him, mouth open for a second, and then cracked up laughing.

"The lady I found to do it locally has me back for another dye before the Grand Final," he said, ruffling it. "Not to be vain but she says I can't enchant Europe if my roots are showing."

"Should I get my roots done for our performance, Caleb?" Lachlan asked.

"What roots?" Caleb asked. He meant it sincerely – Lachlan had a full head of, as far as he could tell, perfectly fine hair – but Lachlan laughed gleefully.

"Right answer!" he said. "Anyway, we can't look finer than we do or we'll just be needlessly upstaging Caleb," he said to Ava.

"As if anyone could," Ava replied, shooting Caleb a grin.

"Mind you, I do have to look good for the man who's going to steal me from my husband," Lachlan said, striking a little bit of a pose. "If I'd known Mika was hosting when we had the National Final I would have insisted on competing, just for the chance to gaze into those big brown eyes of his and allow him to whisk me off my feet."

"What does Stephen think of this?" Alanna asked, amused.

"Stephen will understand, and heal in time," Lachlan said loftily.

The conversation moved on, but Caleb didn't pay much attention; his breathing had settled, and he was trying to enjoy the moment. Here was a table filled with friends, people who were openly, defiantly weird, or subtly weird, who were simply here having fun, with Caleb, who was also enjoying himself.

He leaned gently against Buck. "Thanks for coming."

"We should enjoy it while it lasts," Buck said. "Gimme a room key."

"Give you a what?"

"Room key. You have two, right? I always ask for two," Buck said. Caleb did have two keycards; one was in his pocket, the other stuck into the corner of the door of his room, so that he'd see it and remember to take one with him whenever he left. "Gimme one, so I can come find you when I have some time off."

"What makes you think I'll have the same time free?" Caleb asked.

"You won't, but if you aren't there I'll just eat whatever food I find and nap in your bed," Buck said.

Which sounded...remarkably nice, actually.

"Okay, but other than the food, don't mess with my stuff. And you're going to have to come back to mine to get it, one of them's in my room," he said.

"I'd make a joke about what a trial that would be but you might take me seriously and I'm not going to endanger my chances of scoring that key," Buck said. "I will absolutely come back to the room with you to get the key and also offer you a blow job."

The last was said very, very quietly in Caleb's ear. He couldn't help the grin it caused on his face, and he didn't bother to try. From down the table, Jerry caught his eye and grinned too, glancing at Buck.

"We should take an early night," Jerry announced. "In the absence of the actual family patriarch, it's my job to remind everyone to hydrate, take your meds, eat at least two meals a day, and get at least five hours of sleep."

Thank you, Caleb mouthed at him, as they began rising to leave. Jerry winked and turned to say something in Alanna's ear.

The opening ceremony was the following night, on Sunday, and from there on the pace definitely picked up. Caleb was performing in the second semi-final, so Monday and Tuesday were quieter for him, but he made a point to attend the various first-semi events, and starting on Wednesday he had to perform in the jury show; Thursday he had to go twice, first in the dress rehearsal and then in the live semi-final.

"By Friday it'll be done for me, at least," he said to Buck, over breakfast on Wednesday, waiting for the rest of Strangelust to roll in so Buck could drag them off for a few hours of last-minute rehearsal and a presser. "I'll be out after the semis, and then I can just go watch you win the Grand Final."

Buck laughed. "Maybe. I've seen the competition up close now. Pretty sure I'll make it near the top, but Serbia's a sleeper hit. Sweden's bound to make it through, she'll be tough to beat. Huge bisexual energy on her so, you know, solidarity."

"How can you tell?" Caleb asked. Buck squinted at him. "I think I have a permanently broken gaydar. Permanently broken anythingdar, really."

"Never really deconstructed it," Buck admitted. "She might not be bi, I haven't investigated, but the *song* has that energy. There's something about...I don't know, not to be all Tragic Queer about it, but wanting to grab what happiness you can when you know it won't last."

"There's nothing uniquely queer about that, though," Caleb pointed out.

"Not uniquely, I guess, but everything's harder when you're with someone the culture doesn't really approve of you being with. It doesn't always make for strong relationships."

Caleb wondered if now was the time to bring up the possibility of discussing their specific relationship, again, but not with Strangelust arriving any minute – and perhaps that was a conversation for somewhere more private. Or perhaps they should just...wait until after the Grand Final. A lot was up in the air for Buck, until then.

"Are you coming to the semi-final tomorrow?" he asked instead.

"Course. I'm coming to the jury show tonight, too," Buck said, frowning. "I have to cheer you on, right?"

"I mean, you don't have to."

"I'd like to. Unless you don't want me there."

"No!" Caleb shook his head. "That's not it at all, I just know you must have a million other things to do."

"Well, that's the nice thing about Grand Final rehearsal,"

Buck said, leaning back. "There's a trifle more professionalism. The bloody jacket trick is going off without a hitch at last, and Strangelust is in good shape."

"Glad to hear the jacket's not giving you any more grief."

"Shame we couldn't do the whole act," Buck said. "I wanted to have breakaway trousers, too."

"You did not!"

"Did. That was the idea, like how the invisible man was only really invisible when he was fully naked. I mean, you can't flash your bits at Eurovision but a pair of briefs and a fig leaf? Could've maybe swung that. Missed chance, too much trouble," Buck shrugged. "Anyway, why shouldn't I go to the jury show? I have the time, and I want to."

Caleb smiled over the remnants of his breakfast. "I'll be glad to have you there."

Strangelust showed up then, making noise and generally drawing attention; Caleb nodded at Buck and waved him off, watching as he left.

It was a good day, overall. Dress rehearsal went fine, even if everyone had to put up with Patrice being an audible, ongoing diva the entire time. Caleb hoped Patrice wouldn't go to the Grand Final, so that at least Buck wouldn't have to deal with him anymore. Afterward, Caleb got an invite to dinner with the delegation, but nobody seemed surprised when he begged off, needing a little quiet time before that evening. He got a bowl of cacio e pepe for a very early dinner, and when he got back to his room with the food, Buck was asleep in the bed.

More importantly, Buck had actually not messed with his stuff, which was a true relief.

He sat in the little wing chair in the room, legs crossed, and ate his pasta, letting Buck sleep. When Buck's phone went off like an *air raid siren* just as he was finishing his dinner, Buck sat bolt upright, eyes wide, and Caleb nearly dropped his pasta bowl.

"You're here! I'm awake!" Buck announced, hands going to

his hair, finger-combing through it.

"These are both true," Caleb agreed.

"Sorry – set my alarm to definitely wake me up in time to get showered and put on clothes," Buck continued. "I mean. I have clothes," he said, pointing to the shirt he was wearing. "But nicer clothes. Slightly slutty. Because it's Eurovision."

"Why change now?" Caleb asked. Buck blinked at him.

"Was that *shade* from Shades?" he demanded.

"I had known you at least a week before I saw you with a shirt on. You looked like a different person," Caleb told him.

"This is the Shivadh in you. Brutal," Buck announced. "Okay, fuck. Uh." He rolled out of the bed and leaned over Caleb's chair, kissing him. "Gonna run back to mine. See you onstage. Can I come to the dressing room after?"

"Don't see why not, just knock first."

"Mm, and I will also knock after," Buck said, grinning at him, still bent to be on a level with his face.

"Was that innuendo?" Caleb asked, genuinely unsure.

"It was. Unless you have groupies lined up to fawn on you, in which case I can take a ticket and wait my turn."

"You realize that what you just described is a horror story for me," Caleb said.

"Good," Buck told him, turning to head for the door. "I'm gone! Get in the zone, Shades, you have to dominate tonight!"

Caleb hadn't really spoken to anyone except Jerry about what he'd felt, that first time he'd performed *Young Prince* at the National Final. It felt like if he talked about it he'd maybe ruin it. Every time he got on a big stage, in front of a dark room absolutely packed with people, he expected the panic. But each time, with the monitors in, with the sunglasses on, with Lachlan and Ava there to ground him, all he felt was elation. Getting offstage could be difficult, and if he was made to stay onstage (as he had in one of the rehearsals, to check a lighting cue) it was excruciating.

But by now, the performance was the perfect mixture of novel and rote. He knew exactly where to go, what to do, how to sit and stand, how to play, and Ava and Lachlan did too. The subtle differences, the way the audience reacted, the little timbre shifts he was discovering in his own singing – those were always new, but the good kind of new. They kept the routine from being boring, but still existed within it.

"Holy shit, Caleb," Lachlan said, as they came off the stage after their performance that night. It was late; they were nearly last, and Caleb could feel that most of his energy had gone into the performance. "You sang the hell out of it. Save something for the actual semis."

"It felt good," Caleb agreed. "Was it? Extra good? It's tough to tell sometimes."

"My husband says he used to pretend to be in Eurovision when he was a kid," Lachlan said. Caleb, not sure where this was going, kept his shades on and his head down as they went through the post-performance gauntlet, stifling his instinctive reaction to people touching him to take his mic and monitors off. "He loved all the glamor of it. The wilder the performance the better he likes it. But there's something really…intense about this one. It's not fancy, there's just a lot packed into it."

"Not sure that does us any favors, but Caleb doesn't want to win anyway," Ava said, gently stepping in front of someone who was reaching out to mess with Caleb's hair.

"I can do that, thank you," Caleb said to the woman, who glanced at Ava, then nodded at him. "Thanks," he added to Ava.

"I'm here to look pretty and body-check the hair-touchers," Ava told him, laughing. "Let's get out of the monkey suits. Buck's coming back to see you, right?"

"Probably not until after the last – " Caleb began, because he assumed Buck would want to see the whole show. But there was

Buck Haverd, leaning against the door of the Shivadh dressing room, messing around on his phone.

"Hey, hot ticket," Lachlan said, and Buck looked up sharply, blinking. "Some men are just too easy," he added to Caleb.

"Nobody's ever accused me of playing hard to get," Buck said, pocketing his phone. "Nice job out there. Prince," he said, giving Ava a nod. "Queen number one," he added to Lachlan.

"It's so nice to be remembered," Lachlan sighed happily, giving him a gentle push out of the way so they could actually get into the dressing room. "Give me ten minutes to put my face on and then I'm all yours."

"He's joking," Buck said, because Caleb's expression clearly reflected his bewilderment. "Go on, get changed and do whatever."

Caleb nodded, taking him at his word, and slipped into the dressing room after the others. Buck stayed where he was; Caleb could hear, through the door, the occasional beep-boop of some phone game being played.

Lachlan and Ava were shedding their "royal" uniforms, hanging them up so they could be cleaned before the semi-final. Caleb changed out of his suit, into his other, slightly shabbier suit.

"Someday, when you're a famous Eurovision winner and have to perform onstage all the time, they're going to do one of those human-interest piece things," Lachlan said, as he pulled on a t-shirt that read *Askazer-Shivadlakia is for ~~lovers~~ people who like to say difficult words*. "They're going to talk about how your new stage show has eighteen costume changes but nobody can tell because it's the same costume eighteen times."

"And I look amazing in all of them," Caleb replied. "When you find something that works you have to stick with it, Lachlan."

"I'm married, so I understand the theory, but I'd lose my gay card if I didn't tell you that you'd do numbers in booty shorts."

"Would the numbers be enough to cover the therapy after?" Caleb asked.

"You keep doing you, king. And maybe do the boy waiting sadly outside your stage door, before he gets any sadder," Lachlan said, helping Ava into her jacket. He opened the door and put his head out. "Sad boy waiting outside, you can come in now."

"Don't bother," Caleb called. "I'm done, we can go before the crowd lets out."

"I'm not sad," Buck said, confused.

"Lachlan is a spirit of chaos, I don't know why we're friends," Caleb said, as Lachlan blew him a kiss and wandered off with Ava.

"A little chaos is okay," Buck said.

"Speak for yourself," Caleb told him. "Coming back to mine?"

"If it's on offer. You should take a look at your Photogram tag, you're very popular," Buck said. "They're saying if you don't do well in the semis tomorrow it's because the voting is rigged. I say we start a scandal and make sure you don't do well because you were out all night partying with me."

"But then I'd have to go out all night partying with you," Caleb pointed out.

"A fate worse than death," Buck said, laughing. "Fine, let's stay in and party. I'm yours until morning. Been thinking of a song like that, actually," he added, as they headed for the exit. "Something about finally getting all night with someone. I'll play you what I've got later."

Caleb beamed at him, delighted by everything: Buck mostly-placidly following him home, the implicit promise of sex, and the explicit promise of getting to help write a new song afterwards.

CHAPTER ELEVEN

THAT MORNING FELT like the best kind of limbo.

Caleb had nowhere to be until noon, and after that his time wouldn't be his own until he was free of Eurovision completely. Buck had nowhere to be until the evening semi-final, having given Strangelust some time to indulge themselves in Turin. So they both got to sleep in, and when they did wake up, Buck played "my favorite instrument, naked guitar" to share the song he'd thought of. Caleb had gotten up to dress, briefly – to put on his binder and some underwear, at least – but now he was listening lazily from the bed, pretending he didn't have to eventually face the world.

"I can see some ways to tighten the sound of it," he said, when Buck was done. "But you can't do it without sacrificing the meter of the lyrics on the one line where you shouldn't."

"What? Why?" Buck asked.

"Oh, well, it'd be a shame to cut the line, but I don't think you need the key change there, and if you take out the key change…" Caleb hummed what the line would sound like, if altered, although he couldn't quite maintain the low register Buck sometimes wrote in, and his throat balked at one or two notes. "You get the idea."

"I could lift the whole thing earlier," Buck said, trying some alternate chords on the guitar softly. "Can you sustain that whole line at the higher pitch?"

"Who, me? Sure," Caleb said, lying back to stare at the ceiling. "Anyone with decent breath training should be able to as long as it's in their key. But you could breathe on the third beat too, if you wanted." He turned his head to see Buck regarding him.

"Can I ask you a weirdo question?" Buck said.

"About breath training?" Caleb asked.

"Not really, but kind of? More about anatomy."

"Anatomy," Caleb repeated, a little wary now.

"Yeah, but you can tell me to fuck off if you want, I won't mind. 'S just since – well, the Turin pre-party, I've been wondering. About the binder," Buck said. Caleb, who had been expecting pretty much anything but that, frowned. "You had to undo it when you had the panic attack, right?"

"That's why I buy this kind," Caleb said. "They're not the most effective and they cost a lot more to get good ones, but I need the easy release."

Buck nodded. "But does it interfere with your lungs, when you sing?"

"Not really," Caleb said, pushing himself up on one elbow. He pressed his hand to his chest, over his binder; he'd left it a bit loose but it was still fastened, and he demonstrated how to inhale and exhale freely, breathing from the belly. "I mean, probably a little, but if so, I don't notice the difference. I'm not singing opera – especially when I'm writing my own songs. And I haven't got much to bind to begin with," he added, a little amused. "Fortunate that way. If I had a bigger chest, it would maybe cause problems."

"So, and this is the real fuck-off-Buck bit, why not just…" Buck made a chopping motion, clicking his tongue in a soft *pop*. "They say Askazer-Shivadlakia has great gender affirmation surgeons."

Caleb laughed. "Buck." He clicked his tongue in imitation of the popping noise Buck had made, rolling his eyes. "Really?"

"I don't know the medical terms," Buck said.

"I suppose most people don't. Just a clue for future, maybe google that first," Caleb said gently. "Honestly, I don't know, it hasn't seemed especially necessary. I don't mind my body, in and of itself, I just don't – always like how it makes me look. For me at least, easy fix, between the binder and the T. I might get some stuff done, someday. But it's a big step, takes a lot of recovery time, and it's really permanent."

"Guess it's a little more drastic than a tatt."

"A lot of people don't like binding, and it can be hard on the body, but I sort of enjoy it. It's like having a weighted blanket – the pressure can be familiar, reassuring. Grounding."

"Huh." Buck considered this. "Like a corset."

"Not…quite. In terms of sensation, maybe. Never worn one, couldn't tell you."

"I did for a concert once. Didn't care for it, but it wasn't very well-made. Can I ask…" Buck pressed his lips together briefly.

"Hey. I know you're in good faith. And even if you were asking…bad questions, I'm prepared to give you a little slack. But you haven't," Caleb said.

"I haven't?"

"No," Caleb replied. "I think you really don't care about it unless it involves the music. And…when people ask about the music, usually they want to use your music against you. Try to convince you not to be who you are because *you won't be able to make music anymore*."

"That's…" Buck frowned. "That's monstrous. You can't just threaten someone with not having music anymore."

"I know. They didn't manage it, anyway; I'm too stubborn, and I knew it was a lie. And that's obviously not why you want to know, so go on, ask. You have my permission," Caleb said, waving his hand grandly.

"It is about the music. Like, so…I'm guessing you weren't always a tenor."

"Only in my heart," Caleb said, smiling. Buck smiled tentatively back. "Yeah, that's the T. Took me a while to adjust. But pretty much the same as you probably had during puberty."

"Guess it's similar," Buck said.

"Besides, I was eighteen when I started T, my body'd been

fucking with me for years already. And look at me now," he finished. "Singing at Eurovision as a tenor."

Buck nodded, but Caleb wasn't sure he'd heard half of what he said. He seemed to be considering something, deeply. Caleb let him be silent.

"Am I the first trans person you've been with?" he asked, after a while.

"No. I have been with…a lot of people in a lot of different shapes," Buck said. "But most of them were one-night stands, and I never thought about the music part of it before. I shouldn't have asked, probably."

"I'd rather you ask than wonder," Caleb said. "The problem is that most people who ask aren't wondering. They're just invading your privacy, trying to gauge how human you are by their yardstick. You can't pay them any mind, or at least I try not to. Whatever I do, I do because it's worth it, to be myself. I change for me, exactly as I please, and not for or because of anyone else."

Buck blinked at him, digesting this.

"Can I say I like your body?" he asked, voice low.

Caleb laughed. "Sure can, bud. As long as you don't try to tell me what to do with it. Beyond the obvious," he added. "Here, c'mere."

He held out his hand, inviting Buck back to the bed; Buck set the guitar aside and joined him, sprawling out on his stomach, head turned to regard Caleb's face.

"Every part of my life's been a balancing act," Buck said, and Caleb thought of Jerry, of his remarks about Buck's high-wire walking. "And when you're struggling – I mean life's not perfect now, but it's pretty good. When you're really struggling, trying to make gigs and earn enough to keep fed, you start to think everything in life is a negotiation. There's always a trade-off. Which is exhausting," he said. "And you're so mired in it you think, well, nobody has it as bad as me, nobody could possibly understand. And then you meet someone and you realize you've been negotiating for pocket change while they've been making like, nuclear treaties."

Caleb laughed. "You think I have a nuclear treaty with my own body, Buck? It's not like that."

"No, I mean, I'm not trying to pity you. I'm saying...you get it, you get that there's always a price to be paid. And I think maybe...a lot more people get it than I thought." Buck shrugged, a wriggle of shoulders, chin pressed into the blankets. "But still I don't know if just anyone would get it like you do."

"Well, I'm an extremely perceptive and handsome man," Caleb said, and Buck laughed. "Very good at pattern recognition and I look great with a ukulele. I've been told I'm quite the catch."

"You are," Buck said. "I know you're joking a little, but it's true. And," he added, rolling over, half-on-top of Caleb awkwardly, while Caleb laughed, "After Eurovision, I'm gonna cut that album and your name'll be all over it."

Caleb shoved, rolling them both into a more comfortable position, and curled around Buck with a satisfied sigh.

"What do you suppose everyone else is doing today?" he asked. Buck kissed him and grinned.

"Couldn't begin to care," he said. "Let's make you late for rehearsal."

"Buck, no!" Caleb cried, but Buck was already getting handsy, so he went with it. But he made sure that he could still see the clock, just in case.

That Thursday in Turin was sunny and pleasant, if rather crowded because of the semi-finals. It reminded Michaelis of Fons-Askaz at the height of tourist season, bustling but cheerful, and he'd always been willing to walk a little slower behind strolling visitors, wait a little longer at a cafe, to know that the city – which he thought of as *his* city – was full of people enjoying themselves.

The students from the Maritime Academy were less patient, but well-behaved kids on the whole. He'd taken on minding them so that Jes could get work done; they were nearly adults in any case, and didn't need hand-holding. Besides, he found that he liked Noah's friends and was happy to see Noah thriving. He knew that Noah was being considered for officer's pips on the *Dychev* next year, although only because Jes had accidentally let it slip, but it was easy to see why. The boy was a natural leader when given the chance, and in Turin the others had taken to looking to him for guidance – what they should do next, where they should eat, whether they should buy this or that souvenir trinket.

At the moment, all of them were visibly proud and feeling very grown-up, sitting at their own table in the trattoria for lunch, pretending to be adults while Michaelis and Jes kept a discreet eye on them from a few tables away. The trip had been budgeted by the Palace, so Noah had Michaelis's government credit card, and seemed especially pleased to have gotten through paying for lunch without incident. He carefully folded the receipt into his wallet, then got up when the others did, but came over to their table instead of following the rest of the students out to the street.

"Here's your card back. Thanks for letting me use it," Noah said, dropping into one of the empty chairs at their table, offering Michaelis his card.

"Have a good lunch with your friends?" Jes asked. "Where are they all off to without you?"

"Eurovision Village. I've been a bunch of times already, so I said I'd pass," Noah said. "I'll go back to the pensione or something. Maybe practice my Italian, talking to strangers," he added with a grin.

"Like you don't talk to strangers all the time in English?" Jes asked, eyebrow lifting.

"I can get extra credit if I do a whole podcast in Italian," Noah said. "Immersion is supposed to be the best way to learn. Why, what're you up to?"

"The same, mostly," Jes said. "Interviews for the Eurovision episode, some for the episode about Turin as the motor city."

"What about you?" Noah asked Michaelis.

"No particular plans. Might take a stroll. Terrible as it is to contemplate, I might also take a nap before this evening's revelry. Must be fresh for cheering on Caleb." Michaelis regarded him, then glanced at Jes, who made a little motion with one hand. "Wouldn't mind company, if you want to come for a walk. I've been wanting to speak to you, but it's not urgent."

"Me?" Noah asked, glancing between them. "Am I in trouble?"

"Why, done something you should be in trouble for?" Jes asked.

"No, you're not in trouble," Michaelis said. "Nothing upsetting. It can wait, if you'd rather not."

"Now you've got me curious," Noah said. "Boss?"

"Go on. See you this evening if not before," Jes said, waving them off. Michaelis kissed their cheek, rising, and Noah trailed him out of the trattoria, still looking pensive and curious.

"Did you ever get those postcards you were going to buy, for everyone who couldn't come along?" Michaelis asked, as they stepped onto the street.

"Yeah, did that yesterday," Noah said. "That's not what you wanted to talk about, is it?"

"No, not directly. Though I was thinking we're going to have to send you somewhere more interesting than Turin before long," Michaelis said, guiding them down a side-street, away from the busiest traffic.

"Send me?" Noah asked.

"Well, perhaps take you. But you'll be doing your gap year soon, and I doubt you want us along for that," Michaelis said. "You should consider where you'd like to go. You could always just bounce around Europe, but I think a lot of young people these days go to Japan. I'd favor Aotearoa-New Zealand myself."

"I…wasn't aware I was doing a gap year," Noah said slowly.

"You don't have to, of course. I just assumed," Michaelis said. "Gregory worked his way across Europe and down into the Holy Land, came back very tan and proud of himself."

"I don't know if Boss and I have the money for that."

"Ah," Michaelis said. "That brings us to the point of the matter, actually."

Noah looked at him, alarmed. "It does?"

"You and Jes are important to me, and you both put up with a lot of nonsense from the press because of your association with the royal family. All of this," Michaelis waved his hand, indicating Eurovision, Caleb's song, the publicity surrounding it all, "wouldn't be happening to you otherwise."

"But I like 'all this'," Noah said. "How many kids my age get to go to Eurovision?"

"Not many. But the fact remains that outside of Eurovision, you are paying most of the penalties and reaping very few of the rewards," Michaelis said. "And if you wanted, there are ways that could change."

"Like what?"

"You could be officially acknowledged by the Palace," Michaelis said. "The title of prince isn't a meaningless one, not for Shivadh. It has a very specific legal standing. It means you have to put up with a lot, and in return you are awarded certain perks and protections."

"Yeah, we had that in civics class. Like Gregory would still be a prince if someone else became king instead of him," Noah said. "Because he grew up in the public, because you were king. But I didn't, I just got here."

"True – and I'm not the sitting king, but I am still a former king, and I still work for the Palace. And, unavoidably, so do you. This would…announce that you have a fixed place in the royal household. Medieval as that sounds."

"This isn't some weird way of asking my permission to marry

Boss, is it?" Noah asked. Michaelis laughed.

"No. If I want to marry Jes, I'll ask them, not you," he said. "And that's not really a concern for either one of us. Jes can look after themself. I know you can too, but you're young to have to."

"But what does that mean like…for you, or for Gregory?" Noah asked. "Would he be cool with it?"

"For me, you would be acknowledged as a son – not quite an adoption, but similar, in terms of legal duties you'd perform as the son of a king. Nothing between us would change unless you wanted it to. I'm not attempting to encroach on Jes's parenting. As for Gregory – well, first, we're adults, and our feelings are not something for you to worry about. But I've spoken to Gregory, and he wouldn't mind; I think he'd rather like to have a brother. He likes you, you know. He might ask if he can start giving you work to do," Michaelis said. "It's what it means for you that matters – both what you'd gain and what you might not wish to gain. You have a parent, you might not want another. You might not want royal responsibility beyond what you have now. But it would mean the Palace could act in your interests, protect you from the media, provide you with support. And it comes with things like funding for a gap year."

"It'd be dumb to take it all on just for gap year money," Noah said with a grin.

"Yes, that's not bait," Michaelis said. "Just an example. I believe there's also a ceremonial knife. There usually is."

"Oh, well, now I'm sold," Noah quipped. "Seriously, though, are you sure?"

"Me? Yes. But it's ultimately up to you, and it's only an idea. There's no need to rush to a decision," Michaelis said. "I wanted you to know the offer was there."

"You said you're not trying to be a parent," Noah said. "But you do that a lot. Parenting, I mean."

"Does that bother you?"

"No. I like it."

"Good."

"But..." Noah seemed to be working out how to say something. "You said I'd be your son but nothing else would change. What if – I mean, if I wasn't just legally a prince, if you weren't *worried* about anything changing...?"

Michaelis studied him, slowing his pace further until they came to a stop in the shade of an awning.

"That's Jes's call as much as yours," he said. "If you want more from me as a parent – and I confess I don't really know what that would look like – then we'd need to speak about it, all three of us. But there's very little I wouldn't do for you, in the way I would for Gregory and his cousins, or for Theophile. If there's something specific you want, you only have to ask, regardless of whether you become a prince. Nothing is conditional on that."

Noah nodded, clearly deep in thought.

"What would you like to change?" Michaelis asked quietly.

Noah shrugged. "Don't even know. Maybe just...calling you my stepdad, that kind of thing. I'll have to think about being a prince, but it doesn't sound awful. Prince Noah Deimos. That's a name like out of a scifi novel," Noah said. "Would Gregory really give me jobs to do for the Palace?"

"If you tell him you're open to it," Michaelis said. "We're already representing the royal family here. He might send you to, say, the birthday parties of other countries' young royals, or ask you to serve on various youth councils. It's tedious work for the most part, but not without its rewards. And in its way, something of a mitzvah. Public service."

"Could I be a spy?" Noah asked, holding his hands up and pressing them together like he was James Bond on a movie poster, holding a gun.

"Not in peacetime," Michaelis said, smiling. "Though he did send Alanna and Gerald as spies to Galia. There's bound to be some sort of intrigue you could cause."

"I think I get fired from being a prince if I actively try to start shit," Noah said.

"Not so," Michaelis shook his head. "Once a prince, always a prince, Noah. When you become part of the family, it's not a hired position. You can't lose your place."

"Huh," Noah said. Michaelis looked at him, eyebrows raised. "Are you going to make caez official too, for Jes?"

"Caez doesn't exist, not as a legal position. I made it up for them."

"Really?"

"Well, I stole and corrupted some Latin. I suppose I could ask Gregory to add it to the royal protocols. He has that authority, like he had to make Theophile a duke. I don't know if that's what Jes wants, to be honest, but it wouldn't be a harm to ask," he said thoughtfully. "Might annoy the scholars of royal etiquette and I do enjoy that. How does one address a caez?"

"Carefully," Noah said. Michaelis ruffled his hair.

"Think it over. Talk to Gregory, if you want. He'd tell you what it's like to be a prince."

"So could you!"

"I could tell you what it's like to be a prince in 1975," Michaelis said. "Not as helpful. Life was a lot simpler, and simultaneously much more complicated, before Photogram."

"Tell that to everyone who's bitter I'm an influencer and they aren't."

"Don't let it go to your head. Gregory says being an influencer's easy when you have access to a palace."

Noah cracked up laughing. "He's not wrong!"

"He rarely is," Michaelis agreed.

"It would be weird to have a brother that much older."

"I always found it comforting. My brother Eitan was a bit older than Gregory is now, when I was your age. I knew if I couldn't tell our father something, I could go to Eitan with it. He'd know what to do and he wouldn't snitch."

"Kinda like Uncle Lachlan. Or Jerry."

"Why, what've you been telling Gerald?" Michaelis asked, raising his eyebrows. "No – don't tell me. That's the point, and in any case he needs the practice for if he has children of his own."

"What's the opposite of a helicopter parent?" Noah asked, as they began looping slowly back towards the pensione.

"I think they're calling it free-range parenting these days. But you know, your upbringing – in New York as well as Askazer-Shivadlakia – that's how Shivadh think the thing really should ideally be done. Lots of different people, everyone looking out for the children in their own way, no one hovering too closely. So you can make your own mistakes within reason, and if you can't tell Boss something, you can go to Lachlan, or Gerald or Gregory, or your great-aunt Carla. Or me."

"That's why you made that joke about adopting Buck and Caleb, isn't it?" Noah asked. "Caleb's got nobody. Buck might as well have."

"That's not true – they both have friends, and family they found in Askazer-Shivadlakia. Caleb perhaps a little more so, but he's been home longer. Now they simply also have the Palace, much as you do. Though I don't think I'd make Buck Haverd a prince. Lord knows what mischief he'd get into, and unlike you, he'd do it on purpose."

"I haven't caused a single building collapse in almost a year," Noah pointed out.

"Only because you destroyed more buildings in your first six months here than I did during the first twenty years of my reign," Michaelis told him. "Hang on, there's a shop around here…ah," he added in satisfaction, peering down another side-street and indicating a little storefront. "They've been selling bootleg Eurovision shirts. They've got one with the phonetic spelling of Askazer-Shivadlakia on it, which I want, and I promised Theophile I'd get him one as well."

"Whoa, look at the shirts with Buck's hairdo on them!" Noah said, pushing hastily into the little shop, which was crammed floor-to-ceiling with shirts and smelled like cotton dust and silkscreen paint. It took roughly thirty seconds for Noah to find the best shirt in the shop – a stylized drawing of Caleb, in his performance outfit and shades, captioned *Too cool for school.*

"Caleb's pretty relieved he's out after tonight," Noah said, making a messy pile of shirts on top of a slightly neater pile of shirts, while Michaelis signaled to the shop owner and asked for two of the Askazer-Shivadlakia shirts. "I bet these sell out anyway, they're awesome."

"Put them over here, I'll pay for them," Michaelis said, gesturing at the shirts Noah was piling up. "Sell a few at a profit back home, as I think you're planning, and pay me back," he added. Noah looked like he'd been caught red-handed. "You'll get a good price for them on the national app's sales page."

"I was just gonna sell them at school," Noah said. "We could have Mr. Canto Shirt Day."

"Ah, yes, that instinct for chaos? That's the Shivadh in you," Michaelis replied. "In any case, Caleb seems oddly certain he won't make it past the semi-finals. I suppose it's a rational belief; his performance isn't as dynamic as the others, but one simply never knows. Yes, all of these," he added to the shopkeeper, who rubbed his hands and began ringing up the shirts.

"I'm glad the Maritime Academy students didn't get picked this year," Noah said. "It seems like it must be really stressful. Better to have a good time."

"Well, let's hope Caleb agrees," Michaelis said.

There was a moment, just a bare second, during the end of the semi-final concert on Thursday night, when Caleb felt a slight twinge of disappointment. He'd given his last performance and thought he'd done a serviceable job; he was glad it was over, certainly, but also – he had loved performing, in a way that had never happened to him before. And here was where it ended, at least for now. If he wanted to play like this again, it would have to be something he chose, and that would be monumentally different.

The Shivadh green room sofas were full of people – Michaelis and Jes, Noah and the Maritime Academy students, the Duke of Shivadlakia and the Lady Alanna, Davidson from the RSBA; Caleb, Lachlan, and Ava, all three still in their performance outfits. Everyone seemed to be enjoying the show, though some were more visibly tired than others, and he could tell some were hoping they'd hurry through announcing the artists going on to the Grand Final, so they could go home. Buck, over in the artist VIP seats, was wearing a shirt for the occasion – Shivadh blue, with the orange star on it, which he must have bought when he was still in Fons-Askaz.

"The ten finalists from tonight will proceed, with the ten finalists from the first semi-final, to the Grand Final," one of the hosts, Alessandro, was saying. Caleb, sandwiched between Noah and Ava, tapped the strings of the ukulele on his lap and felt his chest ease. He let the noise wash over him, becoming one big white roar of sound he didn't have to worry about.

The first semi-finalist to advance...our second advancing semi-finalist...the third country to join the Grand Final...the fourth...

Finland. Serbia. Australia. Estonia. Romania. Poland. Czechia. Sweden (Buck would be pleased). Tolot (Buck would be livid; Caleb was certainly irritated).

"And our last performer to proceed to the Eurovision Grand Final is...Askazer-Shivadlakia!" Mika announced. He pronounced it just slightly wrong – it sounded like he said *Skazzer-Shivadokia*, one of the more common misreadings.

Annoyed, Caleb thought, *It's said exactly how it's spelled, it's really just not that hard*, and then the words caught up with him – at the same moment they hit everyone else.

Jerry jerked upright, turning to Caleb with wide, startled eyes.

Ava, sitting next to Davidson, grabbed his arm in surprise, and he turned to Caleb as well. Noah went straight to his feet, jumping up and down with the other students – and with Lachlan and Jes, in amongst them. Alanna was clutching Michaelis's sleeve. Michaelis himself looked faintly amused, not even surprised. He turned to Caleb, even as Jerry was yelling something in Caleb's ear that he couldn't hear over the roaring, and mouthed, *Tough break.*

Suddenly there were a lot more people there than there should have been – Strangelust had gone right over the barrier in front of the artist seating, breaking into the green room area, and in their rush to the Shivadh couches they'd dragged Sweden, Serbia, and Finland along with them.

In the melee, Buck found Caleb and pulled him in by the arm; Caleb clung tightly to his wrist, letting Buck buffer him from the two dozen other people suddenly celebrating a win with the littlest country that had the hard-to-say name.

"You're going to the Grand Final!" Buck shouted in his ear.

"I know! I'm completely fucked!" Caleb shouted back.

Getting out of the concert hall was a mission in itself. Everyone wanted to congratulate Caleb, and the internet had lit up: Askazer-Shivadlakia's first-ever entry, a weird sunglasses-wearing guitarist who didn't even dance, just sat on the stage and played his song, was going to the Grand Final. At least, people said, everyone else seemed really happy for them. The debates on social media about who should have won and who did win went long into the night.

"Listen," Buck said, as they tried to push through the crowd. "I'll run interference. You go home. Meet you there, yeah?"

"Are you sure? It's already late – "

"You want me there?"

"Yes," Caleb answered, without even thinking about it.

"Then I'm sure. Don't stop anywhere, I'll bring stuff."

"You'll what – " Caleb began, but just then Jerry cut between them and, with a glance at Buck, began herding Caleb away. They must have communicated somehow; Buck stayed where he was, drawing attention, and the delegation made its escape.

He had a noisy, excited, and overtired escort almost all the way to his door; after all, the entire delegation was staying in the same pensione. He was trying to figure out how to untangle himself from the celebration in the lobby, since politeness wasn't his forte and rudeness frankly wasn't working, when someone yelled, *Oi!* and the noise dimmed considerably.

Buck was standing in the entryway, incongruously holding a greasy-looking paper bag.

"Don't you all have a Grand Final to rest up for?" he asked, and everyone cheered. "No, shut up! Fuck, you Shivadh are noisy. Go, go on, shoo," he said, pushing his way through the lobby, sending people off with gentle shoves. He reached Caleb and placed the bag in his hands. It was warm.

"Brought dinner," he said. "I'll fuck off if you want some peace, because LORD KNOWS NOBODY ELSE WILL," he added, and people began to disperse a little faster. "Sorry, some of this is probably my fault," he added, more quietly. "When Mika said Askazer-Shivadlakia *and* said it wrong, I lost my shit a little."

"I got so mad he said it wrong I didn't even realize what he'd said!" Caleb said, laughing.

"Right? Like, practice the words a few times," Buck said, as Caleb led the way towards his room. "Stay or fuck off?"

"Stay, please," Caleb said, unlocking his door.

"Good, because half the food in there is mine," Buck replied. "The cacio e pepe is for you. Got two beers but I'll drink 'em both if you don't want one. You like cacio e pepe, right? You can have the truffle pasta if you want."

"Cacio e pepe is fine," Caleb said. "Noted my taste for cheesy pasta, have you?"

"I think you must be an expert in it," Buck said, following him inside and offering him the top carton from the bag.

"Thank you, I'm starving," he said, dropping onto the bed, propping the carton of pasta on his crossed legs. Everywhere was still a bit rumpled from that morning, but Buck had done some of that, so who cared? Buck rummaged in the bag and pulled out a beer as he stepped out of his shoes, then came to the bed and settled next to Caleb, turning to rest his forehead on Caleb's shoulder. There was a space of quiet, of breathing.

"I can't believe Patrice made it through," Buck said at last, and Caleb laughed again.

"I guess I'm glad I did, if Patrice did," Caleb said. And then everything felt...normal again. Buck launched into a monologue dissecting the performances while Caleb ate, and drew him into it eventually as a discussion. It felt almost unreal, cut off from the madness of the last hour or so. Outside didn't matter; here it was just the two of them, eating pasta and talking over their day, even if their day had been *weird*.

And then, at a moment when the food was gone and the world was dark and quiet, Buck took the empty carton out of Caleb's hands, put it with his own to one side, and came back to settle into his lap, with a daredevil grin and light in his green eyes.

"I had a question about your suggestion that perhaps I shouldn't party the night before a show," he said, wrists resting on Caleb's shoulders. Caleb tucked his hands up under Buck's shirt, fingertips resting on warm skin. "Does sex with a hot rock star count as partying?"

"We should find out," Caleb said. "You know any hot rock stars?"

Buck laughed and inched forward, craning his neck down a little for a kiss. "I'll introduce you," he said solemnly. "How about tonight we stay here, and later you and I do glorious battle for all of Europe as a prize?"

"And Australia," Caleb pointed out.

"Yes, my brilliant one, and Australia," Buck agreed. "Sound good?"

"Are you sure you can stay?"

Buck shook his head, face falling a little. "I can't. Not like last night, not until morning – I don't want to be seen sneaking around, and there'll be stuff I have to do before the Grand Final. You know for us it starts at like nine in the morning."

"Are we sneaking around? People seem pretty...aware of us."

"To an extent. What's out there now is just rumor. Might be best if it stayed rumor, at least until Eurovision is over. Unless you want to *really* be in the public eye."

"Point," Caleb said, nodding. "But you don't have to go yet?"

"No. I can stay a while," Buck said, leaning in.

"Good. Then stay."

In another part of the hotel, Alanna had finally managed to corral Jerry out of the lobby and into their shared room; once she was sure he would both sit and stay, she took a quick shower, happy to wash off her makeup and rinse away a whole evening of Being An Official Audience Member.

By the time she emerged, swaddled in pajamas, Jerry was lying on the bed, phone resting on his forehead, bluetooth headphones in. He pointed to the phone and mouthed, *Palace*, then said, "I mean, I don't know, how many sheep does one country need?"

She was becoming accustomed to these calls; it turned out that when he didn't have the party life to distract him, Jerry did not do terribly well when he was separated from home. Half the family was here, of course, but the other half wasn't, and she could tell Jerry missed Gregory and Eddie. And, eternally, Simon's cooking.

Still, it was past midnight, and now they were talking about sheep? She made a questioning gesture, which he acknowledged.

"Someone's done math on that?" Jerry asked. "Hang on, I'm putting you on speaker. Al, you're not going to believe this."

He flipped the phone over so he could see the screen, then tapped a few times; he set it back on his forehead, face up, and popped the headphones out of his ears.

"Al found the guy who did the math for me," Gregory said, as soon as he was on speaker.

"Oh, is this the sheep per capita whitepaper you requested? Yes, I did organize that," Alanna said.

"Greg, I love you, but what is it you actually do? Seems like Al's the one doing all the running around in this administration," Jerry said.

"I have very important thoughts," Gregory said.

"I don't even have that, I'm purely decorative," Eddie added. "Hey, Al."

"Hi, cuties," Alanna called. "Did Jerry wake you?"

"No, we were watching the concert, and now we're having champagne to celebrate," Gregory said.

"By champagne, he means cheap Shivadh beer and a midnight snack. You all have fun?" Eddie added.

"Yes, I think so. Caleb looked like he might have a heart attack, but Buck's got him calmed down, I believe," Alanna said.

"Calmed down is a euphemism for what Buck's got him doing," Jerry added.

"Really?" Gregory asked, sounding intrigued. "He's all right, Haverd, isn't he? Dad likes him."

"He's fine, Greg, but also that's pure speculation," Alanna said.

"I think it's pretty well supported," Jerry protested. Alanna picked up her own phone and snapped a picture of him, still in his concert-going attire, phone on his forehead.

"This is the man you're trusting to feed you intel," she said, dropping the photo into group chat. Eddie cackled.

"Anyway, we'll be in Turin another day or three," Jerry said, sticking his tongue out at her as he sat up, catching his phone deftly. "I should maybe ask Palace comms to prepare a press release, just in case Caleb wins."

"I'll handle it," Eddie said. "If he does, what do we do about next year?"

"Either we shuffle the budget to build a venue big enough to hold the Grand Final, or we say we can't and pass it back," Gregory said.

"I can take a look at the budget if you want," Jerry said, and then blinked. "Gregory, did those words just come out of my mouth?"

Gregory laughed. "I love you, Jerry. Al, put him to bed before he panics."

"Oh, suddenly it's my job?" Alanna asked.

"You're wearing the engagement ring," Gregory said. "I'm over here being a grown-up, ruling the country, while you two are gallivanting around Eurovision with a couple of twentysomething musicians."

"I am *super grown-up*," Jerry announced. "I just said I'd look at a budget!"

"You're both my favorites. Now go sleep," Gregory said. "King's command. Have fun tomorrow. Eddie and I'll be watching."

"Night, Greg," they chorused, and Jerry hung up the phone.

"Do Buck and Caleb make you feel old?" he asked Alanna.

She smiled and bent down to kiss him. "What's making you feel old is that you're now a responsible adult," she said. "Keep it up, I like an older man."

"Hm. When I go gray before forty I'll remind you that you said that," he said. "Right, okay. Let's get some sleep."

CHAPTER TWELVE

CALEB WOKE IN the darkness to rustling, and movement in the bed; he turned his head to find Buck, rolling onto his side, kicking the blankets off himself.

"What time is it?" he asked in a hushed voice.

"Little before three," Buck said, turning to face him. "Got about half an hour before I have to find my trousers and go home, I think."

"Sorry you can't stay," Caleb said.

"Me too. Feeling ready for the Grand Final?"

"I'm going to have to keep reminding myself there's really no stakes," Caleb said. "I'm not meant to win, and I don't care if I don't. What about you? You're the one under all the pressure."

"Yes and no," Buck said. "It's not like anyone expects the UK to win. Our record's abysmal."

"But you want to win."

"Of course I do. I want to win Eurovision and sell a billion albums and be famous and do weird music videos," Buck said with a smile. "Eurovision is a big bet for me. But I never put all my money on one horse."

"Hm. If you don't win, what then? The album?"

"Yep," Buck replied. "I'm going to ask Jes about recording it at Reverb. Their mixing is great and it's like. Impressive. Being produced by Reverb. Because it's all intellectual and that."

"So the month did you some good," Caleb said, grinning.

Buck nosed in and kissed him.

"You did me some good," he said. "The month was a bonus.

Fons-Askaz is fine, I like it, but it's not a bustling center of artistic inspiration."

"You need those bright lights."

"On occasion, anyway," Buck agreed. "But they do get blinding after a while."

Caleb raised his hand to press his thumb to Buck's chin, rubbing his lower lip. Buck lay still, watching him.

"I have a question," Caleb said at last. "You don't have to answer it. But I need to ask it before the Grand Final."

"Fire away," Buck said, and Caleb pressed his thumb in quickly, denting Buck's lip, then drew his hand back.

"Why did you really come to Askazer-Shivadlakia?" Caleb asked.

"I told you. I needed time and quiet."

"Maybe, but it wasn't just that. You still posted on Photogram, you didn't cover your tracks. People could have found you if they wanted. And I don't think it was for me," he added lightly.

Buck's jaw tightened a little. "It wasn't *for* you," he said. "You were a factor."

"I was?"

"Yeah, because like…" Buck considered things. Eventually he rolled onto his back, stretching his arms up over his head, staring upwards. "I mean, it's not the best reason. But remember when I was a dickhead to you and you just mocked me by being yourself?"

"Difficult to forget, yes," Caleb replied.

"Someone else at the sound check heard me telling someone about — well, some prick from some unpronounceable country who pulled that shit on me," Buck said. Caleb smiled. "Sorry. Anyway, the guy who overheard me said it sounded like I'd just been assaulted by the Shivadh sense of humor. He said it's not mean, it's just surreal. He said it was like…someone knows when you're behaving badly and they aren't even going to get mad, they'll just laugh at you."

"And that was an *attraction?*" Caleb asked.

"Sort of."

"I didn't think you were an actual masochist."

Buck laughed. "I'm not. But I thought about what set me off so badly, why it was just so irritating when you put those glasses on and made fun of me. It made me really stop and consider," he said. "And it made me wonder. Maybe I could do with being laughed at. I didn't like yelling at you, I didn't like myself when I was doing it, and there were a lot of moments like that, this last year. Times when I didn't like what I was doing as I was doing it. I thought, maybe if I was somewhere nobody took my shit for a while, it might snap me out of it."

Caleb considered the past month. "Did it work as planned?"

"No. Absolutely not. It was much more horrible and effective than I expected," Buck said. "Not only did none of you take the angry shouty shit, none of you took the terrified insecure artist shit either."

"How do you mean?"

"Fuck, I don't know how to say it…I started playing gigs at fifteen. Cut my first album at nineteen, next one at twenty-three. But I've never just been a normal adult. You're expected to act like an adult but you're also treated like an adult, right?"

"Yes, that's…what being grown-up means," Caleb said, perplexed.

"That's never happened to me. I get either-or. I get treated like the boss because I call the shots, but I don't get expected to behave well. Or I'm expected to be mature and well-behaved but I don't get to make any decisions, someone else at the label calls the shots. In Fons-Askaz, nobody gave a shit, even people who knew who I was. And like. You expected me to be a whole person. Everyone I met expected it. That never happens to me."

"That's a true shame, Buck, because you're very good at being a whole person," Caleb said.

"I am now, maybe," Buck said. "Can't take full credit. Got myself to Fons-Askaz, everyone else did the rest."

"No, I don't think that's true. We don't just become better because we're told to. We have to put the work in." Caleb smiled reassuringly at him. "I'm glad you came, whatever your reasons were. I hope you come back, though I know that's a complicated proposition."

"You believe I want to, right? Come back, I mean."

"Yes, I do have some faith in you," Caleb told him.

"Why?"

"Why do I have faith in you? You've given me no reason not to. I've seen you act with a good heart."

"I mean, thanks, but I wasn't fishing for compliments," Buck said. "Like, why...I guess, why would you be patient with someone who was gone? Why would you be with someone who isn't there? You're not...you don't get their company, and it's not like you really know what they're up to. There's not a lot on offer, it seems like."

"You don't think you're worth it?" Caleb asked.

"Do you? You've known me six weeks."

"Maybe I'm a generous man, but if I'm not positive you're worth it now, I'm close enough that I'm willing to find out," Caleb said. He studied Buck's profile, sighing. "And if you don't want to have the relationship talk we haven't found the right time for, now's the point when you may want to change the subject."

"It's not that I don't want to have it," Buck said. He turned his head a little. "We should – whatever this is, we should at least make sure we're off the same page about it."

"Did you mean *on* the same page, or was that a fun riff?" Caleb asked.

"Riff. How'd it land?"

"Middling," Caleb said, grinning. "Look, neither of us brought it up. It makes me nervous too. I'm just saying, if we want to continue to not bring it up for a while, we should talk about something innocent and harmless, like sex, or Eurovision National Final scoring practices."

"I didn't know if I wanted more," Buck said.

"Okay, guess we're talking about it," Caleb said.

"Not because I didn't like you or anything, really wasn't about you at all. I just…I've been in business for myself since I was a kid, and I'm used to knowing that anyone I depended on could pull out pretty easily, because they often do. To the point I stopped thinking I could depend on anyone. I am not a truster."

"I remember. You've said a couple of times, someone in our line of work has to depend on themselves."

"What do you think?"

"I think it's a terribly sad way to see it, but it comes from experience, so I can't condemn you for feeling that way," Caleb said. "I like to think I don't do that, though. Flake on people, I mean."

"You don't. And that's a little terrifying."

"Well," Caleb said. "I don't like hearing that."

"I want to – trust you. And I want you to trust me. But I'm not like you. The things I'm trustworthy about are all business. I show up on time and I do the work and I pay people when I say I will. The rest…I drink a little too much and I play music a little too loud and I'm out until morning, and that isn't for you. It shouldn't be, you should have better. I'm not here to decide that for you, I'm ready to grab this in two hands, but it's hard, Caleb."

"I'm not asking you to change," Caleb said. "I find change very unsettling, and I like you the way you are."

"Maybe now. But no matter what happens tonight, I'm not going to be in Fons-Askaz much longer if I go back at all. There's business in London, I have to do industry stuff – even if I'm back to record the album, eventually I'll go out on tour again. What are you going to do, drop your students and come with me?"

Caleb laughed. "No. I have a job, and a life that I love, and also I want you to imagine how well I would deal with travel on the level of a concert tour."

"Relationships like that don't work though, do they? What happens when I do something stupid and sleep with someone in a club or something?"

"Are you planning on it?"

"No," Buck said.

"Then don't do it. It's not a hurricane, Buck, you control who you have sex with," Caleb replied.

"I don't usually make that kind of good decision," Buck said. "I can't promise I'll get better at that just because I really want to be."

Caleb heaved another sigh and pushed himself up onto one elbow. Buck watched him, a little wary. He felt, and he was pretty sure he had the observational data to back it up, that Buck wasn't actually the kind of guy to sleep around. He was giving every signal of being the kind of guy who, once he found the right person, was inclined to tell groupies how great his boyfriend was, drunk in a bar at two in the morning.

"Answer something for me," Caleb said. "When you have sex, when you go out on the pull, what's the goal?"

"Uh," Buck said. "If you don't know, we're both in trouble, Shades."

"Obviously," Caleb rolled his eyes. "But what I mean is, are you having sex because you like sex and want to have some, or are you doing it because you want a connection with someone, and you don't see any other way of getting it?"

Buck opened his mouth, then closed it again. He was quiet for a long time.

"That's fucked up of you to ask," he said finally.

"Is it? Why?"

"I don't know, it just is."

Caleb tilted his head. "I think it's maybe because you don't want to think about it or answer. Which is kind of an answer anyway. It's not like you haven't said flings are simpler. And they are, but. I don't think they're ever going to give you what you want."

"And you're an expert in what I want?"

"I'm very focused on it, actually, yes," Caleb said. "Because I'm trying to figure out if I'm it."

If it were anyone else in this situation, anyone else lying in bed with him, he might have tacked an affectionate *dumbass* onto the end – to imply that it was obvious that he cared about Buck, that Buck should find it self-evident. But Buck was touchy about that kind of thing, and it might hurt more than it helped. He just let that hang there between them instead, tantalizing.

"You think you get me that well, that you could just stay in Fons-Askaz, keep teaching and living your life, and let me go off and tour without you?" Buck asked.

"If I don't trust you, I won't trust you anywhere – not when you're with me, let alone when you're gone," Caleb replied. "But I do. I don't think you'd hurt someone you cared for. And if you do, well, I've been hurt before. I know how to survive it."

"I know your life hasn't been easy, but I wish I had your serenity about it," Buck said.

"There are trade-offs. My point is, I think even if I'm not there, if you know that I'm somewhere, that you can always text or call – if you know that at the end of the journey you can come home to the harbor, then yeah, I don't mind that. It means you belong to me," he finished. "I get to have my life and you. You get to have your life and me. If it doesn't work, we figure something else out. But I think it could work."

"As long as I don't hurt you," Buck said.

"And I don't hurt you. If you're gone six months of the year, you don't know what I'm up to," Caleb said, grinning. Buck shoved him gently and he flopped back into the blankets. "You take all the responsibility but you don't know, I might run around town picking up dates."

"Kinda hot, actually, I'd dig a threesome."

"No, my own," Caleb said. Buck laughed.

"You really want to try this with me?" he asked. Caleb put his hand over Buck's heart. His thumb brushed the line that Sister Rosetta sang: **99 ½ WON'T DO.**

"I would love to try this with you," he said.

Buck nodded, almost absently. "I should get back. I — there's…morning stuff I'm gonna have to do."

Caleb kissed him and then let him go, watching as he rolled out of bed to dress. He meant to watch until Buck left, but he was still tired and there was a charming arrhythmic buzz to the rustle of Buck's clothing, the soft muttering as he looked for his phone and wallet. He fell asleep before Buck found his phone, and didn't feel the kiss in his hair or hear the click of the door swinging shut.

The day of the live Grand Final was long, full of rehearsals and last-minute panics. Caleb, with his simple performance and small delegation, assumed he'd spend most of it sitting in one audience or another, waiting for his turn, but the drama arrived at eleven in the morning, with a call from Lachlan's husband Stephen.

The entire delegation was supposed to be on hand, although Noah and the other students had wandered off to make mischief, nominally supervised by Jes, who wanted to fully absorb the ambiance of their last day at Eurovision and maybe buttonhole some performers for interviews for the podcast. Davidson had spent most of the time on a tablet or his phone, keeping the home office updated.

Jerry, Ava, and Michaelis were debating the merits of various cars Jerry was still considering buying. Alanna, leaned up against Jerry, was reading on her tablet; she might pretend it was some kind of important document for the king, but every time she opened her reader app Caleb saw the book's cover, which said

Brotherhood and had a picture of two men holding lightsabers, who looked like they were possibly sharing a single brain cell between them.

Lachlan, whose opinion of cars began and ended with whether or not they had seat warmers, was scrolling Photogram when his phone rang.

"Hey, hon," he answered, sitting up a little, leaning away from the conversation. "Sorry, it's loud in here. How's your d – "

He broke off, then, and stood.

"Okay, sweetheart, talk a little slower," he said, walking away. Caleb looked after him, curious and worried; Alanna was watching too, and so was Jerry, ignoring Michaelis and Ava arguing about manual transmissions.

"Gerald," Michaelis said, trying to get his attention.

"Sorry, something's up with Lachlan," Jerry replied, as Lachlan walked up the central aisle of the green rooms, dodging people in costume and the everpresent stagehands and cameramen. Michaelis turned too, head tilting; Davidson looked up from his tablet. "Looks like whoever called him upset him."

"It's Stephen," Caleb said. "At least I think."

"Stephen's a very competent person," Michaelis said. "Put together. He wouldn't call today of all days unless there was an emergency."

He was just starting to rise, clearly to go after him, when Lachlan reappeared, jogging back towards them; he was paler than Caleb had ever seen him.

"Everything all right?" Michaelis asked, catching him by the elbow.

"It's Bonnie," Lachlan said, voice wavering. He looked at Caleb. "She's sick – Stephen's really worried – "

Caleb felt a spike of panic – at the idea of Bonnie, a sweet baby he'd met once or twice, being sick, but also because there was clearly only one way to handle this. "Go," he said.

"But – " Lachlan looked around like he wasn't sure what to

do. Caleb wasn't sure either, but fortunately neither he nor Lachlan was alone, and Michaelis spoke before Caleb could again.

"Lachlan," Michaelis said. Lachlan and Caleb both looked at him. "Go home and look after your daughter. One of us will take you back to Fons-Askaz, the rest will sort it out here."

"Come on, I'll help you get packed and get you a car," Alanna said, taking Lachlan's arm gently, pulling him out of Michaelis's grasp.

"I can go," Ava said, glancing at Caleb. "I can drive him, he shouldn't have to drive."

"Thank you," Caleb said to her, still barely coherent over the thoughts whirling in his head. "I owe you."

"Honestly, my legs keep falling asleep during the song," she said, giving him a hug around the shoulders. "Are you sure?"

"It'll be fine," Caleb told her, not at all sure that would be the case. Ava ran to join Alanna, who half-turned.

"Jerry?" she called.

"I'm all about it," Jerry called back, taking out his phone. "Get them on the road, Al. Don't worry, Lachlan. Travel safe."

"That's both your performers down," Davidson said, as soon as Lachlan was out of earshot. Caleb's breath came short, but he realized with gratifying speed that he didn't have to have an answer. He just had to ask the question –

"What are we going to do?" he heard himself say.

"My first choice would be panic," Jerry said, which was reassuring, "but I'm going to skip that part and make a phone call. Rob – "

"You shouldn't have any trouble putting in substitutions," Davidson said, but he took his phone out. "If there's any pushback, the RSBA can get involved, but I don't think it'll be necessary."

"Okay, let me work my magic first," Jerry said, putting the phone to his ear. Caleb stood there, letting it happen around him, intensely grateful for Jerry in that moment. "There are rules about substitutions, aren't there? It's clearly a family emer – Denise," he said, into the phone, interrupting himself. "It's Gerald ben Eitan from the Shivadh delegation. I need you to save me. It's within my power to grant boons if you can."

He walked away, still talking to whoever Denise was, and the foggy, panicked feeling rising in Caleb's chest began to recede.

"They don't sing or dance or anything," he said to Davidson, trying to stay rational about it. "We can just – I mean probably we can hire someone, right?"

"I think so. We'll see what Jerry says," Davidson said.

"A year ago I would have laughed to hear myself say this, but trust Gerald – he'll get the job done," Michaelis told them.

"And worst case, you just don't go on, which is very unlikely," Davidson said. He probably meant it to be comforting. Caleb was still working out how to respond to that when Jes arrived at a brisk pace, Noah with them. Both looked upset.

"I just saw Lachlan and Ava leaving with Alanna, they said Bonnie's sick?" Jes asked.

"We don't have any details," Michaelis said. "I'm sure we'll get some. Stephen wants Lachlan home but it sounds like Young Father Panic to me."

"Stephen doesn't usually panic," Jes said, looking worried. "Oh, no, Caleb," they added, worry deepening. "Your – your king and prince!"

"We're fixing it. Well, Jerry's fixing it," Caleb said, as Jerry came walking back. "Maybe."

" – take a few seconds to talk to Caleb?" he was asking into the phone. "Thank you. I won't leave you waiting long." He held the phone away from his ear and muted it. "Organizers say family emergency is grounds for substitution, so we're okay as long as we've got someone to put in, but if it's going in the media materials, including the – whatever they show during the show, the subheads or whatever – it's got to get submitted in the next half hour. Do we have any idea of who it's going to be? Caleb, do you know anyone who could – "

"Noah," Michaelis said. Noah, who was leaning against his parent worriedly, looked up. "He'd fit Ava's costume, or Alanna would. Gerald or I would fit Lachlan's."

"I can't, I'm Delegation staff," Jerry said.

"But you could?" Caleb asked Michaelis.

"You're not staff," Davidson said. "No rule against it."

"It may be better to see if we can hire someone. It's not entirely my call." Michaelis tilted his head at Noah. "No pressure, Tavat," he added.

Noah seemed to consider it, looking at Caleb, then at Jes. They gave him a *your choice* gesture; it was clear something else was going on, but Caleb didn't need to care about that right now as long as they figured out something.

"I'm in. Not unless you are, though. Is that cool?" Noah asked Michaelis, who nodded. "That's really…thematic, huh?"

"You two," Jerry said, waving his phone between them. They nodded. "All right, if you're sure. Noah, how do you want credit?"

"Noah Benyamin Deimos. Benyamin with a Y," Noah said.

"Uncle Mike? Are you His Grace Michaelis or Michaelis ben Jason or do you want the full treatment?"

"King Emeritus Michaelis ben Jason," Michaelis said.

"Ah," Noah said. "Uh. Jerry?"

"Make it fast," Jerry told him, not unkindly.

"Prince Noah Benyamin Deimos," Noah said, voice small. Caleb looked at Michaelis, curious.

"You don't have to, Noah," Michaelis said.

"I want to. If it's okay," Noah said, looking at Jes. They kissed his cheek.

"Michaelis asked me about it first. It's fine by me, Wild Child," they said.

"I'm getting back on the phone and my short-term memory is extremely limited so make any changes now," Jerry said, raising the phone to his ear and unmuting it. "Denise, I've got names, are you ready? Substituting for Lachlan Hines, King Emeritus Michaelis ben Jason – *I know* – and Prince Noah Benyamin Deimos, that's Benjamin but with a Y. Do you need – oh, ah. Hm. It's complicated. Indeed, so am I. Put you on hold again? Thank you."

He muted the phone a second time and frowned at it. "Possible issue with the titles – Eurovision has rules about politics and the titles get…uh, close to the bone on that one. Let me pull out the big schmooze guns, but if you have to be just Michaelis ben Jason and Noah Benyamin Deimos, is that okay?"

The two looked at each other; Michaelis shrugged and nodded. "I prefer the title, but…"

"It's not even really mine yet," Noah added.

"Well, I like it. Prince Noah Deimos means bonus cousin for me, so I'll see what I can do," Jerry said, putting the phone back to his ear. "Denise, hi, thanks. How much of an issue do we think this might become? I mean, even if we don't use the titles, they have them. I can't un-king the king emeritus," he said, chuckling and stepping away again – it didn't seem like he needed the privacy, just that he was someone who couldn't stop walking around while talking on a phone.

"It's fortunate one of us is charming," Davidson said, watching him walk away. "No offense. I meant I'm not," he added to Caleb.

"None taken, I'm definitely not." Caleb rubbed his face. He watched Jerry's face go through a number of emotions, mostly positive it seemed like, and then he was returning, nodding, giving them a thumbs up.

"Okay, great, that'll work perfect. Do you need proof Noah's sixteen? Sure. I promise my word is good but I'll make sure the documentation gets to you. I'll send flowers too. Okay, ciao."

He hung up and immediately opened something on his phone. "Nobody talk to me, I'm making notes. Denise…send Noah's ID…and flowers." He put the phone in his pocket. "Well, that entire conversation was actually much easier than I thought it would be. Titles probably won't be a problem, if they are they'll just drop them without needing to ask."

"Very nicely done," Michaelis said to Jerry, which seemed to be a bigger compliment than it sounded, by the way Jerry grinned proudly at him.

"So you two are my new royalty?" Caleb asked them.

"Oh man, I'm gonna be in Eurovision, the other Academy kids are going to lose their minds," Noah said, already digging in his wallet for his Shivadh Youth Worker's ID. He passed it to Jerry, who snapped a photo of it with his phone.

"Come on, let's go collect the costumes and make sure Lachlan's okay," Jes told him.

"Should I go with you?" Michaelis asked Jes.

"No. Stay here with Caleb and Jerry, brainstorm every single way this could go wrong," Jes called over their shoulder.

"Well, that sounds like fun," Caleb said.

"How difficult can it be? All we do is sit down. Spent forty years doing that for a living," Michaelis said. Then he tilted his head, clearly reconsidering. "Actually, I should practice that. Knees aren't what they once were."

"I wonder if we could get a throne at short notice," Jerry said.

"I barely used the one we have in the palace. Big uncomfortable thing. No, the floor will be fine, the less we change the better. If I'd known, I'd have brought my uniform. Caleb," he added, turning back to him. Caleb nodded. "Worries? Concerns?"

"Not that I can think of, but this is very distracting," he said, gesturing around him at the Eurovision madness. "Maybe we can find somewhere quiet to think up ways things could go wrong?"

"Good idea," Jerry said. "And you can practice sitting, Uncle Mike."

"One of the things I liked best about being king was the sheer variety of challenges it presented," Michaelis said to Caleb. "I wish I could say sitting practice was the strangest thing I've done in life, but I don't think it even cracks the top ten."

"You keep writing that chapter of your memoirs, I'm going to find us a spot," Jerry said. "Caleb, stand by."

Caleb watched him go thoughtfully.

"You know, when I came to Askazer-Shivadlakia I knew almost nobody," he said. "I did not think this is where I would end up."

"I can't say I had you in mind when I expanded our extremely liberal citizenship and immigration policy," Michaelis said, "but it seems to be paying off marvelously. Now, you do a very tidy thing when you sit, one ankle over the other, but I'm not sure which foot should go front…"

Buck caught up with Caleb two hours before they went live; Caleb had an apple he'd taken from catering and scurried away with, hiding out in a corner of the big backstage hall where the food was. Buck had also stopped at the catering table and every pocket he had was stuffed with granola bars.

"There's a shitty rumor going around about your performance, are you okay?" he asked, shoving half a granola bar into his mouth.

Caleb held up a hand to indicate he was chewing, swallowed, and nodded. "I'm fine. Show's fine. Lachlan's daughter's sick, Ava took him back to Fons-Askaz. He texted, she's not dying or anything, but he and his husband are freaking out about it."

"Shit! Ava drove him? So – who's playing your king and prince?" Buck asked, through a mouthful of food.

"Noah fits Ava's costume, mostly. Someone's letting the hems down. Michaelis and Lachlan are about the same size, so he's playing the king."

"Huh."

"Noah called it thematic," Caleb said, because he could see

Buck was struggling with a way to remark on that.

"Yeah, really." Buck unwrapped a second granola bar and started on it. "Are you freaked out, though?"

"I mean. I don't like change. But I wrote the song *about* them, and we've rehearsed it a few times. I spend all of twenty seconds actually interacting with them on stage. And it's not like they're not trustworthy. Noah's not going to pull faces or anything."

"That kid has crammed a lot of life into sixteen years, and I say that as me," Buck said, finishing off the second granola bar. Caleb offered him some water before he choked. "Thanks." He sipped, handed it back, and unwrapped a third granola bar.

"What are the rumors, anyway?" Caleb asked.

"You know how musicians talk. One said someone died, which – I like to think I'd have heard if that happened. One said you were changing up your show for the Grand Final, they thought you were bringing in dancers or something." Buck grinned. "I knew you wouldn't do that, but imagining a chorus line of Shivadh kings was pretty funny. But a bunch of people are saying you had to scramble last minute for some reason, like things were happening. Wanted to make sure you're cool."

"Yeah, I'm…I mean, worried for Lachlan and Stephen, otherwise I'm okay."

Buck nodded, rocking on his feet, clearly not entirely reassured. Caleb wasn't sure what else he could do; sometimes Buck just got in his own head about a thing.

"You're going second. They say second is the death slot," Buck said at last. "It's unlucky. Nobody wins in the death slot."

"Thank fuck," Caleb said. "I love a bad omen."

"Well, that's the thing, isn't it. You weren't supposed to do Eurovision at all. You replaced that other guy."

"Ill-fated Kairao, yeah," Caleb said.

"Then you got picked to go to the semis, and then you passed the semis," Buck continued. "And I'm not gonna say you aren't a good musician, because you are, but you're not generally what

Eurovision looks for."

"I never tried to be."

"I know! But you're still *here*. That's improbable, right? That's narrative," Buck said, clearly struggling to say what he meant. Caleb waited. "It's like. What if you break the curse? You're...you're that kind of legend, Shades."

"I'm not a legend, I'm just me," Caleb replied.

"I just wonder. What happens if you win Eurovision?" Buck asked.

Caleb gave him a dry grin. "Don't catastrophize."

Buck snorted. "Fine, dodge the question. What happens if I do?"

"You tell me," Caleb said, although even he could tell that had mostly been a joke. "You said you'd like to win. Have you actually entertained the idea that you will?"

"Doesn't feel like that kind of thing happens to anyone," Buck said. "It's hours away, but it's not really real. I know it must happen to someone, someone wins every year, but nobody thinks it'll be them. It'd be nice to be the special one, but I dunno."

"You don't think you're a contender?"

"I thought I did, but some of these people...I'm not educated, I'm not the brightest man on Earth – and I'm still not looking for compliments," he added, when Caleb opened his mouth. "Maybe I've got a bit more talent than some. Decent looks. Doesn't mean much when there's bucketfuls of people like me out there. There's a bucketful of them waiting to go onstage tonight, but I'm not like them. I'm just lucky."

"But you're not just lucky," Caleb said, and Buck snorted. "Some of it's luck, maybe. Not all, though. That's not me trying to be nice to you," he added, waving that away when Buck looked ready to disagree. "There's real proof, I'm not saying that because I like you."

"You don't say anything just because you like someone," Buck said.

"You're proving my point," Caleb told him.

"Fine, sorry."

"It's just...not everyone can play guitar like you, even with practice. Most people can't compose music, especially not the way you can, instinctively. How many famous songwriters are there in the world who actually perform their own music? Really, honestly, how many do you think there are? Like – Billy Joel, or Muddy Waters, or Leonard Cohen. How many alive at any given time?"

Buck shrugged. "Twenty? Thirty? At the level of the guys you're naming." He shot Caleb a grin. "Gotta put Taylor Swift in with them, your list is a sausagefest right now."

"Fine! But how many Taylor Swifts are there? Not that many. And you got famous from nothing on the strength of the fact that you're one of them. Even being generous, say there's fifty people in the world who can write poetry, write music to put it to, and perform that music not just competently but...charismatically enough to get to Eurovision all on their own. You don't think that's special?"

"I don't know if it's special enough to win," Buck said.

"Blows my mind," Caleb muttered. "Patrice didn't do this to you, did he? This weird strutting insecurity of yours?"

"No," Buck said. "He was just one in a long line. I think I've mentioned that I don't trust especially easily."

He looked like there was something else he wanted to say, but instead he lifted a hand and rubbed his eyes.

"You have a way of flipping the lid off something hard enough that it goes flying across the room," he said. "Half the reason I like you so much is you're so damn uncanny about it. Just rough being the target is all."

"Maybe I shouldn't have said some things," Caleb said.

"No, I was asking for the Caleb Canto one-two punch," Buck replied.

"Well, if you listened to that you have to listen to this, too: you wrote a song and you sang it all the way into Eurovision,"

Caleb said.

"So did you," Buck replied.

"And what is your opinion of me?" Caleb asked. Buck glanced sidelong, then leaned in and kissed him, quick, tasting like granola. "Sneaking around, huh?"

"You knew I had no self-control when we met," Buck said, which wasn't true, but Caleb wasn't going to call him on it. "Look, I think the…the fame, the prestige, doesn't even matter to you," he added. "You're so far above the politics. You said it yourself, there's no stakes. But you're so comfortable with that, I think people might do one of those Mandela Effects things. People might think you did win anyway. Twenty years from now you're gonna be the guy who won Eurovision, even if you didn't."

"A very Shivadh situation, really," Caleb said. "So. You think I'm special and handsome and a winner?"

"I do," Buck said, clearly thinking this was a flirtation.

"And you're here with me, someone I chose, out of everyone I could have. So what does that make you?"

The shock on Buck's face was fleeting, but intense. His eyes went distant, flicked up to Caleb's face, unfocused again.

"What if I did win?" he asked.

"You should consider that," Caleb said.

"Ah, fuck!"

"There you are," Caleb said, amused. Buck ran a hand through his own hair, making it stand on end briefly. "If I win, I'm going to be the most reclusive Eurovision star in history, which is fame in its own way. If you win, that's one more stepping stone to the platinum album and the expensive Ferrari. If I don't win, I go home to somewhere I love and go back to teaching. If you don't win, come home with me and make an album. There is no downside to anything that happens tonight." He set his empty bowl aside. "Anyway, Amani – Noah's friend? – Amani's doing the math on the Grand Final scoring for a project at school. They say that mathematically, it'd be difficult for either one of us to win, but only because of past voting blocs. If anything changes this year, they've run some models, and we both have a shot, but my odds are a lot longer than yours."

"What would it take for one of us to win?" Buck asked.

"You'd need to somehow beat Italy and Spain, and like two other things would have to happen that you don't have any control over. Amani could explain it better than I could."

"Don't want me to throw the competition for you, do you?" Buck asked.

"Don't even talk about it," Caleb said. "If you did I'd have you expelled from Askazer-Shivadlakia permanently."

"You've got the ear of the king, you probably could," Buck said. "I won't, Shades. I wouldn't insult you by trying. I hope you do really well, though. I won't be mad if you beat me."

"Why would you be? Talent knows talent," Caleb said. Buck laughed and brushed his hand up Caleb's leg.

"I need to go think about all this. You probably want some quiet. I'll see you after, yeah? As long as Patrice doesn't win, it'll all be fine."

"I talked to Amani, they say they can't even calculate the odds, they're so long on that happening," Caleb said.

"Hah! Should have led with that, Shades. Okay. Off I sail. Tell Noah I said not to fart onstage," Buck said. Caleb nodded, laughing, and Buck gave him a Shivadh bow, which was a little thrilling, before running off.

CHAPTER THIRTEEN

IN THE EUROVISION Grand Final that year, in front of over a hundred million viewers, Caleb Canto performed in the second slot, walking out on stage in a three-piece suit, a pair of mirrored shades, and some worn Chucks.

Two people were already standing on stage, in the black uniform of Shivadh royalty, trimmed in white instead of the traditional gold. One was an older man, with gray hair and dark eyes; the other had the gawky body of a child not quite yet done growing into an adult, but with an adult's bearing already.

Out of view of the cameras, Michaelis tipped Caleb a wink. Caleb, careful of the guitar in his hands, put one foot in front of the other and sat, cross legged, guitar propped on his thighs. The other two sat as well – Michaelis a little more slowly than Noah, but both with a reasonable amount of grace. The old king turned to look at Caleb fully, watching intently, and the newest Shivadh prince, not even legally a son of the Palace yet, followed.

Technically, of course, the music was pre-recorded, but Caleb still played as he sang. Nobody would hear it and he barely even heard himself, but it mattered. If only because his playing demonstrated a kind of ownership, or at least an authorship. Noah, in a move that looked casual although they'd rehearsed it, propped an elbow on his own knee and his chin in his hand, continuing to watch as Caleb sang. Michaelis, hands folded in his lap, looked occasionally from Caleb to Noah and back.

Aware of the audience but unable to see or hear them, Caleb still felt himself pulling on its threads, tugging their thoughts and emotions gently towards the conclusion, that the cycle of life inevitably includes the passing of the crown – wisdom, adulthood, however one wanted to read the metaphor.

> *I could never live forever*
> *Never really wanted to*
> *And I know it good, and true*
> *How the crown has passed to you*
> *Tavat!*

When it was over, he could see Michaelis suck in a breath, the same way the audience did at the National Final – like they were coming back from somewhere else. Noah straightened his back, and then stood up; he gave them both a nod, then led the way off the stage. Caleb waited until Michaelis was standing, just in case, then followed Noah, Michaelis trailing after.

Backstage, Jerry caught Noah up in a hug, laughing; Michaelis was already undoing his cuff buttons and loosening his collar, ruffling his hair out of the gelled order someone had put it into.

"You were great! Every time I see that I get chills," Jerry said, setting Noah down and coming to clap Caleb on the shoulder. "I mean, it's still not the king and the evil vizier, which would have been so much more interesting, but it's on-brand."

"Your delight in holding the wickedest job in the Palace really is concerning," Michaelis said, not sounding at all concerned. "More relevant to the moment, Caleb, that was very well done indeed. Hopefully we didn't look too foolish."

"You looked very dramatic. I mean that," Jerry said, his face going serious. "That said, Uncle Mike, no passing the crown anytime soon, huh?"

"Passed it to Gregory already. Now I'm going to live forever," Michaelis informed him. Jerry smiled.

"See that you do," he replied. "Come on, let's get you guys to the green room, we have to celebrate!"

"I'd be happy to get the makeup off my face," Noah complained, then laughed when Jerry handed him a pack of wipes, offering them to Michaelis and Caleb as well.

The little clutch of sofas that made up the Shivadh green room was a fascinating study in contrasts; almost everyone was excited to see Caleb and in high, noisy spirits, but Jerry guided Caleb to a specific sofa, blocked off a little by a potted plant. Davidson was sitting at one end, still at work on his phone, though he gave Caleb a nod and an encouraging thumbs-up. Amani was sitting in the middle of the sofa, a laptop bag tucked between them and Davidson, though the laptop was still in its pocket.

"Designated quiet couch for deep thinkers and anxious musicians," Jerry said. Caleb gave him an unimpressed look, given the constant roar of the crowd around them. "Relatively speaking," Jerry qualified, and gave Caleb a gentle nudge towards Amani's other side, perching himself on the arm nearby.

"Which one are you, deep thinker or anxious musician?" Amani asked him boldly.

"The exception that proves the rule," Jerry told them. "How's the math coming along?"

"Won't be going at all until the jury scores come in," Amani said, turning to give Caleb a bright grin. "Relieved to have it done, I bet, Mr. Canto."

"You have no idea," he said. "I wish I could sneak off, though. I've seen everyone's performances so many times, at this rate I could sing along. Except the big five, and even then I've seen them like three times each. Buck's poor disappearing jacket must be just about coming apart at the seams, it's been pulled off him so often."

"His odds are steady, same as yours," Amani said. "I thought I might try and predict who'd get what votes based on my opinion of their performances but there wasn't room in the spreadsheet."

"You know, I have known some real nerds in my time, but I think you're the nerdiest," Jerry said. "No room in your spreadsheet, that's a terrible thing to have to say."

"In ten years, I bet you offer me a job," Amani told him.

"I'd offer you one now, kid, but I don't know what we'd do with you."

"You will, in ten years," Amani said confidently.

"If he doesn't, look me up," Davidson told them.

"Maybe Noah'll have your job by then," Amani continued to Jerry, teasing.

"All I get is lip," Jerry said, pretending to be affronted. "I blame Uncle Mike, teaching you all poor manners."

"Go easy," Caleb said to Amani. "He has a delicate ego."

"I'm going to go make noise with the cool kids over there," Jerry said, mock-pouting, and got up. "You sit quietly and think about your life choices."

Caleb would have liked to ask Amani more questions, but Eurovision could not be stopped. He'd seen all the acts already by now, but it was respectful to watch, and modeled good behavior for the students. When Amani saw him, they turned to watch as well. Noah wandered over and shifted Amani's bag, tucking himself in next to them, eyes also fixed on the stage.

He could almost tell, as song after song played past, why he'd done so well in the semi-final. Eurovision was a stage drama writ large, lights and theatrics, and that was beautiful, but there was something restful about what he'd done. You couldn't make a whole evening out of something like that, but it was a quiet moment in the loudness.

Then Buck strutted on stage like a bookend – second to last, mirroring Caleb's slot – and the noise amped itself up.

Buck barely remembered the performance he gave at the Eurovision Grand Final. It was like his adrenaline-fueled brain refused to record all but the most important moments. He recalled hopping up and down on the balls of his feet backstage, trying to manage the nervous energy coursing through him, and being barely able to wait for his cue to go on.

When the lights dimmed, he ran onstage, heading in one direction; a stagehand, running the other direction, hooked the wires into his jacket seamlessly, and Buck faced front as the lights came up.

You couldn't really see the audience, even without the sunglasses Caleb wore; it was just one big mass of humanity, heaving like the sea. The best part about being where he was, doing what he did, was that he got to conduct the sea – like the sorcerer from the old Disney cartoon, or one of those van-art wizards waving a crystal-tipped staff over a surf wave. Which was a nice bit of poetry, part of him thought, while the rest of him struck the Devil's Interval on his guitar.

The Clash maybe could have gone harder…but they did have a point about knocking 'em dead in under three minutes. He'd made his bet on Eurovision, and Caleb's words hit home.

What if you win?

He remembered the opening chord; he remembered the jerking physicality of the jacket being pulled off his body. Aside from that, there was a yawning empty gap until he took a bow and left the stage.

He instinctively looked for Caleb backstage, even as he was being accosted by well-wishers and slapped on the back by his bandmates; it took him a second to realize of course Caleb wasn't there. He managed to get his hands on his phone and snapped a picture, texting it blurrily to Caleb as they made their way to the UK green room in the artists' seating, set well back from Caleb's, which was closer to the front. He was just arriving when the reply from Caleb came in on his phone – *Hey bud. What if you win?*

He grinned crazily and texted back, *What if you do?*

Caleb tagged an emoji of a bomb onto the response, and Buck laughed, settling into his sofa.

Forty-five minutes later, after the televote had closed and with the jury score announcement underway, it seemed much, much less funny.

They brought up the house lights after the last performance, probably so that the audience could see to get up and go to the bathroom or get some refreshments while the voting was taking place. Caleb knew the tension was manufactured, but that didn't make any of it less tense.

Half of the points being awarded would come from juries in all the participating countries, including countries already eliminated in the semi-finals. Amani had assured him and anyone else who would listen, with the righteous annoyance of the young, that a lot of that was fixed, pre-set, by both legal bloc voting and occasional pre-arranged vote swapping that wasn't legal but wasn't formalized, so difficult to catch or regulate. The other half of the points would be, essentially, viewer's choice: drawn from the televote in Turin and across Europe, tabulated by country. It was intimidating to think about seeing his own name in the little voting app on everyone's phone, so he tried not to.

Amani had their laptop out now, anticipating the jury score, and Caleb was glad to be sitting next to them. Nearly everyone else was crowded around, trying to discern what Amani was doing with their neat columns of numbers and probability calculations.

"So when the jury scores come in from each country, I can plug them in here, and all of these – " Amani scrolled to a second tab, pointing, "adjust accordingly, so you can tell when someone's basically out. Or when someone's pulling ahead. I made some predictions, so those won't change, but I can compare them to the real scores as soon as we have them."

"That's some nice programming," Davidson said, his voice approving.

"There should be a point during the televote announcement where you can tell who's going to win – or at least who's going to lose badly – because some acts just won't have the numbers," Amani continued. "If all the big blocs vote like people think they will, anyway."

"What if they don't, though?" Alanna asked, leaning over the back of the couch to peer at the screen.

"Then life will get really exciting really quickly," Amani said. "And I might get extra credit for being wrong."

"Wish I got extra credit for being wrong in school," Jerry announced.

"In maths, it's as important to know when and why you're wrong as it is to be right," Amani said.

"Very like life," Jes said from the next couch over. They were sitting with Michaelis, apart from the crowd around Amani. Caleb thought they both would probably rather be home in bed, like he would. Michaelis had even unbuttoned his costume jacket, something he'd infamously never done when he wore the real thing as king. Under the jacket he wore a shirt with the phonetic pronunciation of Askazer-Shivadlakia printed on it.

The drama, of course, was hardly over just because the performances were. Each country's jury score was reported by that country's chosen representative by video; the video would come up, the representative would give a little speech, and then depending on how much of an ass they were, they'd give a lengthy, suspenseful pause before announcing which country got their country's twelve points.

It was annoying Amani particularly, but most of the children were impatient to some degree. Even Jes, normally placid about such things, looked irritated by it. Caleb was restless from the start – he kept taking his sunglasses out of his pocket, fiddling with them, putting them back, then taking them out again, the world's most obvious fidget toy.

He was just wishing he'd brought his ukulele, because

Republic of Tolot was making a real meal out of announcing who got their twelve points, when he heard *Askazer-Shivadlakia* and his head jerked up.

"Did they just say – " he started, and Amani bounced sideways to stare at him, then back to stare at the screens onstage, which were showing Caleb's shocked face.

"You got Tolot's twelve!" Amani blurted. "That's awesome!"

"Awesome," Caleb echoed. His phone buzzed.

Patrice shitting a brick right now, Buck's text read.

He was more concerned Patrice might try to actually murder him, but he tried to keep that worry off his face until the screens onstage mercifully cut back to the next country calling in to award their points. Once he was positive he was off-camera, he looked down at his phone and just texted back, *SAME.*

After that, he tried to pay more attention; only the twelve-point awards were announced by the representatives, but he was pretty sure he was getting smaller amounts of points here and there. One or two more twelves for him went past as well, although it was mostly a blur of adrenaline and confusion by then.

"Huh," Amani said, about halfway through the jury vote announcements. They tilted their head, studying the numbers.

"What is it?" Noah prompted, as the other students sat up and began to pay attention to Amani's spreadsheet again.

"Remember when I said it'd depend on whether they voted like we thought they would?" Amani asked.

"Aren't they?" Caleb asked.

"Mostly," Amani said. "But also…not." They looked at Caleb. "You're stealing votes."

"I'm what?" Caleb asked.

"That's not actually possible, unless you have a hacker I don't know about," Davidson said.

"Not literally," Amani corrected. "Every country is almost giving numbers I expected, right? But not *quite* like I expected. It looks like everyone did the same math – they figured they could give their bloc partners just slightly smaller scores and give you the extra. You're splitting the vote. You're getting – I couldn't give you a number, but you're basically getting a percentage of whatever points everyone else was going to get, on top of what you would have gotten anyway."

"I hate to say this after you sassed me, but I'm going to need it dumbed way down," Jerry said. Caleb saw Alanna elbow him. "Sorry. Not dumbed down. Simplified for someone who is not naturally gifted at math."

"Better," Alanna told him. People really could be fascinatingly weird sometimes.

"Basically, Caleb's not getting a *lot* of twelves, but he's getting five or six points when he should be getting four – just for example. Surprising number of tens, too. He's pulling points in from acts that everyone thinks can afford to lose a few." Amani stared at the big screen on the stage, brows drawing together in perplexity. "But…"

They looked back down at the spreadsheet, flicking through the various columns, clearly looking for something.

"Nobody's cheating, are they?" Michaelis asked.

"No, not at all, it's just mathematically…everyone's choosing who he takes points from based on the performances, I think. Like. He's taking them from Finland, or Sweden."

"Sweden?" Caleb asked. "Buck'll be mad, he likes her."

"No he won't," Amani said. "Because nobody's taking votes from him. You and Buck are pulling ahead because everyone else figured you wouldn't."

"Noah, I hate to kick you off the sofa, but I'm pulling rank," Alanna said, coming around and nudging him to one side.

"You can't pull rank, I'm a prince," Noah said, laughing, but he stood and moved so she could sit.

"Watch yourself, Tavat, a prince makes gracious way when he isn't needed," Michaelis said.

"Everybody shush," Amani said, then looked up in alarm,

realizing they'd just shushed the king emeritus. "Sorry, Your Grace, I – "

"No, by all means, let the math come first," Michaelis replied.

Caleb watched, following for the most part – at least, probably following better than Jerry – as the votes continued to come in, and continued to fill the spreadsheet. He was so engrossed in it that the voice announcing "Askazer-Shivadlakia," came as a surprise. He looked up to see Gregory, video-chatted in on the screen onstage, standing on the *Dychev*, which was lit up with electric lights. He was wearing the royal blacks, the real ones tipped with gold. The audience in Turin roared.

Ta-VAT! Ta-VAT! Ta-VAT!

"You all right?" Jerry asked in Caleb's ear, crouching at the end of the couch. Caleb nodded, eyes fixed on his king.

"Good evening, Turin, Europe, and the world!" Gregory said, with his best royal smile. "Askazer-Shivadlakia is incredibly proud to be a part of Eurovision at last. We thank you so much for your warm welcome into this musical tradition. And for the first time ever, I am delighted to be here to announce our choice."

His voice audibly slowed, and Amani groaned. "The twelve points from Askazer-Shivadlakia go…to…"

"Dear lord, get on with it," Michaelis grumbled through Gregory's dramatic pause, though he looked amused.

"…the UK!" Gregory finished.

Only the authorized announcer was supposed to appear on screen, Caleb knew that, but just before the camera cut away, perhaps predictably, Eddie Rambler popped into view, throwing the camera out of focus and calling, *"Yeah, Strangelust!"*

Gregory, laughing, shoved him back out of frame and yelled "Ejechev Eurovision!" before the cameras cut.

"Blatant favoritism," Alanna announced. "Love to see it."

"It wasn't favoritism, he didn't choose who got our points. Anyway, I raised Gregory better than that," Michaelis said. "I think Buck did a fine job, well-deserving of twelve points."

"Yeah, but also blatant favoritism," Jes said. "King or country, one way or the other."

"It's not like he's embezzling money somewhere, it's only Eurovision," Michaelis said, sitting in the middle of a Eurovision audience, with a Eurovision performer, having just come from being in Eurovision.

The Shivadh twelve points bumped Buck up to the number three spot – but there were still more countries to go in the first half of the voting.

When they were done, Caleb was, inexplicably, in first place. The camera cut to him, wide-eyed, surrounded by students, and the chant started up – *Ta-VAT! Ta-VAT!*

Amani hit enter on their spreadsheet. Half of it lit up red.

"Those are the countries that are realistically out of the running, unless something really weird happens," they said. They tapped another key, and a handful of lines lit up blue. "Top contenders for first place, but that's guesswork. Good news is, you probably won't place lower than sixth," they said to Caleb.

"Bad news?" Caleb asked.

"You are very…televote-friendly," Amani said carefully. "People, in general, like your song a lot. So you might win. Condolences," they added drily.

Caleb turned to Noah, who had settled on the floor next to Amani's feet.

"I realize Lachlan's the one who made me stand in for Kairao, but he's not here, and you are," Caleb said. "So if I win, little prince, I'm blaming you."

"Legit," Noah said, grinning at him. "If you win, I'll buy you an apology bouquet. I bet Jerry knows where to get the best ones."

"Harsh but true," Jerry agreed.

Caleb's phone buzzed; another text from Buck.

shallow 2 laugh but tolot has nul points, it read. Caleb looked up at the screen and gaped. He hadn't even noticed, but Republic of Tolot – Patrice – had zero points from the jury vote.

He wanted to reply, but there wasn't time – the televote was fully counted and the numbers were starting to be announced, appearing on the leaderboard. Caleb watched, eerily calm – a small part of him thankful that his body hadn't chosen now to panic – as the scores came in.

Twenty-five countries were competing in the Grand Final, and each had a score from the televote. They were announced in order from whoever had the lowest to highest score from the jury, Caleb assumed for the drama of it all. But somehow the simple announcement of the number score for each performer seemed to take eternally longer than the jury scores had. Caleb watched numbly as countries moved up and down the leaderboard.

When the televote for the UK was announced, third-to-last, Buck's flag bounced up into first place. *Strangelust for the United Kingdom...208 points from the televote for a total of 450 points.*

Amani made a soft choking noise.

"What is it?" Noah asked. Caleb saw himself back on the big screen; before he could react, Jerry leaned over the back of the couch, face hovering above Caleb's shoulder, and made an exaggeratedly excited face, waving a little Shivadh flag vigorously.

"187 points," Amani said, looking at their spreadsheet, then at Caleb. He hoped the camera, which was just *staying* on the Shivadh green room, wasn't going to drift over to where they were visibly agitated. "You need 187 points to beat the UK. Between 162 and 187 points and you're second. Anything lower and you place third. There's 342 points left. So if Sweden gets – "

"More than 180 points, I place third," Caleb said.

Sweden...168 points.

"Holy shit," Noah said. "Caleb, you're second. But that means..."

"I think so," Amani said, frantically typing on the laptop, opening new sheets to redo and confirm the math. Jerry and Alanna were both visible on the big stage screens with Caleb now, distracting the cameras from drifting towards Amani. Caleb wished they could get the camera off him, too, but he suspected that was a losing battle.

"I'm not sure, don't quote me," Amani said at last, looking hesitant. "I just – "

They were cut off by the final announcement:

Askazer-Shivadlakia…174 points.

The Shivadh flag, up on the leaderboard, skipped above Sweden, landing in second place. The board, flanked by screens now showing Buck's startled face, read

```
United Kingdom - 450
Askazer-Shivadlakia - 438
Sweden - 413
```

There was a moment of silence, and then the UK flag at the top flashed green, signifying the win, and Turin *lost its mind.*

Jerry, perhaps remembering the panic attack from last time they were in Turin, pulled Caleb against him, left ear pressed to his shoulder, right ear covered with his palm; Caleb appreciated the gesture, but he reached up to pat Jerry's chest, gently disentangling him. The students were piled on top of Noah and Amani, a mass of cheering, laughing teenagers, while Davidson tried to dodge elbows and knees. Alanna tugged Jerry away and pulled him into her, kissing him.

Caleb, confused, looked instinctively at Michaelis and Jes; the old king was very still, but he met Caleb's glance and nodded approvingly, the tip of his finger against his lips. He tucked his finger in against his palm and then turned his thumb outwards, eyes shifting to the left, and Caleb realized where he was pointing.

At Buck.

Who had just won Eurovision.

By twelve points.

The noise and chaos rushed back in abruptly, and Caleb turned. Mika's voice filled his ears.

Strangelust has won the Eurovision Song Contest for the UK for the first time in over twenty years! The audience is on its feet for bright-haired Buck Haverd!

Caleb was on his feet too, running before he thought about it; there was no conscious decision, he was just suddenly in motion, dodging people in the aisle. Buck was standing in the middle of a screaming, jumping, flag-waving crowd, looking tragically bewildered, shocked to have actually won.

Caleb vaulted one of the low sofas and hit Buck like a wave, slamming into him and throwing his arms around his shoulders. Buck's arms came up automatically, but it was a second before he looked down and blinked.

"Caleb – " he said, swallowing. Even amid the roaring noise, it felt like they were outside of time, like everything around them was in slow motion, a chaos they couldn't touch. "I'm sorry, I took your win – "

"Shut up," Caleb said, kissing him. Buck leaned into it, shaking. The volume of cheering seemed to dip momentarily in surprise – he heard someone over the sound system say *Well, it does not seem that first place is something Caleb Canto strongly regrets losing* – and then it surged back even louder.

Caleb broke the kiss and pressed their foreheads together. "You won, Buck!"

"WHAT?" Buck yelled.

"You deserved it!" Caleb said, louder, leaning back. "You deserved it and you won!"

"But you – "

"I didn't want to win," Caleb reminded him. "Nobody, including us, wanted us to win!"

"Come on, Buck!" one of the Strangelust guys called. "We gotta go – Buck, come on, stop kissing your boyfriend, we have to do the encore!"

"Fuck – ah, fuck, my jacket," Buck said, seeming to cast around for a second before realizing he was wearing it. He turned back to Caleb, green eyes intense. "Stay here. Don't go," he yelled, and squeezed Caleb's shoulders before running off. Caleb found himself enveloped in a UK flag, one of Buck's delegation handing him a water bottle, just as Jerry arrived.

"Get that *off of him*," Jerry yelled, laughing, and hit Caleb in the face with a Shivadh flag. "We haven't been a commonwealth in centuries! You can cheer him all you want but you're Shivadh, Caleb!"

Alanna pulled the other flag away, and Caleb wrapped the blue-and-orange over his shoulders instead, just as the lights flicked down.

"*Grazie Turin!*" Buck yelled above the noise. "Can't do this trick twice so – "

He shrugged out of his jacket, held it up, and lofted it into the crowd.

Strangelust struck up that eerie opening chord, and Caleb watched as Buck strutted, shirtless, hair hanging in his eyes, the wings of his tattoos dark smudges on his skin. Jerry, assured that Caleb was properly attired and not in any immediate peril, turned to watch as well.

"That's mine," Caleb yelled, leaning up to Jerry's ear to be heard over the crowd. "Him on stage there. All mine."

Jerry grinned at him. "Glad you noticed," he yelled back.

Caleb watched the rest of the chaotic night later – first in news footage and Photogram videos, then eventually in a documentary, though that was a few years away.

The madness of post-Eurovision partying, the exceptional ebullience of every UK supporter in Turin, Buck giving his press conference and then immediately popping up in half a dozen nightclubs in the next few hours – all of it was happening, but Caleb wasn't aware of it at the time. Not even the two reckless, beautiful minutes Buck gave to the international press about winning out over his boyfriend, who he announced was brilliant and talented and helping him write his next album.

Caleb saw it all eventually, but not that night, because he was asleep – curled in a nest of blankets in a dark room with the incessant, soothing roar of the celebrations going on outside his window. You couldn't really ask for a better white-noise machine.

After Buck's encore, Caleb had been caught up briefly with the UK delegation when they were ushered backstage. Alanna had managed to catch up to him and grasp his elbow, pulling him away; he could hear Jerry's voice amongst the UK delegation, but Alanna wouldn't leave Jerry if she didn't want to, so he followed her out to the waiting cars. He ended up in a car with Alanna, Jes, and Davidson; Michaelis had taken a second one, herding the students into it.

"Second place! Gregory will be thrilled," Alanna said, on the ride away from the concert hall, a slow progression through the crowds beginning to fill the street. "Never saw a country so happy to lose, but I suppose it is all the perks of first place with none of the duties."

"Buck's in for a hell of a ride," Jes added.

"He likes it, though," Caleb said. "It'll be fun for him. Couldn't pay me."

"Some people are made for louder lives," Jes agreed.

"Jerry's enjoying the chance to do a little yelling, I think," Alanna said, consulting her phone. "Can't wait for him to get home from that and crash for twelve hours."

"This reminds me," Davidson said, turning to Caleb. "I don't suppose I could have my sunglasses back, now that your stage performances are done?"

All three of them stared at him.

"Those were yours?" Caleb asked.

"Yes – theatrical lights are so bright, you know? I usually have them on when I'm helping set up filming in a venue like that. Once everything was arranged I put them down somewhere, and I guess you found them."

"Lachlan did," Caleb said, fumbling in his jacket. "Why didn't you say anything? I've been trying to figure out how to get them back to the owner for weeks."

"Didn't need them," Davidson said, as Caleb dug them out of his pocket. "Seemed like you did. Bit of a lucky charm, eh?"

"That's more restraint than I'd show if my sunglasses were suddenly famous," Alanna observed.

"They're only sunglasses," Davidson said, as Caleb passed them over. "And now they're a nice souvenir. Might have them mounted on a little plaque in my office. Unless you still need them, of course," he said to Caleb.

"No, I think they should retire," Caleb said. "Thanks for letting me use them."

"My pleasure," Davidson said, tucking the sunglasses into his breast pocket. Caleb was about to ask something else, he wasn't even sure what, when his phone buzzed. He looked down at it to see a selfie from Buck, smile wide, Jerry peering over his shoulder.

Going out. Duty calls, Buck wrote. No apology, no guilt; Caleb felt a rush of relief. *Be my harbour?*

Caleb smiled. *Good sailing. Don't get Jerry into too much trouble.*

And then he went off to bed, the happiest second-place in the history of Eurovision.

The sound of a shower woke Caleb early, and a warm, damp body landed on the bed shortly after. Buck wrapped himself around Caleb like an eel and sighed happily.

"Enjoy yourself?" Caleb asked, amused.

"It was the best," Buck mumbled into his cheek. "Being famous is brilliant. All the movies lied."

Caleb laughed. "Wouldn't think you'd even bother coming

home. They must have you booked straight through the night, all of today, and into tomorrow."

"I do what I want, I'm a rock star," Buck said. "Actually they said the BBC has some kind of interview lock with me for tomorrow morning, so I get four whole hours of sleep, four and a half if I push it. Almost five if we don't fool around first."

"Sounds suspiciously wholesome for Buck Haverd, giving up on sex to be well-rested for his interview," Caleb said.

"You take that back."

"Won't," Caleb said, patting Buck's hair. "Do you want to make out or do you want delicious sleep?"

Buck's sigh could have moved mountains. "I got drunk. I want sleep," he admitted.

"I think that's a good call," Caleb said. Buck's breathing slowed, and Caleb slowed to match it. "Besides, we could sleep now and just wake up a little earlier for making out."

"Sure, wake me up early. You ever shagged a Eurovision Song Contest winner?"

"Yeah! I came second," Caleb said.

Buck laughed – high pitched, exhausted – and slumped into him.

"Came second," he repeated, relaxing a little further. "I like your style, Shades."

"Fortunate for all of us," Caleb murmured. "Go to sleep."

Buck grunted, and did so with relative efficiency after that; Caleb, having already gotten a few hours, stayed up a little while to be sure he wouldn't wake, then closed his eyes as well. Outside, the party went on without them.

Much like Caleb, Alanna woke early that morning to the sound of running water. A few minutes later, Jerry emerged from the bathroom, face scrubbed and hair damp, shirtless.

"Hey," she said, as he hunted through his luggage for something. "What time is it?"

"Not even five yet. Sorry, I didn't want to wake you," he said, shedding his trousers.

"It's fine. I'm not the one who's been out half the night," she replied. He kept poking around in his bag, then checked under the flap of hers. "What are you looking for?"

"Comb? I thought I left it in the bathroom like a rational person, but – "

"You did," she said. "It's probably under my makeup bag."

He disappeared back into the bathroom, giving a soft *ha!* of discovery as he found it and began taming his hair.

"How'd it go, taking Buck out to celebrate?" she asked.

"Great, actually," he said, emerging. "I just dropped him off at Caleb's room, so my responsibilities are done," he added, sitting on the edge of the bed, turning to brush a lock of hair out of her eyes.

"You enjoy yourself?" she asked.

"I did. I forgot how much fun clubbing can be."

"Missing the old days?"

He contemplated this. "Not exactly. I don't miss most of my twenties. I don't *remember* a lot of them. I like who I am a lot better, now. But, eh, turns out even when I'm sober and medicated, I still like loud music and a dance floor," he added, grinning.

"I always liked you regardless," she said, matching his grin.

"Then I'm a lucky man dating a woman with dubious taste," he replied. "Budge over, you're on my side of the bed."

"If this relationship ends it's because both of us want this side of the bed," she told him, scooting the bare minimum. He slid into the bed and pulled her up against him, bumping his forehead against hers.

"I'm sure we can work out some kind of arrangement," he told her. "You're well-rested and I'm still amped, want to have victory sex?"

She laughed. "I hate to remind you, but we didn't win."

"Okay, want to have consolation sex?" He composed his face into a rough approximation of sadness. "To come all this way only to lose…"

"Ridiculous man," she said, and kissed him. He made a little noise of triumph. "You're lucky I find your wiles seductive."

At some point in those first few days, Buck really wasn't sure when, someone asked him for the first but certainly not the last time, "What are you doing next?"

"Oh, you've got to tour, haven't you?" he said. "UK first, and then Europe, maybe America. I'd like to get some of the other acts to tour with me. There's huge talent in Turin right now."

"Including Mr. Canto?" the interviewer asked slyly, and Buck shook his head, grinning.

"Nah, Caleb's got a much more important job," he said. "He's back to teaching. Got to bring up that next generation of Eurovision stars, right?"

"You haven't asked him to tour with you?"

"He'd say no. He'll tell you that himself. Haven't asked because I knew the answer," Buck said easily, shoving his hands into his pockets. "You bother yourself with me and let him alone."

"And what about this rumored new album?" the journo asked Buck, sensing he was on thin ice.

"There'll be a delay, but you can't tour forever. We'll do summer, maybe autumn," Buck said. "Then…probably back to Askazer-Shivadlakia for winter. Stitch up the album with Reverb Studios. Do some surfing, eat the best fish I've had in my life."

("That's yours, you know," Gregory said when he saw the film clip, nudging Eddie.)

("The kid's got good taste and I'm the whole package, what can I say?" Eddie replied.)

"How do you make it work with friends and family, being away on tour so long?" the reporter asked.

"Guess we'll find out, won't we?" Buck replied, and changed the subject to his newest tattoo: *What if you win?* scrawled across the inside of his left arm, covered in clear bandages.

Buck was already working out how to manage this new level of fame. His time was no longer his own but it felt brilliantly illicit, every moment he stole for Caleb, to drag him to the tattoo studio or have a last meal with him, or to see off the Shivadh delegation as they left for Fons-Askaz. He barely made it to an interview on time the evening they left, busy texting Caleb to be certain he got home. He went into the interview cheered by the news that Bonnie was better, no longer in peril from her bout of croup.

And, once the loudest shouting about Eurovision had died down, Buck told his agent to talk to Eurovision and plan the tour, and then bolted for a week's rest in Askazer-Shivadlakia.

In true Shivadh fashion, the people he'd previously rented from refused to rent to him again, at least at first. They said he was a messy pain in the ass, which was true, but he'd been defending himself to them on the phone for almost a minute before he realized they were laughing. After he stopped his defense and started abusing them instead, which only made them laugh harder, they let him have the week, on the condition that he'd scrub the bathtub this time.

"Your national fucking sense of humor," he said to Caleb, recounting the story as Caleb rocked with mirth.

"You asked for this," Caleb told him. "Next time don't leave hair dye stains in the tub."

The fishing lodge on the palace grounds got unexpected visitors with relative regularity; the royal family didn't stand on ceremony or, generally, knock when they arrived. There were people coming and going to the studio in the bunker, of course, but tourists would also roll up to the lodge's front door occasionally, clutching printouts from Atlas Obscura, asking if they could see the wine cellar.

That said, generally anyone showing up at seven in the morning was family, so it was unusual to get knocks on the door over breakfast. When the knock came, Michaelis looked up from his crossword, Jes from their coffee, and they exchanged a glance.

"Were you expecting anyone this morning?" Michaelis asked, craning his neck to see the door from the kitchen breakfast nook. Jes shook their head. "Hm. Delivery, perhaps."

He got up and left the kitchen, heading for the front door. When he opened it, Buck Haverd was on the other side.

"Buck," he said, eyebrows rising. "This is a surprise. Come in, we were just finishing breakfast. There's plenty for you if you'd like some."

"We heard you were back in town," Jes called, getting up. "Should have said hello sooner. Though we did start renting your studio to other people again, on the grounds you'll be touring."

"I can't stay, actually," Buck replied, looking oddly nervous. "On my way to Nice to get a plane. Tour rehearsal's starting up, they want me back in London."

"Of course. Exciting days for you," Michaelis said.

"Yeah, it's going to be...a whole lot," Buck said. "Listen, I just had – uh, something to bring you."

He reached into his jacket pocket – a new jacket, one that actually fit him, with the signature orange cuff-stripe of a Shivadh leatherworker – and took out a slightly crumpled fold of paper. Michaelis accepted it, tilting his head as he unfolded it.

Spread out across the first page was sheet music to an unfamiliar song. The second page had what looked like the same song, written out as plain lyrics with guitar tabs.

"The sheet music's piano. It's scored for your voice," Buck said. Michaelis looked up at him. "It's obvious you trained as a singer. Your vocal tone's…unique. Kind of thing I love to write a song for. So. S'for you."

Michaelis looked back down at the notation, humming a few bars. "That's an interesting melody you've put down."

"Caleb did the notation. He might've added some flair."

Michaelis grinned at him. "Just what we need in our lives, eh? More flair."

"I'll be back in a couple of weeks anyway," Buck said. "To see Caleb. Between concerts. I'll come by."

"I hope so. We'd like to see you too." Michaelis held up the music. "And thank you. This is beautiful."

"So I'll see you," Buck said.

"Buckley," Michaelis said.

Buck looked up at him, half-turned to go. "You've used up two of your three Buckleys, now," he pointed out.

"I know. I wanted your attention. We have your touring calendar – Gerald weaseled it out of your agent somehow. It's on the bulletin board downstairs. I expect to hear from you when you safely arrive."

"Arrive where?"

"Everywhere," Michaelis said. "When you change cities, I expect text messages at least. So that we know you're safe."

"Pretty sure it would make the news if I wasn't," Buck ventured.

"I don't care if they skywrite it over the harbor. I expect to hear from *you*," Michaelis replied. "Understood?"

Buck nodded slowly. "Yes. Uh. Understood."

"Then travel safe. We'll see you when you come back."

Buck nodded and backed away, turning to trot down the porch steps and off to the waiting car. Michaelis leaned in the doorway and watched him leave, Jes hooking their chin over his shoulder, arms around his chest.

"Another tavat for your collection," they said. He smiled.

"People should know they're missed, when they leave," he

said. "Caleb can't be everything for that one, and he shouldn't have to be. Buck will settle down once he discovers none of us are going anywhere. Interesting times when he does, I imagine. In any case," he added, leaning back and closing the door, gently dislodging Jes, "it appears I'll need some rehearsal space. Not every day Buck Haverd and Caleb Canto write one a song."

"Do you even play guitar? Or piano?"

"I had piano at school, ten thousand years ago. As good a time as any to brush up on it. I did think retirement would be quieter than this," he mused.

"You were miserable when it was," Jes reminded him. He leaned in and kissed them.

"Better keep me busy, or I'll do as Gerald suggested and enter Eurovision myself next year. I'll call Caleb later and see if he wants to give me piano lessons, that'll keep him from moping that Buck's gone. Meantime, refill on the coffee?"

"Yes, I think so. Need all the caffeine I can get, these days," Jes said, following him back into the kitchen.

EPILOGUE

Home From Home: Eurovision Champion Buck Haverd On Touring, Songwriting, And Adulting His Way Across Europe

Strangelust frontman and pop bad boy Buck Haverd has been performing since he was 15, but claims that at 26 he's finally done 'the most adult thing' and bought his first house. Hot off his win at Eurovision and in the middle of a spectacularly successful European tour, Haverd made time to purchase a seaside villa – but not in the UK.

No, this white-stucco dream home is on the Riviera, tucked into a cliff in Fons-Askaz, the capital city of Askazer-Shivadlakia. It's the same city where his fellow competitor and boyfriend Caleb Canto, who met Haverd while they were both preparing for Eurovision, has returned to teaching after his top-of-the-pops adventures.

Between tour dates, Haverd has been in Fons-Askaz to work on his next album, which he'll be recording at small but prestigious Reverb Studios this winter. Samples already released, including Photogram sensation *Shower Drum Solo* and prospective single *Poster Boy* – as covered by Canto in the Eurovision Solo Sessions – show a promising mix of hard rock, razor-sharp satire, and just a hint of bubble gum to lighten the load.

We caught up with Haverd on a breezy

late-summer afternoon, dressing for a party.
Not in his honor – the locals treat Haverd as
a curiosity, and aren't overawed by his
presence – but a friend's birthday party,
being celebrated at Reverb Studios. Haverd
was just one of a Who's Who of local
celebrities, including King Gregory III, King
Consort Eddie Rambler, and the Palace's
newest addition, King Gregory's stepbrother,
Prince Noah...

IT WASN'T THAT Caleb didn't like Buck's new villa – it was gorgeous, perfect for Buck, and had an amazing view of the harbor. They could sit out on the terrace in the early mornings, before Caleb left for school, and watch the fishing fleet come in; on Fridays they could watch the *Dychev* put to sea in the morning, swarming with Academy students, with Noah somewhere down on the foredeck calling orders as newly minted first mate.

It was more that Caleb was still attached to his room in the boarding house, with its recently repaired roof and all his familiar things. He didn't mind staying in the villa, but they'd developed a ritual that Caleb liked best: Buck would text from Nice, saying his plane had arrived, and two hours later Caleb would meet him at the train station and walk him home – to Caleb's, where they'd have a meal and Buck would wash the road dirt off. They would have one quiet, private evening together, for Buck to catch his breath and Caleb to welcome him back. He liked waking up with Buck in his bed, in his home.

On the other hand...the villa had its charms.

They'd been to a party at the lodge the night before for Lachlan's birthday, which had been fine, if a little stressful. It was a mixture of people Caleb knew very well and not at all, which was always unsettling. He'd expected to leave early, and for Buck to follow a few hours later, but Buck had leaned over him just as he was getting tired and said, "Want to go?" and they'd made their excuses (or rather told Jerry, who would make their excuses) and vanished. They'd gone to bed in the villa with the windows open, salt breeze blowing through, talking of how big Bonnie was getting and how funny it was to see Noah in official royal black.

The windows were still open, though the breeze was gentler now. Through the window he could see the faint seam where sky met water, and next to the window was Buck's acoustic guitar on its stand, his song notebook tossed carelessly on the floor nearby. A man could get used to waking up like this, he thought.

Buck was lying on his back, still asleep, when Caleb rolled over. His hair was getting long, and the brown roots were showing again through the teal. Maybe he was growing it out, though Caleb suspected he was waiting until the tour was over before bleaching it and dyeing it some other color. He reached out and fluffed up the hair just above Buck's ear, gently.

"Hey," Buck rumbled, eyes opening. He stretched his neck, tipping his head into the pillow. "What's the time?"

"Coming on six."

"Huh, novel to see dawn from this side of the bed," Buck said. "I'm beginning to see the value of sleep."

"Oh you are, eh?" Caleb asked, raising an eyebrow.

"I still like a party – I liked last night's! – but I didn't realize a tour, a real rock star tour, would be like it is," Buck said. "I feel weary sometimes. Glad it's almost over."

"One more leg. Then you're home, unless they send you to America."

"No, I've had that discussion – didn't I say?" Buck said, rolling to face him. "American tour's after the album drops. So in another three weeks, I give the last show in London. Stop in Newport to see the family, maybe get some things out of storage there. Then I close up my flat, move all my muck out here for good. Once I arrive, I'm in Fons-Askaz until spring."

Caleb beamed at him, pleased. "That's great news. You'll get so much work done on the album!"

"Well, yes," Buck said, inching closer to kiss him. "And also

I will be here with you. Pestering you. Breaking into your home and eating your food. Touching your stuff – "

"Nooo," Caleb groaned. "Not my stuff!"

"Okay, I won't mess with your stuff," Buck agreed, pulling him closer. "But I will be here. Put up in harbor for the winter. What's winter in Fons-Askaz like?"

"Not that different from summer, except fewer shops are open," Caleb said. "Sure you won't miss the bright lights?"

"Not for a while. Maybe eventually. But it's not like there's nothing to do. Nightlife here's fine. I could teach that class at the Academy. Paris is a day away. Rome too. I'll take you with me, or bring you presents back," he said. "Bribe the Academy kids to sail the *Dychev* to Cairo."

"Cairo's inland, you can't get the *Dychev* to Cairo."

"We can if we sail down the Nile."

Caleb rolled his eyes, and Buck laughed.

"How about, for today, I run out and get us breakfast," Buck said. "You play me what you've been working on. We'll go to the beach and get fried breakfast for lunch, and this afternoon – "

"Naked guitar," Caleb sighed.

"Naked guitar!" Buck crowed. "I'll dazzle you with my latest, and after you tell me what's wrong with it, I'll seduce you."

"I can think of worse ways to spend a Saturday," Caleb admitted.

"Then I'd better get dressed," Buck said, rolling out of bed. Caleb watched him go, knowing that eventually, and probably sooner than expected, he'd return.

Liner Notes

The "music" in this novel owes a great deal to a number of artists:

- *Young Prince* is inspired by *Forever Young* by Rod Stewart; the opening is inspired by the opening vocals to Sting's *Desert Rose*, as sung by Cheb Mami.
- *Invisible*, by Buck Haverd, was inspired by (and steals the coat-vanishing trick from) *Jezebel*, the 2022 Eurovision entry by The Rasmus, representing Finland. It wasn't until after writing this book that I found out that The Rasmus was so good that it just *looked* like the coat was pulled off by wires – it was actually a skilled bit of stage-and-camera foolery.
- Buck Haverd's tattoos (to an extent) and his general demeanor were inspired by the career of pop icon Robbie Williams over the last 20 years. The tattoo **99 ½ WON'T DO** is a lyric from a Sister Rosetta Tharpe song of the same name. (The G7 chord is just because G7 is my favorite.)
- Caleb is his own being, but his success at Eurovision is in part inspired by Sheldon Riley, the 2022 Australian Eurovision rep, who performed *Not The Same*, a brilliant artistic examination of his experiences as an autistic man.
- I first encountered *Long Hot Summer Day* as covered by the 23 String Brand on the Woodsongs Old Time Radio Hour, which is great fun if you like corny jokes and folk music. *Mingulay Boat Song* was covered by Richard Thompson on the Rogue's Gallery 2006 compilation album, an excellent introduction to sea ballads and shanties.
- For years, I thought "Money for nothing and your kicks for free" were the real lyrics to the Dire Straits song *Money For Nothing*. Like Buck, I discovered very late that it's a much more off-putting song than I had thought.

Content Warnings

This list is to the best of my ability and is made in good faith.

- **Public performance and social anxiety:** Throughout the book (particularly in Chapter One) Caleb performs publicly while dealing with social anxiety; he agrees to perform of his own free will but people who have issues with public performance and coercion may wish to read with care. The most difficult moment is in Chapter Two, when Caleb is briefly laughed at while on stage; Gregory puts a stop to the laughter immediately, and there's no lasting trauma or embarrassment.

- **Panic attacks:** In Chapter Four there is a somewhat lengthy description of a panic attack; throughout the book, Caleb occasionally feels the onset of one, but only the panic attack in Chapter Four is shown.

- **Alcohol and drug misuse**: There are several brief mentions, primarily in Chapters Two and Three, with passing mentions in Chapters Six and Eight. None of it is shown directly.

- **Biphobia and Transphobia**: In Chapter Seven there are brief mentions of internet trolling involving biphobia and transphobia, although the characters are not severely affected. Chapter Eleven contains discussion of gender transition related to Caleb's ability to play music; this is a sensitive subject, as questions about transition are often used against trans people to pressure them into non-transitioning or de-transitioning, or simply as a bullying stick. In this case it is not used in that fashion, but please read with care.

- **Child in peril:** Briefly referenced in Chapter Twelve; no injuries or lasting trauma involved.

www.ingramcontent.com/pod-product-compliance
Lightning Source LLC
Chambersburg PA
CBHW070850260626
47170CB00007B/2565